FLOE

ARLAN ANDREWS, SR.

WOODS
PUBLISHING

CONTENTS

Floe

This is a work of fiction. All the characters and events portrayed in this book are fictional, and any resemblance to real people or incidents is purely coincidental.

Print versions by Woods Publishing

ISBN Paperback 978-946419-60-6

ISBN Hardback 978-946419-61-3

Note: Distance units used herein—miles, yards, feet, kilometers, meters, centimeters—refer to roughly equivalent values in the societies they are used in. Those different societies will use their own names for these units of measurement.

BEGINNINGS

CHAPTER ONE

General Thist breathed in the salt-tinged spray of sea air, luxuriating in its scent. Almost absentmindedly, he kicked a piece of a broken pink marble sculpture near his foot and watched as it plunged over the cliff just a meter in front of him, splashing into the turbulent sea fifty meters below. *The Cold Sea is beautiful from up here*, he thought as he stood amid the shattered ruins of a pink marble balcony, being careful to avoid the other broken fragments scattered around him. Looking out over the Cold Sea to the east, he saw, and smelled, the continual surf below, spreading its foam over broad white beaches. *The Princess must have loved this view—before my siege leveled her palace.* As the mild sea breeze caressed his face, Thist found that he loved the moist air, a new experience for him, the darting seabirds with their raucous calls a reminder that Nature could shower beauty on the world, even as Man ravaged it. *One good thing to come from this siege; I had never seen an ocean till coming to the Sisterdom of WaterEdge. To destroy it.*

Turning around, his view encompassed even more destruction. *That vast plaza down there must have been beautiful,* Thist thought, *before my catapults and trebuchets cratered its maze of flower gardens, smashed its white adamantine pavement tiles, laid waste to its forest of graceful marble statues.* Gazing around his surroundings at the smoking ruins of the huge, pink-stoned palace, he looked down past concentric tiers of burnt gardens, now reduced to long arcs of smoking ash and scattered accumulations of broken pink stones. *All was beautiful here before my army laid waste to this, the magnificent Pink Palace of WaterEdge.*

Sighing, Thist regretted that all the work of centuries, of untold thousands of hours of slave labor, now lay waste. *This is not all my doing—rebellion and treason do have their consequences. And it will all be rebuilt, but this time by free men!*

Standing in front of the general, towering over him, was the tall, pale woman to whom all this desolate beauty had once belonged, until today. Her wrinkled, blue-veined white arms were held tightly by two large Mothersmen, their black-leather armor a stark contrast to her sheer sky-blue godscloth raiment, now splattered with blood. The body of an olive-skinned man lay at her feet, in several parts, gruesome pieces of him staining his voluminous green robes.

"General Thist," Princess Sathronin said, unable to stop weeping. "You have killed my priest here, my best friend, Loranthip Kech. Without him, my Sisterdom is lost. And so I offer you my total surrender. Please be merciful to my surrendering guardsmen, my nobles, my citizens—and to myself." The graying middle-aged matron may have loomed over Thist, twice his height, but she was the conquered, he the conqueror. Her royal clothing, godscloth robes now stained with the blood of her deceased Kech priest and confidant (*And probably her lover,* Thist thought), were wrinkled, pitiful. *As is she.* Obviously weary from the stress of the weeks-long siege, her makeup smeared from tears and sweat, the soon to be ex-princess reeked of fear and desperation, no nobility evident at all.

She really is just an ordinary old woman, the diminutive general observed. *Without her company of armed guards, with their commander now dead at her feet, she has no power.* For the thousandth time during his two years in Motherland, Thist wondered how such weak, incompetent women were ever allowed to be powerful princesses, each of them ruling with absolute life-or-death authority over hundreds of thousands of citizen-slaves in their sovereign Sisterdoms. But even in his silent thoughts, he knew the disgusting answers: they were all heiresses of a corrupt, millennia-old matriarchal power system, descendants of one crazed Mother or another, each one approved and appointed by some despotic Mother Herself.

To the defeated and despondent princess, Thist looked up and said gently, "You are now deposed, no longer a princess. You will return with my men and me to Mother's City, there to await the judgment of Our Mother Perneptheranam, whom you betrayed with your treason and rebellion." As the woman broke into sobs, almost collapsing, Thist motioned for the Mothersmen to take her away; other soldiers quickly picked up the priest's bloody body, gathered up its various pieces, to spirit it all out of sight. *Feed him to the sharks,* Thist thought, but did not say aloud, just turning his eyes toward the cliff. His men nodded; they knew what to do.

As Thist watched, the ex-Princess was escorted in chains down the hill past ruined gardens and across the plaza to a mobile horse-drawn cage, where she would remain confined until his twin, Thusk, arrived in Una, their big green flying machine. Then they would all fly back to Mother's Palace for a quick trial and probable execution. *Mother Pernie is sometimes more lenient than other Mothers were, I know, but treason is treason, and this is the second rebellion in a year!* He did hope Pernie wouldn't insist on a public burning. *A private beheading is more dignified,* he thought, *And probably less painful.* Though he himself had killed many men in combat, he would never get used to Motherland's casual violence, the killing of those who could not fight back. A whisper in his mind seemed to say, *"Yet you remember one Miran Kech?"* Thist quickly dismissed that reminder, choosing to concentrate on serious matters at hand.

Looking down over the ruined courtyard in the hot

bright sunlight, Thist surveyed the hundreds of blue-jacketed emu-riders who surrounded the site, dark little men—*And women!* he reminded himself—who, like Thist, were immigrants from their northern homeland near the glaciers, The People's Lands. Those bird-warriors now formed the fast-moving shock troops of Mother's Army, having proven themselves for the third time to be as fierce in combat as they were placid on their new farms in the Republic of ShadowFall.

Herded in by that slowly closing ring of springbow-wielding warriors on their war-birds, dozens of finely clad, elegantly coiffed and manicured citizens of WaterEdge—former aides, nobles, and courtiers—anxiously awaited their fates. Sighing, General Thist adjusted his scarlet godscloth regalia and with the long golden staff of Mother's Authority in hand, strode down the hillside, through the rubble-strewn paved walkway, and over to a large tree-shaded oaken table where a specially built raised chair awaited him, as did several junior officers and scribes who were standing at attention. A black-hooded headsman stood nearby, ominously resting his as yet unbloodied axe on a deeply stained chopping block. For the remainder of the daylight hours, General Thist knew, he himself would remain seated in the cool shade, dispensing ultimate justice as he saw fit, while his mewling charges would remain in the shadeless open plaza, surrounded by the armed bird-riders and sweating from more than merely the heat of the sun.

Seating himself comfortably, Thist drank deeply of an iced wine. He wrinkled his nose at the wafted odor of emu shit emanating from the war-birds, knowing that the birds often anticipated violence, and that their defecation before fighting and afterwards was an instinctive response. *I wish I understood humans as well as I do these birds!* he thought.

As he awaited for the chief scribe to introduce the first of the fearful assembly of former notables of the Sisterdom—shortly to be the *Republic*—of WaterEdge, Thist thought over what he had done, and where he had been, since first arriving in Motherland. *Here I am, sitting in judgment of all of these rich and formerly powerful folk, people twice my size and three or four times my age in some cases. And just two years ago I was a nobody, a barbarian boy riding emus up north in The Tharn's Lands under the Misty Sky, hunting velks with spear and bolo, exploring The Ice at the End of the World. The glacier.*

I was just one lucky adventurer, he recalled, *riding a berg from The Tharn's Lands down to God's Port. Then as a refugee, escaping from those brutal Solar Priests downriver to ShadowFall over that high cliff. And then meeting Wakan Kech and Princess Pernie—now* Mother Perneptheranam.

At that recollection, another unwelcome memory emerged: of himself fighting on emu-back at the Motherland Game, killing a dozen men with springbow and bolo and sword. *And losing my damned left foot!* Unbidden pain from that long-detached appendage still accompanied his recall of the berserker rage he had unleashed that fateful day. He would never get used to an ivory foot! And he had hoped never to release that wild rage again. Yet during this siege of WaterEdge he had barely been able to contain his anger at the contemptuous Loranthip Kech, the arrogant priest and advisor from a mysterious place called the High Antis. *Loranthip Kech was one of Wakan's men,* he thought, *almost all of whom are assets to their princesses and to Motherland. But not all Kech are as honorable as my best friend, Wakan,* he thought, remembering Miran Kech, whom he himself had executed, *and none are as smart!*

Then, just months after ShadowFall had been saved from General Creesile's invasion, after Mother Pernie was inaugurated, another Sister tried to take advantage of the chaos to break away, slaughtering emissaries that Pernie had sent, almost killing Thist himself and her priest, Wakan Kech, in the ambush. Pernie's retaliation had been swift—and sickening, Thist remembered with a shake of his head. That Sister was burned naked in public, her name purged from all Motherland records and histories, her palace site plowed under, its stones used to construct numerous public toilets; that entire Sisterdom was erased from history, its lands absorbed by its neighboring princesses. Over a hundred of her loyal guardsmen suffered brutal public castration before the mutilated survivors were sentenced to a lifetime of enslavement in the salt pits. *Which miserable actions I had to order and oversee*, he thought with a grimace. *I always thought Pernie and Wakan would be more forgiving of enemies.* Though he was now General of the Motherland Army and thus the third highest-ranking person in the nation, Thist knew he was not truly heir to the thousands of years of their land's brutal traditions, nor would he ever get used to the casual cruelty. *Fortunately!*

As if to rescue Thist from his disturbing memories of dark deeds, the chief scribe spoke the name of the short, obese, bearded man who stood trembling and tearful across the table from Thist. "General Thist, this man, Lord Timmar, is accused of conspiring with the late priest, Loranthip Kech, to incite the former princess to rebellion. Here are the charges and the witnesses." Thist listened intently, trying not to be prejudiced against a helpless noble, though he already knew he was going to cut off this slug's head. *And he will go first, immediately, as an example to the rest of these parasites!* But in his mind, Thist recalled his own rebellion against the late Mother Messinex just the year before. *If we at ShadowFall had failed to defeat Creesile's Mothersman Army, I would have been across a table like this back then, awaiting a headsman like the one waiting here! And my ashes now fertilizer.*

As the scribe continued with the long list of Timmar's other abuses—incestual rape, flaying alive of slaves, drunken murders of entire innocent citizen families on his lands—Thist's involuntary reverie was taking much of his conscious attention. *Just one year ago*, he thought, *I myself was considered a traitor, defending what is now the Republic of ShadowFall—*

then, the Sisterdom—from General Creesile, an old man who was acting under the orders of the Mother's corrupt Kech priest, Miran. He relished the memory of throwing Miran, that piece of ox-dung, out the door of his flying god-machine, Una, from a hundred meters up, splattering him at Creesile's feet on the battlefront, during the siege. That was one way to dispirit an enemy commander!

I treated Creesile better than he deserved, he recalled. *I argued for his life in front of Pernie and Wakan.* "The man was only following orders," he had pleaded back then to the Mother and her Kech priest. "He is defeated, ruined. But, and I say this as one who fought his invasion of ShadowFall, the man has courage, strategic vision, command authority, and a vast knowledge of our country's military strengths. And weaknesses."

Pernie, then brand new to her position as Mother, had leaned toward Wakan Kech, as if in doubt as what to do. Just days into her Motherhood, replacing Mother Messinex, who had been slain accidentally by Creesile's attempt to destroy Una, Pernie was unsure as to the effect of having the general executed.

Wakan had no such qualms. "Thist, as long as the man lives, he is a threat. I say we should publicly execute him forthwith, a warning that our new Mother severely punishes the enemies of Motherland."

Thist replied, solemnly, "Mother, Wakan, if you kill him now he will become a martyr for some other military figure to use as a rallying cry. If we just imprison him, limit his access to the public, we can announce your sympathy for a good soldier who was following the lawful commands of his Mother." He snorted, "Even though we know it was Miran Kech behind the invasion and the atrocities."

"Mother, he does have a point," Wakan said, reluctantly. "Showing your benevolence could temper some of the frustration that his troops felt when they weren't able to sack ShadowFall. And those same soldiers know that if their commanding general is forgiven, then they themselves have nothing to fear for their own part of that war."

Pernie sat quietly while Wakan and Thist debated the details of how and where Creesile might be held prisoner, and what restrictions he would be subject to. *I don't want to wantonly slaughter people like my Lordess Mother did,* she thought. *So perhaps giving this general back his life, milking out all of his knowledge, letting Thist learn the ins and outs of Motherland's military capabilities, that could be the best solution. But he has to be punished somehow.*

As the three sat at her conference table, Pernie saw Thist unconsciously rubbing his left foot. *But it is only an ivory foot,* she remembered, *made by Healer Fyth to replace the one he lost in the Motherland Game, two years ago. Fighting for ShadowFall. For me!* At that moment she envisioned Creesile's appropriate treatment.

"Wakan, Thist," she said in a stern voice. "Creesile shall be stripped of all military rank. He shall be confined in a small set of rooms in our dungeon; given comforts, good food and drink. His sole contacts to the outside world will be with whomever you two so designate." At Wakan's and Thist's nods and smiles, she added, "However, to prevent any possible acts of treason —and if he acts against me, this time it *would* be treason —I order that his *other* leg shall be removed, as painlessly as possible, above the knee, the result to be at stubs of different lengths." Smiling without humor as her two advisors gasped, she added, looking straight at Thist, who now was openly rubbing his false foot, "And no artificial limbs or crutches shall be provided him. I think that no Motherland soldier will follow a man who has to crawl to use the toilet."

And so Creesile remained, a gruesomely crippled prisoner, but alive. Nonetheless, within months the sad ex-General of the army somehow smuggled out letters inciting rebellion, missives posted surreptitiously all over Motherland, resulting in thousands of his ex-soldiers flocking to one Sister in open rebellion. *I was wrong again,* Thist thought. *Even without legs, the man could stir up passions in his former troops. And did.* Thinking back over the war he had had to wage against —the Sisterhood-That-Is-No-More—he was lucky that his intimate relationship with Mother Pernie existed. *Otherwise I could have been executed, too, for woeful miscalculation.* As it was, Creesile would have been better off being swiftly killed rather than the month-long horror that Pernie subjected him to when his treachery was uncovered. *Wakan's death-herb poison has to be the worst extended torture ever invented.* Thist tried to suppress the thoughts of the atrocities he himself had committed, at Pernie's order, against the hundreds of rebellious soldiers after their bloody defeat. He would never erase the feelings of the initial fury, nor the lingering guilt, of the results of Creesile's deviousness.

And then, overwhelming those disturbing feelings, from somewhere arose the completely strange memories of sitting on the Mother's taboo Crystal Throne and unexpectedly communicating mind-to-mind with that Moon-girl, Mienne. *Mother Messinex's throne back then,* he thought, *before she was killed at ShadowFall, before Pernie became Mother. Back when we thought the Crystal Throne was a pathway to the gods, not just a communication device left by the ancients all those millennia ago.* He recalled with a shiver the shock of seeing the bright colored lights across the face of the Moon, those eternal, constantly illuminated beads, being flashed on and off by that Mienne, up there, as he had asked her to do; all of which seemed unreal now. The effect had disheartened Creesile's troops, a resounding success, demonstrating (they thought) that Mother Messinex, and then Pernie, had such cosmic power. Sometimes, were it not for the fact that his own twin, Thusk, was now allowed—and actually *encouraged* by Pernie!—to sit on the Crystal Throne himself to visit that Mienne from time to time, Thist would not have believed his own memories.

But the Moon is Thusk's concern, not mine! Shrugging off such issues, Thist quickly turned his attention to the blubbering fool in front of him. *This will take all day and night,* he thought, *but I have to be just! And swift! My mirror-men have sent messages for Thusk to bring Una here to pick up the princess and me, and I expect him here by morning.* Thoughts of the dark past behind him, Thist returned his full attention to his duties as conqueror and judge, nodding seriously at the nervous crowd in the courtyard, his mind full of the serious matters of retention, reassignments, promotions, fines, confiscation, imprisonments—and decapitations.

"Off with his head," General Thist commanded.

CHAPTER TWO

"*I*ncoming!" Captain Lork screamed, jerking the *Ice God*'s tiller hard right. He felt the godspring blade slice glacial ice, and yelled again. *"Duck, you icers!"* As his crew scrambled to hold fast to rails and masts, their ice-craft spinning around, Lork felt the port outrigger lift from the ice, his ship heeling dangerously to starboard. A stinging ice spray peppered his face and he thought in anger and fear, *By the gods, I hope we don't capsize, not with enemy fireballs coming down at us!* With a *whoosh!* and a *crash!* the flaming ball of stone and hay from the sky smashed into the ice mere yards away, disgorging chunks of the Ice Sea, ice-shrapnel that pierced one of his sails.

Next to Lork, holding onto the taffrail with both hands as the boat lurched, First Mate Attuk yelled back, "Cap'n, we needs ta back off. They's got our range, damned Mounties!" As the *Ice God* righted and swung away from the mountain fortress of Dvora, Lork nodded, his face transfigured in a mixture of ferocity and disappointment. Three of his fleet of ice ships were afire, now blazing furnaces, their doomed crews scattered across ice in the distance, like embers from a bonfire. *Half my ships*, he groaned. *Probably thirty men dead. And for what?*

Lork had been told that Dvora was supposed to be an easy target: a fertile valley, hundreds and hundreds of lush acres of farmland and abundant crops, populated by a few thousand farmers, led by one dissolute and drunken noble, a mere duke; a tempting target if there ever was one, like the legendary low-hanging fruit from the Tree of Life. All Lork's pirates had to do—or so he had been informed by a traveler he thought was a reputable spy—was to get past a small stone fortress atop the bald hill at the entrance and then slide up the frozen river. "Tons of grain, hundreds of sheep, cows, other meat animals," the itinerant had said. *If I ever find that liar, he will be dismembered, a joint and a tooth and a nail at a time!*

Lork and his crew chiefs had planned the raid well, he thought. *But nobody told me about the damned fire-throwers, that the drunken Duke of Dvora could hit us half a mile away!* Accustomed to quick in-and-out, smash-and-grab action, Lork's raiders had never encountered such a well-defended fort or such fire-weapons; typically his sixty well-trained and experienced sword-bearing warriors, toughened by cold years and emboldened by heated anger, could overwhelm any small village or even a provincial militia, in short order. And their godspring-loaded harpoons could take out defending ice craft at a hundred yards. *But this?*

Raising coded pennants, First Mate Attuk signaled *Retreat!* to the other boats and the three remaining ice craft tacked against the wind, heading back north to their home, Stonehaven, a heated valley two hundred miles away. With the winds the way they were, it would take ten to twelve hard hours of difficult tacking, Lork estimated. *We'll even have to row a bit, and the crews won't like that.* But when Attuk roared out the command, his men grudgingly went to their positions and manned the skritcher camshafts fore and aft.

As the ice ships headed northward, Lork wondered how he was going to be able to face the families of the lost men. His usual *Win some, lose some* shrugs probably wouldn't save his captaincy this time. Maybe not even his life! *Not with my animal cages and grain bins all empty!*

As if the day wasn't already a disaster, the easterly winds quickly picked up to storm gale intensity, driving Lork's fleet to the west, overpowering the skritchers, which he finally had the crew withdraw from contact with the Ice Sea. He had been warned before leaving Stonehaven that the winds over the Ice Sea this late in the season were unpredictable and dangerous, but the public larders were running low, the proposed raid target seemingly a pushover—*And I had my own reputation to make!* he admitted to himself. Though a respected icer, he had very few recent glamorous victories to his name, and several younger rivals were vying for the position of fleet captain.

Besides that, it seemed the last few years that the old predictions of wind directions and speeds were no longer reliable; something was happening, some change somewhere. *Or maybe the Wind Gods are just having fun with us?* He wasn't sure that those particular deities even existed—after all, the Heat Goddess, Hillmork, was quite visible with her high, conical shape on the far northeastern horizon marking the boundary of civilization, Her continual eruptions providing life-giving warmth for all of Na Saam's valleys and melt lakes and ice ports. But nobody ever saw Wind Gods; they could be felt, they could be tamed in ice-craft sails, but yet remained invisible, unpredictable, unreliable, unknowable.

Today the Wind Gods, whatever they were, proved that they could be unfriendly and even vicious, blowing Lork's remaining ice craft westward at higher speeds than he had ever known. The fleet's only hope had been to tack northward and row with the skritchers, but the winds were too strong for that, so his crews finally reefed the remaining sails, hoping for the best. But as the incessant wind force pushed the hulls ever faster, Lork feared the ships' outrigger skate-rails would not hold, and especially prayed to those nonexistent gods that his ships wouldn't hit any melt ponds, crevasses, protruding rocks, or cracks in the glacial Ice Sea. Even the *Ice God*'s massive caltrop ice anchors failed to hold, barely slowing the ships down, so he had them pulled back in, lest a sudden catch or snag subject the hulls to breaking stresses.

AFTER TWO FULL DAYS AND NIGHTS OF UNENDING WIND fury, the raging storm began to subside one eventide, but *Ice God* and the other ships were still skidding across the glacier. Exhausted and barely awake, Lork saw only fog and wind-driven ice-spray in all directions, *Fortunately no ponds or rocks or crevasses. One bit of good luck.* He numbingly acknowledged First Mate Attuk who was yelling, "Cap'n, we might be pushin' our luck. Surface might be crackin'; we have to stop afore we drops!"

Lork yelled back. "All right, Attuk, sound the horns." The first mate cranked the bellows-driven loud-horn, giving the orders to ice-down. Lork ordered the crew to launch the *Ice God*'s powerful godspring-driven ice spikes swung over the sides and ejected downward to stop his ship. Using the one-time, last-ditch effort, Lork prayed to Hillmork and Tag that they would work. To his relief he felt the *thud!* and *scrape!* as the pikes hit, and waited anxiously as their heavy ropes pulled his ship to a slow stop. He could see the other ships, the *Hillmork* and the *Fyorn,* likewise coming to a halt a few hundred yards out. *There'd better not be any more storms like that,* he worried, *because our spring spikes only work once!* He hated to abandon those big ironworks to the Ice Sea when the ships departed, but they had done their duty. Attuk would have to locate them on his charts for others to avoid from now on. *Wherever it is that we are. We came a long way.*

Lork was concerned: so many hours at storm-driven speeds would have put the fleet far beyond any recorded distance to the west, into unknown regions. Like the cursed little stronghold of Dvora, all of Na Saam's traditional icer raid targets were to the south and east, typically mountaintops standing above the Ice, dotted with villages and farms that were readily plundered. "Go east, young icers!" was the perennial rallying cry before an expedition. "Nothing but Ice and Ice-End out West," was the common knowledge.

"Where are we, Attuk?" Lork asked, as the first mate fumbled with a fist-sized brass mechanical device, all gears and wheels. "Are we close to Ice-End?" he added, almost as a joke. *The End of Ice and the End of the World, for all I know*, he thought. Like all ice ships, *Ice God* carried an ancient metal-map, of course, the one showing in detail the locations of the ice ports of Na Saam, and of many other communities south and east, including traditional plunder routes and even some no longer to be found. Information about prevailing seasonal winds, stone islands, dangerous mountains, crevasses and cracks, and other important navigational hazards, had been engraved by ancients many centuries before. Another mystery, Lork knew: the metal of the maps could not even be scratched by any of his iron tools. Like the godspring metal, useful enough in its springlike form, but which could only be bent and formed using fresh Hillmork lava and the strongest contraptions of the smiths. *If we only knew what all the ancients did*...was his thought, a thousand times a year.

Prominent on the metal-map an indeterminate distance to the west was a slightly blurred area labeled *Ice-End*, usually thought of as thousands of miles out, but never accurately mapped in modern times. There were legends of seas of melted ice out beyond Ice-End, but those stories were difficult for Lork to believe.

Our volcano goddess, Hillmork, provides us with the long lakes of fresh melted ice that we in Na Saam use for agriculture, for drinking, for seals and fish. If there were vast seas of melt beyond Ice-End, then there'd have to be so many more Hillmorks to keep them melted that we would see their eruptions, feel their heat, tremble at their tremors. The western night sky would be lit up like bonfires and the whole cold world would shake. So those are children's stories; it's only logical! Without knowing it, Lork was thinking only in the terms of what the wise men of his nation of Na Saam had memorized and repeated; he had never considered why Ice-End was so named and what might exist where The Ice didn't.

Attuk said, "We pro'lly be very close." He held up the disk-shaped assemblage of gears. "The ancient integrator here, it takes our directions and speeds from our wind tube array, figgers in the times from our mercury-drop timer, tells us where we is." The first mate took in a deep breath. "Cap'n, sir, I plotted our course out here and this map ain't so precise out here so far west, but I believe if we'd'a gone on much longer, we'd'a been—" He paused, pointing at the left edge of the meta-map. "Past Ice-End!"

Lork cursed, then sighed, shivering at the map. *If the metal-map had been off by a few miles, we'd be—What? Dead? Disappeared? That's all I need, to lose more ships—or myself!—out here. A complete failure, that's me—bad raid, bad luck, and now, bad navigation!*

"Not a word of this to the others, Attuk. Set the night watches and signal the others that we all sleep tonight, and return home tomorrow, Wind Gods willing." With that acknowledgment of the possible powers of unknowable deities, Lork thought, *Time for some hard liquor and a long night's sleep!*

CHAPTER THREE

I'm going to die here, today! Altamun Kech screamed silently, his breath too precious to waste. Swimming for his life, the ice-cold seawater draining his bodily heat, his energy, Altamun knew he could not last much longer. The damnable thick fog around him, the high, rough waves, were keeping him blind. *I thought the shore was over this way when the ship sank, but now I see nothing.* But there, looming through the fog, close by—something sticking out above the water! *Dry land? Or at least solid land,* he thought, feeling a welcome relief as his knees slammed against a hard surface, scrambling up as his feet caught purchase on a sandy, pebble-strewn slope.

Can I get above the waves? Drenched, freezing, he crawled out of the surf to the top of a smooth stone outcrop high above the crashing spray, finding a welcome cave of sorts, more of an extended overhang. *Not dry, but not getting any wetter*, he thought. Looking around inside the expansive rock shelter, he was grateful: *No other occupants, either—no people, no animals. Good!*

Exhausted, Altamun Kech, lately the advisor to Captain Noor, Supreme Lord of Sea Lords, wrapped his wet godscloth robes about his body, crossed his arms tightly, pulled up his legs to keep as warm as possible, and fell into a wearied sleep.

Hours later—the next morning, he realized from the rising sun to his left—and shivering from the cold, Altamun awoke, miserable with aching muscles but grateful to see that the fog had lifted, the sea somewhat calmer, though, with noticeable surf. His green godscloth robes, as usual, had shed all moisture, leaving him at least dry and significantly warmer. Being of only leather, his boots were still drenched, however.

The sky itself was radiant blue, only a few clouds scudding off the nearby glacier to the north, behind him. Rays of the rising sun were bringing even more welcome heat, competing with cold winds pouring from the enormous wall of ice down to the stony beach where he found himself. *Stranded?* he thought. Scanning the horizon over the sea, there was no sign of any survivors, nor any wreckage of the Sea Lord's ship, *Free Brother,* itself. *Sixty crew, gone like that?* Altamun groaned. *I told Captain Noor we shouldn't come so near The Ice, but of course as a god on his ship, he knew better.*

"Altamun," the captain had said, right before the crash, "my old maps show there is a big crack along the front of this glacier, maybe even a valley. Got trees and a river; might be a good place for a settlement. Maybe even a base for raiding hereabouts."

The Kech priest had studied those same maps, documents so old they had been copied and recopied on whale skin for centuries. *I told him that the glacier ice was melting, according to older maps that showed it much farther to the south.* "And melting means icebergs and worse, Captain." *But God-Captain Noor spied the valley crack in the glacier, saw trees in the distance, and figured we could anchor Free Brother nearby, come ashore in long boats, claim a new land for the Sea Lords. And as captain, of course he knew everything— except for the unseen iceberg that ripped out our hull in the fog!*

Altamun had not been so trusting of the accuracy of Noor's ancient maps or of his navigation abilities, so was prepared with a sealskin life-preserver pod when the calamity struck. *Even with my pod, I just barely made it alive to the foot of this glacier*, he thought. *And looking at the barren rock in all directions on this shoreline, and at the endless miles of high ice, east to west, behind me, I might yet starve. But that valley, or crack, or whatever caused us to sink, that's my one chance.* The only signs of life were raucous white seabirds, darting down at him as if he were food. *Unless I die here, I won't be food for you, but if I can make a sling, you'll be food for me!*

He estimated the slumped glacier wall to be a half=mile north of his rock shelter, across strewn shore through which water gurgled from the crevasse. From the *Free Brother* yesterday, miles away, the ice presented a deceptive, even attractive and pleasant appearance—a three-thousand-foot high wall of white, stretching east and west to the horizons and beyond. The one exceptional feature of course being the half-mile-wide valley where the ice had cracked and melted in ages past. *Like other attractive crevices that appeal to men*, he thought, *this one led us to our doom. All but me. So far.*

Up close, Altamun saw that the glacial wall was not pristine at all, but more of a fractured facade, large shards of it splitting and falling into the sea where the glacier met the water, other pieces already down and melting where it encountered stony beach. Directly in front of him lay the half-mile-wide crevasse where titanic forces had created a slump-walled valley deep within the mass of ice, extending on into a distant fog that obscured its end. *If there is an end*, the priest thought.

The sea empty of ships, the rocky beach desolate of any vegetation, Altamun decided to explore the valley as his only chance for survival. He knew that he would never be able to catch any fish in the continual surf at the foot of the beach, so his chances of finding other food than seabirds had to be better ice-ward. *Maybe something I can eat in there—small animals? Fish in a stream? Wood to burn?* With no warm clothes and no way to produce fire, he preferred not to think about another night in his new environment.

PAST THE GLACIER WALL, ALTAMUN KECH WALKED alongside a slowly flowing river some hundred yards wide, which played out in multiple streams over the stony beach and into the sea. "Fresh water, not salty," he murmured after tasting it. "At least I won't die of thirst." Around him, between the river and the sloping glacier walls, sparse vegetation dotted the stony ground. Scattered patches of grass and peat mottled the valley floor and thin underbrush huddled around the few trees. A flock of dark birds hovered up high, mist-like, level the upper glacier surface, he estimated. *What do they find to eat up there?* He would never know; he would never even try to scale those steep, treacherous, icy walls.

"No tall trees like Captain Noor wanted," he said aloud just to hear a human voice, "but only bent and twisted scrub oaks, none over three meters high. Nothing to build houses or ships with." He grabbed a thin limb, working it back and forth until it broke loose. *An interesting odor in the sap of this tree,* he thought, and *something to chew on until I find food.* The limb proved a tasty chew if not nourishing. *Now if I can start a fire with some of this underbrush, the wood will keep me warm.* He looked around for loose rocks that might spark when struck together but none looked promising, so he continued up the valley.

After an hour's slow trek Altamun calculated he had covered over a mile, finding nothing significant that would help him survive. The slumped walls of the valley actually separated farther as he went on, the valley widening, but the scrub trees, grass, and underbrush did not change. Once he thought he saw a rabbit or some small animal dart between bushes, but he wasn't sure; shadows and reflections played tricks. He did spot fish in the narrowing river, so he kept on walking toward its source, hoping to find a spot where the river was only a stream, and he could either grab fish or perhaps make a net of his clothing and catch some that way. He was surprised that the air seemed warmer as he trudged on, definitely not as cold as the winds around his overnight stay in the rock shelter or at the valley entrance.

The location of the sun told Altamun that his Ice Valley, as he now called it, ran almost directly north-south; the quick shading from the eastern wall told him he'd better find or build some shelter before night set in. So he chose the largest tree he could find, halfway between the river and the valley's eastern ice wall, then worked off enough limbs from other trees to build a shelter of sorts around it, large enough to lie and sit in, covering it all with brushy bushes he pulled out of their stony plots of dirt.

Satisfied he had a place to sleep, no matter how uncomfortable, Altamun took off the cloak of his godscloth robe and fashioned a net by tying its corners to a long limb. Finding a convenient spot on which to sit next to the river, hours passed before, exasperated, he finally landed a fish. Raw fish was not to his taste, but his stomach appreciated it. *I won't starve to death, either*, he thought miserably as darkness covered Ice Valley. *But I might perish of disgust!*

As the sun passed overhead the next day, Altamun discovered why his location farther up the alley was warmer than closer to the entrance at the sea. *Sunlight is reflecting off the sloped walls*, he realized, *so I will get about two hours of sunlight heat each day here. Not bad!* Attempting to reach the far northern end of the valley was a disappointment; no matter how far he traveled, no end was in sight, nothing but more of the dark crevasse, and more ice on either side. *Although if the path continues sloping upward, I might eventually get to the top of the glacier. But then what? Endless miles of ice?* He dismissed that possibility and returned to his tree shelter.

Given the choice of where to try to eke out an existence, Altamun decided he would remain where he was for a while, close enough to view the sea yet far enough in to claim the few hours of extra warmth during the day. When he could find the strength, he would go back to the shore and build a fire, hoping to draw the attention of a ship. He knew, however, that if he was rescued, it was just as likely to be by a slaver or some other enemy of the Sea Lords. *Not everybody who sails the Cold Sea recognizes the Sea Lords as their masters!* Thinking over Captain Noor's fate, the first mate wondered, *Will any other Sea Lord come looking for him? Who might replace him?* With a frown he thought over the possible candidates, concluding that another civil war would wrack the Lordship Islands. *That's all they know, the barbarians! They have no Mother to lead them.* Such matters of state mattered little to the priest at the moment, however. *I have to make do here!*

WITH HALF A DOZEN FISH NETTED AND IMPALED lengthwise on limbs split by stone tools, Altamun searched diligently for flint, finally locating several candidate stones. After an hour of trying, he generated enough sparks to light the dry underbrush kindling, and so had a fire. *So I won't freeze, I will have hot fish and clean water,* he snorted. "All the comforts of home!" he said aloud.

With the thought of *home,* Altamun sighed, letting his mind wander back to memories long repressed. *But not forgotten—never forgotten!*

OVER TWENTY YEARS AGO, HE RECALLED, HE HAD accompanied the Kech leader, Wakan, on an expedition from their homeland in the High Antis, thousands of kilometers northward searching for lost antiquities. *When the Mothersmen Army captured the lot of us High Antians by that crystal-domed ancient pyramid in the highlands south of Motherland.* Remembering the slaughter of his expedition's dozen or so guards by the barbarians led by that Mothersman Colonel Creesile, he shivered. *But at least Wakan was able to speak to them, and to keep us alive. And to let us keep our*—Without thinking, he cupped his genitals with one hand. Most foreign male captives of the Mothersmen Army suffered brutal castration. *But not us. Wakan convinced that officer Creesile and then the Lordess Mother to keep us whole.* In fact, Wakan Kech had been responsible for all the Kech priests becoming highly valued advisors among Motherland's princesses. Altamun Kech, youngest of the group, was gifted by the Lordess Mother to Princess Sathronin of the Sisterdom of WaterEdge. Because all "citizens" of Motherland were the private property of the Mother and her princesses, Altamun had had no choice in the matter.

And there I prospered for eighteen years, he thought, groaning aloud. *Until that damned Noor and his pirates came.* The memory of that day a year ago was still as sharp and as awful as ever; it returned unbidden and unalterable.

"SAILING SHIP ON THE HORIZON," A WATEREDGE sentry had yelled. "Prepare for defense!" Responding to the tolling bells along the several piers that provided loading and unloading of freight above the eternally rough surf of the Cold Sea, Altamun had escorted the Princess to her safe room and then saw to the stationing of palace guards at all entrances. As he looked out from a turret above the seashore palace, he observed a dozen of the dragon-prowed sailing ships rapidly converging toward the piers. *These raiders have attacked us before, sometimes with success, but not this time!* Grimly, he dressed in leather armor, cocked his springbow, and went down to the beach to greet the potential invaders.

Along the beach and atop the three piers, the guards had unlocked the pre-positioned catapults, their oil pots already boiling, ready to drop fireballs on threatening ships. *With two hundred trained fighting men,* he remembered with pride, *and six catapults, we won't be a pushover again!* And a thousand ordinary citizens now swarmed the beach between the sea and Princess Sathronin's Pink Palace, men and women with swords, spears, axes, rakes, and hoes. *I was touched by their willingness to fight for WaterEdge,* he remembered. *Citizens with no rights, but still loyal.* He rightly presumed that peace and prosperity were worth fighting for.

To Altamun's surprise, the pirate fleet stopped about two kilometers out, dropping a longboat into the sea. A white flag flew from that boat's tall mast. At first suspicious of the barbarians' intentions, Altamun reluctantly gave orders to hold fire. "Let me talk to that boat," he told his lieutenants, who immediately spread the word.

The longboat pulled up to the pier where Altamun and ten archers stood, ready to fire. Five men sat in the boat, four of them rowers. A tall man, older, with long white hair and striking albino-white skin, dressed in a rainbow of finery and audacious jewelry, waved at Altamun, speaking loudly in perfect Mother's tongue: "Ahoy, I be Captain Noor, Supreme Lord of Sea Lords. I come in peace, to parley, not to fight. Might I be allowed up this ladder?" Spreading empty hands, he shouted, "I am unarmed. May I speak with one in authority here?"

"Let him climb up," Altamun told his archers, "but keep your weapons aimed at the others."

Once on the pier, the tall pirate smiled broadly at Altamun, bowing low. *The man reeks of sweet perfume,* the Kech thought. *But underlying that—fish? Whale oil? Disgusting!* Trying not to wrinkle his nose at the malodorous creature, Altamun said in a stentorian tone,

"Who are you and what brings you to our—*peaceful*—Sisterdom?" At that, the pirate waved his arms as if to say, *Peaceful, you say, with this army behind you, ready to attack?*

"I hight Captain Noor, Supreme Lord of Sea Lords, from the Lordship Isles, a thousand miles southeast over the Cold Sea." As the Kech nodded in recognition, Noor continued. "You see my fleet out there? I know we have on occasion visited here under less friendly circumstances, but I assure you my intent now is purely commercial. I offer myself as hostage." Rummaging through a sea bag under the suspicious glare of the guards, Noor pulled out a glassy twenty-five inch diameter sphere and held it in both hands for Altamun to see. He said, "Kech Priest, this is why I came to Motherland."

Ten minutes later, Captain Noor ordered his men to return to their ship and await his return. As Altamun and his guards escorted Noor and his several large trunks to the Pink Palace, the pirate said, "You know, of course, Priest Kech, that unless I present myself here in four weeks' time, conditions will revert to the old ways."

Altamun nodded. "Yes, Captain. But this time, *we* will be even better prepared." He gave quiet orders to his second-in-command to retire the main defensive force and send the civilians back to work. "But keep a sharp eye out for those criminals in the fleet yonder," he said. "And set the catapult ranges to hit them if they try to come in closer." Turning toward the Pink Palace, he set his mind to advising the Princess and if asked, Mother Messinex, on how they should respond to Noor's outrageous claims.

CHAPTER FOUR

Mother Pernepthéranam, the young woman who was now ruler of all Motherland, laid aside the inscribed golden plate and sighed deeply. Around her on the walls of her private room, bright gas lights illuminated colorful embroidered tapestries, the largest one a colorful wall-sized map depicting her domain. An incense burner in one corner added its piquant aroma, intended to stimulate her contemplation of the ancient records, *But it's not that much help right now*, she thought. *I could do better with a glass of wine*. With resignation, she gazed at the thirteen multicolored Sisterdoms that defined the span of her Motherland—a vast, oval-shaped basin surrounded by almost inaccessible highlands. *A basin that once was a sea*, she thought, *thousands of years ago, or so I am told by the archives in the godspheres. Called in ancient times Gufffov Mesikko, according to my little lovers Thist and Thusk, who study such details as revealed by their flying god-machine, that Una*. Now all of that ancient sea was a great basin called Motherland, a country of more than ten million people, one nation, where she ruled as an absolute matriarch.

Sighing, Pernie (as she called herself, and allowed only three others to do likewise) wondered how she would be able have the tapestry map rewoven in secret to reflect new names and borders—the year-old

Republic of ShadowFall, the impending Republic of WaterEdge, and—*How do I erase the one defunct Sisterdom completely? I've already ordered that all traces of it and its princess be obliterated, discarded from history. Someone here in my palace must know how to make those changes. Or should I just keep this one hidden here for my own historical purposes and create a whole new map? A lot more changes are coming—ten more republics to be started up.* Thinking of the capabilities of her lovers, Thist and Thusk, and their flying machine, she concluded, *They could produce a new map, a realistic one, as seen from the heights they fly at.*

Pernie told herself that she would remember to task them with that when the twins from the Dark Highlands each returned. *One coming home from a war, the other from internal troubles at ShadowFall, hopefully not yet a conflict.* A year ago when she was just Princess Pernie of ShadowFall, she had no such worries, such problems. A part of her grew instantly nostalgic for that more innocent time. *But that was then,* she thought. *If I am to rule as Mother, I have to let that time go.* But an ever-present rejoinder arose from another part of her mind: *I am only twenty-one years old, with all this responsibility. I might live another fifty or sixty years. How can I possibly endure all of this stress for that long?*

To ease her mind, she looked at other, more pleasant, tapestry scenes from Motherland's long history adorning the remaining walls—the white-skinned, copper-haired First Mother hosting a feast of thanksgiving for the peace and prosperity She had brought to the unified land in the far distant past; other redheaded Mothers, over the centuries, holding their beautiful young girls, all portrayals of smiles and softness, reflecting tranquility. "Peace and plenty, happiness and love; these pictures are beautiful," she said aloud to herself, "but the actual history written in these golden plates shows me that I have inherited a seething mess of squabbling Sisterdoms, a nation with a murderous and hidden past."

Holding her head in her hands, she sobbed quietly. "I wanted to be benevolent, democratic, a ruler with a light touch. But, seeing how we all came to be here, doing what we're doing, I don't see how we can ever pretend to be something we've never been."

During her year's tenure as Mother, Perneptheranam had lived in Mother's Palace, in private rooms formerly occupied by the late Mother Messinex. Late one evening during her first night in those spacious and luxurious quarters, an elderly woman, whom she recognized as one of her Secret Sister Language teachers from her early school years, had brought her a sealed envelope. Telling the woman to open it for her, Pernie asked who had sent it.

"Mother Perneptheranam," the teacher replied, "Mother Messinex left this to be opened only by her successor, should anything happen to her." Pernie noted the tears in the old woman's eyes. *So she actually loved my Sister Messinex, my blood half-sister, and the previous Mother? Maybe I should replace her with someone loyal only to me?* Pernie disliked her own increasingly paranoid thoughts on the matter but knew that as Mother she needed to recruit her own handmaidens and servants, those who owed no respect to the memory of a dead and gone Mother. *Even Messinex, the best Sister, my favorite.*

The note was written with a flourish, in golden ink on private stationery and in the secret language known only to the select few teachers who in turn educated each princess-to-be. The intent and the practice were clear and successful: if any such private correspondence ever found its way to unauthorized persons, it could not be read or deciphered. *The teachers told us that it was based on a prehistoric script, one to be read with eyes only, having no spoken version,* she remembered from her elementary school years, *but that didn't keep us girls from making up our own speech from it!* That was the only fun that the princess school had ever offered, the rest of the severe curriculum consisting of being drilled in Motherspeak, in the traditions of Motherland, in maths and geoms, in accounting practices, and a rigorous, detailed review of military strategy and tactics.

Having been years out of practice in the Secret Sister Language, it took Pernie a few minutes to remember the forms of the script, the grammar rules, and to be able to read Messinex's note.

DEAR NEW MOTHER,

If you are reading this, I must have gone on to that reward the priests keep telling me will be mine for ruling our nation and its peoples so magnificently. I trust that is so. I wish we had had time to discuss everything a Mother must know. There is so much.

My first request is that you soon write a similar letter for your successor, and ensure that it will be passed on to her by one of the Teachers. You may think you will have ample time to pass on your wisdom, but I tell you that you may never know when disease, illness, or an assassin will lay you low.

But first, let me tell you secrets. One is that when you sit on the Crystal Throne you may hear voices. Myself, I only ever heard nonsense noises, but kept that from all the others. They think we are receiving actual instruction from the goddesses; that is the basis of our power and we must never betray the trust of the Motherhood. Only the faith in the Throne and the Mother bind our Sisterdoms as a nation. We must maintain that facade or we will devolve into small fiefdoms continually at war. From the history plates you will find and read that warfare, those raids, were the common condition for centuries before First Mother finally consolidated our nation and began ruling all from Mother's City. You will learn, in time, that what we as young girls thought brutal and restrictive, is necessary to rein in the ambitions and greed that underlie every single Sisterdom in our nation. I pity you, as I do myself, when it is necessary to use force or even cruelty to maintain our dearest Motherland. But do what you must, else our Motherland will devolve into savagery and barbarism, as are the conditions of the foreigners in the highlands around us. I pray that your reign will be successful.

Next, in this envelope is a key to the golden archives kept by Mothers since time immemorial, thousands of years. When you have time, it may be of interest to you to peruse them. Other than learning of our true and violent history, I found very little of use in them, but you may.

Here is how you enter the sealed room, which is located behind the mirrored wall in your private office...

THEREAFTER AS HER DUTIES PERMITTED, MOTHER Pernie spent every free hour reading those inscribed golden plates, rereading them for blatant facts and nuances. She kept the very existence of the private room and its plates secret from even her advisor Wakan Kech and her twin lovers, General Thist and Advisor Thusk. Getting away from her handmaids, demanding privacy, she was able to access the plates almost daily.

Like Messinex before her, and every other Mother for centuries back, she was alternately enthralled or bored by the hundreds of ancient reports inscribed in the Secret Language by those matriarchs themselves. A bundle of sharpened scribing pens nested in the copper chest, as was a stack of blank plates, but Pernie was not yet moved to record her own history; she would wait until current matters were resolved before adding her own words to those remaining plates.

Not at all interested in the mundane activities of running Motherland—taxes, crops, promotions, executions, all of which made her eyes glaze over with ennui—Pernie quickly scanned over those, instead concentrating on the plates that dealt with wars, strategies, rebellions, treachery, assassinations. Of these latter, every single Mother had reported either a succession of violent incidents or prolonged conflicts among the Sisterdoms, some even aimed at The Mother Herself and the Palace. Pernie felt that much of the written information was merely the boasts of the winners rather than accurate history. But no matter; the details of the unending brutality and fragility of the participants, their incessant struggles to keep power and occasionally, only secondarily, to do some good for ordinary citizens, began to weigh on her.

With General Thist away for some weeks now, putting down the rebellion at the Sisterdom of WaterEdge, and with her advisor, Thusk, trying to smooth over problems with his immigrant People having their troubles in ShadowFall, Pernie had been alone too much recently, and was feeling unfulfilled physical stirrings she could no longer ignore. "Nights without loving, I don't like," she whispered to herself while taking out another handful of unread plates from the massive copper chest. "I'd like to bring in one of the handsome guards or even a clean stranger from the city for a night, but I don't want to sacrifice him the next day as we did in ShadowFall." She shuddered at recalling the gruesome ceremonies at the Stone Arch there. "Or like my Lordess Mother did to every one of her lovers." *Including my own father, whoever he was, I'm sure,* she thought, *like all the hundreds of others.*

She would ask her chief priest and advisor, Wakan Kech, about it; with his knowledge of his native High Antian herbs and medicines, he had provided her with pregnancy prevention herbs since her menses began. So as long as a chosen lover was inspected and found to be clean, she was in no danger of pregnancy or disease. "I don't want them killed, but I also can't have men bragging that they slept with me, either." She tried again not to remember the ShadowFall sacrifice ritual, *But that truly was an effective way to stop gossip and any claims to fatherhood, if any lover tried such.* To her disgust, she could at last understand the old traditions; she still didn't like the choices. *But I am in a fiery mood, desperate now,* she thought, *and I must find a way.*

Turning her attention to the inscribed plates at hand,

she read several more and then said to herself, "Wakan needs to know all of this history if he is to help guide me in our revolution." Thinking about how to inform him, she said, "But only I and the other Sisters can read and understand the script." *And the half dozen Secret Language teachers,* she recalled. Her next thought, unbidden, was *If I have all of the Teachers—er, dismissed—then because I am the youngest blood Sister, in a few years, after I depose the other Sisters, only I would have access to all this history, this secret knowledge. What would it be worth, knowing what no one else knows?*

Immediately she thought of Wakan's possible reactions to more executions of people he considered innocents. *What* would *my Kech think? Maybe if I do share all of these plates with him, perhaps I can dictate our true history in Motherspeak to scribes, for him and others to read. Maybe I shall edit them, or even change them. But who else needs to know? Who can I trust not to share history's secrets?*

Her own biological mother, the Lordess Mother—whose princess name, she learned, had been Noomeet—had left scant records of her own accession to the Crystal Throne, only terse intimations that *her* Mother was "a scheming bitch who deserved what she got." Pernie knew from traumatic personal experience that her Lordess Mother had been prone to irrational fits of violence and cruelty toward Messinex and Pernie and all the other princesses living in the palace, but until reading the plates she had not thought the woman capable of matricide. *She killed my grandmother?*

"This is all but a confession," Pernie said quietly, guardedly, even in her most private surroundings. As the impact of the accumulated strata of violent ages accosted her mind, she shook her head, despairing of the waste of centuries and of lives that had created the Motherland of which she was now absolute ruler.

Standing up, she carefully stacked the inscribed golden plates back inside the chest and locked it. "I will have to talk to Wakan about all of this. He and I must chart a new course for Motherland. We cannot afford to be gentle, not if we are bringing about revolution to princesses and people who don't want it. But I hate to be brutal. There must be a way to unify my people, my princesses, in something they would all support, a cause bigger than themselves and their petty greed, so that we can all struggle toward a common goal."

Then she remembered a phrase from an earlier Mother, one whose name was lost in time, not even recorded on the golden plates.

She said it aloud. "War is the health of the Motherland."

CHAPTER FIVE

Enraptured by the lunar surface sights she was viewing, Mienne sat at a console in the center of the dark, ten-meter-diameter hemispherical dome, its surface illuminated by a panoply of three-dimensional digital and video displays. Choosing her favorite scene to encompass the entire dome, she watched the live video feed from the surface of the Moon, hundreds of meters above her underground location. She never tired of the white-and-blue disc of Motherth high in the sky, bright against infinite blackness, nor the jagged, speckled, gray crater wall that spanned the distant horizon from left to right.

Mienne had discovered this place a year before, after she and her armless friend Wayer escaped from the confines of the Niche of Disabled Children, kilometers away down in the tubes of Community, in Shinyeen City. Looking around the selection of smaller digital displays available on her console screens, she scanned for updated videos and text messages. After her initial discovery of the Control Complex back then, over the intervening time she had nursed back into operation some ancient off-line cameras and sensors, with the knowledge and assistance of the complex's Developing Intelligence system, DI. DI was a widespread distribution of quadrillions of "qomps"—quantum computers—that had survived the millennia since Sun raped Motherth and Moon. Qomps, she learned, were as near as anything could be to eternal machines; they didn't wear out, they didn't degrade, and the nanomachines that provided their interfaces to the macro-world were likewise nearly indestructible.

As she read and watched, Mienne spoke to her little armless friend across the room. "Wayer, we are now getting new pictures and data from DI. Its minibots have dug down to the lower levels, and is showing us that our complex has a lot more ancient machines in the places we haven't been able to get to." Wayer came over to look.

Mienne pointed to the screen. "See? Why don't we try to get down there ourselves and find out what other kinds of magic the ancients had?" Wayer laughed at the word, as neither of them actually believed in magic anymore; the DI's tutorials had taught them what Technology and Science and Reality were. They were still impressed, though, by the bewildering and numerous artifacts, machines, and videos they uncovered and which DI tried to explain.

Wayer, now outfitted with DI-printed goggles that enabled her to see what her tall friend did—"What they call my *visible spectrum*, Wayer; different from the limited range of infrared colors all of you down in Community see with," Mienne had told her—enjoyed the camera views. Whatever the goggles did, the short albino girl was impressed; the colors she had never experienced before remained a fascination for her. She now gazed at what Mienne was excited about—a colorful, three-dimensional maze of tunnels and rooms that extended down many levels below their own location, which was marked by a flashing red dot of light.

"But we've walked for kilometers in all directions, Mienne, found hundreds of rooms with machines and displays we still don't understand. And all the elevators and escalators five levels below us are collapsed. We could never get down there. DI's little digging minibots can dig, but we can't. Not through piles of rock and mooncrete rubble, through thousands of years of dust and dirt."

Mienne smiled at her. "No, you and I can't, but thank Creator there are engineers who can."

JOLAN KEESH AND LEDD MERNAN, COMMUNITY'S leading engineer-tunnelers, rode on their electrical transporter, a two-person vehicle usually utilized for rapid inspections of small tunnels or newly discovered voids in Infinite Rock. This day they were en route to visit their friends Mienne and Wayer, in the control complex some horizontal kilometers away from Community. The men felt a special affinity for both Mienne and Wayer. Three years before, while tunneling to create new living space for an expanding Shinyeen City, they had encountered a slanted shaft that intersected their horizontal excavation. When the roof of their tunnel collapsed, they discovered in the debris a strange tall child, Mienne, who inexplicably had fallen from that upper void, where no life was supposed to exist. The Elders always taught that Infinite Rock extended around and below them but "Upward is the End of Rock, there the Vac that takes life. Creator demands that we do not tunnel Upward."

But in front of them, fallen from forbidden Up, lay life—a young girl half again as tall as they, but female and immature for all that. Because the girl was nearly blind—"My range of visible light was just different from yours," the child, now a young woman, later explained—the engineers had delivered her to Elder Myuk, keeper of the Niche of Disabled Children in Shinyeen City. He had seen the child only occasionally over the intervening time, during brief visits to the niche to check on her condition.

Then much later when both Mienne and her truly disabled friend, armless Wayer, had been judged unfit to live—one supposedly near-blind, one actually armless— and were scheduled for Reprocessing, Jolan and Ledd helped them escape to the place Mienne had discovered because of her ability to sense ancient displays. *She was never blind,* Jolan thought. *Being from the surface of Moon, UpTop, there above Infinite Rock, as hard as that was to imagine, she just saw differently than we do. Her vision responds to a different range of colors than ours. The control complex was made for people like her—tall and different-sighted.*

Both men remembered the first time they had visited Mienne here in her new domain, many months later. The girls had met them in the hallway where Mienne took them by the hand up dark escalators to the domed room that Mienne called the Control Room. At that time she had asked something called "DI" to adjust the displays so that people like themselves could make out what was being presented on the glass-like screens.

"We're going back to the control complex, Ledd," Keesh was saying as he drove his electric vehicle through the infrared-lit tubeway to what had been called the "Hall of Whispers." "But this time we have these goggles that Mienne sent us, to let us see everything just as she does. So now the Hall of Whispers should just be a long hallway of digital displays, lots of them in realistic three-dimensional form, she says."

As they parked and approached the arcade-like entrance to the tunnel, Keesh saw the unmoving giant of a Nuuk guardian standing watch next to the doorway. Both men shuddered as they walked past the tall, unmoving, red-armored figure holding a coiled whip in its hand. Whatever Mienne had done to control the big red thing, the Nuuk no longer attacked unauthorized people as it once had. Yet, at a massive two and a half meters in height, it remained impressively ominous. Keesh wondered if it were alive as People were or if it were just something artificial and mysterious that the ancients had built. *Just one more ancient mystery,* he thought.

Once inside the arcade-like tunnel, observing multitudes of colorful, three-dimensional moving images, Keesh said, "I would love to know how the ancients built all of this. Imagine what we could do with it." *The place has a strange aroma,* he mused, *the smell of centuries, the odor of eons.* His engineering knowledge of materials, though, informed him that not all of the devices and displays were quantum- and nano-based, and therefore they were subject to aging by the simple escape of volatile compounds from surfaces. *After so long,* he concluded, *almost anything will stink!* As he noticed a slightly higher humidity that persisted throughout Community, he wondered, too, if all of the environmental maintenance equipment in Mienne's complex was still functioning. *Thirty thousand Motherth years? It's a wonder anything at all still works. Those quantum and nanomachines are just incredible.*

"I don't know, boss," Ledd replied, dodging numerous tall, solid-looking human images in the hallway who were speaking noisily in an unknown language, "I mean, I enjoy seeing this stuff, especially the new colors and all, but I'd rather find the old digging machines that enlarged the natural tubes and sealed and built the first Community habitations way back when. That's what we really need."

Taking the continually operating escalators up five flights, the two pale little men, dressed in their dark brown work clothes, met a welcoming Mienne, now clad in a shimmering pink silklike shift dress, clothing that accentuated her blossoming femininity. She stood much taller than her Community friend and the two engineers. Keesh was momentarily taken aback; the girl had always been just a tall, skinny stranger. And now she was…something more. Paying close attention to her appearance for the first time, he saw that the young woman's height, dark hair, dark eyes, and olive skin were a striking contrast to her armless friend's blue eyes, albino hair, and matching skin color. Mienne was fascinating in a way he hadn't considered before. When their eyes met, holding contact for a few seconds, he felt that she recognized his new interest. *Efficient medium that, light!*

"Hi, guys," Mienne said without any further

reaction, motioning them to the new display discovery, which by her hand motion now covered the ceiling of the control complex dome itself. "There we are, at the flashing red dot," she said, "and here, far below, DI says there are a bunch more rooms, big ones, with all kinds of ancient machines. DI can't access them electronically yet, so we don't know what they were used for."

The engineers whistled at the three-dimensional representation that floated in front of them. "That must be hundreds of meters below us," Jolan said, Ledd nodding.

"How would we get down there, Engineers?" Wayer asked. "Surely you know how."

The men asked Mienne to zoom in on the details, trying to find a path of least resistance. "Elevator shafts? Escalator flights?"

"All collapsed in ancient times," Mienne said. "I have already asked."

Thinking for a moment, Jolan Keesh asked, "Have you inquired about the possibility of natural tubes or fissures that we could dig into and go down that way?"

"No, I didn't think of that," Mienne said. She pointed to the display. "DI, show us any natural tubes or fissures that are close to the levels now blocked off by rubble." Turning to Keesh she asked, "How did you think to ask such a thing?"

Keesh smiled. "Everything you've shown us so far has been man-made—tunnels, rooms, tubes, even those empty cities on the surface. I never saw any naturally occurring features. It didn't hurt to ask."

Smiling, Mienne said, "I know that the Elders have forbidden anyone to attempt to use any ancient machines for upward excavations, for fear that they might breach the Five Cities tubes into Vac and lose all our air. But there is no restriction on us—you—clearing out shafts or digging tunnels in the *other* direction, downward. That would at least let us get down there to see what was once used. Maybe we could all learn something more?"

To get a different viewing angle, Jolan Keesh drew

closer to Mienne, pointing out a series of voids that could possibly be of use. Being very close to him, almost touching, Mienne noticed something different about the handsome little engineer this time. Although she had known Jolan Keesh since he rescued her years before, she figured the man must have applied some kind of musk today, an intriguing odor that stimulated strange thoughts she had never experienced. Shaking her head she pulled away. Jolan acted as if he hadn't noticed her reaction, which she hoped was true.

As the DI escorted the viewers on a virtual trip down through envisioned potential digs and connecting natural cracks and voids, the engineers were intrigued. Already, Mienne's initial discovery of the control complex had led the population of Community to the true knowledge of the Sun's cataclysmic eruption long ago that destroyed the Ancient Worlds on both Moon and Motherth; in a series of meetings, she had shown the Elders their true place in the vast Universe. Some of those facts had been hard to accept: that Community, all five cities of it, the hundred thousand inhabitants, occupied underground lunar tubes originally enlarged and finished by ancients, thirty thousand years before; that Infinite Rock did indeed end where Vac began; and that Moon and Motherth were big rocky orbs situated in an infinite void of Vac—called appropriately, *Space.*

The religious impacts of Mienne's discoveries were still reverberating among the Council of Elders, while ordinary citizens had taken the revelations in stride. The Council remained fearful of unleashing unknown ancient forces, hence the taboo on doing anything other than monitoring the digital and video displays. For purposes of survival and access to provisions, Mienne had accepted that restriction, while knowing that no Elder and no citizen of Community would ever comprehend her discoveries. And the complex held more secrets, she was certain.

As if knowing Mienne's mind, Jolan mentioned the crystal chair in the adjoining chamber. "I take it you still haven't informed the Council about what that chair does, how the man from Motherth communicates with you, in your mind?"

Mienne laughed. "No, nor have I told them I was able to flash the city-dome lights to help friends up on Motherth. It helped Mr. Thist win a conflict there. So, not yet. Wayer and I don't think the Elders are quite ready for that much truth just yet. You do know that they don't even like to come visit here? Which is fine by me. What they *don't* know is that I have the ability to turn off any or all of the New Vision goggles you all have. If I want to."

At that, the engineers each touched their goggles involuntarily. Without them they would be effectively blind anywhere in the complex, lost in absolute darkness. To ensure that no one in Community could find their way to her Control Room and do mischief, Mienne had seen to it that infrared illumination did not exist anywhere in her domain; she didn't trust the same Council who as a group had once voted to Reprocess her and Wayer. The engineers nodded in understanding.

"Good, then, Engineers. Show us exactly how we can get through those collapsed shafts and tunnels. I want to know about those ancient machines down there."

Over the next hour, Keesh and Ludd closely examined the sizes, shapes, and characteristics of the lunar strata and voids around the levels of interest. "We have some exploratory shafts in tubeways near here," Keesh said, pointing to a series of zigzag lines radiating from a major tunnel. "As your DI shows, going from this one," he said, indicating a flashing rectangle, "to these small voids"—scattered dots—"we should be able to excavate and seal a new shaft that will let us get down there."

Ludd nodded. "Can't use our bigger digger, but our two-man cutter should do the job. Three days it will take, if we don't hit any big metal lodes along the way."

"Do what you can, boys. Wayer and I will be patient." *This is something to do,* she thought, *while I wait for my Mr. Thusk to return to me.* She felt that strange warmth, the yearning, once again. *Hurry, Thusk!*

IT IS TOO DARK AND CLOSE DOWN HERE, MIENNE thought as she stood up, her head almost touching the top of the roughly-hewn lunar tunnel. *So different from Control Center. I hope the deeper levels are lit up better.* After all the time since descending into the tunnels that made up Community, even after living there, she still felt the occasional twinge of claustrophobia. *In Control Center I can see the whole of Sky and stars and Motherth and mountains and illuminated cities. Down here, now, only rock, right in front of me.*

Hundreds of meters below the surface of Moon, the tall Mienne and her small armless friend Wayer had just exited a downward-slanting natural crevice leading into a horizontal tunnel, where the similarly small tunneling engineers, Jolan Keesh and Ledd Mernan, were waiting. The two men had finished excavating a passageway with their small burrowing machine, which was now stored in an unlit niche behind them. "Dark down here, Jolan," Mienne said as she arrived. "And I'm glad I can stand up now; that maze of little tunnels you made to get us down here was hard to get through without hitting my head."

The three small Community people laughed. "It's our small world, after all," Wayer said with a grin now illuminated by a head-mounted gaslight. "Big people just have to learn to fit in."

Gaslights now lit, the four could see before them a long hallway with doors on either side. *Fortunately, the ancients were tall, like me,* Mienne thought as she stretched strained muscles. *I would hate to have to walk more kilometers in such a cramped position.* Though unspoken, the three Community people were recognizing the same size difference: *Our ancestors, like Mienne, were giants compared to us. And they could build incredible structures both underground and on the surface, Up past Rock, UpTop, in Vac. Why are we so small in comparison? And Mienne so big?* Everyone recognized the reactions of the others, but such questions were avoided. Things were what they were, and had been for thousands of years. Even DI would not shed any light on the matter.

Mienne found a panel on a wall, its metal door ajar. Shining her gaslight into it, she saw handprint-like outlines. Pushing on one with her palm, she was gratified to see the hallway light up. "I did it, people. It turned back on." As they watched, a sequence of glowing overhead illuminators began lighting up along the length of the hallway into the far distance. Some of the walls even became transparent, more light pouring into the hallway.

"Well, Mienne," Jolan Keesh said with a grin, "Glad we had somebody here with big hands to enlighten us."

"Looks like a lot of these rooms were dormitories or barracks," Jolan Keesh said during their lunch break, as they dined on the bread, cheese, and jerky from the larder compartment on their digger. "Hundreds of people must have lived down here; this big table we're eating at, these benches, accommodated a lot of them. But what interests me most is that big room with the high ceiling and all those dozens of compartments with the gurneys outside them. Any ideas?" He passed around the jug of sweet water for all to drink.

After several attempts, Mienne had finally been able to access the DI, which had been intermittent during their descent. She guessed that qomps were not distributed outside of the complex construction, that the bare rock and undeveloped cracks and fissures were not instrumented. But when she actuated the palm-press panel, some connectivity occurred. Though somewhat erratic, the DI's voice came through. "Yes, Mienne… now accessing your…level…transported soldiers were…nano-optics disrupted…qomps now self-repairing. Full…capabilities…soon."

"DI, what is that big metal wall, with all those doors and compartments and gurneys in the large domed room down here?" They had found one area at least thirty meters square with a ceiling over fifteen meters high, seemingly more like a factory than a research or maintenance facility.

"Mienne…avatarobots…only one now undamaged…for full qomp communication…Do not activate…will demonstrate later…"

AFTER THE NEXT WAKE PERIOD, JOLAN KEESH AND Ledd Mernan made their excuses. "We had to take off a week from our current projects for this, but the Council will require us to get back to work. Your displate showed other voids down here that we can explore and excavate later, and we will ask permission to return and investigate." Mienne felt that same unknown sensation as Jolan reached up to touch her hands to say goodbye. *What is this?* she wondered. *I've never felt this way before.*

Bending over, Mienne gave the engineer a hug of thanks, noticing a truly warm, unexpected reaction from Keesh, who in return held her just a little longer than a friend would. *I never noticed, but could my rescuer have physical feelings for me, after all this time?* Her own response to that realization was also unexpected—a sudden warmth in her groin. *Oh my, is this what some of those strange videos meant, the things I watched ancient men and women do?* When she had first uncovered those video archives her first thought was embarrassment: *Why would people do that? It looks unwholesome. Then after DI explained the reproductive act, of course, I felt nothing.* But the feel of Jolan's strong arms around her, the sudden warmth, his *aroma,* if that's what it was, the *need* that came over her, was not embarrassing at all. *Is* this *what happens?* This *is why?*

Wayer picked up on the awkward situation, saying too loudly, "Mr. Keesh, Mr. Mernan, we are so happy you could dig us a tunnel to get down here. We will be happy to tell you and the Council what we find. The ancients did so many wondrous things!"

At that, a blushing Jolan Keesh released Mienne, who stood up and patted him on the head. Their eyes met in mutual understanding: *We will meet again, alone.* Slight nods acknowledged the agreement.

AFTER THE ENGINEERS LEFT, MIENNE SAT IN FRONT OF another console, this one in the large room with the high ceiling, looking at the array of metal doors and gurneys in front of her. Wayer had been asking her over and over, "What was that between you and Mr. Keesh? Were you both getting shocked, or sick?"

Mienne sighed; she knew that her little friend had never developed any feminine curves, had never begun her menses, whereas she herself had been experiencing them for over a year, sometimes with flashes of inexplicable yearnings she didn't understand. Once in the shower in their living quarters in the complex, she had accidentally touched herself *down there*, quickly manipulating a tender spot and immediately feeling an overwhelming sensation she was not prepared for. Upon again viewing the few videos of nude men and women in various reproductive acts, she intellectually understood the biological drives underlying the actions.

But until today, with that embrace of Keesh, she had not experienced the *need. But I will find out, somehow. I will get together with him and, and...what?* She hoped that the older man would show her.

"No, Wayer, it was just the realization that we are...*friends*, that's all." Inwardly, she was thinking, *And we will be much closer friends soon, I hope.*

FIVE DAYS LATER, JOLAN KEESH MET MIENNE ALONE IN the newly excavated lower level of the control complex, where she stood in front of an opened metal door and a covered gurney. The place smelled slightly of mold and ash, a familiar odor to Jolan. *I've encountered many such ancient voids in my excavations over the years,* he thought, *and all have the odor of ancient life and death.*

"Is that somebody under that sheet?" he asked.

"A body of sorts," she replied, pulling back the cover to reveal a nude body—very notably, a male. Embarrassed at the nudity, Keesh thought, *A giant at that, in all respects. Pale, like me, but tall and dark-haired, like Mienne.*

Keesh stood open-mouthed. "Who is that? How did he get here? How did he die?"

Mienne gave a half-smile. "Jolan, these machines here, these banks and racks of machines, they *create* bodies. Only one of those compartments still works, though. When I asked, DI ran its processes. Hours later, this is what came out, through that open metal door." Running her finger over the figure's lips, chin, and chest, she said, "DI tells me that it is made of nanoparticles, with quadrillions of qomps acting as nerves and organs and more. It does everything a human body can do." She blushed slightly at her own words and moved the sheet to cover the lower portion of the figure.

Keesh took the nearest chair, hoisting himself up for a closer look at the artificial human, a body nearly twice his height. "Mienne, I will never understand the technologies of the ancients. But I *would* like to know why they would go to the trouble of building...a *dead* man."

"But it is *not* dead, Jolan," she said in a low voice. "It lives when a man is transported into it. Here, watch. DI, show him."

As they viewed a wall-sized screen, the DI said, "The *avatarobot* is a fabricated approximation to a human body, though with certain features and capabilities enhanced for its military operating environment. Through its extremely large complement of qomps, the avatarobot is also a receiving terminal, capable of containing the quantum analog of a human nervous system. A human on one qomp terminal may feel as if that person is transported from their original location to the destination location, awakening in the avatarobot. This room and its facility were created to provide numerous enhanced military personnel—soldiers—for reasons not available in existing archives."

The video showed a human man sitting naked on a crystalline chair identical to the one in Mienne's Control Room. Adjacent to it on a gurney was one of the artificial bodies, this one similar to the one in front of them. After a moment, the crystal chair swirled with internal vortices of colors, the man slumping to unconsciousness, at which time the avatarobot shook its head, flexed its arms, and rose from the gurney to stand up.

"This transference of the human nervous system is accomplished by quantum entanglement. Some theorists maintained that the communicant exists at both locations simultaneously, but for the purposes of this demonstration only the *avvy*-bot is shown.

"According to available but incomplete archives, this system was in operation only a few months before the Solar Emergency that terminated all qomp communication among Earth, Moon, Mars, and asteroids. This particular installation was intended to provide, instantaneously, a number of highly trained and specially modified security forces from Earth to this control complex. The barracks on this level were intended to house them. I literally cannot speculate on the reasons for establishing this installation."

Jolan sat quietly, thinking. *I will never be able to do what those ancient engineers did. I should feel inadequate, but* my *world is still here. For all their incredible achievements,* their *world is gone except for the bits and pieces we can find and operate. I want to know more, so much more. Maybe this is the way to do that?* "Mienne," he said, "you said before that this is the only machine still working? The others here in this room are all broken? Really, after all these millennia, I am surprised that anything still functions here."

"But Jolan, those diggers you use, they are ancient too, aren't they? And they still work."

"Yes, but..." He stopped, an idea forming. "Can we take this...body...up to your Control Room? We can transport it in my two-man vehicle."

"JOLAN, I DON'T THINK THIS IS SUCH A GOOD IDEA," Mienne said, as they struggled to lay the avvy on a gurney in the room adjacent to the Control Room. "This hasn't been done in thousands of years."

Ignoring her, the engineer tied restraining straps to the body's arms and legs. "DI says there is no reason for this transfer not to proceed; the avvy is fully operational, and my D-N-A—whatever that is—is compliant with your crystal chair.

"I'm tying this avvy down in case there is a problem. But your friends from Motherth have visited you in your mind many times, from their crystal chair up there down to you here in your Control Room, right? And it worked well all those times. Besides, DI assures us that the short distance between these two terminals— that artificial body and your crystal chair—gives a good safety factor for the test. It should be about like taking a few steps across the floor here." With that, he left and walked through the open door to the Control Room to the crystal chair that Mienne had used in her mind-mixing. Her first time, she said, was with that Thist, and afterwards, numerous times with his twin, Thusk. *The men from Motherth, or Earth as they call it,* Jolan thought. A twinge of jealousy arose unbidden from somewhere deep in his mind. *If they can do it, so can I. But far better—I won't just be in somebody's mind; I will have another body!*

Mienne sighed. "If you say so, Jolan. Walk up these stairs, here. When the colored lights start moving, you are ready to sit. Make sure your bare skin touches the surface, either your arms or, or"—she smiled—"your bottom." As Jolan stepped up, the colored lights in the risers flashed. He turned and sat, slipping his work pants down to expose his buttocks to the cool crystal seat.

"I'm ready. What happens now?" Jolan sounded fatigued, if not overly concerned.

Mienne herself would never have done such a test. *But to each his own,* she thought. *I'll never understand men.*

"The avvy is strapped down on its gurney and you are in your chair," she said, watching the artificial body through the open door. "If this works, you might get to wake up in that body. We'll have to see." As she turned to watch Keesh, though, he was already unconscious, surrounded by swirling patterns of rainbows of all shades.

Mienne didn't know if the transference would be instantaneous, so she paid close attention to the avvy. The designed body was very handsome, she thought, the physical features, perfection, decidedly—*Very much!*—all male. But lacking life, any appeal. *I wonder how Jolan will feel, if this is successful...*

The still avvy body began to breathe, sharp intakes of air, then coughing. Opening its eyes, it turned toward her. "Mienne, am I here? Did this work? You won't believe what I went through—a kaleidoscope, a separation, strange sounds and new colors and wonderful odors—so very weird." As Mienne undid the straps, the figure sat up, trembling, the sheet now sliding off the gurney onto the floor, revealing a moving, living body, all of it.

Mienne was stunned by her own unexpected response: *With Jolan inside it, the avvy looks so* alive, *so —handsome—so* appealing. *Why am I feeling this warmth, this desire?* Remembering the videos she had seen of human lovemaking, she thought, *I know what I want to do!*

As Jolan-*avvy* reached to embrace her, Mienne breathed in; feeling his kiss, the embrace, with Jolan's entire new body pressed tight against hers, it was extremely apparent that the avvy indeed did simulate very important human physical reactions.

CHAPTER SIX

Odel M'ridge jumped from the top level platform of the hundred-foot-high wooden tower at ShadowFall, trusting his life to the structural strength of the tri-wing glider craft that kept him aloft, his latest design. Behind him, the lieutenant commanders of the Aerial Force of the Republic of ShadowFall, affectionately called "the AFORS," leapt from that same launch tower in sequence, quickly arriving in formation.

"Lookin' good, boys and girls," Odel shouted as his lieutenants drew up their craft alongside his own glider. He loved the feel of the wind in his face, the bright sunlight of a cloudless Motherland day, and the piebald blanket of ShadowFall's fields far below him. *And it takes a little away from my damned lower back pain, he thought. Those stressful hours in the fight for ShadowFall, then months later, the war against The-Sister-That-Shall-Never-Be-Named, and then weeks ago at the first assault on WaterEdge.* Though he had never complained, those campaigns of aerial warfare, dropping flame-bombs, firing springbows, dodging arrows, had wrenched his spine and its muscles beyond easy repair, not to mention his peace of mind.

Oh well, I ain't young no more, but this here flyin's the best life for me, long's I kin do it. No more cuttin' stone in no quarry back home, not fer me! Occasionally, he had to admit, he did miss the lush green hills of his property in God's Country, although he had been an exile there when Thist and Thusk first flew to his quarry in that Una machine of theirs. *Una made my little flyer look poorly by comparison, but then I built mine myself; they* found *theirs, built by ancients, in a melting glacier in their cold home country.*

Then again, it was because of inventing and flying those very winged machines that he had been ejected from his original home in Great Woodland, hundreds of miles east of God's Country, and made his way to the profitable hillside quarry. *At first I despised those backwoods preachers that ran me out for bein' a heretic, flyin' my gliders and all, but later I was glad they did. I liked runnin' my quarry just fine, supplying cut stones for the big buildings in God's Port. I only wish that those miserable Solar Priests didn't run everything— taxes, laws, executions.* He grimaced, remembering the fate of his mate Razzo in God's Port, incinerated by the focused solar mirrors of those priests. *Just for the theft of a spool of godscloth!* Thinking of a more recent memory, his frown turned to a smile. *But I am pretty sure that those old solar boys didn't like it when they heard I had flown my tri-wing over the great falls and down here into Motherland.*

His position in Motherland as chief of the Motherland Aerial Forces, reporting only to General Thist, was significant. His aerial warriors had performed well, *Heroically, actually*, he thought, reviewing in memory how, being towed slowly by that Una, they had flown over Princess Sathronin's Pink Palace in a show of force. General Thist had thought that having a dozen tri-wings darting around in the sky might be enough to force an immediate surrender, since most of WaterEdge soldiers had never seen people flying anything. *But that damned Loranthip Kech, the bastard, had already recruited deserters from the army who had fought at ShadowFall, and they were prepared for us!* He grimaced at recalling those catapult-launched buckets of small, fiery stones that killed three of his flyers.

Nevertheless, his surviving AFORS tri-wings had

then flame-bombed the defensive catapults and trebuchets that were entrenched around the Pink Palace grounds. *We took out their long-range weapons that first day,* he exulted, *and then we were through, with no place to launch from. We saved lives of our soldiers, but could have done more. If only we had engines like those we see in that Una's video archives, but nobody knows how to build them or even to get started in that direction.* Thinking more about those Una videos of the wars of the ancients, the destruction of entire nations, he knew he didn't want Motherland's enemies to be able to use aerial craft to wipe out entire cities. *I'm not even sure I want us to have that capability, either. I love the flying, but the constant killing, no.*

Bringing his attention back to the urgent present, Odel watched closely as each AFORS flyer dived below his craft, inspecting that glider for weaknesses and strengths of design in flight. *And of the pilots, truth be known!* he thought. After all four had passed beneath him, he flew below them in turn, inviting their inspection of his own craft's performance. *And of me, too, I'll bet!*

With thumbs-up signs all around, Odel gave a hand signal and a shout: "All right, light 'em up!" At that, each pilot turned, scratched a fire-starter, and lit the short fuse of a ceramic cylinder the size of an arm. As his own firepowder booster ignited, Odel heard the *whoosh!* of its nozzle exhaust and felt the jerk as his craft suddenly accelerated; controlling his attitude, he directed the rocket-powered flyer as it rose higher and higher, rising another thousand feet in seconds. As the firepowder rocket burned out, Odel's world was quiet, peaceful. Looking around, he confirmed that his aerial fleet had made it as well. *Great! We really are an aerial force. These new craft are larger, faster, can carry bigger loads. They will serve us well, next time we…*

He didn't want to think further on it, that such beautiful machines could cause so much carnage. *And as much as I care for my friends Thist and Thusk, and love this gorgeous land I'm flying over, none of it is really my war. If I wanted to fight, I'd go back to God's Country and take on the obnoxious Solar Priests. But...*

Putting thoughts of war out of his mind, Odel waved to his companions. Practicing maneuvers over the next half hour, he finally gave the "Recall" signal and returned to the landing field next to the tall Wakan's Tower from which they had launched. The new aerial craft design had worked very well as had his little pilots —that wen, Mox, especially. Tying her own craft down securely, she came over and hugged him around his waist. Odel lifted her so that their faces met, delighting in the smell of her sweet sweat, yet another unique characteristic of her People. *Like...other...physical features she has that our big women here don't*, he reminded himself, almost blushing. He never could figure out why it was that his friends Thist and Thusk seemed to prefer women not of their own kind, but large ones like the Princess. *Ah well*, he thought as he put Mox down gently, still holding her tiny hands. *To each his own; no accounting for tastes. But my little Mox tastes sooo good!*

As the other pilots converged, giving the ancient thumbs-up signals, Odel's field instrumentation technicians strode across the field, smiling broadly. "So did we reach over two thousand feet altitude?" he asked as the men cheered in answer. Smiling, he began to plan another mission. *Could I really fly up over the cliff top, into the Dark Highlands? Maybe go back home?* He was anxious to discuss all of this with Mox, his little companion from the land of the glaciers. She had not been happy in Motherland, given the recent ongoing tensions between her People and native Motherlanders, the Originals. Liberating ShadowFall from General Creesile's invasion had not been enough of a feat for Mox and her countrymen to earn the permanent gratitude of the tall Motherlanders; others of her People wanted to work out a solution, but she just wanted out. *And I'll take her out of here, one way or another,* Odel thought. *Flying home in that Una would be the best and fastest, but maybe these tri-wings can get up to the height needed..* As he envisioned lighting up his rocket booster, an idea came to him: *What if we added two or even more rockets? Bet we could get up over that cliff, east or west of that Mother of a waterfall, onto dry land. Something to think about!*

7.

Four weeks after the albino pirate had first come ashore at WaterEdge, Altamun Kech was again on the same prominent pier, this time with an unhappy and quite furious Captain Noor, who was once again guarded by half a dozen Mothersman springbowmen.

"Dammit, Priest!" Noor spit out, "your Mother Messinex would not even listen to my claim. The godsphere that floated up ashore on my island clearly shows that all of your so-called 'Motherland' was once under many hundreds of feet of sea. And since"—he drew himself up, chest out, jewelry clinking—"we Sea Lords have dominion over all seas, it is only natural that these *bottomlands*"—the tone was sneering—"that you call a 'nation,' belong to us. The ancients said it, we believe it, and that settles it!" *The man's eyes are near afire,* the Kech thought. *Good thing he has no weapons!*

"Captain Noor," Altamun explained calmly, hoping to temper the pirate's wrath (*After all, those ships of his out there could still pose a real problem*), "what's past is past. The Mother speaks for us all. Just be glad she allowed you to return. In one piece." The pirate nodded in recognition; from the gruesome sentences that Motherland criminals often suffered, he knew the Kech was not exaggerating.

But Captain Noor continued to fume and curse as the longboat was rowing toward the pier to pick him up. "That Mother of yours, she even kept my godsphere, Priest, and my maps! That is not acceptable! I should have something in return, you know."

"Such matters are above my station, Captain. I only follow orders."

Noor grew quiet, then whispered, "You know, from what I've learned in my trip to Mother's City, talking to the coachmen and guards and others during these weeks, you Kech priests are the true secret weapons of this Motherland. Your knowledge of all things." Conspiratorially, he spoke even less loudly, "And if the stories are true about your magic monkey-men and their big green flying cucumber god-machine? With them, that, and you, mate, we could conquer the whole round world!" Laughing, the pirate slapped Altamun Kech on the shoulder and clambered down the ladder to the waiting longboat. Angry or not, the priest was happy to see the pirate leave. Four weeks of that weird spectrum of fetid aromas and unceasing chatter en route to Mother's City and back, in a confined coach, were enough for a lifetime!

Altamun waited until Noor was aboard his flagship and the entire fleet of barbarians had sailed over the horizon. *What does that criminal plan to do?* he wondered. *I have the impression that he could bring a hundred ships to invade us. We will need more defenses if they do. I will talk to the princess about recruiting—impressing—another thousand men, training them, arming them. We have to be ready!* Thinking of the crazy pirate's insane claims to all of Motherland itself, the priest concluded, *This Sea Lord threat affects more than just the Sisterdom of WaterEdge; it is a national crisis—Whatever is happening in the rebellion in ShadowFall, Mother Messinex must supply us troops!*

OVER THE NEXT WEEK, ALTAMUN KEPT EXPLORING HIS ice-crack valley, hoping to find means of escape, but the only way out was still the opening onto the stony shore. Recognizing that his marooned situation might be for a considerable time, he pulled up enough peat moss to pack around his brush-built shelter, expanding it to have a place to stand, a place to lie down, and a central fire pit. An opening in the top provided ventilation. Picking and choosing among the infinite supply of broken stones on the valley floor, he assembled a tool kit of rough cutters and scrapers and used them to fashion branches into short spears for fish and sharp-pronged gigs for frogs. A stone-headed club and a long pointed spear for small game rounded out his inventory. A warren of rabbits did exist, he soon discovered, and their meat provided a welcome break in his fish-and-frog diet.

Though surviving, Altamun wanted to get back to civilization. He dreamed of soft beds, warm women, cold wine, books to read, reports to write—and just some ordinary human companionship. To his regret, the morning smoke fires that he laboriously arranged daily atop his original rock shelter attracted no ships. "I could be here for years," he said aloud, "and no one would know. In fact, I doubt if any other human being has even been in my little valley." By this time, he would have welcomed even those dreaded slavers. *At least I would hear human voices, something—anything!—other than pounding surf and whispering wind!*

As weeks passed, the daily reflected warmth grew less and less, and Altamun became concerned that a cold winter might freeze him or his river and drive off whatever small game he could find. *Freeze to death or starve to death! What a choice.*

ALTAMUN AWOKE TO THE ROAR OF A STORM. HURRYING out of his wattle-and-daub hut, he saw that the sky overhead was dark, with fog and clouds scudding over the valley, kicking up a mist of snow that blotted out most of the darkness above it. Looking seaward toward the valley opening, he saw the east winds kicking up enormous waves and crashing surf.

I'll just stay inside and hope for the best, he decided. Keeping the fire going, attempting to pad his fine godscloth robe with layers of rabbit skin and peat, and just staying alive, became the sole focus of his efforts for the two full days and nights the eastern storm blew without ceasing.

WHILE THE DARK STORM RAGED OVERHEAD, ALTHOUGH Altamun's survival activities kept him busy, his mind was bored. Used to the thousand and two things in a Sisterdom that kept a Kech priest busy—attempting to temper the outlandish and expensive whims of a spoiled princess; overseeing the construction of bridges, canals, roads, and piers; ensuring plantings and harvests; sitting in on trials and executions of criminals and political activists; and other minutiae—none of those existed here in his valley, and he only had his memories to review. *And this one is the worst of all—my capture by Noor's pirates.*

THE NIGHT BEFORE APPROACHING WATEREDGE WITH HIS pirate fleet, Captain Noor had secretly landed small boats north of the harbor, out of view, far from the piers. Those twenty men made it ashore in the dark without being seen. They successfully infiltrated the city, mimicking the local clothing and speech, renting temporary quarters without drawing attention. *I should have posted watchers in watchtowers all along our coast,* Altamun thought regretfully. *And planted more spies in the population. But I didn't, and the old sea dog outsmarted me! And I paid the price! Taken captive in my own mansion on the grounds of the Pink Palace, even as I slept!*

"I even bribed your loyal guards, Kech man," Noor had bragged to his face in the captain's own cabin aboard the *Free Brother.* "It's amazing how little coin it takes when the main incentive is to live as a free man, beholden to no princess, no Mother. And no damned olive-skinned Kech priest from an imaginary land."

Altamun had not replied; he was Noor's now, no question about it. A hundred kilometers at sea, en route to the Lordship Island, a den of pirates and barbarians. "But why me?" he asked, "Why not kidnap the princess?"

Noor laughed. "She's too old for fun, and too

brainless to matter. Even though I am contemptuous of your so-called 'Motherland,' I don't wantto be at perpetual war with its millions of people. So, Kech-man, I took you—brains, knowledge, experience. Your Mother won't go to war over a priest who can be quickly replaced, and by another who is much more friendly to us Sea Lords. One such as your friend, Loranthip."

At Altamun's shocked face, the pirate laughed again. "You don't think my agents haven't landed at that WaterEdge city before? Maybe years ago? How did you think we pulled off those profitable raids over the last decade? Your assistant, Loranthip Kech, has been a most valuable spy and agent."

Altamun was crushed. Loranthip, a traitor? A few years older than himself, the man was an exemplary Kech—educated, a quick learner, skilled in court and national political matters. Why had he betrayed Altamun and the princess, and the Motherland?

Captain Noor volunteered the unasked-for answers. "You Kech priests, for all your intellectual knowledge, sometimes overlook the obvious." He looked Altamun straight in the eyes and said in an earnest manner, "Altamun, first realize that you are never going back to WaterEdge, unless it is as an ambassador for me." At the Kech's sniff of diffidence, the pirate continued, "I want you to be my first mate of land affairs, so I will tell you this. Your Loranthip felt like he was passed over for a younger man; he resented reporting to you. And unlike many of you others from whatever strange place you call home, Loranthip never accepted his kidnapping out there next to that weird pyramid, if that story is even true. So he had no true loyalty to any Mother or princess.

"Such tensions will tear at a man; if you know how to evaluate them, you can tell who is vulnerable and who is not. Some years ago, my agents in the city sussed out the issue with Loranthip and gradually brought him —and *bought* him—to my side.

"And I offer you what I offered him—riches beyond

your dreams, freedom as a free man, and someday, somehow, a return to your High Antis homes. If we can find them." Noor let those thoughts sink in. Chuckling, he said, "I never really intended to try to find that place, but the stories of Princess Pernie's monkey-men and their flying green whatever-it-is, make me think we just might be able to fly there. What do you think?" Altamun acted insulted by Noor's offer, but admitted it had its temptations.

UPON ARRIVAL AT THE INCREDIBLY BEAUTIFUL LORDSHIP Island, with its white sand beaches framed by high gray cliffs and overhanging palm trees, Altamun was surprised at his treatment by both the captain and the island's inhabitants. Rather than the den of cutthroat thieves he had expected, the locals seemed like ordinary citizens, *But much happier and more relaxed than in WaterEdge,* he thought. *And more colorful in skin and dress and even gaudy street decor. So many albinos like Noor, but also those reddish men and the dark black ones, even some like me.* Street musicians, literally unheard of anywhere in Motherland, strolled slowly down broad avenues, playing soft, lilting tunes, accepting donations from onlookers and passersby. To Altamun, they were the final assertion of a better way of life than he had ever known. *Is this what freedom means?* Even though he had thought himself "free" in his High Antis homeland, the customs, costumes, and austere traditions in that mountainous nation were not as amenable to individual expression. *There is joy here,* he saw. *These people are truly happy!*

AFTER BEING SETTLED IN A SPACIOUS AND PLUSH SET OF rooms in a large whitewashed stone house of his own, complete with shelves of books and scrolls and ancient mechanical artifacts he didn't recognize, Altamun knew that Captain Noor was being true to his word. *He has provided everything—a mansion, research materials, and a promise of servants and even voluntary concubines if I want. But I am still a captive, still taking orders from Noor. I may have more personal freedom on the island here, but am I truly free, if Noor commands my every action?* Over the last year he had never pressed the issue, resolving to adapt to his new situation. His one nagging concern was how the traitorous Loranthip, known to Altamun to be ambitious and reckless, might mislead Princess Sathronin. Especially with his seditious suggestion during the ShadowFall rebellion that WaterEdge might want to side with Princess Pernie against Mother Messinex, taking advantage of the turmoil among the Sisters caused by General Creesile's imminent invasion of Pernie's Sisterdom.

I tried to shut down all such seditious talk when I was high priest and advisor, but with Loranthip in my place, who knows? Well, all of that is in the past and thousands of miles away in another land. Another place where I was a kidnap victim! He laughed at his own thoughts; he was unconsciously even thinking in miles, not kilometers, after all his time with pirates. "Because that was a year ago," Altamun said to himself, remembering his time in the Ice Crack.

BACK THEN, HE HAD BEEN TALKING TO HIMSELF ONE day, trying to make his voice heard over the howling winds buffeting his tree-branch-peat-sod shelter. "The adventures I had with the Captain—fighting real pirates, exploring highlands, finding those ancient ruins—would fill volumes, if I had any writing materials in this cursed hut. I really was freer then than I had ever known. If only we had not ventured north, looking for this miserable valley. Damn that man's curiosity!" Outside, the storm raged, though Altamun thought he sensed a diminishing strength in the winds that were trying to destroy his shelter. The fire was going strong, he was relatively warm, and still dry, and well fed. Drifting off to sleep, he dreamed of white sandy beaches and palm trees and warm island women.

The next morning, the winds ceased and Altamun roused himself to go outside. The air was fresh and sweet; overhead, the sky a deep blue. As he congratulated himself on surviving the worst night of his many weeks of marooned solitude, a distant human voice echoed in his valley.

In a moment, everything changed.

CHAPTER SEVEN

*T*he Universe seemed to swirl around Thusk and within him, stretching his body and his inner self *in all dimensions—not in pain or pleasure but in a kind of tingling near-ecstasy, of new belonging, of*—fitting. As those sensations wafted away, Thusk returned to his normal senses of sight, sound, pressure, temperature. *And heartbeats,* he thought, *and muscle strain, and headaches. I don't care for the stress of returning to Earth, detached from that Mienne. I've done it half a dozen times before, but* this *time was really different*!

And here he was again, his vision returning, sitting on the oversized transparent crystalline chair that was the Crystal Throne in Mother's Auditorium in Mother's Palace. *With Mother Pernie looking up at me from the bottom of the stairs, as lovely as ever.* As his lover and confidant over the last year, young Pernie's ever-so-shaded ivory skin, moss-green eyes, and copper-red hair were welcome and familiar sights. *Just what I need, her beauty, to anchor me back in reality after this wild ride back from the Moon!*

"Thusk, my love, what do you think of my Crystal Throne?" Mother Perneptheranam asked the small dark man just now clambering off of the cold stone seat, as he stood on the narrow ledge around it. Alone with her little lover in the vast Mother's Auditorium, save for two large black-vested Mothersman guards, she anxiously awaited Thusk's report of his activities on the Moon. "And what is happening up *there*?" she asked, pointing toward the high domed ceiling of the auditorium. But Thusk knew she didn't mean the fabulous historical paintings on that painted tile surface a hundred meters above them, but far beyond it, out to Earth's satellite, from where he had just "returned" after occupying a *qomp* system avatar—*My Moon body!* he thought, *Tall and thin like Mienne, my…friend…up there, who was born there. Mienne, who is quite the woman now!*

Thusk answered Pernie haltingly, trying to control his speech. "Mother, riding the Crystal Throne is always quite an adventure. But it is better to *have ridden it* than to *ride it*!" Pernie chuckled and after Thusk's polite bow toward her, he walked down the thirteen transparent steps as a rainbow of colors swirled within them, trailing his passage.

He would have to give Pernie a full report later, but a carefully edited one. *I can never tell her what really happened up there this time*, he thought. *Not about how Mienne is now a grown woman. Not only is there another whole round world up there, but a new body for me and a whole different way of life. In fact, one much better for me there, than here!* His own thought, almost treason that, surprised him. Would he rather stay up there with Mienne, forever destined to live underground in the vast subsurface lunar tubes that were Community's living spaces in the Moon? Would he be satisfied using that avvy body, spending his time exploring the hundreds, maybe thousands, of kilometers of abandoned tubes branching out from Community, or even those on the devastated Far Side? Or attempt to make a life on the surface of the Moon, in one of the largely abandoned yet still functional dome cities? How would his Earthly body be sustained if he did? He smiled, wondering what those ignorant sun-worshipping Solar Priests at God's Port would think of him, living inside the jeweled necklace of the Moon goddess they called the Pale Lady of the Night.

For Thusk, the visits between the worlds had begun a year ago, shortly after Pernie was inaugurated as Mother following the Battle of ShadowFall and the untimely death of Mother Messinex at the battlefront there. Upon setting up residence within Mother's Palace, Thusk was anxious to repeat his twin, Thist's, experience on the legendary Crystal Throne.

"I found out about that Mienne girl and talking to the Moon, just by accident," Thist had said back then, "when we were searching for Mother Messinex, before the Battle of ShadowFall. Nobody was in the auditorium but me, and when I brushed against that big transparent chair, it lit up with all kinds of colors. It seemed to beckon me, inviting me up those crystal stairs and into the seat. Wakan and Pernie once said that the Lordess Mother—her biological mother—always sat on it with her bottom bare, so I did, too. I hoped to learn what the Mother did, maybe be able to find Messinex."

After which Thist described the sensation of leaving his body, of his mind mixing with that of one Mienne, a young girl who lived on the Moon. Or rather, *in* it; "She lives in a large underground cavern up there, a *tube,* she said. Lots of ancient made-things in them. I could see through her eyes, feel what she felt, and let me tell you, being in a female's body is really strange. Mienne was in a room with its own Crystal Throne. But those big crystal chairs were just used by the ancients up there to communicate with us down here on Earth. That's all they are—communication devices, not anything godlike at all." Thist said he did not want to try it again, that it all was too mind-bending, too exhausting. "And for what?" he had asked his twin. "Thusk, I am just too busy here in Motherland to go up to the Moon again. There's nothing up there that anybody down here needs, anyway."

Thusk agreed with most of that; he knew Thist was overwhelmed with new responsibilities in the new regime running Motherland, that Pernie and her chief priest, Wakan Kech, were urging him to take over all military matters for Motherland, now that ex-general

Creesile—"No-legs" was his taboo whispered name—was in the dungeons under Mother's Palace. But for Thusk, the appeal of the unknown, the exotic, was too great to resist. "I've got the same *Dee-Enn-Aee* as Thist," he told Pernie one night in bed. "And Wakan says that it is what enables Thist and me both to activate so many ancient godspheres—we are more closely related to the ancients who made them, *purer* if you will, than most other people in Motherland. So it is logical that if Thist can sit on the Crystal Throne then so can I, and experience what he did."

After some persuasion, Pernie—Mother Perneptheranam now—had finally agreed to let her little lover attempt the contact. Sitting up with pillows behind her back and sheer godscloth sheets drawn up across her breasts for feigned modesty, she said, "You know that Wakan believes the throne is what drove my Lordess Mother, my true mother, insane, and finally killed her. In the half-year that my sister Messinex used it every day, she, too, changed from a beautiful loving woman to something horrible; she was showing signs of irrationality and instability there at the end." With a frown, she added, "Probably that is why she authorized that horrible Miran Kech to send General Creesile to invade my ShadowFall. I hate to think of all the misery that throne has caused, all the Mothers it drove insane, over hundreds or thousands of years."

Thusk nodded in sympathy. He knew that simply by being a princess, Pernie had been happy reigning in her Sisterdom of ShadowFall, had not sought out the Motherhood with all its vast problems and concerns. Certainly, he himself would have been satisfied to stay at ShadowFall as her advisor and lover. *And Anklya's, too.* He smiled, remembering vividly the tall beautiful blonde handmaid he had rescued there and taken to his own homeland. But now Anklya was a powerful person in those faraway People's Lands next to the northern glacier. Princess Pernie was elevated to Mother of all Motherland, and his twin was presently the important *General Thist*. He himself, Thusk, was officially the

Special Advisor to Mother Pernie. *And her lover, too,* he thought with a smile. *Especially that!* He was somewhat thankful that his two lovers, Pernie and Anklya, were separated by over two thousand kilometers. *I don't think Pernie is jealous, but with her life-or-death power over every person in Motherland, I don't want to chance it.*

In a pensive mood, Pernie went on, "Apparently the throne was originally set up for ancients with a certain DNA, which Wakan tells me is the code that builds the cells our bodies are made from. We moderns here in Motherland are not that much of a match for the ancient code because since ancient times we have intermixed and mutated. So the Crystal Throne messes with our minds when we use it. Wakan and I decided that I would not sit on it every day; we would avoid that old, old tradition so that I would not become insane like my predecessors. But Thist—and presumably you—have more of the same ancient blood, that DNA stuff, than we do, so the throne worked for him, and most likely will for you, too.

"Thusk, my love, you are a great scholar and your talents in archiving our history from the godspheres and old books—as well as your, er, ah, *talent* here in my boudoir—are greatly appreciated. As are your diplomatic skills handling the difficult relations with the Republic of ShadowFall. But for myself, I'd like to know more about what's going on up there on the Moon and in it. Maybe there are things up there that can help us here on Earth. As you always say, 'Knowledge is important. Especially when other people don't know it.'"

Thusk grinned; his Sire, Reader Thess, would have been pleased to hear his advice being echoed by the most powerful woman in the most powerful nation in the whole round world.

"So if you want to go up to the Moon and explore it, and if the Crystal Throne will enable that, I hereby appoint you Motherland's very first ambassador to the Moon!"

THUSK'S FIRST TRIP ON THE CRYSTAL THRONE THE YEAR before had to be experienced to be explained; no words could impart the feeling of *otherness,* of detachment from reality. But once he had made mind-to-mind contact with that Mienne, the girl on the Moon in her own crystal chair up there, the intimacy was beyond belief—a *oneness* unlike anything he'd ever felt, a *unity* of two minds, two souls. He did not like to admit it to himself, but he felt her physical desires as well. *She is young,* he thought. *Yet when our minds mix, I sense her maturity, her needs. Maybe on the Moon they age differently?*

"Mienne," he had said by merely thinking/feeling, "is this what the ancients did, when they used these chairs? I mean, this is more than just talking, it is like, er, making love, only more than that." There! He had broached the awkward subject, and waited for her response.

The girl's reaction was confused and confusing. "Mr. Thusk, I feel a strangeness with you that I did not when first—*speaking*—with your twin, Mr. Thist. I can't explain it, but it is a—" Abruptly, the connection broke, leaving Thusk disconcerted, unable to think. As the quantum communication, the *qomplink,* disestablished itself, he went through the swirling, disorienting, kaleidoscopic return phase, finally feeling the coldness of the crystal chair against his bare bottom. His tunic was covering his surprising physical response to Mienne's enticing tone. Glancing down at Pernie, he was grateful that she was not standing beside him but was down at the foot of the illuminated stairs; he didn't want her to suspect his otherworldly desires. *Pernie is my lover, and I hers*, he thought, *but even though she is so young, she still has ultimate power over me!*

BUT WHAT THUSK HAD ENCOUNTERED ON THE MOON

during his last visit, he hadn't told Pernie, and only briefly mentioned to a disbelieving and doubting Thist. "Another *body*, Thusk? Mixing *minds* I know happens, I've been there. But popping into a human *body* up there on the Moon? You're just hallucinating, is all." Thusk knew that his twin believed his story, though; among their People, lying was almost unheard of. Between siblings it was a near impossibility.

When Thusk had sat on the Crystal Throne that last time, instead of experiencing the familiar and ever more sensuous mixing of minds with Mienne, he awoke in another body, not his own! Standing over him was a tall, dark-haired, and olive-skinned young woman, slender and attractive, in a pink shift-like dress that did not hide her modest curves—Mienne? *She is as tall as Motherlanders, and so am I! But how do I know this, and why do I feel so big myself?* Next to her was a shorter, very pale, almost albino, young girl, wearing a similar close-fitting green garment, but with no arms!

In a state of near shock, Thusk's immediate concern was with the body he was in. *How did this happen?* he asked himself, and then repeated the question in the deep voice of the strange body he inhabited.

The dark-haired girl answered, "You are in the *avatar* mode, my friend from Motherth. Since you last visited, we have uncovered the incredible nanofacturing capabilities of this site. Some of the equipment still operates. From the archives the DI reconstituted what it says is an *avatarobot*; we call it an *avvy*." Smiling broadly and suppressing a giggle, she said, "Now you can not only speak to me here in Moon, you can walk around, touch, smell, do *everything* just like we do!"

Thusk thought the room smelled faintly of the odor that Una, their flying machine, emitted upon takeoffs and landings; a bit acrid but not unpleasant. He tentatively tried to move his limbs, successfully sitting up and swinging his legs off the low-lying gurney he was on. "This feels strange, miss. You, you, are *Mienne*, I take it?" He thought he recalled seeing an image of her on Una's video screen months ago, but at the moment his memories of such images were not as sharp as the sights he had actually experienced in real life. He recognized that fact but had no idea why, except: *Maybe a person has to become accustomed to video images from an early age?*

"Yes, I am." Mienne smiled knowingly. "Welcome to Moon." Touching the shoulder of her armless smaller companion, she said, "And this is Wayer, my best friend." Thusk then recalled having seen Wayer through Mienne's eyes during one of his previous visits. His memories seemed vague, incomplete. *Maybe this body's brain remembers different from my own?*

Thusk nodded toward both of them and then stood barefoot on the surprisingly warm floor. In a light blue formfitting shirt and matching shorts, he could see that his arms and legs were a very pale pink. Flexing his arms and legs, he felt unusually strong, yet a little off-balance, and much lighter on his feet. "How does this body, this *avvy*, work, Mienne? Is it like my real body? Are there any dangers I should know about?" He was fascinated to be looking at a tall person eye to eye, rather than up at them. And enjoying Mienne's appearance. When only their minds had mixed on his previous "journeys", he had not seen Mienne in the flesh, only out through her eyes, and for some reason, not much of her surroundings or of her friend Wayer.

Mienne said, "Here in the Control Center, we have experimented with the qomp chair, which apparently is a kind of transmitter. According to DI, the avvy body itself acts as a receiver, being built of the same qomps and nanotech.

"A small man in the Five Cities down in Community, Jolan Keesh, was able to transfer himself into the avvy." She shrugged. "He...*liked* it, being as tall as me." Blushing, she shook her head, not wanting to say what she and Jolan had done while he was in the avvy. "All told, the test was enough to prove it works, but I especially wanted you Motherth people to use it. Particularly *you,* because with our mind-mixing, I feel that I already know you well."

There it is, again, Thusk thought. *If that's not an invitation...*

"I want to show you our world, to walk with me through it. And if you have avvys up on Motherth, I'd like to visit you up there, too."

"Mienne," Thusk replied, trying to modulate the avatar's voice to a less deep tone, "we have nothing like this. Only a Crystal Throne, and just the one. Until recently, it was used only by the Mothers of Motherland, for thousands of years." Shaking his head, he said, "And it drove all those poor women insane, unfortunately."

Led by the hand by Mienne, with Wayer tagging along, Thusk walked around the large room in which he had awakened in his new body, resisting an urge to lope, to take long steps. What Mienne called the Control Room was a hemispherical dome about ten meters across, with glowing digital displays scattered all over the inner surface. In awe at the scenes in and around the Moon, of the tube cities of Community inhabited by other small people like Wayer and his own original size, he tried to take stock of his feelings of the new body he was immersed in. The first thing was, he still felt very light on his feet. Was it the avvy body or something else? As he tried absorbing his surroundings, Mienne demonstrated for him the marvels of her Control Room and its capabilities, finally blacking out all the interior lights to let the imported lunar surface image emerge all around them. And there in the distance, rising up over sawblade-sharp mountains, was a blue-and-white disc standing out against a velvet-black sky sprayed with tiny lights.

Thusk gasped. "And that is Earth, up there? That is how it appears from here on the Moon?" That image, he knew, would be burned into his mind for the rest of his life. "I've seen it in simulation, even in some of the *videos* that our aircraft, our Una, has shown us. But, but, seeing it this way, against the fullness of infinite sky, is indescribable." Trembling, he motioned to sit on one of the padded benches.

After accepting some tangy liquid nourishment from

Mienne, Thusk asked, "This body I am in. I don't know what qomps really are, or what *nanotech* means. Is it all biological or just robotic, mechanical? Our Una has tried to describe such differences, but right now I feel completely biological, and very lightweight. And if I can drink this juice, it must also mean I have to excrete wastes, too?"

Mienne laughed. "Mr. Thusk, this body you are in is both biological *and* robotic, with quadrillions of built-in qomps that are neither. It can do anything—*anything*—your body up on Motherth can do. Remember that our gravity down here is but one-sixth of yours up there, so you will feel lighter. And as far as food and drink, the ancients designed the avvy such that all nourishment entering is used up almost completely, any remainder being expelled through sweat and breath. So no need for bathroom breaks. According to our archives, it is also self-repairing and much longer-lived." Blushing, she added quietly. "That one local man found out that certain—*other*—biological functions are available as well."

She didn't elaborate, but Thusk quickly touched his groin. *Yes, those parts are there, too, though they feel... smaller.* Then he thought, *But why have them in a body that is just for communication? Maybe the ancients had other uses planned?* Nothing came to mind, so he decided, *Something to ask Una when I get back to Earth.*

THUSK AND THE TWO TUNNELING ENGINEERS, JOLAN Keesh and Ledd Mernan, accompanied Mienne and Wayer as the two girls showed the newcomer around the various areas of what they called their "Control Level," a three-dimensional maze of illuminated hallways, elevator shafts, escalators, and doorways. "There are at least ten levels in this complex, hundreds of rooms," Mienne said as they passed by transparent walls that revealed strange equipment and large machines of unknown use. "We are on the top one. Not all of the moving stairs or elevators below here are functional, and there were many cave-ins and slumped walls, so there were still some levels we couldn't get to and explore." Smiling, she touched Jolan Keesh on his hard hat. "Until our marvelous engineers found a way to dig down to them.

"And in one huge room far below here, we found the laboratory and the avatar-making nanomachines. Many of them no longer functioned, or at least did not respond to us. But one of them did, and to our surprise when activated, the DI produced the avatarobot body you now occupy. How, I do not know." Thusk wanted to say that he had not volunteered for a new body, but thought better of it. He was becoming acclimated to the constructed device—*Suit? Clothes? Body?*—and was looking forward to seeing what the rest of Mienne's world was like. As long as his avatar body was comfortable and safe, he would focus his attention externally. *What do these people have that we can use down on Earth? That avatar machine, for one. What others?*

"THIS WAS CALLED 'THE HALL OF WHISPERS,'" Mienne said, sweeping her arm to indicate the wide tunnel, its tiled arch at least five meters high and its length disappearing into the distance. Now a riot of colorful holographic images displaying dozens of sites of the small Moon people at various activities, a subdued babble of overlapping voices, music, and electronic sounds, echoed through the arches. "The people of Community could not sense the visible spectrum as you and I do, so to them the images were meaningless wispy blurs. And they do not process all of the voice frequencies of the accompanying sounds, either."

Thusk laughed. "So, 'Hall of Whispers.' Just think of how many years of progress were lost until you came down from the surface and found all of this." Mienne blushed.

Wayer said, "But the qomps made what they call 'contact lenses', small goggles, so I can see what Mienne does, you know. Many in Community wear them now, like these engineers here, but some of the Elders don't, or just won't." She laughed. "I read somewhere that 'There are none so blind as those who will not see.' A perfect description of most of the Council."

"But even those people are welcome to see the truth here anytime they want," Mienne said with a laugh, waving the group on. "Let us take you to Shinyeen City, one of the Five Cities of Community, where you can see how Wayer and I lived before we found the Center last year."

As they left the hall, at the exit door stood the once-formidable Nuuk, a tall figure completely covered in what appeared to be dull reddish metal armor, with only a horizontal slit in the head area to indicate where eyes or a face might be. In all the millennia up until Mienne activated the Hall of Whispers, the—person? robot?— had brandished a long whip with which he/it drove off unauthorized people. Mienne was happy to see the creature apparently disarmed and inattentive; she had barely escaped that lash on her first unauthorized visit a year before. She never had received an adequate explanation from DI about what the Nuuk was and whether it was sentient or merely robotic. But as long as it remained stationary and nonthreatening, she could ignore it.

After the two-kilometer walk through the dim red lights of the tunnel to Shinyeen City, Mienne stopped outside the entrance to an irregularly shaped opening into a cavern extending at right angles to the main tube. There she introduced Thusk to Elder Myuk, the extremely wrinkled mistress of the Niche of Disabled Children, neglecting to tell him the nickname she and Wayer had used for their guardian. This aged Elder having been so protective of them when they were scheduled to be Reprocessed, the girls were now embarrassed that they had ever called her "Ugly Elder." From Thusk's facial reaction, Mienne guessed that he would probably agree. *But a person's looks do not reveal what's inside them,* she thought. *I think it says more about us who judge them that way.*

In their workshop area of the city, Ledd Mernan and Jolan Keesh were enthusiastically professional in showing off their stable of excavation equipment to Thusk—drills, dozers, lasers. And the Earthman was more impressed than he wanted to let on. He said, "I've never seen machinery like this anywhere on Earth, in my travels. So huge, so complex. Our Una is an ancient machine that can fly and hover and has, I believe, an intelligence of a kind, but this," he said, rubbing his palms over the smoothly machined finish of a massive earth mover, "this is magnificent. What roads and canals and tunnels we could build!" The engineers were all smiles; the man from Motherth envied their machines!

Hours later the group finished off a spicy meal with members of the Community Council, who Thusk could tell were all wearing the dark contact lenses that enabled them to witness ubiquitous overhead digital displays in their city. Thusk thought it strange that in all the millennia the people of Community must have lived underground, that nobody had ever seen the ceiling screens that displayed scenes from hundreds of other sites in and around the Moon. Many of those screens were blank now, or dark, and others only showed ruined domes or cave-ins; there was no sound. *But if you can see only in infrared,* he thought, *these displays are invisible and useless.* He wondered whether there were phenomena he himself was missing, either physically or metaphorically. *How do you ever know what you don't know?* He dropped that train of thought; he had too much to learn about Mienne's world and its capabilities.

BACK IN CONTROL ROOM, MIENNE SHOWED THUSK

where she and Wayer were living, then took him to a separate room. With a simple mattress and bed located in a niche, and with utilitarian toilet facilities, the accommodations were not nearly as plush as in his and Pernie's room up on Earth, but then nothing else in Motherland was, either. This would do for his new body.

Taking the one chair in the room, Mienne sat and talked as Thusk sat on the bed, his back against the wall, leaning across the narrow mattress. "Mr. Thusk," she began (rather timidly, Thusk noted), "I have something I want to say to you, alone. We have shared—minds, I suppose—over the qomp communication system. During those times I was able to glimpse some of your memories. You are eighteen Motherth years of age? And you have a friend, Anklya? And one named Pernie?" Drawing in her breath slowly, she said, "They are both exceptionally beautiful."

Thusk nodded dumbly. He had not experienced Mienne's memories during the mixings, yet she knew about his lovers? *How much did she see? I think I know.*

"So, Mr. Thusk, I have come to know you well, though we have never really met, until now. other than that mind-mixing way." She looked at him in a way that with any other girl—woman?—he would believe was evidence of increasing passion. *But with this avatar body?*

"Yes, we have, Mienne. I think I have come to know you well, too." Thusk was growing slightly uneasy at her tone, but his new body was beginning to respond physically to her overt seduction. *Do these Moon people have such rapid reactions, and hook up so soon after meeting?* He realized then that he had "known" Mienne for a year, sharing minds more intimately than any other two lovers ever had. *At least since ancient times,* he thought, wondering if fully functional avatar bodies had been used by the old civilization for such very intimate "communication."

So it's not a rapid relationship, but a long-standing one. Intellectually, he was not all that interested in the slender young female who now got up from her chair and sat beside him, stroking his face, but his body was responding involuntarily. Mienne's shift was drawn up high above her knees now, her breasts heaving. Thusk accepted the fact that Moon people had different customs than Earth people, but some things were the same. A voice seemed to whisper, "When on the Moon, do as the Moon people do."

Mienne spoke softly, seductively. "Thusk—may I just call you that?—I told you that your avatar body could do anything your Motherth body can. I know that because, well, it was one of my first—experiments?— that I tried after this body you now wear was activated and occupied by a man from Community." Sighing, she kissed him. "And it was wonderful. So I am already attracted to this body, but I think I am also in love with you, your mind." Huskily: "I want you, now."

Thusk gulped, "But how old are you, young woman? Should you be doing this sort of thing?"

Stroking his groin lightly, Mienne just smiled. "Ugly Elder had my age all wrong, because we UpTop people mature at different rates than you do here, DownUnder. By Motherth measures, I was fifteen when I fell into Community. I am over eighteen now, as old as you. Is that old enough, Earth-man?" she said, squeezing him *there*.

To his delight, Thusk found that it was.

CHAPTER EIGHT

"Mother Perneptheranam!" the fat man in the blue velvet suit shouted, his raspy voice echoing off the polished marble walls of the Mother's throne room. "ShadowFall has serious problems! These little dark people from the Dark Highlands, like this one here beside me are, are, just—"

"Quiet!" Wakan Kech raised his voice, motioning to the tall, armor-vested Mothersmen guards to silence the offender. "Who dares speak to our Mother that way? Out of the throne room with him!" Glancing up to Mother Pernie on her throne, he saw her nod slightly, then continued, "Guards, this one is never to be admitted to the Mother's presence, ever again. Permanently barred." Wakan was pleased to see that as one guard muzzled the complainer with a big hand over his mouth and an arm around his neck, the other guard picked the man up and together they roughly carried him out of the Mother's presence.

Raising a palm toward the target of the portly man's displeasure, a plainly clothed immigrant whom Wakan recognized as one of General Thist's little dark-skinned bird-riding warriors, the priest smiled and said, "And your response to your, er, *fellow* ShadowFaller is?"

"Mother, Wakan Kech," the small man said, bowing as he spoke. His Motherspeak was almost fluent, revealing to the Mother what she had known about

Thist's and Thusk's diminutive countrymen: they were all very fast learners, within barely two years' exposure now speaking Motherland's language better than many native citizens. "I am Thetten, once a peat farmer in The People's Lands. I enlisted as a bird-warrior with General Thist's troops when we liberated your former Sisterdom. Now I'm a farmer again, but in the general's armed reserves." In a quieter voice he said, "We fought in the next campaign, too." Frowning, Thetten went silent; that conflict was never to be mentioned.

Seeing that both the Mother and the Kech priest were waiting for him to finish, Thetten said, "In the year since the republic was founded, we folk from The People's Lands have conducted ourselves as promised. Coming from our poor cold country of receding glaciers, we found Motherland to be a warm paradise. For our war efforts we were granted possession of the republic's easternmost lands and have learned to farm the virgin prairies and to fish the rivers." He paused. "And the problems my, er, *large* countryman spoke of, well, we People work harder and raise more crops, and have begun to trade with other Sisterdoms down the river." Palms up, he shrugged. "This has interrupted the trade monopoly the former nobles used to have."

Wakan commented, "And that is the basis of the ShadowFall Republic's issues? Trade? Money?"

Thetten hesitated briefly, then nodded.

Mother Pernie spoke, clearly, *And with an edge,* Wakan thought. "Please deposit the papers that you and that high-living countryman brought as details of your claims and defenses. You shall have a resolution decision soon," adding with a smile, "Thank you for your aid in liberating ShadowFall. And please congratulate your People for increasing ShadowFall's crop production. Because of recent…issues…that food is needed elsewhere in our country."

Thetten bowed, turned on his heel and departed. Though Wakan wished the day were over, he could see another dozen or more anxious citizens standing outside the throne room door, awaiting their time to make pleas, accept promotions, or offer suggestions. With a weary voice the Kech commanded, "Let the next one enter."

I AM CONCERNED ABOUT MOTHER PERNIE, WAKAN KECH thought as he watched the day's final petitioners and new appointees depart Mother's throne room, ushered out by the Mothersman guards. *Though she is only twenty-one and in good health, I fear that the burden of sudden Mothership may have been too much to lay upon her. I do remain hopeful, though, that she does not use the Crystal Throne any more. That thing made previous Mothers turn mad!*

As if reading her priest's mind, a wearied Mother Perneptheranam walked down the steps from the raised throne platform and onto the marble floor, where Wakan took her in his arms, fatherly. *Like a daughter I could never hold,* he thought.

"Dear Wakan," she whispered, "Do you think we have tried to do too much, too soon?" Sighing, she said aloud, "How did Messinex, and before her, our Lordess Mother, and all those other Mothers, century after century, how did they ever handle all of this, day in, day out? Did they have some magical strength potion one of you Kech gave them?"

"Mother," the Kech replied, smiling, "I know of no such potion. If I did, we'd both have it!" They both laughed. "But I will say, those other Mothers were not attempting to reorganize a whole empire like we want to do. It's a challenge going from Sisterdoms to republics, from absolute to distributed power. Those old Mothers let traditions and institutions do the heavy lifting, and allowed each Sister to worry about the details in their own lands." *And most of them were horrible tyrants, too,* he thought. *Very few complainers ever lived to present their cases to the Mother in person, as was done did today.*

Mother Pernie nodded, motioning for Wakan to join her in smaller private quarters adjacent to the throne room. There, as they both lay on soft couches, handmaidens massaged their shoulders and calves, rubbing perfumed lotions on Pernie's tired muscles and a strong liniment on Wakan's. More handmaids brought in fresh fruit, cheeses, and a selection of sweet wines from the famed vineyards of Three Rivers. Incense vapors wafted by palm fans permeated the room, adding a literal atmosphere of tranquility to the surroundings.

After relaxing a bit, Mother Pernie said, "You know, Wakan, Thusk has been spending a lot of time on his Crystal Throne trips lately, in communication with the qomps, presumably visiting the Moon girl, that Mienne. I do have guards standing by there, to help him each time he comes out of that…trance. After a year of doing those trips, half a dozen now, he stays longer each time. Hopefully, the reason he stays so long is because he is learning things on the Moon that we can apply down here. Otherwise…" *Though I have a feeling he might like it up there a bit* too much. *Or maybe it's that Mienne girl, the one who lives there?*

Wakan nodded. *I hope Thusk is not becoming addicted to whatever—or whomever—is up there,* he thought. *We need his brains and creativity down here.*

Pernie continued, "I want Thusk to return to ShadowFall right away and see what he can do about the troubles there that we heard about today. Thist sent me a message by the mirror towers you installed, saying that Sathronin has surrendered, so he would be back in a few days, once he has…executed…the transition to a republic." Wakan just nodded, grimly. He suspected that WaterEdge's population of nobles would shortly be diminished. *Or should I say, 'diminished shortly,' knowing of Thist's penchant for decapitation of traitors.*

"My plan is to put Thist and Thusk together again, to work as a team. They have been apart too long in my opinion, and that Captain Noor pirate business— kidnapping that Kech advisor last year, the outrageous claims to Messinex with that godsphere or whatever—is a good excuse to arrange that. There is no predicting what they will find out there in the Lordship Isles and wherever else they may choose to explore. I don't want them competing with each other, because together they are unlike anything Motherland has ever known."

She smiled, thinking, *Certainly in my bed they are unlike any others.* But that thought brought on the familiar nagging yearning. *Thist has been gone to WaterEdge for weeks now, and even when he is here, Thusk is becoming…more distant. I find myself needing —wanting!—the touch of other men.* Wakan had long before told her that such desires were normal in any young woman in her early twenties, that she should not feel guilty or ashamed. "You are a healthy woman, Pernie, with physical needs." She hoped he remembered that advice.

Wakan Kech nodded, peeling a long yellow fruit. "Yes, Mother, they pulled off a fairly peaceful democratic revolution in their northern homeland, and with their Una machine successfully defended your ShadowFall. As your general, Thist has put down two rebellions; and as a Moon explorer through his qomp communication on the Crystal Throne, Thusk has opened our eyes to a whole new world. Literally."

Mother Pernie smiled. "Once they have…*solved*… the current troubles in WaterEdge and ShadowFall, I will want them to use their Una together to go exploring over the Cold Sea. To find out what kinds of strength those Noor pirates have, how they operate. Why they have raided WaterEdge for centuries instead of just trading with us." Growing grim, she said harshly, "If that pirate chief kidnapped Sathronin's Kech advisor, I want him punished. As just as importantly, Una and the twins might be able to find those so-called 'Lordship Islands' of legend and story."

Wakan noticed a sudden serious expression on Pernie's face a transformation. *She's going to say something she doesn't want to,* he thought. *And probably I won't like.* "Wakan, I've been thinking, if they do find those islands and if those places amount to anything, there will be new territories, new people, to trade with. Maybe, if we're lucky, they can even furnish us with new crops or fruits or meat animals. But first, I want that albino bandit's head on a spike!"

Wakan smiled weakly. In the year since Pernie became Mother after the death of Messinex during the final battle of ShadowFall, she had exhibited exemplary powers of ruling—assessing disparate facts, assigning appropriate discipline and restrictive measures when necessary, rewarding performing bureaucrats, dismissing corrupt ones, balancing the precarious ambitions of a dozen absolute princesses and their privileged nobles. And executing only the most disloyal, egregious, and self-serving parasites in the palace and across Motherland. Those, he recalled, did number in the hundreds, *But a small price to pay for the welfare of millions/*

Wakan had been happy that under his guidance, based largely on his own homeland's meritocratic culture in the High Antis, his protégé Pernie had been pursuing the principles of literacy, equality and democracy for all citizens of Motherland. *But it is taking longer than either of us wished; some people have to be forcibly removed from the conversation.* Changing over from an absolute matriarchy to a semblance of a democratic republic was an entirely new concept in the millennia-old empire she had inherited.

I taught her these principles, so I am ultimately responsible. But the cost... For the most part, she has been relatively benevolent, even kind. For the most part. Yet my spies in the Sisterhoods tell me of more discontent in every princess's domain, even among some ordinary citizens—Mother's slave property!—who prefer not to change. I can't tell Pernie that yet; she has enough to worry about. Thinking over the sage decisions and decisive actions that Thist, the little man from the Dark Highlands—now *General* Thist—had demonstrated during his two short years in Motherland, Wakan told himself, *I will need Thist's counsel, his wisdom, on how to handle our revolution. We expected some resistance to our democratic changes, but did not think it would be so vicious.*

What had surprised Wakan occurred when the Sisterdom-That-Shall-Never-Be-Named revolted only a few months into Pernie's reign, before Motherland had completely settled down after the war on ShadowFall. Thousands of Motherland troops, disappointed that they were not able to sack ShadowFall's riches, were secretly recruited by that Sister and her Kech advisor, who thought they were merely continuing the incessant inter-Sisterine wars, a traditional pastime of the petty matriarchs. That late Sister and her Kech had committed a fatal error by not realizing the extent of Pernie's strength and determination, which by then comprised not only a large and loyal part of the Mothersman Army, but was buttressed by the presence and skills of Thist and Thusk, their flying Una machine, the tri-wing aerial force of Odel M'ridge, and the hundreds of small but battle-hardened, bird-riding People's Lands countrymen, immigrants from the far north.

"Wakan," Pernie had said back then, furious when the first rebellion broke out, "this outrage must be more than just punished. I want her burned alive, naked, in front of her citizens, her palace plowed into the ground, and her lands divided among my other Sisters who have adjacent lands. Her citizens will be divided accordingly." Wakan had never seen such rage, not even when she was awaiting General Creesile's final attack upon herself and her palace.

"And I want every reference to her and that Sisterdom of hers erased from all records, everywhere—statues, tapestries, books, street names, *everything*! She will not have existed!" And so Mother Pernie had had her revenge. But when the Sisterdom of WaterEdge likewise rebelled during the same year, Wakan was able to prevail upon Pernie to be more merciful. That Sisterdom contained Motherland's only seaport as well as fertile croplands; he didn't want to lose those resources and alienate its citizens. And from her mellower mood during this private conversation, she appeared to be mellowing. Somewhat.

Sipping a glass of wine, Pernie said, "Wakan, I don't

want to kill Sathronin; she was once a nice Sister to me, when I was a little girl here in the palace. I don't know what happened to her, why she fights me."

"Thank you, Mother, I understand your mercy." While he was eating grapes, Wakan knew he was supposed to ask *What else?* but was reluctant to inquire about further details.

Pernie said, "Once Thist returns her here—and I have confidence that he will—she will be kept in comfortable conditions in one of the cottages on the palace grounds for the rest of her life." *Merciful,* Wakan approved. "But she must be punished, as a reminder to her and all who might want to support her again."

Wakan's voice broke. "But, Mother, you aren't considering punishing her as we did General Creesile, are you?" He remembered with a frown how Pernie had wanted General Creesile burned publicly for his invasion of her Sisterdom. But Thist had argued for the man to be left alive even though he had led the attack. It was only after Creesile's second betrayal that he had administered the death-herb. He shuddered to recall Creesile's month-long agony; the prison guards who had witnessed it likewise shuddered, as did all of the other potential traitors among the disaffected soldiers.

"Creesile was following the orders of Miran Kech," Thist had said forcefully. "Legal orders. I don't think he should be burned alive or tortured to death for that. Besides, he is the most experienced military man in all Motherland, and if I'm going to take over from him, I need his knowledge. Of logistics, of resources, of manpower, of command."

Pernie had solved that problem for Thist, showing her wisdom at such a young age, but a brutal wisdom tempered by the reality of Motherland's history and power structure. "Very well, Thist, Creesile will live, because you have made the case for mining his knowledge and skills. But he will still be imprisoned below the palace, with very restricted access to outsiders, to prevent any treasonous activities. And one more condition..." Wakan Kech gritted his teeth at that memory; he was required to be present when that *one more condition* was applied: when Mother Pernie had Creesile's legs sawed off, unequally, partway between hip and knee, condemning the ex-general to a wheeled chair for life. Wakan knew that Thist often conferred with the mutilated man on military matters, granting the prisoner extra food, drink, and even occasional female favors, in return for relevant and useful advice. Wakan thought, *I think I'd rather have been burnt than suffer that!*

Pernie admonished her priest. "No, Wakan, I would never disfigure my Sister like that. But to ensure she never raises forces against us again, even from the dungeon, you will have her eyes removed!"

Gulping, Wakan choked out, "Of course, Mother. As you wish." *Somewhat merciful,* he thought, *but I* know I *would rather be burnt!*

CHAPTER NINE

Over the next days, in her private quarters, Mother Pernie and Wakan Kech worked on the details of how to transform Motherland's ossified matriarchies into emergent and functional republics. In front of them were stacks of reports from Pernie's former Sisterdom, ShadowFall, which had been operating under the new system of governance for a full year. Not all of the news from there was heartening. Among other priorities, they urgently needed to find a way to reduce conflict between ethnicities, the large and the small people—the original inhabitants and the dark little immigrants from the land of Thist and Thusk.

Wakan proffered one solution. "What if we create a separate republic for the immigrants, in the uninhabited eastern lands? Just separate the short people from the tall?"

Pernie frowned. "Motherland has never *segregated,* if that's the term, its people. But that may be possible." *Identical in every way!* she thought of her two favorite lovers, Thist and Thusk, with a smile. *If all those dark little men are like mine, I can imagine a lot of mixed marriages up there already.* "Let me think about that. It wouldn't solve the trade issues, but might reduce conflicts."

She tossed a sheaf of papers onto their wide work table. "What have we learned from our changes in

ShadowFall, Wakan?" she asked in obvious distaste. "Even outside the trade issues little Thetten brought out, aside from the ethnic problems, even among the originals I see nothing but squabbles, arguments, even some duels. Will they ever learn to govern themselves, or do I have to appoint a new Sister to rule them with an iron hand again?" Shaking her head, she added, "Surely the ancients who existed thousands of years before The Ice came, they dealt with all of this in a rational manner. What did *they* do?"

Wakan thought, *First, they endured centuries of headmen, tribal chiefs, monarchs, wars and revolutions. Then came constitutional governments, and finally they evolved a complex system of distributed democracy made possible by technologies we don't have and can't reproduce. But most of all, they eventually educated the populace. Something we don't have and can't wait for!* "Mother," he replied softly, "they had many hundreds of years to do what we hope to accomplish in our—*your*—lifetime. But we can learn a few simple steps from them." *I don't dare bring up that ancient Constitution of the Union of North America, or that Hemispheric Declaration of Rights. One step at a time.*

"I interpret these reports from ShadowFall another way," he said. "Motherland citizens have been conditioned by thousands of years of servitude; outside of running their shops and trading, they seldom think for themselves, were not allowed to, and were even killed for it. And that is why the trading situation with the immigrants arose—*that* they understand.

"As for the rest, they will have to be taught to adjudicate issues, without relying on a noble or a Sister to settle their problems. But we can take intermediate steps, and set up a hierarchy of persons who can moderate disputes, interpret contracts, make settlements." Taking up another stack of papers, he said, "I have some solutions that the ancients found useful. Summarizing historical findings from the godspheres and from that Una's memory archives, we can establish some new institutions that will help these new republics operate more smoothly."

Mother Pernie scanned the summary sheet that Wakan handed to her. "*Judges*? People trained in the law? I suppose that would help, but first they would have to be chosen and then educated." After moment's consideration, she said, "I can see that; we set up schools to teach the laws, select honest persons of integrity as students, then assign them to the new republics when they're educated."

Wakan smiled. "For the interim, I suggest that you appoint people in each republic and Sisterdom already known to possess those characteristics. As they practice their new profession, they write down their ideas, and these become the outlines for the law-school curricula." He sighed. "It will take years, Mother, but we have to begin somewhere. And such a system will help us transform from absolutism to a democratic system."

"Agreed, Wakan. Pick some of your Kech and ask them to choose the best candidates in their Sisterdoms. You and I will select the first 'judges' for ShadowFall and what will shortly become the new Republic of WaterEdge. And I will insist that the new councils of each republic elect a local council leader to make final decisions at home, and another to represent their republic here in my palace."

Wakan said, "So we will have a Congress of Representatives? Will that replace your current advisors?" He was suddenly concerned about his own position as Mother Pernie's chief priest and advisor.

Pernie laughed. "Yes. Those representatives will more fairly gain Mother's attentions, don't you think? No republic will be overlooked if it has a squabbling, whining man or woman here, complaining or begging every day.

"But your services, Wakan, they will be needed by me as long as you live." Suddenly frowning, she said, "Or as long as I do."

Wakan nodded, acknowledging with Pernie that their Motherland was still far from becoming one of those ancient democracies that elected its leaders, that violence was a long and still honored means of succession. He tried to suppress the next thought, but could not: *With at least ten remaining Sisters, still absolute rulers in their domains, supported by hundreds of privileged nobles and thousands of unemployed soldiers, all able and probably willing, to attempt an assassination at any time!*

As he watched her, Wakan could see a sudden change in Pernie's demeanor. "Wakan, in some… secret…notes left me by another Mother, I saw the quote 'War is the health of the Motherland.' I take it to mean that conflict involving the whole country against an outside force would unite us as one. So I think that when Thist and Thusk return, we should consider building a navy to go over the Cold Sea and conquer all of those pirate islands we can find. We may have to trade with them first, to see if they will be worth the effort to invade."

Wakan paused, groaning within. He had often considered the same approach, but wondered how such a war could be justified by all the citizens who would fight in it. "Mother," he said, "as we saw at the Battle of ShadowFall, extreme loyalty—or extreme greed— among the troops is necessary. How might we excite our population to support an aggressive navy?"

Pernie laughed. "Wakan, my…records…show that Cold Sea pirates have raided WaterEdge off and on for centuries. Last year that Noor kidnapped Sathronin's chief Kech priest, who is dead now for all we know. If my little general brings that pirate back alive, we will have enough of a story to incite all Motherland. If Noor is dead, then I am sure my little men will have an equally stirring story to tell. Whatever happens, we can proclaim the pirate islands a threat to all, persuade all the Sisterdoms and republics to participate—for a share of the spoils."

"So there will be a war, then, Pernie?" Using the familiar name, rather than her title, told the Mother that

Wakan was asking as a lifelong friend, not just a formal advisor.

Pernie understood his friendly concern. "I see no other way, Wakan. Maybe we forget the trading, just outright invade and annex them to begin with." Her tone became more authoritative, measured, and Wakan knew he would be accepting orders, not suggestions. "Please begin assessing the investment required for providing us a navy, with all the particular naval weapons, provisions, training. Maybe even a way to carry some of Odel's tri-wings along for aerial bombing and some of Thist's bird-riders as invasion shock troops. It's too bad that the Una won't help fight anymore."

"You intend to begin building an invasion fleet soon?"

"Once General Thist and Ambassador Thusk return from their new mission to find Noor." Then she said, hesitatingly, "Wakan, Thist and Thusk will both be gone again for a while, out over the Cold Sea." In a lower voice she said, "I do have…other…needs that we must discuss. I'm sure you understand."

The Kech sighed; he knew that this day—or night—would be coming. *She is very young and very passionate. And I'm not sure that she won't be sending her little lovers away purposely, knowing that she might want to try someone new, experience some variety among the many courtiers and nobles here in Mother's City.* He began mentally to assess potential candidates. *Who can I trust? And, will Pernie want to…dispose…of him afterward? That would be a waste.* Laughing within, he thought, *In one breath we are talking about starting an international war and in the next, finding a man for Pernie's bed tonight!*

Wakan said, gravely, "Of course, Mother. I know of several potential candidates. Shall I provide you with choices or send in a surprise for you?"

CHAPTER TEN

Thusk, Special Advisor to the Mother, departed for ShadowFall on an early afternoon, flying aboard Una, the ancient god-machine he had retrieved from the glacial ice in his homeland. *Only two years ago? It seems like a lifetime.* Looking out through the transparent walls of Una's three-meter-diameter blunt cylinder, he saw the patchwork of crops, the ribbons of roads, and the sparkling rivers that were Motherland's valuable resources. Towns and small cities speckled the landscape—the capitals of the Sisterdoms exhibiting palaces and temples, the smaller settlements merely houses and shops. *And these, her ten million people, are her real strength—if they can ever stop fighting among themselves!* He was on a mission to ShadowFall to help prevent such fighting.

"Una," he said aloud to the Developing Intelligence, DI, which comprised the countless number of quantum computers—qomps—distributed throughout the aircraft's ten-meter length, "please inform me of any significant changes your sensors observe on our trip to ShadowFall. We need to maintain records of crops, irrigation, city sizes, and particularly any large gatherings of people who might be an illegal army forming up." With two rebellions in recent times, keeping a watch on potential enemies was a priority.

"Thusk, in summary, everything is nominal," Una

answered. "All scans are being recorded, collated, and analyzed for your retrieval. No unusual gatherings." As Una's voice emanated from a realistic three-dimensional image of a tall, sensuous blonde woman on the front screen of the cabin, Thusk groaned, *Why does Una always have to represent herself as Anklya, my former lover, now back in my homeland?* Though he intellectually denied having any remnant emotional attachment to the woman he had rescued from slavery in Motherland the year before, she was a constant character in his more erotic dreams, and the vision of her in all her lush beauty brought forth a physical reaction he tried to suppress. Pernie, Mother of Motherland, was his favorite now, and one did not cross the Mother. *And live!*

After Una landed her green fuselage in front of the Palace of ShadowFall, Thusk exited through the lowered side door, taking note of the Arch to his left. He was glad to see that the steel spike that had once occupied a prominent position at the keystone position was now gone. Its former purpose had been to support the grinning skulls of Pernie's annual First Man sacrifices, but now she was Mother and her former Sisterhood a republic, and relics of that royal privileged past were disappearing. *Good; we are removing superstitions and unnecessary deaths.* Smiling as he walked into the palace, he thought, *And I'm especially glad that the reigning Mother does not kill her lovers anymore.*

Inside the palace, Thusk's periodic meetings at ShadowFall were scheduled in Pernie's old throne room, now hallowed for being the very place where Princess Perneptheranam and her war council had stood against the hordes of General Creesile during the siege the year before. Thusk thought the room smelled. *Or is it these council members?* Part of the odor, he realized, was from fresh paint. The walls had recently been decorated with murals memorializing the siege, pictures he had not seen before. He recognized the accurately painted, life-sized renditions of the principals of that battle: the pale princess, the olive-skinned Wakan Kech, his own dark twin, Thist, and himself. *But were we all outfitted in battle armor? Thist and me astride our emus, carrying lances festooned with ShadowFall banners? No way! Artistic license, my ass!* He also disliked the insect-like representation of Una, the savior of that battle. *She is a big green flying cylinder; she does not look like a bug!*

As the fifteen citizens and ex-nobles who constituted the Governing Council of ShadowFall entered and took their places at what formerly had been Pernie's war planning table, Thusk paid attention. He recognized the Council members from his previous visits: a few wealthy merchants in fine godscloth, other tall citizens in a rainbow of colored tunics representing their trades and guilds, and several small People like himself—men and wen alike—in various kinds of dress and uniforms. And at the other end of the table sat a big, red-faced man with matching hair and beard—Odel M'ridge, now dressed in full khaki as chief of Motherland's aerial forces.

Thusk smiled at Odel, whom he considered the best and brightest here today. *And he's from God's Country, hundreds of kilometers upriver, in the Dark Highlands. At least he knows what we fought for here, what we're trying to do for all Motherland.* Odel's aerial force had been instrumental in defeating She-Who-Shall-Never-Be-Named. Thusk grimaced at the memory of that final battle at the obliterated and erased former Sisterhood, where...*No! I will dismiss thoughts of what happened that day! As I'm sure Odel tries to.* When the big man looked at him, nodding with no smile, Thusk knew they were both thinking alike. The aerial force had most recently supported General Thist's suppression of the rebel Princess Sathronin of WaterEdge. Thusk hoped that Pernie's revenge there would not be so gruesome. He himself was scheduled to fly Una to that port city after tending to the business here at ShadowFall. *Hopefully, that princess will be able to return with us to Mother's Palace, still in one piece. But today I have to pacify Pernie's former Sisterdom, the first republic to be established in Motherland.*

Without going through the usual protocols of introductions, greetings, and news updates, Thusk started in on the group, his displeasure obvious from his face and his stance. "I am most disappointed that the first new republic in Motherland is in such disarray," he said sternly. "I am told that there is dissension on account of People from The People's Lands, my former countrymen—People who look like me—and the so-called 'original' inhabitants, most of whom, I remind you, were only resettled from other Sisterdoms all of seven years ago.

"As I understand it, the problems arise from competition in trade. Your representatives, Herren of the west side of the river, and Thetten of the east side, made it clear to the Mother, her advisor Wakan Kech, and me, that this situation cannot stand."

Unrolling a long sheet of parchment, he said, "Therefore, as my aides will present to each of you, I strongly urge you to consider a political separation between a new ShadowFall, comprising all of the original settled lands, and a new independent republic to be established in the territories granted to immigrants from The People's Lands." At the intake of breaths and various other barely suppressed vocal noises, Thusk said, "Let me remind you all again, that we small people from the Dark Highlands fought for you, and with you, against Creesile and his invading armies, only a year ago."

An aide from Thusk's staff set up two tripods and stretched a colorful two-by-three-meter map between them. Thusk took a long, thin pointer stick, touching each designated spot as he described the reestablished borders. "This map is based upon a high-altitude photograph of ShadowFall.

"The new republic has a western border fifteen kilometers east of Mother's River, not touching any preexisting fields and farms. Its eastern boundary is the original ShadowFall boundary, adjacent to the Sisterdom of Ancient Towers. Furthermore, the new republic will be granted a two kilometer-wide strip of land along the southern border of ShadowFall to the Main Road, giving its citizens access to both the Main Road and to Mother's River, for the purposes of trade and commerce."

Sensing that the Council members were somewhat relieved that their lands and resources were not being confiscated or redistributed, Thusk chuckled. "Some of you here may understand the significance of the name of the new political entity being established here. It is to be called the Republic of Thessland."

OVER THE NEXT THREE DAYS THUSK TOOK EACH OF THE Council members on a ride in Una, at altitudes from fifty to five hundred meters, pointing out the boundaries of the new republic, and showing them the vast extent of ShadowFall itself, from the city of the Palace to the northernmost extent—the great kilometers-wide waterfall and its six hundred meter curtain of river water that plunged ceaselessly into Mother's Lake below, from which body of water Mother's River flowed southward. Having never seen their own land and lands from above, the Councilors were shocked and awed in equal measure. Thusk couldn't tell individually whether they were impressed with the natural beauty of their republic or if some of them were mentally planning how to expand their own properties. *Just like everybody*, he thought, *probably both*.

DURING THE FINAL SIGNING CEREMONY THE NEXT DAY, the Governing Council members notarized documents formally agreeing to respect the new charter for the Republic of Thessland. Thusk shook hands with each of them and saw them off. Only he and Odel M'ridge remained in the meeting room. Palace staff emerged from nowhere, lighting a different spectrum of incense burners—*Hopefully to get rid of the paint smells and body odors and perfumes, and to provide us some more relaxing aromas*, Thusk thought. A large assortment of sweetmeats, cheese, breads, and fruit was arrayed on the conference table. "And honeyed wine, you will recall, Odel, something you showed our vintners how to make." Holding up a frosty mug, he said, "We thank you for it."

The big man laughed. "Thusk, my man—or is it Your Highness Thusk, beggin' yer pardon?—you are quite welcome. I believe our two countries have a lot to give each other, a lot we can learn, both ways."

Sensing Odel's reluctance to detail those 'ways,' Thusk said, "It's always 'Thusk' to you, big guy. What's bothering you? You can speak openly here; nobody is around."

Odel swigged his cold wine. "Look, I hope this division of ShadowFall solves the immediate problems here. But there are big and little people, some of them who might want to live on the wrong side of that new border. You *do* know that not all of the issues are to do with crops and trade, right? "

"Such as?" Thusk was genuinely concerned.

"Well, there's lots of folks, both sides, who like to, er, *fraternize* with each other, y'know?" Asked for details, Odel grinned widely and then in exquisite detail described unique anatomical differences and complementary body chemistries between the two 'races,' unloading explicit stories that made Thusk blush.

"Why'd ya think that your Anklya and the princess and them other big Motherland women are so affectionate with you and Thusk? And why did so many of us large folks—including me, I have to say—find your little women so, er, stimulating?" Odel roared with laughter, spewing out a spray of wine. "And *tasty*, too, Thist. That Mox, my tri-winger? Right much."

"I really had no idea, Odel." Thusk was honest. "I *didn't* think." Embarrassed by his own ignorance, he said, "Let's change the subject." But now that his big friend had explained—with extreme precision—Thusk knew that mere signatures on a document were never going to remedy such primal issues.

"There ain't yet been no evidence of it," Odel said with a grin, wiping his lips and taking another drink. "But if it turns out we are interfertile, our young'uns are gonna be somethin' else!"

"ODEL, YOUR AERIAL FORCE IS A SIGNIFICANT FACTOR IN Thist's planning for the new Mothersman Army," Thusk said later in the evening, after much wine and reflection. "He and Wakan Kech want to expand the capabilities of your machines. You can build hundreds of new tri-wings, and train the flyers, my People, if they want to. Or build big ones for folks like yourself. I have had some ideas of providing you with rapidly erected launch towers, based on our experiences with catapults and trebuchets, oxen-pulled wheeled vehicles that can telescope up to twenty or thirty meters, right on the battlefield."

Odel squinted his eyes, his dark facial wrinkles made prominent by the flickering torchlight. "Thusk, hate to tell you this, but my taste for war is 'bout over. That last…campaign…before WaterEdge took a lot out of me. Now I was in the fight against Princess Sathronin that first day, last month, but left the others there to carry on. Seein's how the mirror-men messages are sayin' your twin's won the war down there now, the rest of my folk will soon be comin' back by wagon. Since they's fresh off of a mighty victory, some of them might be feelin' all cocky and all, and willin' to build more fliers, get them field-launchers of yours built. They's young and will be wantin' to be part of your Thessland Republic. But not me. Don't get me wrong, I love flyin'. I love my fliers, my pilots, and I love all that designing and testing.

"But, and a big but, I have had enough killing. Oh, I know it's necessary if you're gonna keep out bad guys like Miran Kech and Creesile and princesses like…"

Both men knew of Whom he would not speak. "But y'all down here in Motherland, ya gotta do it yourselves. Not me, not my homeland. I done your killin' and don't like the idea of it anymore. I don't know why anybody would even try to fight among y'all's selves; there's so much land, enough to go around for ever'body. And I still don't understand why your flying Una didn't help, *don't* help, you fight if ya have to…"

Thusk was quiet for a long minute. Skipping over the Una business as too complex to summarize, he said, "But how about back home, *your* home, in God's Country? You could organize a rebellion against those Solar Priests, the ones that fried your friend." He knew that Odel had never figured out that it had been Thist's theft of that godscloth spool that was responsible for the warehouseman's execution by solar mirror incineration two years ago. *And we'll never tell him, that's for sure.* "Odel, with your leadership abilities I'm sure you are experienced enough now to organize an army of God's Country citizens to overthrow those priests."

It was Odel's turn to rhapsodize on revolution. "Well, Thusk, I was glad to help y'all do most of what ya did in the last couple years, and I occasionally think I'd like to fly over that solar temple and drop some fire-bombs on those guys. But then I think—*What would I replace them with?* I'm not sure that me and my hill folks could come up with anything much better. The problems y'all are having here in ShadowFall, we would have in endless numbers back home, if we didn't have them Solars to bitch about to unify us.

"So I ain't sure that it would be worth all the killin' it would take. I never seen so much blood, so many dead and dying, as down here. I don't believe I could kill a man again, to tell the truth." Putting down his mug forcefully, he said in a loud whisper, "I thank all y'all for treating me so well down here, and I am happy that ShadowFall is free and WaterEdge and…that other place…aren't problems anymore, glad I could help. But I would like to ask one favor in return."

"What is that, Odel?" Thusk braced himself for some impossible demand.

"Please just use your Una to fly us back to my stone quarry in God's County." At Thusk's puzzled look, he said, "Me and my little woman, Mox. And a few of her little friends."

Thusk breathed out slowly, trying to take in his big friend's concerns. "When, Odel?"

"Soon's you can, Thusk," Odel said with a sigh. "Mox and me just want out."

CHAPTER ELEVEN

"Cap'n! Cap'n!" Attuk's raspy voice roused Lork from an exhausting, fitful sleep. His awakening mind wondered *What the Hel is happening now? Can things get any worse?* As he stumbled to the deck and saw what Attuk was pointing to, he said aloud, groaning, "I should never ask that question!"

Climbing out of his modest captain's quarters, Lork wiped his eyes with a wet towel and stood on the deck of *Ice God* and stretched, taking in a deep breath of fresh air. Above him, the blue sky was visible for the first time in two days, with only a bank of low-lying clouds or fog a short distance to the south. With a yawn he followed his first mate's pointing finger, indicating something to the west. "What is that, Attuk?" The dark streak across the span of glacial ice made no sense at first. But looking closer, eyes now focused, he realized what his grizzled first mate was seeing: a wide crevasse in the ice stretching left into the fog and to the right as far as he could see, cleaving the Ice Sea!

"Damn! Attuk, how close did we come?" Lork estimated that they had escaped disaster and death by less than a mile. No telling how deep that crack was!

"Cap'n, I done sent crew over there to take a look, but I reckon we's ony a half-mile from that Crack of Doom." Lork groaned at Attuk's dark humor but acknowledged the pun with an additional smile and nod.

Half a mile! The Wind Gods—in whom he suddenly believed and had always respected—had been benevolent after all. *Excuse my agnosticism,* he thought, *I will make offerings at the temple—when we all return safely to Stonehaven,* that last bit a hopeful deal with those deities to continue their protection.

"Cap'n Lork!" The cry came from the men investigating the crevasse. "You need to see this, sir!" Attuk tossed the rope ladder over the side of the *Ice God* and went down it, holding it in place as Lork slipped on his ice cleats and descended.

"What do you think, Attuk? First an uncharted crack, then something worth my time to go see?"

"Dunno, Cap'n. Our metal map don't show no hazards, jist a blurry bit; but then we be way far'er than anybody ever been, far's I kin tell." Grumpy without his morning chai, Lork tramped over to where his crew stood, waving and yelling, near the edge of the crevasse. A northern wind was kicking up some little ice-dust, beginning to dissipate the clouds and fog; flocks of birds —*Chuffs, like back home,* if memory served—disturbed by the unwelcome humans, noisily complained and flew away, disappearing westward.

Look at what? Lork thought. *Something down there, in that big crack?*

Lork and Attuk stepped through the line of fur-clad crew and looked down into the crevasse. Up close it was much wider than as seen from their ice ship: more than half a mile wide and at least that deep, its sloping walls defined by slumped and softened glacier ice, the place was more of an actual valley of sorts, with a flat, stony floor, patches of grasses and peat, and a fair number of leafless scrub oaks. But what drew their attention, as it had that of his crew, was the conical hut constructed around one of those trees, obviously a primitive shelter for a man. The rising wisps of smoke from an opening at the top showed that its inhabitant was still there.

"Damn, Attuk, but there's a man down there! Send somebody down to check him out. And take swords, in case he's hostile." Attuk gave the orders and turned to Lork, but dropped his jaw, eyes widening.

"Cap'n, Cap'n," the mate croaked, again pointing, but this time to the south. Without comment but shaking his head at Attuk's repetitious gesturing, Lork turned to follow that crooked finger once more.

What he saw, as the fog and clouds moved away, was Ice-End, the End of the World.

WITHOUT HESITATING, LORK RAN SOUTHWARD, followed by all the crew save the four who had descended into the ice valley to capture its lone inhabitant. At yet another glacier edge, they stood looking out over an impossible scene: the solid surface of the Ice Sea was gone! Thousands of feet below them lay a broad ribbon of exposed stone, with a river from the ice valley running over the stones in numerous streams, into—what?

"It be Ice-End, Cap'n," Attuk said in whispered awe. "Never believed in it, but here we are. But what is all that, that sparkly liquid out there? It goes ever'where!"

Lork was speechless; legends older than Time spoke of Ice-End, the boundary of the World itself, beyond which lay no Ice, but only melt, extending into infinite distance. Legendary, but here it was. "A *lake*, Attuk, just like the one at home, melted ice born from Goddess Hillmork. Magnificent, Attuk, just beautiful." He wondered about the salty odor coming from the direction of the huge lake, but dismissed it. *Salty water? Not possible*. Turning to his other crewmen, he said with more confidence than he felt at that moment, "Men, icers—we have made history today! Attuk here will sight in with his Sun-dialer and record our location. We will return home as heroes. For we have found and documented Ice-End. And now we know where the World ends!"

The men were more than a little disconcerted, trying to be cheerful but still looking over the edge at the tremendous ice cliff, then out to the distant horizon, and back again. Lork took command again, once more trying to impress upon them the significance of their discoveries, "So now we know that the Ice Sea is about three thousand feet thick here, and Attuk will chart this Edge of the World. We will create new maps for the Ice Hall Council, and everybody will hail us all as discoverers and as the most remarkable icers who ever lived!" Lork was more satisfied with their response this time; fame back home usually meant more food and certainly more amenable women. He could tell that they had all been worried, as had he, that returning empty-handed after the failure of the Dvora raid would bring embarrassment or worse.

"All right, now," Lork said with a grin, "we have all been privileged to find the End of the World, now let's go back and see about that man—or men—who lives at the bottom of that ice valley, at the bottom of our World."

As Lork and his crew watched from the edge of the crevasse, a tall figure dressed in dark green was walking around the wattle-and-daub hut below on the valley floor. Lork yelled out, "Who are you? Where are you from?"

At first appearing to be suspicious, the man finally waved and yelled back. Either his voice was garbled by echoes or else he spoke in an unknown tongue, but for whatever reason, nobody understood him. It took two hours for the four-man team to navigate the treacherous slumped ice wall, traversing switchbacks, crawling over cracks, avoiding crags, and to get down to the valley floor. Once there, swords drawn, they approached the tall figure, who bowed politely, holding up his hands to show he was unarmed. Lork couldn't hear the conversation, if that's what it was, but the body languages and gestures were plain to see even from thousands of feet away: the man was happy to be found and was willingly accompanying Lork's men back up to the Ice Sea.

"Who's there?" Altamun Kech yelled through cupped hands, trying to get the attention of the figures high above him on the far edge of the crevasse. Waving his arms wildly, he was relieved to see those figures waving back. "I hope they're not slavers," he said to himself, "but if they have decent food and a warm place to sleep, I'll take that much."

But how to get up to them? He had no gear for climbing; Captain Noor had not thought to provide any for what was to have been only a shore landing, and even if he had, their ship *Free Brother* was now in pieces at the bottom of the Cold Sea. Altamun saw the figures waving some more, seeming to congregate as if planning something. No ropes would reach this far down from them. All he could do was wait, so he retreated inside his makeshift hut and cooked a fish. As he chomped down on the greasy meal he wondered about what kind of people could possibly live on top of glacier. Were they true men, or some kind of animal?

He wished that Mother Messinex had not confiscated Captain Noor's godsphere last year; *That globe may have all the information we needed to explain the glacier people. I know it convinced the captain that our Motherland had once been a large sea, that his Lordship Island mountains were once tiny islands strung across the Cold Sea.* "He should not have laid claim to ancient seas, the old fool!" Altamun said; he would not be freezing in a damned glacier-crack if Noor had just been content with lording over half a million happy folks in his lordship. "But here I am, wondering who those glacier folk are and what they might be doing."

Three hours later, the strangers arrived. Altamun had marveled at their descent, using ropes and large springlike coils; anchoring themselves, lowering each other, until four of them were on the valley floor and approaching him. All of them carried short swords, and two had bow-like weapons strapped across their backs. *If they're not friendly, I am doomed,* the priest thought as the short and bearded fur-clad men drew within a few yards of him.

Bowing toward the men (*Rescuers? Slavers? Killers?*) then standing erect with his arms up and palms out, he said in a grave tone of voice, "I am Altamun Kech, advisor to Captain Noor, Supreme Lord of the Sea Lords. Welcome to my humble valley. I greet you in peace."

One of the glacier folk responded, with speech that reminded Altamun of pigs squealing and owls hooting; he understood not a word. *But at least they haven't cut me down on the spot!*

Half an hour of back-and\-forth speech attempts apparently convinced the glacier folk that talking was useless, so they made gestures that showed their intent: they wanted to put a rope around the priest and take him back up with them to the top of the glacier.

"I have no choice, my short friends," Altamun said to their leader, taking the proffered rope sling and pretending to wrap it around himself. "Let us proceed." All the men laughed, which the priest took as a good sign. *I only hope I am not to be a meal, for I have no idea what glacier men find to eat up there!*

The four-hour trip up the glacier wall was something Altamun Kech would never forget, though he wished he could: dangling from a rope hundreds of meters up, scrambling on icy ledges while the glacier men drove coiled springs above, pulling him up, dragging him over rocks embedded in the ice, and more dangling from hundreds of meters up. The sights below might have been awe-inspiring—the infinitely long crevasse valley on one hand, the receding shoreline and sea surf on the other—but to Altamun the hours stretched endlessly, each second full of fear. He had never known he suffered from acrophobia, but by the time the rescuers brought him to the glacier surface, he was paralyzed, eyes tightly shut, breathing erratically.

The glacier men tied his hands behind his back and walked him toward a taller, red-bearded man, obviously their leader. All of the men appeared to be strong, confident, no-nonsense types. *Typical experienced sailors,* Altamun thought, *maybe even pirates, but on* ice?

But what impressed Altamun most were the three vessels tied down onto the ice, wooden constructions with sails, resembling seagoing ships but low-slung, no more than two decks deep. About twenty meters in length, four in beam, the ice ships (as he immediately thought of them) sported huge outriggers with metal blades, with a strange arrangement of spring coils on both sides that looked as if they served like the oars on a water-borne craft. How different! *These are an inventive people, adapted to a world of ice. But how do they live? Where do they live? And most importantly, how do they treat strangers?*

THEY TIED HIS *HANDS WHEN THEY GOT TO THE TOP, I SEE,* Lork observed as the captive approached him, the retrieval crew apparently distrustful of their ward. *And I don't blame them. He is taller than we are, has that not-quite-brown skin, and is dressed in strange wispy green robes. Dirty ones at that, stuffed full of peat and mud. And stinking!*

"Who are you?" Lork asked. The man answered the obvious question, pointing to himself, his speech seemingly grunts and clicks and wheezes, a nonsense sound, "*Alll-mmmm-kessshhh*". Lork said, "I don't understand you, man. Do you speak a civilized tongue?" The man spoke differently in response, but to Lork it was just more unintelligible garble.

"I give up, Attuk," Lork said in disgust, quickly losing interest. "Get him up the ladder and into an animal cage belowdecks. And for Tag's sake, wash off the dirt and the stink from those clothes; give him some old furs to keep warm." Those cages were intended to be filled with sheep, goats, and cattle—*And they would be, but for the Drunken Duke's damned fireballs!*

On deck, Attuk reported that the rescued man had gone willingly into the cage. "He even seemed happy to take our leftover swill, Cap'n," the mate said with a smile. "Must'a been starvin'. Wonder how long he was down there." Attuk wrinkled his forehead. "More'n that, Cap'n, I wonder, how he did *get* down there?"

Lork said, "And I wonder where in Ice did he come from? You think there might be other kinds of people out this way? I mean, look—that crevasse, it extends all the way from that big lake out there, all the way north, far's we can see. Maybe his people live on the Ice on the other side?" Visions of raids on the captive's homeland formed in his mind—*Where do they make that fine material? It would be worth a fortune back in Na Saam.* And since the man's fine-spun clothing was obviously not fit for wear on the Ice Sea, he must have come from another volcanic valley, one with its own goddess of warmth.

New places to raid! Lork exulted. *Not only did I find Ice-End, but whole new lands to plunder. This tall, strange man might be the one who saves this raiding trip. And saves* me*!*

ALL ATTEMPTS AT SPEECH COMMUNICATION FAILING, THE glacier men put Altamun into a cage belowdecks, and provided him with warm furs and a hot stew to eat. Appreciating his respite from the harsh ice valley of the last months, he determined to enjoy the creature comforts, however short his time might be. When one of his captors brought him a mug of a honeyed wine, he was ecstatic, smiling and loudly thanking the man. "You are civilized men!" he shouted in a language nobody else understood. "Wine is the common tongue of humanity!" His captors laughed; they understood that much!

CHAPTER TWELVE

"Thesslanders, follow me!" Odel M'ridge shouted from the platform of the Arch of ShadowFall, his right arm raised high, broadsword in hand. Afternoon sunlight played on his polished sword, a bright reflection that he used to advantage to attract attention. He knew he was an imposing figure, red-haired and full-bearded, taller and more broad-chested than most Motherlanders, and certainly twice as tall as most of the dark little people in the crowd before him. The assembled immigrants from The People's Lands, countrymen of Thist and Thusk, stood in mixed anger and relief as Odel hastily ordered them to gather up their possessions into wagons and follow him out of town and into their new republic to the east.

The people were ready to heed him; independence was not going well for the newly founded Thessland Republic. Violence had erupted the next morning after the separation was announced, with the local guard force seemingly approving of the actions of the original ShadowFallers who attacked their smaller neighbors all over the city. Though the treaty allowed a full month for the separation of the two populations, Odel, seeing that the guards would not protect Thesslanders, hoped to prevent further problems by simply taking the new republic's citizens to their own territory immediately. Among them was his lover, little Mox, who had distinguished herself in the Creesile War as a commander of bird-riding warriors. In the year since then, she had easily become Odel's best tri-wing flyer—and his lover.

Three hours later, as evening shadows fell, the plaza in front of the palace was clogged with ox-drawn wagons, carts, and carriages of all kinds and sizes. Odel and Mox were in front, in a small two-wheel, horse-drawn carriage, their possessions having already been relocated to what had now become Thess City, capital of the Thessland Republic. Many of the drivers carried unlit torches, ready to be fired up should darkness overtake the caravan before they could settle into quarters in the new republic, fifteen miles to the east.

As Odel started his team, leading the caravan away, a band of angry "Originals," as they now called themselves, armed with springbows and other weapons, ran into the plaza, surrounding Odel's entourage, yelling what were meant to be insults and slurs at Odel and the thousand little dark people behind him. Stopping his carriage, Odel stood at full height and drew his sword, waving it high for all the attackers to see. The mob quietened, but the defiance and anger on their faces struck Odel as confusing, irrational.

Brushing aside a long pike weapon held up in front of him, Odel yelled out, "Leave us be, folks. We'll soon be away from here, won't bother you no more!" In the hundred wagons behind his, on the more than a hundred two-leg war-birds packing the plaza, he could see the PeopleLanders pulling out their own springbows, smaller but still lethal. Odel realized that if he couldn't ease the tension, both sides were going to pay a heavy price in lives. As his people stood their ground, sweeping their springbows across the mob, cooler heads did prevail. Odel sensed the change in the atmosphere, and calmly but loudly said, "Remember, everybody, we all fought Creesile together. All of us here still respect our Mother, Perneptheranam, and all of us still honor the two little men who rescued us—Thist and Thusk!" Between the hundreds of ready springbows and Odel's rhetoric, the cursing crowd backed off and dissolved away into knots of grumbling, mumbling individuals.

With relief, Odel said to Mox, "I don't know what's got into these people, Mox, but I don't like it. But you and me, gal, we are getting out of here as soon as we can." Having heard through Wakan's nationwide mirror messaging system that his little twin friends were to go on an expedition to explore over the Cold Sea, Odel realized that he could not depend upon them to fly him or any of his people back to God's Country. He determined that he would begin to make plans to leave without their flying god-machine. "That Una would make the trip in less than half an hour," he told Mox as the caravan slowly made its way toward the new capital city, "but if we can find some kind of valley in the Dark Highlands farther to the east, or if we can build really tall towers to launch from, I can get up to two thousand feet, and I will take you to my home."

As Mox snuggled up to him, Odel put his right arm around her. *My little friends have changed in the time I've known them, so I can't count on them getting us out with their Una. After he was here to arrange the treaty, I realized that Thusk is more concerned with helping Mother Pernie than us. And I know that General Thist is getting too involved in wars. They won't be helping me, but I'll do whatever it takes to get us out of here before it's too late, my little one,* he thought. *Whatever it takes.*

DAYS LATER, AFTER ALL THE THESSLANDERS HAD safely arrived and begun to find temporary homes to share while building their own, Odel M'ridge met in the Thess City plaza with a group of close to one hundred citizens of their new republic. The sun overhead was hot, shade almost nonexistent from the few scraggly pines that defined the extent of the acre of pounded dirt. Sunlight reflecting from whitewashed adobe walls of the surrounding homes and buildings added to the heat, bringing up Odel's unwanted memories of the big polished copper solar concentrators in God's Port, used by the Solar Priests there to incinerate victims. On a more pleasant note, aromas of cooking food swept in from the kiosks of vendors set up around the periphery, while iced mugs of honeyed wine and various beers were eagerly quaffed as the people waited. Odel was glad to see that, while most of his impromptu audience were the short, dark People's Lands immigrants, more than a few dozen original tall ShadowFallers stood out among them, people of both sexes. As he had suspected, mixed-race relationships were becoming a natural development. *I understand quite well, fellows, what you find attractive in the little women. And I've heard of equal enthusiasms from our big women and their little men.* He smiled at a sudden thought: *What a trio—Thist and Thusk and Pernie...*

In the center of the plaza Odel had erected a six-foot-tall wooden model of a launching tower, complete with scale models of the AFORS tri-wing powered gliders. "In real life, I believe we can build one of these Wakan's Towers two hundred feet high," he said, walking around the model, which by design matched his own height. "From the top platform, using multiple rocket boosters, I am confident that I—*we*—can routinely reach over two thousand feet in altitude. Your AFORS pilots and I have already done that, in fact, from an eighty-foot tower back in ShadowFall."

As the crowd of dozens gathered around the model, the question arose, "And why spend all this time and effort, Odel? Only a few dozen of us can fly your machines. Are we going to have to fight again? And against who? ShadowFall? All of Motherland?"

Odel grew grim. "Folks, first I don't believe that signatures on a paper are going to stop the kind of violence against us—and here I include myself, my Mox, everybody here in Thessland—that we saw back in ShadowFall." Loud groans and sighs from his audience soon evolved into complaints and curses, which Odel strived to contain.

"Listen, think what you want, but I have had enough

of fighting. The land I came from, which the priests call God's Country, has not had a war of any kind in hundreds of years." He winced inwardly, glossing over the simmering religious conflicts between his homeland and the Solar Priests, but those border skirmishes were minor in comparison to the bloody slaughters in Motherland the last year. *Which I have been part of,* he thought, *but no more!* "Mox and I plan to return there. I have a plan that will enable anybody else who wants to, to go with us."

This time, the shouts were louder. "The Dark Highlands?" "Over that waterfall?" "Those cliffs are thousands of feet high!" "What kind of people live there" "Is it any better than here, where we were promised peace and friendship?"

Odel held up his arms for quiet. "Listen, folks, weeks ago I asked some scouting crews to explore along the foot of the Dark Highlands, twenty miles east of the great waterfall. And I am happy to say that they have found a valley with cliff walls a little lower than around the waterfall. There is a forest there with more than enough timber to build a full-scale tower like this model. There is a cliff face that I am confident I can fly to the top of."

A red-faced man, an Original, asked bluntly, "Odel, so you can fly to the top with your tri-wing and its rockets. How do you plan to get a thousand or more of us up there?"

Standing beside the model tower, measuring three feet high by six inches in diameter, was a wooden spool with some shimmering blue material wrapped around it. Odel smiled and put his hands snugly into large green gloves. He unspooled a yard-wide bolt of godscloth, its translucence almost invisible to the onlookers. "I think you all may have heard of how our General Thist escaped down from the Dark Highlands, next to the waterfall, a couple of years ago, with this material? Well, I have miles of it on this spool from ShadowFall's warehouse. And the godscloth line can work both ways —to let you down those cliffs, or take you up!"

CHAPTER THIRTEEN

"Look out, *sorihan*! *Sorihan! Cap'n!*" At Attuk's screams, Lork jumped from his hammock, sword in hand, without even pausing to put on his boots. Once on deck, in the light of the rising sun he saw all the harpoon crews uncapping and unlashing their weapons, tracking the giant taloned birds as they drew near. *A dozen really big ones,* Lork thought, *twenty-foot wingspans, and some babies out of the nest, not over ten feet across.* Man-eaters when the occasion presented itself, the flying predators typically went after seals and other prey, but he was taking no chances; he would prepare to fight them.

Glancing up at the barely filled sails of *Ice God,* he yelled out, "Ice anchors, now!" Lork braced himself as the *thud! thud! thud!* of the massive iron caltrops hit the glacier ice behind him, jerking his ship to a standstill. He saw with satisfaction that the *Hillmork* and *Fyorn* were likewise stopping, and that all the harpoon crews were still tracking the sorihans. He was even happier when that flock appeared not to be attacking his ships, but going after other prey out of sight to the east.

"Hold off, men!" he commanded. "Let's see what they are chasing!" But the scene that played out in front of the human crews was something very rare in all Na Saam history: the prey of the sorihan flock was turning back on the birds, as if to fight.

"*Good Tag!*" Attuk swore. "Those are a sloth of ice-bears! Big ones, and cubs, too!"

"This will be something to see," Lork said, hoping that neither of the species would decide to come after the humans in the area. *Maybe I shouldn't have stopped so soon? Well, what's done is done, and we're here and armed to the teeth ourselves!*

"Attuk," Lork whispered, "signal everybody to stand down until we see what happens out there. No shooting; just stay quiet and don't make any moves. Maybe we'll get some fresh ice-bear meat, or"—he smiled—"some big drumsticks?"

As the huge birds descended toward the ice-bears, half a dozen of the fifteen-foot-tall white beasts stood on hind legs to meet them, growling, their claws pawing the air, their smaller cubs huddled inside the circle of bears around what must have been a pregnant female. Lork was impressed that wild animals could present such a unified tactic in the face of an assault on their pack.

A brutal spectacle unfolded before the humans who stood on their ice craft, men transfixed by bloody nature, red in talon and claw. Less than a hundred yards away, ten or more huge screeching sorihan swooped down, talons bared, one bird attacking each of the standing ice-bears, four more going after the female and the cubs behind them. Again, Lork felt surprised that even the sorihan practiced a collective strategy. *Are all these animals getting smarter?* He wondered, *or are the ones this far south just different from those back home?* He knew that both the bears and the birds here were larger varieties than he'd ever heard of, and that they were demonstrating tactics he'd never seen wild creatures use.

Not that any tactic was always successful for any particular bird; with a powerful swat, one ice-bear paw eviscerated an incoming sorihan, strewing its innards across the ice; other birds did better, slicing the white fur of the bears, while three predators were able to drive away one cub from its protective huddle. A large sorihan dropped down, stabbing the cub in the back with its foot-long talons, lifting it from the ice and flying away from the melee. Lork felt some sympathy for the mammal; he hated that birds of any size could kill and eat other warm-blooded creatures.

The battle raged for only a few minutes but it was savage and fierce, ending with four bloody bird carcasses scattered on the ice, and two giant bears down, their eyes torn out and their bodies bleeding from massive, deep wounds. The rest of the sorihan flew away, presumably to share the feast of the ice-bear cub. Lork wondered if the flock of birds considered their attack successful. *I guess the survivors do; they get a few hundred pounds to eat! And so do we.*

"Attuk!" he shouted. "All hands! Harpoon the male ice-bears! Leave the female and cubs!" Without stopping to think of the irony of first wishing the bears victory over the birds, now he was considering the massive bears as prey himself. Bringing tons of bear meat back to Stonehaven would alleviate some of the embarrassment of the failed raid on Dvora.

Ice God's harpooners were nearest, and their six shots wounded each of the male bears. But the tallest white beast, suddenly recognizing the threat of the iceboats and the harpoons, charged Lork's boat, the closest. In fear, the harpooners quickly loaded and released two more bolts, one of which caught the ice-bear in the chest but did not stop him, the creature continuing his headlong dash toward them. Lork watched in horror as the giant bear's bloody claw raked above the gunwale, catching one transfixed icer and taking off his head. "*Good Tag!*" Lork yelled, swinging his sword at the bear's massive head, "This one's *big!*" The captain's blade crunched against the bear's neckbones as the creature fell backward onto the bloody ice, moaned, and lay still.

The other crews' harpoons finished off the remaining males, while the female, recognizing her situation, trundled off across the glacier with the four remaining cubs. They had taken a minute or more to bite into the dead birds; out of hunger or revenge, Lork couldn't guess.

"I wonder what these ice-bears feed on," Lork said to Attuk, "and how they and those sorihan grow so big. They must have some place around here to hunt, and to live." *Maybe another place for us to raid, for food?*

"I'm making notes, Cap'n," Attuk said, manipulating his astrolabe. "We still be near two hundred miles southwest of home." Looking at the departing bears, he said wistfully, "If only we could follow them critters, no telling what we might find. More mountain islands, I'd bet."

Lork said quietly, "And maybe more monsters?"

Attuk smiled, turning his attention to retrieving the bear meat.

As the *Ice God* crew rotated the spring drum to bring in the first giant carcass, Lork's mind snapped back to future matters. *Now if these harpoons could go out half a mile instead of just a hundred yards, I could go back and visit that Drunken Duke.* But he knew that not even the specialized high-altitude sorihan-shooter 'poons at Stonehaven could reach up much over three hundred yards with their much smaller bolts; anything flying higher than that could not be reached. He shuddered at the thought of those huge birds and their man-snatching talons attacking again while his fleet was on the Ice Sea, but knew that few of the flying creatures had ever ventured out over the ice around Na Saam. *Some say they are sent as punishment by Hillmork when Na Saam is too sinful. But we who are without sin, out here on the unknown Ice, were we guilty? And were those ice-bears also guilty?* He usually left religious thoughts behind at home, finding no practical use for them while raiding.

As Lork watched the crews expertly skin and dismember the giant creatures, he thought, *A few thousand pounds of ice-bear on each of these critters. At least we'll bring home some tons of bear meat.* Looking out over the Ice Sea for other possible targets, he thought, *I hope there are no more surprises along the way.* But days more along their return, The Ice revealed no more living things.

During the days that followed his *rescue? capture?,* Altamun Kech was let up on deck to see the ice world around him, to observe the captain whose name he found to be "Lork," the mate, "Attuk," and the dozen others who manned the ice ship. Though he remained hand-tied while not in his cage, the priest watched with interest as the crew sailed their ship on ice as skillfully as any sea-ship sailors he had ever seen. The tiller mechanism, cutting into the ice surface, he didn't understand any more than the oar-like "skritchers" driven by hand-cranked camshafts, but all in all the ice ships moved swiftly across the vast unending expanse of glacier ice..

Three times the fleet halted to hunt down huge white ice-bears, which were killed by spring-driven harpoons. Allowed on deck to watch, Altamun marveled at yet another application of what appeared to be the godsmetal of his homeland's springbows. The Kech leader Wakan knew the secrets of forming those thin arcs of metal into useful implements; he had studied such techniques back in the High Antis while most of the rest of the priest class avoided anything requiring manual labor. *And Wakan made the springbows that kept ShadowFall free. But those were simple constructions. Wakan should see these mechanisms, the intricate moving parts. These barbarians have taken godsmetal-working to a fine art.*

As Altamun watched with interest, the large animals were expertly skinned and their pelts stretched out to dry on vertical racks, while their salvageable meats were packed in salted drums belowdecks. *Tons of fresh meat,* Altamun guessed. *Enough to feed quite a mob.* He estimated that the ice ships had sufficient storage space for hundreds of such kills, and wondered why they were all but empty. And the huge barrel-like containers farther back from the cages appeared to be storage bins, for such as corn and grains. Maybe they were not out hunting for a few animals, but for something else?

A strange thing Altamun noticed about his rescuers —captors?—was that after the first attempts at speech failed, the glacier men showed no further interest, while he himself listened intently, pairing sounds with actions, especially names, nouns, and commands. After less than a week's captivity, he knew all of the crew's names, what their devices were called, and what the captain's and mate's shouts meant. And though he could pronounce the names of the ice ships, he had no idea of their meaning. To him, *Eye-ess Gott, Feen-yor,* and *Hyeel-Moork* were only tongue-twisting sounds.

***

SAILING BACK HOME TOOK SEVEN MORE LONG DAYS, because Lork slowed his fleet twice to kill more ice-bears, a species smaller than the first monstrous ones. And he stopped every night, fearful of yet other unknown crevasses in this uncharted region of the Ice Sea, and of other possible dangers. Harpooners kept watch in the dark, their weapons fully loaded and uncapped, with many torches lit to keep away any huge ice-bears, sorihan, or any other unknown denizens that might inhabit the uncharted region they were traversing. Fortunately, no storm winds blew, only favorable breezes that kept their sails full as they headed northeast to Stonehaven.

Though Lork was fairly confident that their discoveries of Ice-End and the vast melt lake beyond it, plus their tons of bear meat and the strange captive, would gain them some forgiveness for the failure of the Dvora raid, his men were not so optimistic. An ominously quiet group of despondent warriors, they were self-shamed men who had not brought home any trade-good loot, or especially any measures of grain, from their long-distance raid. All of them knew that the coming winter could be close to famine rations unless the icers could find another way to feed their waiting families. Though they had been discoverers of Ice-End and were bringing home some ice-bear meat and the strange captive retrieved from the crevasse valley, they still had no loot or barrels of grain or meat animals to show for their effort and for the sacrifice of half the fleet. Lork knew that his fate was tied up in theirs, and theirs in him.

AS THEY NEARED STONEHAVEN, LORK PULLED THE crews together for a final briefing. "Men, we can't hide the fact that thirty of us died by the treachery of that lying traveler and the Drunken Duke. But do not go into detail. As laws allow, I—and I alone—have to answer to the Old Men in the Ice Hall Council. I alone will bear the responsibility. By law, I have three days to prepare. I won't let you down. Remember, we are the crews that found Ice-End and the crevasse that splits the world. Our names will go down in song and tales, from this day on. But I must be the one to make our case." Seeing that his crews were not all that convinced, Lork repeated his comments. "I just ask these two things of you—one, do not tell anyone what we found or about our captive. And two: as I tell the tale, be sure to cheer and clap and encourage others of our countrymen to do the same— our fame depends on it!" *And possibly my own life!*

As his men disembarked, Lork heard the wails and cries of newly informed widows and orphans, a new and emotional experience for him, not the least reason of which was that his leadership had failed miserably. Even with the news of Ice-End, the Old Men of the Ice Hall Council might have his head for the disaster, maybe even demand a Slow Death, the most horrible of tortures, a hideous week-long ordeal.

Lork's one hope of redemption was in the *Ice God*'s hold, that tall strange survivor his crew had rescued from certain freezing death, a man who apparently knew no civilized language. *The fellow speaks in grunts and wheezes,* Lork had observed. *Without true speech, I wonder how his kind can even survive? Maybe he's just an animal?* Going belowdecks, he made to let his pitiful captive out of a cramped cage. Lork himself was in no danger from the man; with arms and legs in chains, with bulky warm furs provided for him against the chill, it was all the stranger could do to stand up by himself. Originally dressed in thin clothing totally unfit for the cold, wind-swept world of the Ice Sea, the man stood a head taller than Lork, but was thin and dark-haired, with skin the color of pale oak.

As Lork led the shivering captive off the iceboat, a portly Tag priest came to the dock and covered the man with even more furs, asking, "You poor cold man, do you speak our language?" More grunts and wheezes followed. At the priest's request, Lork released the prisoner into the holy man's custody. Maybe the learned priest or his fellow temple monks could find some way to communicate? Otherwise the Ice Hall might decide that keeping a useless captive alive would not be in Stonehaven's best interest. *Each one, feed one,* the unspoken ancient motto of Na Saam society, still held. The man might be sacrificed.

As the priest and the chained captive walked away toward the Temple of Tag, Lork collected his thoughts: *This savage could yet be my way out. Nobody is supposed to live on the Ice Sea, and nothing is supposed to extend beyond Ice-End. Yet we all saw the huge Melt Sea, and yet here he is, a shivering giant of a man. He has to be from somewhere warmer. A possible raiding target on the other side of that ice valley? I have an idea that nobody has ever had,* he thought, *and I've got nothing to lose by proposing it now!*

CHAPTER FOURTEEN

A s the light of the rising sun angled across the ruined plaza at WaterEdge, an exhausted General Thist was grateful to see the large green bulk of Una coming out of the sky, slowly setting down to hover a few centimeters above the broken tiles. *Reminds me of a leaf being borne by a gentle breeze,* he thought. *But Una is a big girl.* Occupying a volume ten meters long by three in diameter, Una had been most useful in Thist's and Thusk's adventures for two years now, ever since their Sire, Reader Thess, and Thusk retrieved it (*Her,* Thist reminded himself) from the Ice glacier back home. *Long and green, a god-machine,* he thought with a grim grin. *Come to take me and the captive princess back to Mother.*

Flying cucumber, indeed! he sniffed, remembering an insult allegedly made by a pirate captain in this very city, over a year ago. *Una is the living symbol of Mother Pernie's power—as exercised only by me. And of course, by my twin, Thusk, who flew her here.* He unconsciously glanced at the black ovoid atop Una's fuselage, inside of which the mannequin-like White Pilot resided. *I really don't like to see the pilot,* he thought. *But I'll admit he has come in handy, scaring ignorant crowds when needed.*

As if reading his twin's mind, Thusk appeared in the doorway as the doorway opened itself on the side facing him. "Welcome aboard, conquering hero. Our taxi is at your service." Smiling, Thist embraced his twin, then turned to order his prisoner be brought aboard.

Once inside Una with the sobbing, cursing former princess securely chained to a standard-sized seat in the rear of the cabin, guarded by two large Mothersman guards, Thist took his scaled-down seat at the front, sitting next to his twin. "Una," Thusk said to the three-dimensional representation of a beautiful blonde woman in translucent white robes on the large forward screen, "please take us back to Mother's City." Una had fashioned the image from an earlier scan of Anklya, the former lover of both men, a tall blonde woman now residing in The People's Lands. Thist tried, unsuccessfully, to stop memories of that relationship from surfacing. *Neither of us has seen her in nearly a year,* he thought ruefully. *After all this time, she's probably either angry or disinterested. Or found another man back home, somebody to replace Thusk and me. At least she won't be around Mother's Palace for me to see or for her to see me.* He knew that the phrase "torn between two lovers" might not be just a poetic phrase, not if Mother Pernie got jealous!

"As you wish," Una responded. *With a bit of sarcasm,* Thist noted with a grin. *Una has developed quite the female personality these last two years. From an ice-bound tube stuck in a glacier for thousands of years, one that could not think for itself, to a sassy individual DI who likes to argue.* Only that short time back, his twin Thusk and their Sire Thess (*murdered by The Tharn, who Thusk killed for it!*) had removed the flying god-machine from The Ice at the End of the World (*Actually, just the southernmost wall of the northern glacier,* he reminded himself). Since Thusk had flown the big green cylinder down from their icy homeland to the warmer climes of Motherland all that time ago, Una had played a large role in the political and military events of Thist's and Thusk's new adopted homeland, as well as their own.

As Una lifted almost silently into the air, Thist

sighed. *I never will understand her explanation about "micro-nozzles" and "electrostatic propulsion" and "qomp-fusion systems."* The cabin walls went transparent by Thusk's command, revealing to the little men, the pouting ex-princess, and the big, black-leather-vested Mothersmen guards, an aerial view of the ruined Pink Palace and its grounds; to the east, the dark blue vista of the Cold Sea spread out to the horizon. Immediately below them, appearing like swarms of ants from their altitude, were ranks of rapidly dispersing demobilized troops, guards, and bird-rider warriors. *Getting back to normal under the new Kech priest, Awhalpa. I hope! Two rebellions in one year is entirely too many!*

As Una gained altitude, the landscape view began to unroll like a vast plaid carpet, fertile plains dotted by lakes, villages scattered like quilt squares amongst the wide farmlands. Thist asked Una, "Will you silence the rear of the cabin so that we up here may speak privately?" From behind himself, Thist heard a waterfall of white noise, effectively shielding his conversation with Una. He began in frustration: "Una, when I laid siege to WaterEdge a month ago, you know I appreciated your towing Odel's tri-wings to the front; they were a great asset. But when I wanted your assistance in surveillance, you refused even to fly over the palace. I know you won't drop weapons on Motherland's enemies, or kill rebel troops, but surveillance itself can *save* lives."

A year before, when Thist and ShadowFall's citizens were defending themselves from Creesile's invading army, Una's ability to fly over the enemy formations, to let Thist use her loud-talker function to address troops on both sides from above, had been instrumental in the final battle that led to their enemy's defeat. He thought, *You even let me drop that despicable Miran Kech from a hundred meters high, right into Creesile's lap! Well, close to it!*

"Una, you helped me at ShadowFall and at, at, the Sisterdom that shall never be named," he said with a gulp, recalling those gruesome days. "Yet at WaterEdge you sat outside of the plaza and did nothing as we laid siege that first day, and then had Thusk take you back to Mother's City. Please explain to me, if you would."

Seconds passed, Thist understanding that at the speed of Una's collective of quantum computers, her qomps, that period was the equivalent of centuries of human thought. But she answered, "Thist, I have evolved. I have reviewed all of the human history in my data banks and in the godspheres collected from all over Motherland, and records from the Crystal Throne in Mother's Palace. Most of your race's history is a record of violence, killing, betrayal, and suffering. As a nonsentient DI, I was programmed by a modified version of the Asimov–Campbell Three Laws not to harm humans or let them be harmed.

"However, that same review of human history reveals that violence, when properly limited, intelligently directed, and judiciously applied, can be an effective weapon when one's enemies are wantonly murderous and their victory would increase human death and limit or eliminate human freedoms. Thus, I allowed you to liberate ShadowFall from the certain massacre of its citizens—and yourselves—that General Creesile was planning under orders from Mother Messinex's corrupt priest, Miran Kech.

"As you recall, in the last rebellion before WaterEdge, I refrained from any direct harmful actions as well. That entire situation was political and did not necessarily threaten lives. Its outcome would not have altered the course of Motherland for long. As for WaterEdge, my component qomps decided that you and the tri-wing aerial force were to be allowed to be transported to the front line, from where you conducted your campaign. I had nothing further to do with it."

Thist sighed again, recalling the stubborn refusals of Princess Sathronin and Loranthip Kech to negotiate; followed by the subsequent aerial force attack by Odel's tri-wings (*And his unfortunate losses,* he thought, sad for those deaths but grateful that he hadn't lost his big friend from God's Country). Followed by the siege, the catapulted fire-stones, the final mass charge of Mothersmen and emu-riding warriors. Una's assistance could have reduced the time fighting from a whole month down to probably a day or two, given the ability to drop bombs, do surveillance, and intimidate the opposition through the loud-talker. Even just letting the White Pilot be seen addressing rebel troops might have been enough. He would never understand the machine's reasoning. Didn't Una realize that all wars, all rebellions, all human armed conflicts by any name, required killing people and breaking things? He hoped that this last demonstration of Mother Pernie's absolute military power would be the last, that all of the Sisterdoms becoming republics would minimize the centuries-old feuds and civil wars that had wracked Motherland. He himself was close to refusing to lead any more battles, kill any more people.

But somehow I know that is a forlorn hope, he thought, *having power over other people's lives is an addiction of the worst sort. Once tasted, the appetite for it will never be satiated. Only Death can cure it!* Pernie and ShadowFall were very lucky that the High Antis foreigner, Wakan Kech, had been raised and educated in a free and tolerant culture, far away from Motherland's reach. *Or had they been lucky?* Part of his mind argued, *Without Wakan's insistence on democracy and the rights of citizens, ShadowFall would have remained an absolute matriarchy for decades more, under Pernie's rule. A tyranny, perhaps, but a benevolent and peaceful one. No rebellion, no invasion, no thousands of dead on both sides. Was it all worth it?*

Already Mother's Palace had been rife with rumors from the year-old Republic of ShadowFall that trouble was brewing up there, fights between its original Motherland peoples and the several thousand immigrants from Thist's own homeland in the far north, now called The People's Lands. *Short, dark, and hard-working people, that's us,* he thought. *Who incidentally fought and died by the hundreds to hold off Creesile's invasion!* But, as he had learned in two hard years of faithfully serving Princess—now Mother—Perneptheranam, in politics and war, there was no such thing as gratitude, only the next big issue.

He was glad when Thusk told him how he had resolved ShadowFall's particular problem, the separation of the two peoples up there, and he warmed to the naming of the new republic after their Sire, Thess. But he felt that his twin was not forthcoming about all the issues there. "I am a bit surprised about Odel," he told Thusk. "I figured he would want to stay here as head of the aerial force, to grow it into a huge armada. I was hoping that Una, here, would teach him about how to make those engines to keep those tri-wings up in the air for hours."

But Thusk ignored the question; he was thinking not about Odel any more, only about Anklya and Pernie, the similarities and differences in their mutual lovers, trying to assess what Odel had alluded to. Their most recent mutual lover, Pernie, had been acting strangely lately, and he was not anxious to find out why. *I guess we'll know soon, now that we are both going back to the palace. I hope it's nothing we've done.* He didn't believe that Pernie knew anything about his feelings toward that Mienne on the Moon. *I hope...*

———

CHANGING THE SUBJECT, THIST ASKED, "SO YOU'RE going to report to Pernie on what you accomplished at ShadowFall, Thusk?" Unconsciously he was comparing his own ostentatious scarlet godscloth regalia and robes to his twin's neat but workman-like tunic. At Thusk's nod of agreement, he said, "For me, I will condense the WaterEdge story for her to two words: 'We won'. But I'll tell you some details. WaterEdge put up one hell of a fight," he said with a frown. "Never understood why. When you and I were fighting Creesile's invasion at ShadowFall, we knew that if we lost, we would all be killed and Pernie taken captive, at best—fight or die, we had no choice. But WaterEdge? Last year, after Mother Messinex…died…their princess, like all of the Sisters in Motherland, surrendered gracefully and swore allegiance to the new Mother, our Pernie. Then she revolted in spite of her oath of loyalty. What a waste!"

Thusk nodded, acknowledging that his twin was the more action-oriented of the two sons of their late Sire, Reader Thess. After all, Thusk had prevailed in the brutal and lethal Motherland Game for Pernie while fighting on his emu war-bird, and had fought with honor (and a bit of berserker) at the Battle of ShadowFall. Furthermore, as the new general of the Mothersman Army, Thist had completely erased the rebellious Sisterdom-That-Shall-Never-Be-Named six months ago, and just yesterday had finally reconquered WaterEdge for Mother Pernie.

Thusk thought, *And here I have spent most of* my *time since ShadowFall studying godspheres and books and maps down in the dungeons and tunnels below Mother's Palace. I may have saved Pernie a civil war in ShadowFall, so there is that. And I* have *visited the Moon half a dozen times. So I'm diplomat and space traveler both, and Pernie named me Ambassador to the Moon.* Smiling, he thought, *I did have quite some incredible Crystal Throne body-sharing encounters there with that lovely Mienne. Especially that last time with the big avvy-body. I really can't talk about that, though, not even with Thist.* He realized with a faint smile that Mother Pernie would probably be scheduling both of her lovers to make their different presentations, one after the other, in front of herself, Wakan Kech and the court, having them compete in a fashion. Too bad he could not be telling his whole story. *Not and stay alive!*

But that's all right with me, Thusk mused, *Because I did my diplomatic chore, and I'm not into wars and court politics, and have no desire to do anything other than learn about the ancients and explore the whole round world. And eventually, go back to the Moon and somehow get back into that avvy body and be with that Mienne again.*

RETURNINGS

CHAPTER FIFTEEN

Altamun Kech was on deck with all the crew as Captain Lork steered *Eye-ess Gott* into the ice-port pier slot, his icers expertly slowing their ship to a stop with the skritcher springs and crankshaft. As the other two ice ships pulled in alongside them and the men disembarked, Altamun heard both cheering and screams. *What is wrong?* he wondered, but as crying women and children pointed out to the horizon of ice, then fell down in misery, he thought, *These people are mourning! This fleet must be missing ships!*

A quiet Captain Lork led Altamun onto the pier, from where the priest could view the ice port that Lork called "Stonehaven", a collection of hundreds of one- and two-story gray stone buildings with thatched roofs, a few sporting colorful tiles. At the center of the city loomed a tall gray spire of a tower with a plus sign atop it. As Lork released Altamun from his wrist shackles and walked onto the pier, a fat, balding man in a fur robe came up and spoke briefly with the Captain. Altamun could not understand the conversation, but it seemed friendly enough, punctuated with emphatic finger-pointings by both men, at him. Lork shrugged, smiled and nodded at his captive, then left to confront the crowd of onlookers. The fat man embraced his foreign guest, covering him with yet more furs. Altamun was made to understand he was to accompany his benefactor. For what purpose he didn't know, but nodded toward the departing Lork and left with his new companion.

TWO DAYS LATER, ALTAMUN KECH WAS SATISFIED THAT he had learned enough of the speech of Na Saam to try to converse with the friendly fat man, whose name, he learned, was "Eki." While the Kech was being housed in a simple but warm room in that tall spired building and being fed simple but filling meals, his host, apparently some functionary of the tower place, had been pointing to himself, to objects, and acting out action verbs, saying words each time, all apparently in an effort to teach his involuntary guest the rudiments of Na Saam's tongue. With his week aboard the *Eyess-Gott*, supplemented by Eki's instructions, Altamun was confident he knew enough of Na Saamese to sound intelligent to the locals.

The man Eki sat across a table from Altamun, drawing in and exhaling sweet-smelling smoke from a long pipe. The Kech had never seen or smelled anything like Eki's smoking, but wanted to learn more. Up to this point, he had only revealed his name, which Eki continued to mispronounce as "Alty-Moon-Keks," despite repeated attempts by Altamun to correct him. Otherwise, the Kech had made no attempt to reciprocate with words in Motherspeak or Lordship; he thought, *I learned long ago not to give up secrets for nothing*. But now Eki had also brought in a hard black loaf of bitter bread and a mug of that honeyed wine, so Altamun decided to show his appreciation by talking.

"Eki," Altamun said aloud, holding up the wine mug, "Altamun thank you for drink. Enjoy it. Bread too hard, but fill me." As he watched, Eki's eyes opened wide and he withdrew the pipe from his mouth.

The Kech could interpret Eki's meaning, if not every word: "Good Tag! Alty-Moon-Keks, you learn fast! I have a thousand questions!"

As Altamun washed down the tough bread with wine, he gathered that Eki wanted to know where he was from, how he got to where he was found, who his people were, what they did for commerce. *The same questions I would ask, were one of these Na Saam folk to be marooned on a Lordship Island or...or even on Motherland.* From his friendly treatment, he knew Lork, Eki, and probably the other Na Saam were not slavers; but he had heard enough aboard the *Free Brother* to understand that Lork was a pirate returning in shame from a failed raid. At first he worried that they might want to raid beyond their glacier, but quickly put that thought to rest. *Even if they wanted to, how would they get iceboats down hundreds of meters into a real ocean? Their dinky boats would not survive even a mild storm on the Cold Sea.*

As a courtesy to Eki, Altamun engaged the man in deeper and deeper conversations. *These people have found godspheres*, he discovered, *but they are merely objects of curiosity; not one has ever spoken to them.* Eki volunteered that their iceboats utilized godsprings found in abundance at the bottom of their melt reservoir, Lake Perdis. (Altamun thought it interesting that the Na Saam had no separate word for "water," only "melt"). Eki related that Na Saam blacksmiths had learned in ancient times how to re-form godsprings by dipping them in the lava ejected from the active volcano they worshipped as Goddess Hillmork. Developing an unexpected respect for Na Saam technology, he mused, *To think, in Motherland and the High Antis, we have to use whatever forms of godspring we find, but these —barbarians—can reforge it in fresh hot lava, and shape it as desired.* Thinking of what that process might entail, he thought, *I wouldn't want to be one of their smiths, though!*

In so many words and gestures, Eki let Altamun know that they would be present at a meeting where Captain Lork would be judged by a council of elders, for his failed raid on a mountain island kingdom hundreds of miles southeast of Stonehaven. Apparently, losing ships and men and returning with empty hulls was a serious offense.

"Altamun help Captain Lork. Lork good man. Save me."

Eki sighed. "I hope you can, Alty-Moon. He may die."

CHAPTER SIXTEEN

In his position as the third-highest-ranking member of the hierarchy of Motherland, General Thist was first to speak to the several dozen notables assembled in Mother Perneptheranam's throne room. Bowing in the accepted manner toward first the throne, then to Wakan in his adjacent but lower chair, and finally to the Court Assembled, he spoke loud enough to be heard through the hundred-foot-square room. "Mother, Wakan, my twin Thusk, and all court here today, I bring you the news that the rebellion in WaterEdge has been quashed. The former princess, Sathronin, is in custody in the chambers below, awaiting the judgment of our Mother and the court."

At the smiles and polite applause, he continued, "All of the leading rebel nobles have been, ah, *disposed*"—he had not enjoyed the decapitations, but those were his orders from Pernie and Wakan—"and their assets distributed among those identified as remaining loyal to our Motherland. A temporary administrator, one Awhalpa Kech, is now in place there, and the rebellious troops are being interrogated for potential war crimes." He hoped for no more executions, since even enemy troops usually had little choice in whom they fight. "Known loyal officers from here in Mother's City are now in command of the proven-loyal troops there.

"As to why the former princess acted in a treasonous

manner, I have come to believe that her chief priest and advisor, Loranthip Kech, led her astray. Possibly with the connivance of the pirates from the Lordship Islands. We heard rumors to do with a godsphere the pirate chief Noor brought here to the palace sometime back. Further details will arise, I am sure, from the continued…*questioning*." Knowing that the newly appointed Kech, Awhalpa, would use whatever means necessary to get to the truth, he dismissed that disturbing thought.

As General Thist related more details of his victory, Wakan Kech, the tall, long-time priest and advisor to Mother Pernie, grimaced at the news that yet another of his countrymen from the High Antis had acted the traitor. When Thist had thrown out the late Mother Messinex's Kech priest, Miran, from the Una flying machine, from high above the ShadowFall battlefield, Wakan had hoped that was the end of the corruption of the group of educated men he had led all the way from the High Antis to captivity in Motherland, over twenty long years before.

At Mother Pernie's nod, Wakan Kech bowed to her and turned to Thist. "General Thist, we thank you once again for your invaluable service to our Motherland and our Mother. We trust the new administrator will quickly enable WaterEdge's transition to republic status." Wakan opened his arms to include the court. "The Republic of ShadowFall was only the first Sisterdom to modernize, and so far the citizens—and the remaining nobles—seem to have adjusted to their new roles and responsibilities, after some negotiation, as Advisor Thusk will elaborate." He winced internally at his outright lie. Only Thusk's diplomacy had prevented imminent civil war there. "Other Sisterdoms are likewise changing to meet Mother Perneptheranam's decrees. It is unfortunate that a few, including WaterEdge, chose other paths, engaged in destructive resistance."

Bowing to Thist and the Mother, Wakan called for Thusk to make his presentation. After the protocolic introductions, Thusk said, "My report concerning ShadowFall was what we expected. After some initial hesitation, both sides realized that separation into two republics was the optimum solution for the ethnic issues there. I trust that all parties will adhere to the agreement they signed. The separation is to begin immediately." Bowing toward Pernie, he said, "That's one republic that won't be rebelling. Two, actually. Maybe we can use those lessons learned to prevent other such problems around the country.

"Which is why I was very interested in hearing General Thist's report on WaterEdge's motivations for rebellion. You may recall that the Sisterdom's former Kech priest, Altamun, disappeared some fifteen months ago. At the time it was thought he may have drowned, but my research suggests that he was probably kidnapped by that big white pirate, Captain Noor, who accompanied him here to the Palace and back to WaterEdge just days before he vanished.

"To refresh the memories of all present, recall that Captain Noor was the insolent Sea Lord who came here to the palace with maps and a godsphere, claiming that the globe told him that all of Motherland belonged to the Sea Lords. When Mother Messinex rejected him, confiscating his godsphere and old maps, he was furious. I feel that he may have abducted Altamun in return."

Standing up from her throne, Mother Pernie spoke sharply, "Wakan, all here, it was that pirate's visit here to my predecessor, Mother Messinex, that the traitor Miran Kech used as an excuse to try to conquer ShadowFall, because as princess there I refused to hand over ShadowFall's precious godspheres, books, and maps." A full minute of silence ensued, broken with Pernie's voice, softer now. "Thist, Thusk, I want you two to confer about this pirate, Noor. Investigate that godsphere, if you can locate it among all those hundreds Thusk has retrieved from the bowels of our palace below. And any maps and books that might help fill in about all of those treacherous pirates—where they reside, how they raid us, how we can best defend against them. Use your Una if she will cooperate; go out and fly over the Cold Sea if you have to. And if you can, while you're out there, try to find that poor Kech, Altamun. Or find out his fate."

Wakan Kech motioned to the twins that their times were up; they bowed and left the throne room, stopping outside to sit on a stone bench in an unroofed atrium. Behind them, Wakan was calling forth several squabbling nobles. Thusk was happy to be leaving the details of governance behind. *Pernie and Wakan are working themselves to death*, he thought. *They both look so tired. I never knew that running an empire would be so all-consuming. No wonder they are desperately trying to get each Sisterdom, all of them, to become self-governing republics! That would save the Mother's time for the big national issues.*

"So, we will be working together again," Thist said. Looking around the open-air, grassy yard, he smiled. "Would you believe that this very atrium is where you rescued me with Una, when you and Anklya appeared out of nowhere and took me away, last year?"

Thusk laughed at the memory; in the many months he had spent in Mother's Palace after ShadowFall's successful rebellion, he had not recognized this particular area. "I've spent half this last year mostly underground, down in the dungeons and tunnels. My staff uses a much larger open courtyard to bring up the godspheres to catch sunlight, and a dozen big rooms for storing all the books and maps. Even quite a few carved totems from our homeland."

Totems? Thist hadn't thought about those small carved cylinders for a long time, since visual reading was now so much faster and convenient. *Thank Una and her laser technology for correcting our extreme farsightedness, so we can read close up.* Both his Carving hand and his Reading hand quivered as he recalled his lifelong habit of inscribing a daily journal of his activities, and then Reading its cuts, twists, depths. His fingers twitched in muscle memory at the thought.

Thusk continued, "Una has said that she can communicate with the 'spheres. It might be faster to let her use her 'radio' system and find that particular one that the pirate brought to Pernie. Then we can ask her directly what that globe has to say. It might not even talk to us."

Thist nodded; he himself had been able to access information from many, but not all, of the crystalline balls that the ancients had left scattered all over the explored world, North and South. Una had tried to explain that, while sunlight powered the head-sized globes, human touch was required to retrieve any messages or pictures from the devices.

Thusk said, "Una told us that different kinds of that microscopic DNA material will open different godspheres, but that no one person can activate them all. The ancients most likely designed them that way to ensure that not one person or one tribe could utilize the information they all contain." Thist nodded, but did not reply that such a limitation made little sense to him.

Standing up, Thist stretched and yawned. "Thusk, I've been away from the palace for a month now, you just a few days. I think I'd like to rest a bit more before we take off and go away again for who knows how long." Pursing his lips, he said, "You can fetch Una and find Noor's godsphere in the morning. Meanwhile, I think I'd like to...*visit*...with Pernie tonight. If she is willing."

Thusk patted his twin on the back, laughing. "And when has she *not* been?"

CHAPTER SEVENTEEN

Three days after Lork's return to Stonehaven, the Council assembled in the Ice Hall, a vast and dark ancient auditorium-like building constructed of some unknown metallic material. One of the very last structures remaining from the Age of the Gods, it was Stonehaven's tallest structure, exceeding in height even the spires of the Temple of Tag. Encompassing a volume large enough for several thousand people to gather, in times of severe storms it served as a community shelter but otherwise was only used for Council activities.

Present this day were hundreds of fur-clad locals and a few dozen people from other ice ports, some holding smoking seal-oil-soaked torches. *Those things stink,* Lork thought, *probably as much as the men holding them, and they blacken the high ceiling here.* He wondered why the ancient builders had not provided more kinds of illumination for the spacious structure, one of hundreds of questions he wanted answers to. *Maybe someday,* he thought. *Surely those old boys left more stuff around, if I could just find it.*

Looking up at the building's high curved interior, darkened by centuries of torch smoke, Lork had often wondered whether the Ice Hall might have been built as a refuge by ancients who feared a devastating eruption of Hillmork. *So far, at least in my lifetime,* he thought, *the lava has not flowed this far south.* Like all of his countrymen, when he thought of Goddess Hillmork, Lork touched his forehead and nodded toward Her, an unconscious gesture of respect and gratitude to the one source of earthly warmth in the cold world that was Na Saam.

Standing in front of the Twenty Old Men who wielded absolute power over the dozen independent ice ports that collectively constituted the Assembly of Na Saam, Lork felt the presence of those esteemed warriors and sages like a weight around his shoulders. *Hel, around my heart and my head, too*, he thought. He knew that the old worthies sitting at the large U-shaped polished wooden table had each brought in fabulous amounts of loot—*and food, lots of food!*—that had kept all of Na Saam well fed and prosperous for many, many years; their raids and conquests were legendary. *And here I failed, on my first long-distance raid!*

At the center of the table, a stout, wrinkled old man, dressed in the once-white fur of an ice-bear, stood up, pointing at Lork. "I, Lord Montrea," he said in a commanding tone, "as elected leader of this Ice Hall Assembly, charge you, Captain Lork, for a full account of your journey. The leaders here assembled"—his arms swept around to encompass the other Old Men—"wish to know your gains, your losses"—a chorus of sobs and raucous yells from the hundreds in the hall revealed their feelings quite ominously—"your expenditures, and your new knowledge, if any."

Lork breathed in slowly. From the grim expressions on the faces of the Old Men, he knew that he was on the defensive, that unless he had a good story he would likely be sentenced to death. The harsh climate of Na Saam had birthed an unforgiving society, mercy an unknown concept for people struggling to survive the cold and ice.

Lork bowed to the Old Men, then turned and did the same to the unfriendly crowd now murmuring loudly, noting that his crews had scattered among them, as he had requested. Turning back again, he faced Lord Montrea. *This is the moment of my life,* he thought. *Let's give them a show!*

"To the Twenty Old Men of the Ice Hall Council, to the Na Saam Assembly, to my fellow Stonehaven kin, to my many friends from all the ice ports"—interrupted by louder jeering and angry shouts, he bowed again, waited for the shouting to die down, then went on. "Word has been spread that our raid on Dvora was unsuccessful." Again, shouts and sobs from the assemblage. "Our traveler spy did not inform us that the Drunken Duke's stone fortress, guarding the river inlet, was equipped with fire-stone-throwing machines, treacherous and unmanly and inhumane giant wooden throwing arms that destroyed three ice ships of the fleet as we tried to enter."

After the resultant shouting and curses and insults died down, Lork went on, slowly acting out his narration, exaggerating his motions—*acting!* "Then, as we attempted to return home, the Wind Gods fiercely attacked, blowing us for two deadly days, dark days and nights of unrelenting storm-level winds, the like of which we had never seen." Looking around, he saw that he was generating interest in the tale he was relating, that eyes were upon him, voices lowered. *Good! They long for entertaining stories almost as much as for food!* Life in Na Saam was always a fight for survival, for sure, but tales of adventure and conquest, typically shared around campfires or hearths, were the spiritual equivalent of food. *If it's food for the soul you want,* he thought, *well then, I've got a feast for you!*

Lork accentuated the rest of his report with wild-eyed passion, shouting as necessary, his voice dropping to a barely-heard whisper at other times. His audience expected such a performance and he was giving them a great one, acting out dodging the fireballs, waving a sword at the enemy fortress, fiercely resisting the efforts of the Wind Gods to destroy his fleet. When telling of the failure of the ice-anchor caltrops to hold, his listeners and watchers grew silent with fear. As he related the desperate emergency effort of firing the spring-loaded spikes into the glacial ice, and the heart-pounding wait for those lifesaving ropes to bring the *Ice God* to a safe halt, he could hear the gasps.

As his rapt listeners waited breathlessly for the outcome—not recognizing for the moment that Lork, the hero of his own story of peril and danger, was standing there in front of them—he concluded in a lowered voice, "And then the next morning, when the warm and welcome sun rose over the Ice Sea, my crew and I found that had we slid just one quarter of a mile more, we would have crashed over a three-thousand-foot crevasse!" The townspeople and Old Men alike breathed again, as one. "Two thousand miles southwest the Wind Gods took us, out beyond where anyone has ever ventured." Lork eyed the unbelieving crowd as if searching their shocked minds at the news that he had traveled almost as far as the Moon above; local religion taught as much. "But Tag and Goddess Hillmork had other plans for us. Plans for all of us, all of Na Saam, in fact, because I bring you wonderful news, a discovery that will change everything: my crews and I have found and mapped—the legendary—but in fact, the actual, *Ice-End*!"

For a few seconds no one spoke. Lork didn't know if he had been believed or if they all thought it just a wild tale, one made up to save him from the consequences of a disastrous raid that cost three ice ships and thirty-one icers. But in those few seconds Attuk walked from the front of the crowd and held up a long sheepskin scroll. "Here be that map, honored Council men. Cap'n Lork found the edge of the Ice Sea, beyond which be a vast melt-lake like our lake Perdis." Waving his free hand, he bellowed, "It is all melted ice, far's you can see! And my new map here shows where it be!"

Pandemonium ensued, wild cheering and shouts of encouragement ringing through the Ice Hall; finding Ice-End meant the actualization of a legend, an affirmation that their hero had now penetrated their culture's undiscovered limit. Only the kin of the lost icers held back but even they were enthralled by Lork's performance. Councilman Montrea stood and loudly called for quiet, which came immediately.

After a full minute, Montrea broke the uneasy silence that gripped the Ice Hall. "Lork, your tale is interesting, and I trust that First Mate Attuk's map is a true reflection of the, the, *Ice-End*, something that has lain unreachable, legendary, for thousands of years. We have never considered what might lie beyond it. And a mile-wide crevasse splitting the entire width of the Ice Sea itself, that is both a wonder and a danger at the same time. But a melt-lake that takes up the whole horizon, larger than our twenty-mile-long, three-mile-wide Perdis, and filled with salty melt, too? Now, *that* is the hardest to conceive." But the old man's wide grin showed that he, too, was believing the formerly impossible.

Feeling that he had nearly convinced the Old Men to forgive his losses, Lork regaled his rapt audience with the heroic tale of the battle with the ice-bears and the sorihan, stressing the gigantic nature of those creatures. "Ice-bears up to twenty feet tall," he lied, "and sorihan birds with forty-foot wings!" Attuk ordered two of the bear skins, complete with enormous skulls, brought out for show. "These are two of the smaller males we killed; unfortunately, the sorihan had torn off the heads of the big ones." As his men paraded around under the skins, the astonished looks on the faces of the audience showed that they would have accepted any tale.

Two more of Lork's icers walked out, each one carrying a sorihan leg bone complete with huge talons, bones nearly twice as long as any ever seen in Na Saam. "And here is what's left of those birds after the bears got to them! The biggest drumsticks in the whole ice world!" Laughing and cheering, the Na Saamese were all were used to exaggeration, but the enormous bear skins and bird legs seemed to back up Captain Lork's wild tales.

Then, as the Council and the crowd of citizens were

assimilating the evidence of Lork's adventures, the captain brought out his final exhibit, hoping to nail down a favorable decision. "First Mate Attuk," he said loud enough for all to hear, "bring forth our visitor from afar!" At that, Attuk motioned to men in a side alcove. Another gasp went up from the Council and the citizens when three icers and a Tag priest walked up to Lork, bringing with them a fur-clad man who was a head taller than even big Captain Lork himself. Lork was happy to see that the man was now washed and clean; he had left instructions that the wonderful greenish clothing underneath the furs be likewise pristine.

As the icers unwrapped layers of fur from the man, the stranger's features became visible—skin pale brownish, with long, shining dark hair and flashing black eyes; but his clothing caught the eye even more: layers of robes of greenish wispy cloth, far finer than any weave ever known in the history of Na Saam, wispily iridescent as it rippled over the man's thin body as if in a breeze, alternately opaque and semitransparent, almost a living thing of itself. And his boots! No simple fur-lined sealskin tubes those, but shiny black formfitting knee-length coverings never seen before in any ice port. Was the outlander some sort of god? A demon? What? Whispers arose, quickly turning into shouts, demands. The strange man had a firm, unyielding look on his long face, as if he were on trial and expecting a sentence of punishment.

Lork waved his hands for quiet, feeling some satisfaction when his command, like that of Montrea, was obeyed by the rambunctious crowd. A quick glance at Montrea and other Old Men on the Council revealed their recognition of Lork's handling of the situation. *Good! They are not objecting. Maybe I will win them over yet!*

"Everyone, this tall man we found living in a primitive hut at the bottom of that crevasse, a valley of stone, peat, grass, and scrub oak. Although he came willingly, in the week it took us to return home, we understood not a word of his speech." He spoke then to the Tag priest.

"Priest of Tag, you have had this stranger in your care for three days now. What have you learned of him, of his people, and *where they are*?" With emphasis on these last words and a broad smile, Lork's countrymen knew what he was thinking, and what a prize the unusual captive might prove to be: *New people, incredible cloth and boots, no telling what else they possessed—new places to plunder!* Laughter and even a few cheers erupted.

The Tag priest raised his own hands for quiet, but unlike Lork, he did not command immediate respect. At Lork's raised hand, all talk ceased; he motioned for the priest to continue. "Council members, Captain Lork, and all people of Na Saam here gathered, all I can tell you is, though he appears to be a quick learner, at this time his speech is that of a barbarian, a child, barely understandable to civilized folk. I present to you, Alty-Moon Keks."

At that, the captive bowed low, his green robes swirling in a hypnotic vortex. *Well practiced,* Lork noted. *This Alty-Moon Keks knows* he *has to perform too!* The stranger had earned his captor's respect, though he was unaware of it. *I almost hate to have to find his homeland and raid it.*

As if to correct the Tag priest, the captive spoke very slowly and clearly: "Al—tah—moon—Kechhh!" Lork laughed; his tongue would never be able to curl up enough to reproduce the sound of that name. Others laughed, too; they knew what the man was doing, and enjoyed the embarrassment of the Tag priest, who muttered to himself.

As Lork started to speak up again, to pull attention away from the exotic stranger, Altamun spoke out himself, in halting, barely recognizable Na Saamese: "People of Na Saam, I Kech priest, from land beyond Ice Sea where no glacier. My people sail large ships, hundred men, not on ice, but on sea of salty melt." He looked straight at Lork, whose mouth was open in astonishment. He had not conceived that his captive had come from the huge lake, but thought only that Alty's homeland was on the other side of the ice valley where they had found him. And the concept of huge wind-driven vessels out on that melt-lake was hard to accept. Perdis, Stonehaven's long, narrow melt-lake, knew sail craft, but none other than small boats for fishing and others to travel short distances between villages, certainly none carrying a hundred raiders. *And again, that idea of salty melt—ridiculous! Then again, I did smell it...*

"We Kech same Old Men here," he said, pointing to his temple and then at the Twenty around the table, "wise, know things. Hear Captain Lork, crewmen, Priest of Tag, I can talk you. Hope we learn from each other, trade goods with ice ports, live in peace."

Looking directly at Lork, Altamun said, waving his hands in the air, "In my lands, have ancient god-machines. They fly. Defeat all enemies!" At that, Lork realized that the foreigner had understood the nuances of his speech. *Alty understands more than he says,* Lork thought, *if he knows of Na Saam's threat to his homeland. Or does* his *homeland now threaten* us?

Breaking the uneasy silence that followed Altamun's revelations, Old Man Montrea called for Lork, Attuk, the Tag priest, and their captive to meet in private. The dismissed crowd of onlookers was of mixed feelings; everybody was excited about the strange foreigner, the new discoveries, the possible new raiding targets, but subdued after hearing that no new food or trade goods had been seized, after losing thirty-one icers. Typically, a failed captain would be drawn and quartered, his body left on a tall pedestal for sorihan bait. Not all were happy about the changes in tradition, but the younger men were thrilled at the prospect of new lands to explore and raid, and huge animals to hunt and kill.

After the hall was emptied of all but Council, crew, and captive, the other Old Men began to grill "Alty-Moon" about details of his shipwreck, his place of origin, the crops and products they had for trade, and other details that didn't interest Lork all that much. He was more concerned with Attuk's new maps, charts showing the Crevasse That Splits the World (now designated "Attuk's Crack" to Lork's distaste, and not only for the obscene pun), and the possible extent of Ice-End (which the captain endeavored to rename "Lork's Cliffs" and so had Attuk inscribe on the sheepskin).

While the Old Men kept busy with Alty-Moon, Lork and Attuk conferred in a side room, under a clean-burning candle light. "Attuk, how do we get across that Crack of yours," the captain asked. "Do you think Alty is telling the truth? Maybe he just doesn't want us to explore beyond his ice valley, afraid we'll find the mountaintop he came from?" Lork could not imagine any kind of civilization that could exist on that vast lake; Alty had to be from an ice port farther west.

"Cap'n," Attuk replied, chewing on a thumbnail, "if'n he's on the other side of the Ice Sea, then we'd have ta figger a way to drop ships down into the valley, then pull them out the other side. Three thousand feet, takes a lot o' men, lots o' work. But could be done." He thought for a moment, then challenged his captain. "Why would ol' Alty-Moon lie to us? Seems log'cal he got throwed up from the Melt Sea on that rocky shoreline, made it to the Crack, like he tole us."

Lork was not convinced. "Do you believe in a melt-ship with a hundred men? Can you see something like that, sailing on Perdis? And it wrecks? Where are the other ninety-nine men, or their bodies? I don't believe it!"

"'S you wish, Cap'n. I am tryin' to scale out the sightings I done while we was down at, at 'Lork's Cliffs,' and add them to my maps. You know," he said with a wistful look in his eyes, "I'm beginning to b'lieve this whole world of ours really is a big ball. Them sightings can only be 'splained if'n we're on a huge, I mean, real big, sphere. A world ball!"

Lork laughed aloud, saying, "Attuk, keep your maps

up to date, but your ideas to yourself!" and waved goodbye as he rejoined the Council in session. Alty-Moon was still speaking. Somehow, the tall stranger's booming voice filled him with chills. *And not from the temperature, either.*

CHAPTER EIGHTEEN

Before dawn the morning of their departure, Thusk boarded Una in the walled field behind the palace, where the god-machine was stored while in Mother's City. Then he flew her over the short distance to land in the open atrium where she had rescued Thist the previous year. As before, the aircraft's green bulk barely cleared the colonnades on either side, remaining just centimeters above the short grass.

As Una opened the access door, Thist came aboard with two large Mother's Guards. "These men will go with us, Thusk. Just in case." The guards took their large seats at the back of the cabin, placing their spears and swords on the floor. The smaller men sat in their scaled-down chairs in the front to discuss the plans.

Thusk thought, *Landing here again, that much was easy. Now comes the hard part—getting Una to do everything else!* Predictably, the god-machine's qomp collective that was the "brain" of Una responded as its usual self, requiring Thist and Thusk to explain and justify their request to locate Captain Noor's godsphere.

Una spoke through the Anklya-image on the forward screen in her cabin. "I will respond to your request for locating and accessing the Captain Noor godsphere. But before departing today for WaterEdge and out over the Cold Sea, you must both assure me that this information will not be used for conflict with other humans, not for planning wars or kidnappings or even just frightening other humans."

As Thusk chuckled at Una's reaction, his twin Thist was thinking, *This machine, these immortal quantum computers, are learning too much about human behavior, almost becoming human itself. Themselves? I, too, want to minimize violence.* But thinking back over the last year of rebellions in Motherland and even the one back home in The People's Lands before those, he recognized that force must be met with force. *Applied force is a fundamental element of Nature, and therefore is also an element of* human *nature. So we cannot seek to eliminate violence, only to direct it, to try to lessen it.*

"Una, I am sure we both agree, Thusk and I, that the godsphere we seek will only be used to discover its controversial message, the one that unfortunately led to the invasion of ShadowFall."

Thusk nodded, adding, "And to discover, if we can, the whereabouts of the priest Altamun Kech, late of WaterEdge."

THROUGH THE SEEMING MAGIC OF HER "RADIO scanning"—whatever that actually was—Una identified Captain Noor's godsphere before Thusk had finished speaking. By chance, the crystal globe was easily located among a stack of such objects in a nearby field outside the Palace proper, where Thusk's assistants had piled ancient artifacts taken from the vast number of tunnels and vaults below Mother's Palace, prior to properly investigating and archiving them. With detailed directions, Thist had the guards go retrieve the godsphere and bring it back to him, which was quickly done.

Seeing that the atrium was clear of people, Thusk gave Una orders to proceed to WaterEdge while the four passengers secured themselves with belts. Through the transparent walls, below them the checkerboard pattern of red-tile roofs, white-stone buildings and houses of the capital seemed to glow in the rays of the rising sun. From the cruising altitude of a thousand meters, before them in three directions lay the flat mottled vistas of Motherland; only on the far southern horizon did low, ragged shadows give evidence of a range of hills in the distance. Much closer and to the southwest lay the Salty Sea, its rippling waters now sparkling in new light.

While gazing out at the landscape, Thist said, "In an hour Una will take us to WaterEdge. We will first stop and discuss our mission with the Kech, Awhalpa, whom I left in charge there last week. I want to see how well he is doing, and I have some questions about the rebellion that need answering before I decide what to do about reinforcing new defenses there."

A slight acceleration, and Una headed eastward. Thusk made the walls opaque for the moment, wanting to get the full update about Captain Noor's godsphere without distractions. The guards, seeing no requirement to remain alert, dozed off.

As Thist talked, Thusk nodded absentmindedly; he was enjoying a view of the dimming video image of the full moon near the horizon. "You know, Thist, that from the Moon you can barely make out any of our gas or oil lights here in Motherland, but from down here we can see those up there, like jewels in a necklace. Do you ever wonder why?"

Thist snorted. "Twin, I have had my hands full here on Earth, you may have noticed? What happens on the Moon doesn't affect me, so I don't pay any attention to it."

"Well, yes, your wars and all of that. What I don't understand, though, is why you stopped using the Crystal Throne after your one experience with it. You're the first one who made contact with the Moon-girl, that Mienne." Smiling broadly, he teased, "You made history. Thousands of years with no one talking with the Moon, and now you were the man from Earth who started it again."

Thist made a waving motion, dismissing Thusk's comment, and turned his attention to the sights below.

As the mottled carpet of fields and forests unrolled under them, after a few minutes of silence, he said, "Look, that one time was enough for me. I felt like I was dying, being torn apart and put back together. So I *was* able to make contact with that Mienne girl on the Moon, so what?" He preferred not to think of the strange sensations, though they had not been totally unpleasant. That tall Moon-girl, that Mienne, she *was* attractive in some ways…

Thusk laughed, drawing the attention of the two Mothersmen guards who were dozing in their seats at the rear of Una's cabin. Seeing no problem, no need for their action, they promptly returned to sleep. *We don't need you just yet,* Thusk thought. *Only if we have to fight pirates.* Thusk said, "What you did, twin, was to get that Moon-girl to flash those Moonlights off and on during the siege of ShadowFall, showing the Mother's awesome power to control even the Moon. That's all!"

Thist chuckled. "Well, so I did. And so she did. But that once was enough for me. But I'm glad you are enjoying your trips Up There."

"I enjoyed *being* there, but not the going to or coming back." He could never tell Thist everything that he and Mienne had been doing on the Moon, but it had been literally "Out of this world!"

"So, back to Earth, Thusk, let's see what that pirate left with Mother Messinex, what caused her and that damned Miran Kech to invade ShadowFall." Thist thought, *For all the death and misery it caused, Motherland is better off that the war happened. Otherwise, Pernie would not be Mother now, and I would not be her general. But why does everything in Motherland have to be decided by death?* Putting those thoughts aside, he held up the godsphere globe, feeling its coolness but not seeing anything within it.

"It's not responding to me, Thusk. You want to try it?" Typically, a receptive godsphere would light up from inside, displaying colorful and realistic miniature scenes of ancient times, occasionally with maps and three-dimensional moving pictures and sounds. *And too often,* Thist remembered, *in languages we have not yet learned.* Neither he nor anyone else to his knowledge had discovered why the ancients had left thousands of the head-sized spheres scattered all over the whole round world, as near as they could tell. One person's touch might set them off, but not everyone could work that wonder, and just because you could light up one globe did not mean that another would work for you; most of them remained either pitch black or presented at most a swirling, milky mist.

A strange reality, Thusk thought, *but there it is. Sometimes they're useful, sometimes not. There must have been some logic behind it all, but it's quite a mystery.* He handed it over to his twin, who pushed it away.

"No, Thist, we have the same DNA, so I won't be able to read it, either. Let's see what Una can do."

Una responded, "Of course I can access the information in this information sphere." After a pause, she said, "It may be useful for you both to know that I have already downloaded all data from this and all the other informational globes in Motherland. Ask and you will receive."

Thist gasped. "You mean you already have this godsphere's information, and that of all of those hundreds of others out there?"

"Yes."

"Why didn't you tell us?"

"You didn't ask."

CHAPTER NINETEEN

"One hundred and fifty feet, Odel," Mox said, pointing to the top of the wooden structure rising high above her and M'ridge. "That's as high as the timbermen will work. No farther. Too dangerous. High winds up there."

Odel looked up to the top of the launch platform he had ordered built, the yellowish bare wood a contrast to the blue sky and white clouds behind it. Though impressively tall for anything ever built before in ShadowFall or Thessland, the tower appeared insignificant when compared to the vertical cliffs of the Dark Highlands just a quarter of a mile north of it. Those cliffs extended westward to the miles-wide Great Waterfall and beyond. To his right, the east, their dark mass was a wall that went on for hundreds of miles, right into the horizon. *Unexplored territory,* Odel thought. *And this little valley, with its forest, has walls two thousand feet high, the lowest spot my scouts could find.*

Odel sighed and looked down at his mate and said, "Mox, if that's all they will do, so be it. I don't want anybody risking their lives for me. I was able to fly my boosted tri-wing over two thousand feet from a tower half that size. The only thing that concerns me is the wind. It seems to roar down from the highlands at times, but sweeps upward other times."

Mox replied, pointing toward separated piles of timber remnants and brush arranged in a line a quarter mile on each side of the launch tower parallel to the cliffs beyond. "I've got crews ready to build bonfires and maintain them," she said. "We will keep records of the smoke direction at the different times of day, and see which way the winds blow and when. You can judge then when to fly."

Odel nodded. "Brilliant, Mox." He said. He thought, *You little people are the most imaginative folks I have ever met. Does that creativity come from surviving locked in by glaciers for thousands of years?* He knew he'd never know the answer to that. *Maybe I should have asked that Una machine of Thist's and Thusk's?*

"Tomorrow, then," Odel said. "Let's watch that smoke all day today and tonight, and then I will decide when to go." Returning to the crude construction hut he and Mox had occupied for the last week, Odel checked the spindle on which he had rewrapped the yard-wide godscloth material. "This measures roughly two miles in length, plenty long enough," he said aloud as Mox listened. "When I make it to the top, I will wrap the line around a sturdy tree or rock and drop this line down. Then I can haul up the pulley system. This bright yellow weight on the end weighs a lot more than all the godscloth itself, but is needed so the stuff doesn't blow away and you all can see it when it comes down.

"Then I will attach the pulley system to the anchor end up there, and drop the other end of the line down. Using that system, we can have an elevator system. One crew using their ox pulls on one end, raising up the cage full of people or supplies on the other end."

Mox nodded, "So those who won't be going with us, they will be the last crew pulling up the cage for the others to leave?"

"Could be. Or maybe, if everyone wants to go, we pull up both the lines to the top and abandon this place. We would need to take all the godscloth with us. Too valuable to leave down here."

As the sun rose the next morning, Odel and his people watched the smoke rising from Mox's line of bonfires, the pungent evergreen fumes being swept by the heating ground below in vaporous sheets, wafting northward and smoothing themselves against the cliff face. "That's what I wanted to see, folks. I can rise on that column of warm air, then back off a bit to get clear of the cliffs and fire my boosters. That ought to get me high enough to get over the top."

To the cheers of the bystanders, he picked up Mox and kissed her. "*Tomorrow*, everybody, tomorrow we begin our journey out of these lowlands and up, up to a new life *there*!"

Through the rest of the day, he and Mox and others supervised the loading of weapons, tools, provisions, and miscellaneous materiel onto skids. The metal elevator cage, twelve feet square, stood nine feet high, with loops of iron through which the godscloth would be run and secured. Odel would take no tools with him for the first flight, minimizing the weight his tri-wing would have to support; tools and construction materials would be lifted up afterwards. He knew that he would have to construct some kind of cantilever system to hang out over the cliff so that the cage would not be bashed against the vertical rock face while being raised and lowered. A sketch to his timber chief described a simple configuration that could be lifted up in the first load before the cage could be used.

"Odel, you've got a lot of responsibility on you," Mox said that night in bed. "Please don't get hurt tomorrow. We can't do this without you. And I would rather stay here and take our chances against the Originals than have you killed trying to get us away."

"Not to worry, hon," he replied. "We'll do it. All of us."

THE NEXT MORNING FOUND ODEL'S TRI-WING SPINNING out of control, dangerously close to being smashed against the cliff face. "Damn, maybe I shouldn't have done this!" he cursed, as his craft jerked around crazily, nearly a thousand feet above the valley floor. "Damn booster didn't light. I've got to gain altitude or get killed!"

Below him, hundreds of Thesslanders watched in horror as their leader seemed to be caught in a vortex, spiraling upward. "But not high enough," Mox wailed. "Fire your next rocket, Odel!"

Swinging his left arm out to a strut holding the second booster rocket, Odel touched its fuse with a firestick. With a satisfying roar, the arm-length cylinder spewed out sparks, then flames, and the tri-wing glider accelerated. Blowing out a breath of relief, Odel quickly pulled levers that allowed the craft to rise almost vertically, to the cheers of the crowd below. As he saw the top of the Dark Highlands in the distance, Odel turned his tri-wing northward, staying above the ground surface there, then gradually descending to earth several hundred feet in, away from the cliff edge. "I made it," he breathed. "Now comes the hard part."

FIVE DAYS LATER, ODEL, MOX, AND THEIR CLOSEST colleagues rested in the shade of large oaks in their newfound campsite a mile inland from the edge of the Dark Highlands cliffs. Breezes rustled the yellowing leaves, bringing with them the welcome scent of grasses and flowers. Standing before the circle of reclining people, Odel said, "Folks, we've got this far pretty fast. Everybody who is coming with us is now here. Mox, how many?"

The little woman said, "Eight hundred or so up here now, big and small." She smiled; more big people than she and Odel had suspected had joined them, nearly a hundred in all. "And I estimate an equal number stayed behind in Thessland."

Odel frowned. "I do hope they do find peace and security down there." Waving toward the north, he said, "We have neither yet, but there's a lot of unoccupied lands between here and God's Country. Anybody wants to stay in this area is free to do so. I plan to return to my land in God's Country and settle down again. I have a quarry there. And even there, you can get land grants for farming and such. We will leave a noticeable stone pile or tree markings every few miles along the way as we go, if anyone wants to follow us later." He picked up a handful of fallen leaves. "It is getting to be fall now, so we need to make plans. Those staying here need to prepare for winter. Those of us going north have to make sleds or carts to carry our provisions and tools. So let's get to it right away."

"I DIDN'T THINK THAT MANY WOULD STAY AT CliffEdge," Odel told Mox as he pulled a loaded sled behind him. "I mean, only fifty are coming with us, and half of them big people?"

Mox laughed and looked up at her mate twice her height. "My dearest, my people and I are from a nation that was separated from the rest of the world by surrounding glaciers for thirty thousand years—or so that Una machine told us. So, stuck in a small country all that time, we are not naturally very adventurous. To us, *adventure* always meant dangers and strangers. You have to realize that the ones who came up to these highlands had already resettled from People's Lands down to ShadowFall and then over to Thessland, all in less than two years. That forest at CliffEdge, with its meadows and streams and fish and wild game animals, is still a paradise to them, compared to the dreary Misty Sky and the ice back home. And now, being up and away from the threats of those Originals, that gives them the peace and security you promised."

Odel agreed. "And I think that more than a couple of your countrymen might just be thinking of how important their location could be as a trading post between the highlands and Thessland. They still have friends, maybe even relatives, down there. And we left them half the godscloth and the iron cage elevator." He laughed. "I tell you, anybody like your folks who can make a living selling icebergs from a river will probably make a killing at CliffEdge. The oak trees there make for better timber than the pines below, and some of the outcroppings look to have mineral deposits for the taking. So there's no telling what all your talented salesmen will find to peddle"

"I RECKON WE'VE STAYED AT LEAST FIFTY TO A HUNDRED miles east of the New River all this time," Odel said at a campfire one evening, weeks after leaving CliffEdge. "Our little expedition is staying well away from the Solar Priests at God's Port. We ought to be less than fifty miles from my lands, due north."

Mox and the other group leaders smiled. "Odel, dear," Mox ventured, "the fifty of us *are* getting restless, they tell me. We've passed through some nice territory coming this way. Valleys and rivers and forests and plains, almost any of those places would make a good place just to stop and settle. And very few people, too." At that, the leaders murmured under their breaths. Twice Odel's entourage had fought off attacks by small bands of near-naked, pale-skinned savages, but springbows and spears had made short work of them.

Odel could tell that the men around the campfire didn't agree with Mox. *I concur,* he thought. *Why settle where savages roam? We were better off than that back in Thessland. The Originals might be savage but they are not savages.* "Mox, hon," he said, "my quarry and farm lands will provide resources and work for this many. And there's lots more, unclaimed, to the east of my place. And no savages—or Originals." *Solar Priests we got, but they're way west.* He would handle those men when any problems arose, but for now he just wanted to get these people safely to his home.

Odel was leading his straggling group of refugees up the access road from the main paved highway to his quarry site, and closely observing changes along the way. "This road has been improved since I left," he told Mox, who was walking beside him, carrying her springbow at the ready. "Paved with flat stones. They will handle heavy loaded wagons better, no ruts and all, but I wonder why."

As he entered the quarry site, Odel was astonished. "Who are all these people?" he asked aloud, to nobody in particular. There before him, his quarry had been excavated to twice the open volume as he had left it, and two dozen workmen were busy swinging sledgehammers against wedges, splitting off slabs of the precious pink granite. As the immigrant group filled in the staging area where wagons were being loaded, the quarry workers stopped and looked on with astonishment. What they saw were a big, bushy-bearded Odel in ragged khakis, several dozen other large people dressed in a motley assortment of tunics and trousers and skirts, and an equal number of short dark people, half the height of the big ones. Although some were dragging sleds behind them, the most obvious and ominous feature of the strange crowd was that almost every one of them was carrying an unusual type of bow. And all of them, now standing and staring back at the quarrymen, were aiming pointed projectiles at the awed onlookers.

"Who's running things here?" Odel bellowed out.

"Yo, stranger," said a big, leather-aproned man, his tattoos and cap insignia indicating his allegiance to the Solar Priest cult. In a defiant stance, he snarled, "I do. I am the foreman of this site. And what is the meaning of this, this, *invasion* of the property of the Solar Temple?"

Odel walked right up to the man and stared at him, eye to eye. "I am Odel M'ridge, and this is *my* property, *my* quarry." Waving an arm back toward his band of refugees, he said, "And I—*we*—aim to take back possession of it, right now."

The foreman started to say something, but sputtered. Seeing the hostility in the faces of the archers pointing their shafts at himself and his men, he calmed down. Bowing slightly, he said, "As you wish, Mr. M'ridge, is it? No use getting people killed here. Me and my guys will leave now, on a wagon if you will let us. I'll just have to report this situation to the priests in God's Port. As I'm sure you know, they won't be happy." He waved to the bewildered quarrymen, who dropped their tools and headed for the largest wagon, a ponderous affair drawn by a team of four oxen.

Odel was shaking his head. "You tell the Solar Priests that Odel M'ridge is back home and wants no trouble. Just to occupy my quarry and my lands. I will also insist on a full accounting of the illegal harvesting of my granite since I've been away. Now, go!" The foreman bowed again and joined his crew on the wagon. Odel was impressed at the man's stoic behavior. *I would've put up a fight, if somebody came onto me like I did on him! But the man was just doing his job.* Odel knew he would have to find out what happened while he was away. *The road was paved so heavy loads of my granite could be transported, I'll bet. But why would they need so much stone?* At any reasonable price, someone had carted off a small fortune. *My fortune!*

Putting down their weapons as the wagonload of displaced workers disappeared down the access road, all of Odel's followers began to take advantage of the jugs of cool spring water and the spread of food laid out on workers' tables. After weeks of wild game, berries, and the occasional beezt meat, the appetizing array of breads, cheese, beans, pork, and sauces were like a palace feast to them. Odel was just glad they hadn't arrived after that food was gone.

But now, though he had promised his people here peace, he was going to have to prepare them once again for a fight this time with the Solar Priests. *Will it ever end?* he wondered. *Will it ever?*

CHAPTER TWENTY

In frustration at Una's flat declaration of "You didn't ask," Thist shouted at the Anklya-image on the front screen of the cabin, "Can't you ever anticipate what we want to know? You knew we wanted all the godsphere information we could access. You have deliberately withheld important information!" Calming down, he addressed the image more civilly. The three-dimensional representation with which Una chose to represent herself was too close to reality, Thist thought, awakening repressed physical memories of the great times he had spent with his and his twin's lover.

Now a political leader back in The People's Lands, their homeland at the foothills of The Ice, Anklya had chosen to remain in that country rather than return to her native Motherland. "Too many bad memories in Motherland," she had said when Thist had left her, "of when I was only a slave. Among your people here in the north, I am treasured, free. You may go fight for the Mother, but I will live here with your birther, Mell. She needs me." Though unhappy with her choice, Thist let her go. But he often missed her, both body and brain. He was sure that his twin did, too.

The collective system of qomps that comprised Una's Developing Intelligence answered immediately, even before Thist's last word had been uttered. "Thist, I am in the process of developing models for human thought and expectations. Human life is not an algorithm, but a chaotic system of unknowable complexity, more akin to turbulent gas dynamics. However, with this latest datum, I will attempt henceforth to provide unasked-for information when a decision is made that it can be done without causing harm."

Thusk laughed at his twin's frustration. "I have been with Una a lot longer than you have, twin. Knowing what questions to ask of her is a majority of the answer. Having her think like we do might be impossible." Turning to the Anklya-image, he said, "Una, please summarize for us what that pirate's sphere had to say."

"Very well. The 'godsphere,' as you call it, originated in what in ancient times was called 'the Caribbean Sea,' deep underground, under the seabed surface, at a nanofabrication facility of a corporate entity called Tagren, LLC. During the Emergency, some humans took shelter in those facilities. After a while, they fabricated an indefinite number of the information spheres with their nanofab technologies. Most of the spheres contain no updated information later than that era. I found that nearly all of the devices ceased data inputs either immediately or within a few decades after their fabrication."

Thist and Thusk could not imagine why the inputs stopped, and that begged the question *What were they for?*

Una went on, answering the unspoken request. "Apparently the borophene globes require direct solar energy input to activate them. Lacking sunlight or its equivalent, they go silent until recharged. Human touch is required to access the information, but not all human DNA will unlock every sphere.

"The sphere that belonged to the pirate, Captain Noor, was actuated by himself two years ago. Among other contents, it is a documentary presentation that shows videos of ancient survivors, an uncatalogued variety of technological information, and several simulations of the expected geological upheavals caused by the solar eruptions that brought on the Age of Ice. Anticipating your possible interest, here on screen are the complete contents of Captain Noor's sphere."

Una's female voice had awakened the Mothersmen guards, who now took an interest in the digital presentation on the screen. Thist smiled; few outside the inner circles of Motherland's rulers had ever witnessed ancient digital technologies in action. Flying through the skies in a big green cylinder? *That* they could accept— everyone knew that birds and bugs could fly, so why not men? But to watch a flat screen with three-dimensional moving pictures, and a beautiful woman who could talk to you? That was not like anything they'd ever even thought of. Dreams were the closest experience, but dreams were not shared. Nevertheless, the soldiers were enthralled. *And right now they're going to witness, with us, secrets that not even Mother Pernie and Wakan Kech have ever seen.*

The opening scene was of a three-dimensional blue-and-green ball, one familiar to Thist and Thusk as representing the round Earth, but as it was before The Ice came. The rough outline of Motherland existed below the brown and green northern continent, but it was all blue—a sea! Gasps from the guards told that they understood part of the meaning; Wakan's crash courses in astronomy and in Motherland geography and geology had been imposed on all nobles, palace staff and military officers, including the guards, so they all knew somewhat of the true nature of Earth and Moon and Sun. But seeing ancient Earth as if from high above in space was entirely new; the Motherland-shaped sea only added to their shock. Remembering his own first reaction to digital simulations just two years before, Thist thought the men accepted both the view and its implications fairly well. *They are becoming civilized!*

As unintelligible characters appeared on the screen, yellow markings on a blue background, a male narrator's voice ("Translated from ancient Spanglish for your convenience," Una explained) said, "July 1, 2135. This information globe is being nanofabricated at

Tagren Laboratories, LLC, two kilometers undersea at our corporate location east of Guantanamo, Republic of Caribbea. It contains information about our present situation. We have no idea as to when global storm conditions will allow us to return to the surface. At the very least, these globes may become time capsules for future generations, if any. We plan to nanofacture and eject as many globes as possible over the next weeks, until the dedicated nanofab facilities here are exhausted. If you are seeing or hearing this, it means we have succeeded to some extent. We hope the background information downloaded from all of our local qomps will be of use to you."

Short video segments of interviews appeared, with over a hundred survivors telling about themselves. After a dozen or so talked about their families and hopes for the future, Thist began to lose interest. "What a waste," he said. "Who cares about their names? We want ancient knowledge, not a list of names for tombstones!"

Thusk hushed him. "They thought it important, so let's listen." The guards in back had no comment, still enthralled by the pictures and sounds coming from the screen. The individuals being shown were fantastic enough in themselves, a range of skin colors like none ever seen in Motherland—yellowish, pitch black, albino white, rainbow glittering—with a spectrum of hair colors and styles, iridescent clothing, internally lit jewelry, even tattoos that *moved and changed colors!* The common message of the people interviewed seemed to be: "If our relatives or friends find these globes, please try to locate us at—" followed by numbers that apparently meant coordinates to the ancients, but a meaning lost in time, as much as the name of their location.

Thist snorted. "Thirty thousand years ago? I don't think anyone they knew is still around!"

Thusk said, "But this is fascinating. So, Una, what else is there? We'll be arriving at WaterEdge soon, and will be busy with other matters. You said the pirate's sphere had simulations of an ancient Motherland Sea?

Captain Noor's claims? And yours, Thist, what you found under the palace, the one that set off Mother Messinex and caused a war?" He was only half-joking.

Thist replied, "Yes, what I found in the old libraries under the palace was one godsphere that showed a map of the world, pre-Ice, and the salty sea covering all of Motherland. When I tried to present the information, she exploded at me, demanding that all the globes and books and maps be taken back below and sealed off forever. That's when she told that slimy Miran Kech to seize ShadowFall's libraries. You and Anklya and Una swooped down into that atrium and rescued me then, remember? I never realized what sent Messinex into such a rage. Of course, we didn't know back then that the Crystal Throne was damaging her mind, either.

"But thinking back on it, that pirate must have shown her the same thing, this view of Earth on the screen, with the sea covering everything. That was over a year ago, when she threw him out and kept this sphere; I must have come into court right after that with my own discovery, which confirmed his claims. No wonder she was so upset—it was proof the pirate was right."

Remembering Messinex's fury and the unnecessary war that followed, Thist shook his head. "But it happened all those centuries ago, before The Ice came, so what? Una, keep on, show us the simulations you promised."

On the screen, the blue-and-green Earth was whipped by intense streams of light and heat—"The solar conflagration as envisioned by the qomps of the survivors who made this video, based on the final data they collected"—followed by continent-sized storms that raged for years, according to the narrator. "Centuries of heavy rain will commence in Earth's temperate and tropical regions, and the polar regions will rapidly accumulate ice, forming glaciers very quickly. As a consequence, global sea levels will drop hundreds of meters; exactly how far we here will never know."

"Una," asked Thusk, "please show what happens to

Motherland in this simulation. The rest of the round world, we can worry about later." Thist asked to include The People's Lands, too. He had always wondered how his people had survived the cataclysm.

In response, the screen was filled with the large northern continent and the sea immediately below it. As swathes of white accumulated and moved southward, covering over half of that land mass, the Motherland Sea gradually diminished, shrinking to a small lake in the southwest, recognized by the men as the Salty Sea, in their time an eighty-square-kilometer lake that marked the southwestern extent of their country. The broad outlines of Motherland became apparent as the surrounding highlands emerged from the receding waters.

The translated narration continued. "This simulation is the best guess of our qomps. Your mileage may vary. The sims forecast a millennium of heavy global rain, and sea levels dropping significantly as glaciers form. How these events will affect human survivability is not predictable. Following are downloads from our qomps —scientific knowledge, engineering practices, artisanal skills, and a bit of history and philosophy and religion. Lots of music, artwork, 3Ds, just a data dump. The eclectic collection here is made up of everything we had up and running in our facility and on our personal qomps. We never expected to become a library."

In the background a voice shouted, "And we never expected to be stuck in a Tagren Nanofab a mile underground, either!" Other voices interrupted: "Do we get overtime, Mr. T?" "Is there a damned world *left* out there?" "Why are we talking into these damned balls? They gonna help us get out and go home?" Followed by darkness.

With the Anklya-image gone and Una's front screen now a grayish blank, Thist sat back in his cabin chair, looking out through the transparent walls at the never-ending panoply of fields, patchworks of variegated crops, and silver rivulets of rivers that unrolled below them. "According to Wakan, Noor's pirates or their like have raided WaterEdge for centuries, usually taking whatever they could grab—food, metals, some people. No wanton destruction, I would presume because they wanted a renewable resource; why destroy your free supplies? The raids never cost quite enough to warrant preparing expensive defenses or trying to build boats and have crews to fight them on the Cold Sea."

Thusk rubbed his chin, agreeing. "Other than a few coastal fishing ships, Motherland has never had a navy, according to the secret histories Pernie says she has access to. I don't know why, except that the Cold Sea has always been rather turbulent and its winds unpredictable. You'd think, though, that somebody would have braved it to go exploring."

"I don't think Motherlanders think like we People do," Thist said. "You've seen how they hold grudges and stew over verbal insults, for years in some cases. Mother's Palace is full of that kind of conspiracy and controversy, especially now with all the newcomers. I believe it's because we who lived near The Ice had no time to waste on nonproductive activities. Our forefathers and birthers worked hard just to survive. After hunting velks and ice-bears for furs and meat, and scratching out peat crops, who had the energy to invest in petty feuds and fights? But when you're rich and well fed, and you are not worried about that next meal or wild beasts attacking you, then you can let your idle mind dwell on unimportant things. Like armies and navies."

Thusk agreed with his twin, but as usual was focused on loftier subjects. "So what is it in Motherland's warlike culture that prevented them from fortifying WaterEdge years ago and just killing all the raiders? Maybe even seize their ships and go invade their islands? Solve the problem, once and for all?"

"Again, Thusk, that's you and me speaking. From listening to Wakan talk about it, Motherland as a whole could easily afford a navy but WaterEdge by itself could not bear the expense—the forests needed for shipbuilding lumber are all in the north, far away from the Cold Sea. And the Sisterdoms have never thought of themselves as one people, one nation. Mothers ruled over all of them, but out of necessity had to pit them against each other to maintain that Mother's power. So no way would, say, Three Rivers and Trader Plains pitch in to finance a bunch of ships they would never use— they have no sea boundaries.

"Wakan and Pernie are trying to forge the ten remaining Sisterdoms into republics, and those republics into one nation, but that requires each Sister to relinquish power to a local Governing Council, and the favored nobles to yield some of their lands and perqs to entrepreneurial citizens and new farmers. As you can see from two bloody and vicious rebellions in less than a year"—here, he frowned and shook his head, staying silent for a few seconds—"some progress has to be made at the point of a sword." Another frown, more silence, then a whisper, "*My* sword."

CHAPTER TWENTY-ONE

Awhalpa Kech, interim administrator of the Republic of WaterEdge, nervously paced the wide tiles of the plaza of the Pink Palace, carefully stepping around the broken ones. Though the sea winds kept his yellow godscloth robes dry, the material's constant billowing was getting on his nerves. *I need my scribe's tunic*, he thought. *Simple and not all tangly.* Around him scurried men dressed like that, his assistants who were making ready for General Thist's arrival.

On Awhalpa's orders, the last week had seen crews of demobilized guards cleaning up and disposing of the debris of the recent battle. *At least the landing area for the general's flying machine will be spotless.* But looking uphill at the ruins of the Pink Palace and the concentric garden tiers below it, burnt to blackened ashes, he was less pleased. *I don't see how we can reuse that beautiful stone, all smashed apart and cracked as it is. But the general has ordered that all of it be carefully stacked and out of the way. Me, I'd just throw it into the sea and make another breakwater out past the surf.*

Waving off the insistent, whining assistants to get on with their jobs and oversee the disposition of the ruins, he turned once again westward, hoping to catch a glimpse of that Una's vast green bulk. Within minutes, the craft appeared below the light clouds, high above the city.

As the Una grew soundlessly closer, Awhalpa squinted to make out its shape, finally grinning as it gracefully touched ground just a few meters in front of him, on freshly swept tiles. *It does look like a big green bug, at that, or even a cucumber.* As did every other Motherlander, Awhalpa knew the hilarious story of how Advisor Thusk had made the Una walk off from the plaza of the Solar Priests in a weird northern place called God's Country, dragging nets and statues and street kiosks with it. *Like a giant green spider carrying off its next meal.* And with that white man-thing sitting on top like a god.

As the Una settled down onto the plaza just yards from his position, that "white man-thing" appeared to Awhalpa's view when the black bulge of a cockpit hinged open back from the front of the green cylinder. Visible only from the waist upward, the familiar white torso turned toward Awhalpa, its featureless face showing only two large black circles for eyes and a black unmoving oval for its "mouth."

That is one creepy thing, Awhalpa thought, but waved at it and bowed as if it were a person. Around the plaza workers were gathering, whether awed at the giant cylinder or its putative "pilot" he wasn't certain. *Probably both, as am I.*

"I am Una," said a loud voice out of nowhere and everywhere, "carrying General Thist, Advisor Thusk, and two Mother's Guards." With that, a door hinged open at the top of the Una, and two small, dark men in blue tunics emerged, followed by their large, leather-armored Mothersmen, carrying springbows unslung as if expecting trouble.

"Awhalpa Kech at your service, gentlemen," the new administrator welcomed his guests. "Please accompany me to our temporary headquarters." Nodding in acknowledgement, Thist told the guards to stand watch at Una's entrance hatch, which by now had closed up. He knew that Una needed no protection —*Except against borophene arrows*, he remembered with a frown. *Creesile could have killed us all if one of his spears had hit Una. Instead of Messinex.* But the presence of two big burly Mother's Guards would serve as a reminder to everyone of their Mother Pernie's power.

Looking around, Thist was pleased to note the progress in cleaning up the site in only a week. *Centuries to build,* he thought, *a week to destroy, and days to pick up the debris. What a comment on human affairs; no wonder our Una does not trust us!*

After chilled honey wine and a selection of cold meats and fruits, General Thist and Advisor Thusk sat at the shaded outdoor table and listened to Administrator Awhalpa's long and detailed report on the political and economic situations in WaterEdge. Things were as satisfactory as could be expected. And boring.

Then Thist asked, "Awhalpa Kech, why did Loranthip Kech advise his princess to revolt? And why did the citizens here put up such resistance?" He had lost more fighters than expected, and many WaterEdgers had refused to surrender, fighting to the death. "Why fight when your leader is a tyrant?"

The Kech spread his hands, sweating. "General Thist, Loranthip followed General Creesile's campaign with interest, and saw how only the intercession of your Una machine prevented his success. Rumors were rife afterwards that your Una could not harm people, what people had witnessed, so its effectiveness was discounted. If it couldn't kill, who would care that it flew around and shouted loud messages from the sky? And that business with lights flashing on the Moon? Loranthip dismissed it; what could anything on the Moon do to harm us down here? We are not a superstitious people." Awhalpa quickly realized that he was caught up in his predecessor's own arguments, perhaps presenting them just a bit too enthusiastically.

Somewhat abashed and now in a calmer voice, he said, "If I may say so with some shame, not only our

Princess, but I and many of the other nobles considered Mother Pernie's rapid succession to Motherhood not quite legitimate." Thist and Thusk shook their heads in disbelief, but the administrator continued. "And after the defeat and crushing retaliation of"—at Thist's raised forefinger, Awhalpa did not name the Name—"of that *other* Sisterhood, I believe Loranthip saw an opportunity for WaterEdge to break away. No one had expected such a scorched-earth policy from Mother Pernie, nor had the other Sisters, so there was nationwide revulsion and dismay. Amidst the confusion, Loranthip spread the word that Mother Pernie was going to use her"—Awhalpa gulped, saying—"pardon me greatly, sirs, her *monkey-men*, to seize and rape the women of WaterEdge, and brutally cut off the genitals of all our men." With downcast eyes, the Kech gritted his teeth. "Sirs, I'm afraid that I, too, also believed much of that story, until I saw how your bird-riders and the regular Mothersmen soldiers behaved during the siege."

Thist let out a long whistle. "So we finally get to the bottom of this. Centuries of cruelty is the tradition in Motherland, so they would believe any lies, and fight to the death rather than surrender. I would do so myself, in their place. But wrong beliefs always lead to unnecessary slaughter." To Awhalpa: "Thank you for your candor. Should any more military force be required again in Motherland, I will make sure that those we fight know the truth." Thist sat back in his chair, taking a long draught of the honeyed wine, an expression of disgust and regret on his face, whispering to himself, "We didn't have to kill all those men, or destroy the Pink Palace and those beautiful gardens after all." He made a mental note that apparently most WaterEdge nobles and courtiers had not seen fit to die as had their troops. He'd have to reconsider some of his drumhead pardons.

Anxious to get information about the Lordship Islands and so continue their exploration over the Cold Sea, Thusk finally asked, "Awhalpa Kech, what can you tell us about that Captain Noor and his pirates? About the islands in the Cold Sea?"

Grateful to talk on a less distasteful subject, Awhalpa said with a sigh, "Thankfully our written archives survived your, uh, *the* fires that destroyed the Pink Palace, kept as they were in the deepest tunnels, in sealed rooms carved out of the living stone of the hill upon which it was constructed. There have always been pirate raids, but usually unorganized and sporadic. More of a nuisance, actually, than an existential threat. They sometimes boarded our fishing boats but hardly ever killed any of our crews. Unfortunately, upon occasion they would abscond with a youngster. Never to be seen again. Nobody ever returned so we knew nothing about their fates." He shrugged. "As you can imagine, the wildest rumors swept through the populace—slavery, cannibalism, human sacrifice.

"Then a little over a year ago, a tall albino calling himself 'Captain Noor' arrived with a fleet of those dragon-prowed ships. Only he himself came ashore, but the visible threat of those hundreds of predatory men offshore were guarantee enough that he would not be harmed. And so he wasn't, traveling all the way to Mother's Palace for an audience with Mother Messinex, then back here. Our chief priest at the time, Altamun Kech, accompanied him both ways. Weeks on the roads." Looking strangely at his two guests, Awhalpa said, "But you didn't hear of his visit?"

Both twins shook their heads with no further explanation. Back then, Thist had been recovering from the loss of his foot in the Motherland Games and while recovering, exploring the ancient tunnels under Mother's Palace for godspheres. And Thusk had flown their Una to Mother's Palace to take his twin and Anklya away, first to ShadowFall and then back to their homeland.

WHILE ACCEPTING PROVISIONS FOR THE REMAINDER OF

their planned trip, the four travelers lodged in the untouched palace of a former WaterEdge noble, a stucco'ed mansion with an interior courtyard, a saltwater pool, and servants. "I'm getting used to all these luxuries," Thusk said to his twin as they relaxed under sweet-smelling torchlights. "I don't know why these nobles, these courtiers, wouldn't be satisfied with all of these huge houses, gardens, rich foods. Back home this would have been beyond belief."

"Greed," General Thist answered softly, quaffing a flagon of honeyed wine, "and lust for power over others. I think our People could teach them a thing or two about getting along." But the recent troubles in ShadowFall between PeoplesLandsers immigrants and the tall Motherlanders put the lie to that. Along with Awhalpa's revelations about Loranthip Kech's lying and insidious propaganda about Thist's bird-rider warriors. With a sigh, he said, "On the other hand, at ShadowFall we have seen that the Originals there don't get along with our People. Or maybe vice-versa?"

With Awhalpa's assistants fetching surviving historical documents, WaterEdge records showed scant information about where the raiders came from. "I'm afraid that all we know is from our far east over the horizon," the Kech explained. "That albino pirate, Captain Noor himself, boasted of coming from over two thousand kilometers east, but that is probably just typical criminal exaggeration. I don't think he'd really want us to know, do you?"

CHAPTER TWENTY-TWO

Departing WaterEdge eastward over the Cold Sea aboard Una, Thist and Thusk and their two guards eagerly watched the sunrise as its rays lit up the sparkling waves a thousand meters below. Overhead the sky was cloudless, and after fifteen minutes of low-speed flight all they could see out of Una's clear walls was sea and more sea, horizon to horizon in all directions. After taking in the spectacular but boring view, the guards dozed off; they would not be needed until—and if—Una landed on one of the islands that Thusk was determined to locate.

"Una, show us the ancient maps of the Cold Sea, and those simulations from Noor's godsphere," said Thusk. Without comment, the images appeared on the front screen—a blue-green background, dotted with brown land masses. Una's position was marked by a small green triangle from which trailed a dark red line marking their route.

"This is our route compared to the pre-Ice map," Una announced, "and we are the green triangle on the simulation." Islands on the first map grew in size as the simulated sea-level drop occurred. Strings of new land masses emerged, stretching far out into the Cold Sea, dozens of specks. The green triangle was approaching the first grouping of islands.

Thusk said, "Go invisible, Una, and hover five

hundred meters over the first inhabited island we come to."

An hour later Una's crew looked down at a bustling port city, spread out below them like a child's playroom: blocks of houses and buildings scattered along a narrow shore, crowded up against high cliffs, continuing up over those heights onto a flat plain, where the majority of the population lived. Sailing vessels of all sizes clustered about piers stretching fingerlike into a sheltered harbor, from their altitude appearing like toys in a stream. From one mast to many, the vessels appeared to be more than mere fishing boats.

Thist whistled. "At least twenty ships down there! They could carry a thousand or more troops, I'll bet, from the size of them. Maybe we have to plan against an invasion by sea?" Already he was visualizing such an attack on WaterEdge and what defenses could be rallied against it. *Catapults, certainly. But what else?* He hated to think of the expense of outfitting and training a naval force, but it might be necessary to protect Motherland. Maybe Odel's aerial force? But how far could they travel over the Cold Sea and still return? Launched from towers aboard ships? The cost in resources and men would be overwhelming. *Let's try for trade,* he thought. *Unless these are the pirates that have raided us for so long.*

But Thusk was scanning the city above the cliffs, and in particular what seemed to be conveyances that ran up and down the steep inclines on tracks of some kind. "Una," he asked, "what are those vehicles? How do they move? And while you are scanning everything here, can you determine if this island was here before The Ice or did it emerge when the oceans dropped?"

"Thusk, those are wheeled carriages that ride on steel rails. They were once called 'funiculars.' They are pulled uphill by cables and lowered the same way. Here, they appear to be operated by animal-powered cable drums at the top and bottom of the routes.

"As far as the island itself, my scans indicate that some of it has been here since before the ice came, but portions of it have risen and others have sunk, in geological response to the weight of northern glaciers. Storms, wind, uplifts and earthquakes reshaped it extensively. Here at its western end, the plain at the top used to be seabed."

In response to Thist's detailed questions about the size and defenses of the island, Una answered, "The population of the city below I estimate at twenty thousand. The defenses appear to comprise catapult-like installations on the mesa above, protecting the harbor."

Thist said to Thusk, "So they have been attacked from the sea in the past, else catapults wouldn't be necessary."

"No argument there, *General*," Thist said, smiling. "Say, Una, can you read any of the flags or banners or signs down there, anything that would tell us if this is where the pirate Noor sailed from?"

"Most of the sailing vessels display flags of an identical but unknown symbol. Only six bear different flags and hull designs. From this, I conclude that the larger number are of one organization, the others commercial ships from elsewhere. Similar flags and banners with the unknown symbol decorate larger buildings around both the lower dock section and the populated area on the upper heights. The apparent lettering on street-level shops does not match any historical iconography records."

"So these people are not related culturally to Motherland," Thusk said. "Interesting; I'd've thought that they would have been sailing for centuries and would have made some kind of continuing contact with our nation." After thinking on it a few minutes, he said, "You know, this must mean that they are related to the people on the other islands farther east. That's where they trade. And probably raid, too."

Una volunteered, "Based on the lettering and the sounds of voices I can detect, a search of the archives suggests that the language is most probably related to archaic Basque and Carib variants. It has no relation to any Motherland tongues. Furthermore, I note that the ships at dock here do not fit the description of dragon-prowed vessels that accompanied Captain Noor, as reported during his visit to WaterEdge.

"So this is most likely not the pirate's home base."

In disappointment, the men discussed other facets of their discovery, Thusk tracing out their route flown with a finger on the forward screen. Una obligingly supplied distance and time notations above the tracing. "A half hour's flight from WaterEdge, Thist, eight hundred kilometers. Two to three days of fair winds to reach WaterEdge."

At Thist's request, Una began updating her aerial maps of the islands and would continue to do so for the remainder of their trip. These islands were going to be important places, the men agreed. "Whether as potential trading partners or possible wild pirate dens that have to be tamed," Thist said, "or as Pernie desires, places to be conquered and absorbed."

Thusk shook his head. "I don't think that trying to force strangers into our nation would be good government, Thist. And without Una's military help we can't reach these places anyhow. No navy, remember? So at least we have to try talking and trading." Pointing at the ships below, he said, "I don't see any that look like they might be warships, so this place might be one to visit when we have time. But for now, why don't we go see what the other islands look like farther out?" Thist agreed, and Una headed east.

As they continued, the Cold Sea appeared fairly calm, few waves rippling the deep blue surface. A hundred kilometers farther out, a small island came into view, one that appeared not to feature such high cliffs, only beaches and trees. Thusk asked, "Una, please scan that place. If it's uninhabited, land in a safe place on its beach, invisible at first." Una descended, hovering just above the white sand, kicking up only a small dusting.

Out of sight of any neighboring land, the isolated island stretched about two kilometers in both directions, its only feature a gently sloping hill and a small lagoon on one side. The surface was almost all white sand, with a scattering of palm trees and patches of bright tropical flowers. Mild surf rolled in from azure seas, and as Thusk looked into the lagoon, he saw water as clear as air. "Beautiful, Thist, the clearest water I've ever seen. You know, living on a spot like this might be attractive."

Thist grunted. "Yeah, as long as pirates don't attack, or any of those huge windstorms don't sweep over you, like they do at WaterEdge in the summer." The two guards strolled in the distance on patrol, ostensibly looking for possible threats, but like Thist and Thusk were glad for the opportunity to be out of the confines of Una's cabin, their feet on the ground, enjoying the bracing sea breeze and the smell of flowers. Declaring a lunch period, Thist had the guards lay out a blanket on the sand and they all partook of a delicious hot meal from Una's heated larder.

An hour later, Una departed once more, this time flying invisibly over a string of islands, each separated by from ten to a few hundred kilometers, most of the larger ones inhabited. The smaller islands typically lacked high cliffs, a few featuring villages with piers and small fishing boats. The larger islands were dominated by the same high cliffs, large cities with stone buildings, obvious walled fortifications, and fleets of ships. Thist ordered a quick scan of each significant island, to be reviewed at day's end for evaluation as to potential threat, trade, alliance, or conquest. And where they might best search for Altamun Kech and his captors.

THE MOST PROMINENT DENSELY POPULATED CITY WAS ON a raised mesa a two thousand kilometers out. Twenty kilometers wide by fifty in length, the island had many villages and smaller towns, with croplands evident in checkerboard patterns. The largest settlement was on the western end, above high cliffs with the same funicular vehicles moving ceaselessly between the plains above and a wide beach below—"And with a shoreline fortified by a high stone wall with openings for their ships to enter and leave," Thist noted—the city appeared to be one huge fortress. "Definitely a city built to withstand siege, an island ready for war. And with those sleek, pointed two-masted ships—a hundred or more of them—I don't think they fish for a living."

As Una's video zoomed in on the details of the layout and potential threats of the island from a thousand meter altitude, the four passengers saw below them hundreds of men in formations, obviously military maneuvers.

"Got ourselves some warriors, Thusk," his twin commented wryly. "I say we do not land in this place. I fear that the four of us wouldn't be very effective against that bunch down there.

Thusk laughed. "Yes, I think they are already going to go fight somewhere. Hmm, why don't we go back to their nearest neighbor, see what they have to say? Maybe if they are in danger from these guys, they'll be willing to talk?"

"Una," Thist said, "you have been scanning all day. Please summarize what you know to be true about this island chain, all of these people."

"Thist, today we have overflown thirty-five inhabited islands. From scanning their banners, their infrastructure, and other visible preparations, I can speculate on their varied cultures. However, these assumptions may be verified only by landing and interacting with the locals."

"Which we may only do after hearing your evaluations first," Thist said.

"The first five islands comprise a kingdom of less than one hundred thousand persons. From their ships I conclude they are fishers and whalers and trade among themselves. They do have defenses, evidence they have been attacked; probably from raiders in these easternmost islands.

"Many of the intermediate islands are either independent or have no affiliation with any groups off their shores. They often raid each other for domestic animals or for mates, but seldom for territorial gain. Several of the larger islands—independent clans or groupings from their banners—occasionally fight among themselves. At present they are banding together to resist the repeated incursions of this eastern island, the fortified one here below us.

"This island possesses several thousand armored warriors and the ships to carry them. I conclude that they are preparing for an imminent invasion of their nearest neighbor to the east, displayed here." Una's forward screen showed an aerial view of the fortress city below them, zooming out until the neighboring island, some seventy-five kilometers away, also came into view. A dozen smaller islands lay between them.

Thist said, "We haven't been that far yet, Una. How did you get the information?"

"After it was activated by human touch, the Noor information globe recorded its position and other information about its environment. That data matches the projected island characteristics of the simulation. If correct, then that island's city is the capital of the Lordship Islands, the home port of Captain Noor."

"All right, Una," Thist said, breathing hard, wishing Una had volunteered Noor's home island first thing. "How long before that invasion fleet down there sails? When do they arrive?"

"I estimate one more day to board. With predicted winds, another day to sail to the Lordship Islands."

After a brief conference, Thist gave an order. "Una, take us to Noor's home port quickly.

"As you wish."

"And..."

"Yes, Thist? Further instructions?"

"Please access all of the languages you can from your records. We want to be able to talk to these island people."

CHAPTER TWENTY-THREE

As Una flew high and invisibly over what they assumed to be Noor's capital, Thist and his twin made mental assessments of what lay below them. Thist said, "High cliffs, again. One of the ancient islands. Those little tracked vehicles up and down to the narrow beaches below. And ships, lots of them, dragon-prowed and with rams. These are definitely warships, pirates. But they are at anchor, some even with no sails. Not at all prepared to fight."

Thusk was puzzled. "I can see the farms and villages scattered around the mesa top too, and some catapults protecting their docks. But why are their people not scurrying around, setting up defenses? Why aren't their ships being readied with supplies and sails? I don't understand."

Thist said, "I don't think they realize the threat from that neighbor. We need to tell them, but because they are pirates themselves, we may not be welcomed; Una is quite a forbidding spectacle.

"I propose that we fly low over the city here, announce our intentions. Then land in a defensible area, like a town square. Use our loud-talker to try to prepare the people and their leaders for what will have to be a shock. Maybe Captain Noor will be there. He will have heard of you and me if he spent time in Motherland, and that could be a good introduction."

Thusk agreed. "If this is Captain Noor's capital city, they may have already heard of Una too, don't you think? Noor was in Motherland for nearly a month last year; surely at the palace somebody would have chatted about us 'monkey-men' and our wonderful 'flying cucumber'?"

Thist groaned. "Twin, Una had not been seen outside of ShadowFall at that time, remember? Even Pernie didn't know about Una until after you rescued me from the palace."

Thusk nodded, remembering how they had intercepted the Princess's retinue as she returned to ShadowFall after the Games and Mother Messinex's coronation. A short invisible ride in Una had convinced Pernie of their capabilities as defenders of ShadowFall. *Yes, that was all before Creesile's invasion, so Noor won't know. So much has happened since then!* "All right, but then what do we say?"

"You and I have been through this same thing before. You in God's Country and at ShadowFall, me in battle. This should be easy."

AT AN ALTITUDE OF FIFTY METERS, UNA FLEW INVISIBLY and slowly over the red-tile roofs of the whitewashed buildings below, scanning for clues of language and culture—and weapons. From above, the town of about twenty to thirty thousand showed wide cobblestone streets, tree-lined avenues, colorful market sections, and people dressed largely in white or flowered clothing. Some few carried instruments of unknown uses, apparently shouting as others applauded them. No one onboard Una had ever seen such activities and wondered what they meant.

"Whatever they are doing, it reminds me of Odel M'ridge's musical instrument. Anyhow, it all looks peaceful and pretty," Thusk said. "Hard to believe it's a pirate den."

Thist laughed, "Well, even criminals probably like to

live well and peacefully, at least when they are home." Then grimly: "I don't think these folks are prepared for an invasion in two days. We have to tell them." He tried to figure out where the pirate chief would be, which building was the largest, most prominent. Two passes over the town didn't show any obvious place, so he said, "Una, can you pick up anything on their speech? Will they understand us?"

"Thist, the speech resembles a derivative creole of elements of ancient Euskara and Kulina, though it has very few remnants of each. I will endeavor to translate between you and the locals, though nuances may be difficult. I will draw upon historical archives that must be augmented by real-time data. To hone the translations, you will need to converse and let me analyze."

"Well," said Thist, "do the best you can. Right now, become visible and let's go down to twenty meters. I assume you've detected no borophene weapons, so we should be safe. Fly from one end of this main avenue to the other end, to that plaza. Let everyone see us; go slowly and let them see we mean no harm. We'll land at the far end and let their leader come to us." At that, the two guards checked their armor and springbows, preparing for further orders upon touchdown. Likewise, Thusk readied himself with a leather armor vest and cocked springbow.

The first reaction of the locals was horror, terrified at the large green cylinder that appeared out of nowhere high above the street market. Shouting, screaming and running away in panic, they showed little evidence of curiosity. As Una glided silently down the emptied main avenue, Thist said, "Maybe I'm too used to Una, but I didn't expect such a massive fright. I thought somebody would want to see us up close."

As crossbow bolts and metal arrows bounced off their flying machine, Thusk laughed. "There's your answer, twin. A typical human reaction—*kill the weird thing!*" The guards tensed visibly; they were prepared to fight or run. *Probably the latter,* Thusk thought. *And I don't blame them.*

Within the several minutes that Una progressed through the town, seeing that their crossbows and arrows literally made no dents in the big flying green thing, some townsfolk gathered in the street behind the phenomenon, following it as it slowly descended into a parklike open space at the end of the avenue.

Thist chewed his lip. "Una, do you know enough now for me to speak to them on your loud-talker?" First, he wanted no confrontation; but next, he felt obligated to warn the islanders of the imminent attack by their aggressive neighbor to the west, and finally, he wanted to see Noor. *And Altamun Kech, if possible. A lot to do in a short time!* he realized.

The main street ended in a tree-lined plaza facing a two-story colonnaded white building. Una descended, hovering silently, one foot above the cobblestones of what the twins were now calling 'Noor's Town.' Through Una's one-way viewing capability, her crew saw an increasingly large crowd gathering, hundreds of people both curious and fearful. Only a few weapons, crossbows mostly, were evident. The crowd was whispering, and shouting, pointing at the big green cylinder that might be a god, or maybe a legendary beast of some kind.

Una said, "As they speak I am learning more of their language. They have nothing in folktales or legends or religion that they can compare us to. The closest they can relate is that maybe we are a flying whale, an large sea creature, but one that swims in the air." Una laughed, an unsettling and rare occurrence for the DI. "They are wondering how to kill and eat us!"

Thist laughed, "If we look tasty to them, then they're not so afraid. Hopefully our lack of aggressiveness will give them confidence that we are no danger to them. Let me speak, through the White Pilot."

As THE NOW-CURIOUS AND CALMER CROWD WATCHED with less fear but increasing interest, the dark bulb atop the big green flying thing began to hinge backward, revealing what appeared to be a white mannequin with a human-shaped head and shoulders, seated within it. As if suddenly awakened, the white thing turned its face outward, its large, round black eyes and mouth like a child's drawing. The creature's visible upper body rotated all the way around as if scanning the onlookers. Though frightened at the un-human appearance, but by this time not having been threatened or harmed, some people drew even closer, in an effort to inspect the strange thing.

Then it spoke: "Is Captain Noor hereabouts?" But the islanders heard it as "Doosh Noor zdess?"

"They're not understanding us," Thusk muttered. "Una, try just saying 'Noor.'"

"Noor, Noor, Noor," echoed over the plaza, reverberating from the walls of nearby structures. "Noor, Noor, Noor." But the crowd grew silent, puzzled. Some of the women were crying, some of the men with bows and spears drawing nearer.

At a loss for what to do, Thist asked Una to pull in the White Pilot but keep the loud-talker on. "Maybe a human voice will be better," he said, then told Una to amplify his own speech.

"People of Noor's Town, we come in peace," he said in his softest voice. "We need to talk to Captain Noor."

Una whispered, "Thist, every time the name Noor is mentioned, the people react in either anger or sadness. I surmise that the man is out of favor, or missing, or possibly dead."

Thist breathed out in frustration. "To come this far, and not be able to find the pirate, or even talk to his people? Disgusting!"

But Thusk said, "Una, how about asking about Noor in all of the current languages, Motherspeak and the others? If some of these men sailed to WaterEdge with him, surely they must know something of our speech."

A frustrating, repetitious, hour-long exercise

followed, during which over half the onlookers gradually went about their business, tired of the loud, garbled voice that spouted unintelligible, word-like sounds, all meaningless except for "Noor." A ripple of interest stirred the crowd, who parted to make way as a young albino man, dressed all in white, escorted a small elderly woman in flowered robes to the front of the onlookers. Eventually one man, a warrior by his look, his rapier, and his gaudy clothing, stepped forward and shouted at Una: "I know your talk. Where our captain? Come out and fight!" Standing over two meters, the swarthy man wore a headband covering of layers of red cloth, a satiny blue shirt with billowing sleeves, tight black trousers and hobnailed boots.

Una whispered, "He could be an illustration from an ancient text, a stereotypical pirate." But the word meant nothing to Thist or Thusk; the man was just another strange character to them, less strange than most.

"So we've found one that understands us, Una," Thist said. "What tongue did he respond to?"

"A Motherland dialect, centuries out of use. Curiously, what was once spoken in the ancient ShadowFall region." To the twins that was a curiosity, but nothing else. Their adopted homeland had many secrets and unknown mysteries; one more made little difference.

"You there, your name?" Una's loud-talker announced Thist's question in the same dialect. Taken aback, the pirate drew a blade and took a fighting stance, looking around for a person.

"Show yourself again, you creature," the man yelled, "I don't talk to spirits." Then, pounding on Una's hull, he shouted, "If this is your ship, come out. Show yourself. Fight me!" The crowd cheered, now swarming around Una, apparently convinced she was either harmless or cowardly.

"Time to step outside, gentlemen," Thist said, unsheathing his short sword. "After me. Open the door, Una, and translate for me." Stepping out into late afternoon shadows, the sun nearly behind the trees around the plaza, Thist first felt the oppressive humidity, and then with a deep breath took in a panoply of aromas —meats cooking, squeezed fruits, even impressive flowerlike perfumes. He quickly made a show of laying down his sword on the cobblestones, then staring up at the audacious pirate who had issued the invitation.

"I be Thist, General of Motherland. This my twin, Thusk. These, our guards. We come in peace."

Apparently confused at the peaceful actions of the weird little dark men from inside the big green flying thing, the pirate nodded, bowing deeply. A hush came over the other townspeople, even as they moved back from Una and her crew.

"I be Curstin," the pirate said, warily looking at the visitors, in particular the two large guards. Una's translation came seconds after the man's spoken gibberish. But he spoke directly to Thist, looking down at him. "Where Noor? Do you have? Do you know?"

Surprised, Thist said, "We no have Noor. He gone?"

The pirate nodded and frowned. "For months now."

"Who is the leader here, with Noor gone?"

"I am," the more smoothly translated speech came. It took the twins only a short time to get used to the delay between Curstin's spoken words and Una's translations.

Thist waved his right arm around, encompassing the plaza and the populace. "What is your town called? Your people?"

Curstin smiled, "This is Noorstown, capital of the Lordship Isles. We people are Sea Lords. We own all the seas."

I've heard that claim before, Thist thought. *It caused a war back home.* "Then we have a lot to discuss, Curstin," he said with a grin, gesturing toward Una's open door. "Will you come inside and have a talk with us?" At Curstin's hesitation, he added, "And you may bring aboard any two other people you like." Pointing down at his own sword on the ground, he added, "But please leave your weapons outside."

CURSTIN BROUGHT IN TWO OTHERS: ONE, THE ELDERLY olive-skinned woman in a flower-patterned dress, the other a young albino man in clothing like Curstin's but all white. After an introduction to the concept of digital technology—they were initially astonished but quickly accepted it as magic of the ancients—the Sea Lords were introduced to Una's unique capabilities of speech and displays. *And without being overawed,* Thusk observed. *These people are open-minded and imaginative. Why are they pirates, criminals?*

As Thist's and Una's introductions finished, the white-haired woman spoke. In a raspy voice barely louder than a whisper, she said in fluent Motherlander, "My name is Myerna. I was taken from WaterEdge as a young girl and brought here to Noorstown, captured by the father of this Captain Noor. I was treated well and that Captain Noor married me. The Captain Noor you now seek, our leader, is my son." Wiping a tear from her eye, she went on, "When your white man-thing said his name over and over, I hoped you were from the gods, bringing him back to me. To us." Sobbing, she stopped talking, Curstin taking her in his arms and comforting her.

Curstin said, pointing to the young albino, "And this is Elmene, my own brother, a pirate like myself. We are kin of Captain Noor, and serve him. Now I have to ask, what do you know of our missing captain?" Waving his hands around at Una's cabin and screens, he said, "And can this incredible flying Una-machine of yours, with its magic moving pictures, can it locate him?"

Thist replied, "We may be able to help, if you tell us all you know. Where he went, which direction? What he was trying to do?" The little man was anxious to get on with the invasion warning, but knew diplomatically that he had to take care of the Sea Lord's immediate questions before getting to that particular item of concern.

Curstin said in a serious tone, looking at Myerna,

"We know he was sailing north, up to The Ice, looking for a valley there, where it splits the glacier. Departed six weeks ago, should have returned a week ago, but no word."

Thusk interrupted, irritating Thist. "Curstin, can you explain why Myerna there, why she was kidnapped from our country of Motherland? And why you are all pirates, preying on innocent people?"

Thist grabbed his twin's shoulders, shaking his head. "Thusk, we have other things to talk about! Why threaten our hosts?" Una didn't translate, but the Sea Lords understood the incident quite well.

Curstin replied, his voice cool and measured, as Una translated: "Little Thusk, our customs are our customs. We have always sought mates from far away. Look at my brother, here. Like our captain, Elmene suffers from the condition that makes his skin pure white. Although it is a beautiful color, he cannot endure long periods in the sun, lest his skin burn terribly. Our wise men say that we must continually mix our blood with those different from us, or we may all become pure white and unable to stay outside long enough to plant, to harvest, and to fight."

Becoming more passionate, the pirate looked straight down at Thusk. "It is true that we are raiders, that we take resources from others. But we never slaughter unnecessarily, never leave devastation in our wake. Our island does not have natural resources or made-things that we can trade with, yet we have many, many thousands to feed and house. It is a natural law, it seems to us, that a family, a tribe, a people, needs first to feed itself. If that troubles you, tell that to the creatures of the sea that eat each other, the denizens of the jungles that prey on others. We feel no need to explain ourselves."

Thist stepped in to intervene, deescalating the situation. "Gentlemen, we are not here to convert anyone, nor to criticize anybody's livelihood, their ways of life." Curstin and his two companions nodded slightly but Thist could tell they were not satisfied with Thusk's critique. And, of course, Thusk was red-faced and fuming. Thist shook his head; his twin was in dire need of learning some diplomacy. He himself could see that, with education and cultural exchanges, the Lordship Islands could become a trading partner; they just needed better access to resources. *But that's for much later. First, first, we have to stop that invasion!*

"Curstin," Thist began, "forgive my twin for his outburst. He sees things differently than many do, even in our homeland. But—important things first. Let me tell you why we are here. And what you should know about a danger to your island."

CHAPTER TWENTY-FOUR

"And now you have seen what we saw, Curstin," Thist said, as Una passed over the mobilizing invasion fleet below, in dimming twilight now illuminated by the torches of thousands of boarding soldiers, "and why we thought to warn you of your neighbor's preparations."

Curstin and Elmene stared down at the armada of ships below, and the thousands of men now boarding their warships. "I can't believe this, Thist," he said, holding his forehead in pain. "We signed a peace pact with Thornveld just last year, vowing not to raid each other's prized lands or capital cities. And yet, we are the only nation near enough for them to attack with such a large force." He explained further, "With peace guaranteed, we have been in fiesta for some time now. With our captain missing, I regret that we have neglected our scouting duties, and our spies have not sent messaging birds for too long. And we are not outfitted for fighting right now, either. Our raiding parties don't typically launch until the outer islands south of here have harvested their fruits, so we are months away from having our ships ready to fight."

At that, Thusk stared. Thist could almost read his mind. *So your raiding other islands for their crops—and women!—is natural, but it is bad when your big neighbor decides to raid* you?Thist shook his head at Thusk as if to say, *No more, not now!*

"And this flying Una, it won't help us fight this treachery? What good is a day's or two warning against Thornveld? We need at least two weeks to call in our departed ships by fire-towers, to mobilize the villagers, to ready the fire-catapults!"

Thist asked Una, "Will you consider just scaring these Thornvelders to stop their invasion, hinder it just long enough that the Lordship Isles can defend themselves?"

A long two minutes of silence was Una's tactic, Thist knew, of making him sweat. Untold billions of proposals and counterarguments were swarming within Una's complex of quantum computers. *It is probably like every citizen of Motherland were screaming at each other*, he thought, *before finally coming to a consensus. At least it'll be a well thought-out answer!* He was wrong on one account: the discussions among the qomps were more numerous than if every person who had ever lived in Motherland over its entire existence, thousands of years, had been arguing.

Una finally answered: "I have concluded that a temporary dispersal of the military force in Thornveld, below, will minimize human casualties in the forthcoming conflict. Therefore, I will execute maneuvers and loud-talking to cause delays in the aggressor's plans. But I will not participate in any further actions."

To the Thornvelders, it seemed as if the gods themselves had descended on their island, Una in full view flying only a hundred meters up, one end of the island to the other, broadcasting in a deep loud-talk voice: "Thornveld, be warned. The Lordship Isles are watching you. If you set sail, your ships will be sunk by demons of the deep, your men will be torn apart by the giant sky-birds, your city and villages will be burnt to cinders by the fire-breath of my fury!"

Ten passes over the main city, the docks, and the individual boats were enough to do what Thist had asked of Una: soldiers throwing down their weapons, jumping off ships already boarded, townspeople in panic crowding the streets, villagers hiding in fields. Some fires broke out in the larger settlements, with Una apparently accepting them without comment as unavoidable and acceptable collateral damage.

"I think we've given you a few days' respite, Curstin," Thist said, laughing as the Thornvelders ran like scattered ants. "They have to be afraid now, especially their troops. This kind of display, the shouting and all, would have scared me to death, back before I knew about Una."

Curstin, too, was grinning. "They do look like scared hares, don't they? Not so scary from up here. Thist, are you sure this Una won't let itself be used as a weapon?"

"No, Curstin, we are lucky—*you* are lucky—that she knows enough about the odds that she would do as she just did." He thought, *Now that I have demonstrated Motherland's power to Curstin, I hope we can work out some kind of deal. At least where he won't be raiding WaterEdge!*

***

LANDING BACK IN THE PLAZA IN NOORSTOWN, WHERE A few dozen citizens had been waiting their arrival, Thist had to insist that his visitors aboard leave Una; their fascination with digital images, particularly the high-altitude videos of the island chain, were becoming almost obsessive. "Look, Curstin, we will return someday soon, and even take some of your people back with us, to learn. In the meantime, though, you have to promise not to raid Motherland, our port at WaterEdge. I guarantee you that you have more to gain by trading and talking with us than pirating against us." The unspoken threat of other, more lethal, technologies like Una lay heavy between them.

Pointing to the recorded video of Thornveld's war preparations, he said, "And you had best use the time we bought you to prepare for your own defense. In a few days, the lord of that place will convince his people that we were a figment of imagination, some kind of trick. They will gather up their forces and try again." *A trick,* he recalled, *like the one I arranged with that Moon-girl Mienne, having her flash the Moonlights off and on to impress and overawe Creesile's army at the Battle of ShadowFall. Sometime such showy tricks work, but they are more effective when backed up with real strength,*

Curstin shook hands with Thist and then offered his hand to Thusk, who only reluctantly took it. "Look, little man, we can have long talks about right and wrong when all this Thornveld stuff is over. But search your own heart and soul; I'll bet there are things you have done that even I would not approve of."

To Thist he added: "And one last thing to tell you before you leave, Thist, in gratitude for your warning of Thornveld's treachery. Please find our Captain Noor; Lordship Isles need him. And if you find him, you will also have that priest you are searching for. Your Altamun Kech sailed with the captain."

CHAPTER TWENTY-FIVE

As Una lifted up, departing from the Noorstown plaza, Thusk said, "I can't say I'm sorry to leave that bunch of pirates. I don't trust them. Imagine, raiding your neighbors for women and food. Like a burglar or a highwayman." Below them, the torchlit streets of Noorstown shrank into starlike twinkles, finally swallowed by darkness as Una gained more altitude.

Thist, though, regretted his own distrust of Curstin and the pirates there. "I would have liked to taste some of their island food; the aroma of meat cooking in those open-pit kiosks around the plaza was incredible, and whatever that bread was, you could almost taste. And their alcoholic drink, 'rum' they called it, that one sip was powerful.

"But I couldn't trust that they wouldn't try to poison us and seize Una for themselves." Thusk just laughed at him; the two guards remained silent as usual, but disappointment showed on their bearded faces—they had not eaten or drunk any of the pirates' offerings, but some of the women in that plaza crowd were especially exotic and enticing.

At two thousand meters, Una hesitated. "Where to, gentlemen? Your instructions?"

By habit of command, Thist replied, "Directly northward, until we find the cracked sea-glacier Curstin said Captain Noor was looking for when he vanished. And took our Altamun Kech with him."

Turning to his twin, he said, "Myself, I would have liked to stay in Noorstown tonight. In addition to the new foods and drink, some soft pillows and a bed would have been more comfortable than here in Una." Looking back at the guards, he laughed. "As I'm sure these gentlemen would agree." The guards broke their standard frown protocols and smiled. "One day I will go back."

Thist demurred. "That Curstin's talk about natural law and predators made me uneasy. It reminded me too much of The Tharn back home; you know, 'the strongest take what they want.' Those Solar Priests in God's Country, they did that. And the Mothers before Pernie acted like it was natural for them to take what they wanted, and kill whoever they liked." He shuddered. "That is no way to live." Looking at the three-dimensional image of the beautiful blonde woman that Una used as an avatar when talking to the twins, Thusk said, "I hope Anklya and our birther and the Council in People's Town don't revert to that kind of savagery. We need to learn more about democracy and peace from the ancient records that Una has, and from those godspheres."

Thist snorted. "Those *wonderful* ancients created weapons that killed millions, burned entire cities. They were as savage as these pirates, more so." He was tiring of Thusk's opinions, and began to think about returning to Mother's City as soon as possible. *I like working in the real world, doing real things, not imagining ideals that can never happen. The real world is a place of strategy, personal, political, even military when necessary; manipulating people at every step. Thusk thinks people are basically good; but I see them for what they are—greedy, self-serving, sometimes even cruel.* Thinking over his own rapid rise to status and riches in Motherland's fossilized matriarchy, *Through war and violence and cunning,* he concluded, *so I must be one of those self-serving people, too!*

UNA CONTINUED A SLOW PACE NORTHWARD WHILE THE guards slept, only a faint whisper of wind noise giving the crew any sensation of movement. Thist and Thusk took turns at two-hour watches at the transparent walls and video screens; two thousand meters below them the Cold Sea turned rougher, wind-driven waves cresting in the moonlight, the occasional streams of bioluminescence shimmering like galaxies of stars. *Probably those big fish they call whales, coming to surface,* Thusk thought. *A fish bigger than Una is hard to imagine.*

"Any activity down there, Una?" Thusk asked quietly so as not to disturb the sleepers. "Any land or ships?"

A barely audible whisper replied, "Nothing, Thusk. Only a few wave-washed reefs. The sea state is getting progressively rougher. We have come close to seventeen hundred kilometers since departing the Lordship Isles. Based on ancient ocean floor charts and simulated geological projections since, I anticipate encountering either glacial ice or risen land surface soon."

He awakened Thist, informed him of Una's remarks, then crawled onto the makeshift mattress pad and fell asleep. But within ten minutes, Thist was shaking him awake. "Thusk! Get up! We have found the glacier!"

Thusk shook a weary head. "Thist, let me get some sleep. Wake me when you find Noor and Altamun!" Behind him the guards had not roused a bit.

In disgust, Thist said, "Una, find a safe place to land. On top of the glacier, away from crevices, but within walking distance of its edge. Then scan the immediate area for possible threats from animals or people." He could not imagine any serious dangers atop a glacial sea, but he had been surprised enough by the world not to be cautious in an unknown land.

As Thist watched both the video screen and through Una's walls, the craft descended slowly, coming to rest on an expansive surface only dimly visible under a wispy cover of slow-moving clouds. Una said, "Thist, I have scanned the subsurface, and it is solid ice below us, a thousand meters of it. I have landed a kilometer inland from the glacier edge. Surface winds are fifteen kilometers per hour, no precipitation."

"Very well, Una, thank you. Please opaque the walls but maintain your sensor scans for any possible threats. Now, I think I'll join these others and try to get some sleep."

IN THE LIGHT OF NEW DAWN, UNA'S PASSENGERS walked out onto the glacier surface under a clear blue sky, the salty tinge of sea air a refreshing wake-up welcome. As the guards patrolled a perimeter several hundred meters out, Thusk asked Una, "Where are we, exactly? Is there land under The Ice here, or water? And is this the same Ice as back home? Or a different glacier?"

Una replied, "Thusk, I am nearly five thousand kilometers east of The People's Lands. The glacier there rests upon continental surface. Below us here is sea ice and a plateau of seabed. Other than seafloor rubble scraped up by the glacier, now providing a narrow shoreline, I detected no other landmass above the glacier for the extent of sensing range."

"Thank you, Una," Thusk said. "Which direction is the edge of the glacier? You said a kilometer?"

With the guards trailing, the twins trudged off to the south following Una's directions. Shortly they came upon the extent of the ice: fifty meters in front of them they could see a fringe of thin cracks apparently leading up to the glacier's edge, beyond which was open air. In the distance, mist was rising from the Cold Sea, which was now spread before them from east to west, horizon to horizon. Walking cautiously toward the rim, they saw below a narrow, rocky shoreline between the foot of the glacier, the surf pounding away.

Backing off to a safer location away from the edge,

Thusk said, "Looks just like the top of The Ice back home, the first time I flew Una up through the Misty Sky. Except there, we couldn't see all the way down, just to the cloud layer."

Thist had them all return to Una. "Let's continue the search after we have something to eat." With a smile he asked, "Una, any chance that your heating oven can produce anything that smells as great as that island cooking in the plaza last night?"

The result was a pleasant surprise for the whole crew: savory sizzling strips of spicy meat, juicy fruits, baked bread, and stimulating chai. As he enjoyed the new meal, Thist thought, *I've always wanted to ask Una how she finds and brings aboard these exotic foods and prepares them in that little steel box, but somehow I prefer not to know. Magic has its place!*

BECAUSE THEY WERE NOT SIGHTSEEING BUT SEARCHING, Thusk had Una rise to and stay at an altitude of five thousand meters; that way she and they could see for kilometers. They tried going east for half an hour—eight hundred kilometers—but the scene below was uniform, just the massive glacier front, now calving more frequently as they followed the rim southward..

"Nothing this way, twin," Thusk said. "Let's go back to where we landed last night and then explore westward. The prevailing winds are from the east anyway, so if Noor and Altamun landed anywhere on this narrow rocky shoreline, they are probably in the other direction."

"And Curstin said Noor was looking at a valley in the ice," Thist said. "Maybe the glacier is split? At least that should be a definite landmark; we know what we're looking for."

Under Thusk's instructions, Una swung around and went at top speed westward, her sensors attuned to finding cracks, crevices, or valleys in the vast sea of ice. As he gazed out Una's walls over the endless vista of white to the north, he wondered, though, if even Una would ever be able to find such a small feature.

It only took an hour, just as Thist took up the watch. "And there it is!" he yelped as Una slowed to a stop, her video screen zooming in on a dark line immediately below them. "Let's land, Una!"

Avoiding a flight up the valley, Thist opted to land on the rocky shore and walk inland. As they made their way over the wave-washed shore, Thusk said, "I see piled stones on that big rock there. Those stacked stones mean it is man-made, for sure." Thist nodded agreement as all four men entered the cleft in the glacier, each of them feeling uneasy about the high walls of slumped ice that defined the east and west sides of the valley. An avalanche of ice might cover the valley floor, they knew. And themselves.

Ten minutes into the ice valley, they came across a strange hut. "We've got a dwelling here, Thist!" Thusk yelled, running toward a lone scrub oak surrounded with mud-daubed limbs and peat-sod fillings. "Somebody built this, and lived here!"

Inside, the two small men saw the remains of a firepit and a makeshift peat-sod mattress, evidence that a human being had once lived there. "Not much of a place," Thist said, "but judging from the fish bones and bird feathers, there was some food to be got." He shivered. "But probably not all that comfortable. Wonder who he was, how he got here, where he went?"

Thusk scratched around in the debris on the floor of the hut. "I think I know, twin. Look at this." He held up a flat piece of tree bark upon which was written in charcoal in Motherland script, *I am Altamun Kech, marooned here—* The bark was broken off at that point.

"So he was here, that Altamun," Thist whispered, "but no mention of Noor. Marooned? Then their ship must have sunk."

"And no human bones about, so he must have left," Thusk said, examining the crudely written message again. "Or was rescued. But by whom? And where would they go if not back south to the Isles?"

Two hours of searching farther up the valley and then back on the shore produced no signs of any rescuers, no more indications that Altamun Kech had even survived. "Six weeks in this place would be hard to take, Thist," his twin said, "but he had the rudiments—shelter, food, water." Looking up at the towering glacier, he said, "Do you think somebody might have rescued him from up there?"

Thusk shrugged. "We can look, but I doubt it."

Back in Una, the searchers rose the thousand meters to the glacier surface, looking for any signs of human activity there. "The winds on this sea of ice will have blown away any footprints," Thusk said. Indeed, the slow but constant winds blowing around their own boots were proving that observation.

"Nothing for kilometers but a sea of ice and that big crack," Thist said. "I can't imagine anybody living up here, much less be able to rescue Altamun all the way down there."

Back inside the cabin he asked, "Una, do your scans show anything that could tell us how Altamun Kech got out of that valley? Where he went? And was anybody else with him?"

"Thist, I have scanned the immediate area from here to the edge of the glacier overlooking the primitive tree-hut in the ice crevasse. There are no signs of life."

"Damn!" Thist snorted. "Where do we go from here?"

"But, there is evidence that humans were here recently. Large iron anchors of some kind are in place at the surface level and there are pitons in several locations down the eastern valley wall. They are not covered by blowing snow. Assuming present wind velocities and ice-dust accumulation, the anchors and pitons were most likely placed less than two weeks ago."

In frustration, Thist started to object that Una could have volunteered this information upon arrival at the valley, but thought better of it. *It is I who has to think like Una, if I am going to take full advantage of her incredible capabilities. Maybe she can learn to anticipate my needs? Or maybe I can learn to ask broad enough questions?*

Thusk came back with the guards, holding two pitons and a length of frayed rope. "They were here," he said. "They must have gone down and brought him up this way." He looked northward across the empty ice sea, a featureless flatness of white, marred only by the dark abyss of the valley. "But where? How?"

IRRITATED, THIST ORDERED UNA ON ANOTHER SEARCH. "Let's go as high as you can, Una, keeping a lookout for humans anywhere in range. We will stay on the eastern side of this sea of ice. If the rescuers came from this direction, they surely wouldn't have crossed that valley again. They've gotta be somewhere out there."

For two and a half hours Una sped northward, as the ice valley crevasse sharply turned northwest, eventually lost in the distance. Then Thusk yelled to a sleeping Thist, "I see movement down there! Una, drop down to a hundred meters and stay invisible!"

Now awakened, a wearied Thist rubbed his eyes, trying to stay awake after boring hours of nothing but ice. But below them now lay a moving sailboat, unlike any the Motherlanders had ever seen: not over twenty meters long and only a fourth that in beam, the craft was held up from the ice by outriggers outfitted by what appeared to be thin blades. A helmsman operated a tiller-like set of blades aft, and inboard from those, some kind of large fast-spinning wheels that moved against the ice.

Thist said, "What kind of boat is that, Thusk? A sailboat on an ice sea? And what are they doing? Where are they going?"

Una answered, "Thist, I can follow their bearing. At altitude I should be able to determine their destination."

"Do it, Una, now!" With that, the men felt the pull of acceleration as the craft rapidly rose to five thousand meters, the iceboat beneath them now just a dark speck on the vast white ice sea.

"Fifty kilometers northeast is a large human settlement. That must be the destination of the ice ship."

The twins looked at each other. "Take us to it!" they said in unison. Their common thought was, *Now we find Altamun Kech. And a new civilization on The Ice.* Without saying any more, as Una approached the ice city at two thousand feet, both men felt an exhilaration of exploration, much like their reactions when first leaving The Tharn's Lands en route to the Warm Lands and finally finding ShadowFall. And each wondered, *Is this cold land a place of welcome, or something else?*

OPENINGS

CHAPTER TWENTY-SIX

A month after Odel's return to his quarry, a delegation from the Solar Temple arrived at the quarryland, unannounced. But Odel, having been acclimated to military tactics by his experiences in Motherland, had stationed scouts along the ridge overlooking the highway in both directions. Towers there and one on the ridge above the quarry site provided line-of-sight communication. Those scouts' mirror messages notified him that a wagonload of robed men would soon be arriving up the road to the quarry. "No weapons, no soldiers," the flashed message said. "Old men in dark robes."

Odel, Mox, six large spearmen and six archers of both sizes met the Solar Priests as they entered the quarry grounds, forming a semicircle facing the wagon. Odel greeted the visitors in a friendly fashion. "What brings you here, brothers? Are you ready to renegotiate our terms of your sale of my granite?" He motioned for the archers to lower their springbows; the several large people with spears drew their lowered weapons upright.

As he assisted the priests down from their wagon, Odel invited them to sit at a table and have refreshments. He knew from experience that the trip from God's Port was a long and tiring trek, with overnight stops at fairly primitive way stations. *And these are old men. Wonder what they will say? Threaten me? What?*

"I am Preesen," the apparent leader of the priests said after quaffing cold honeyed wine, "and we thank you for your hospitality. We are come to rectify an error." Odel's mouth dropped open; no such statement had ever come from the lips of such as these. "You were not present for many months. We needed the pink granite for our project, and so set up this operation to obtain it." Motioning to another priest, Preesen took a scroll from him and read aloud, "But now that you are returned, this deed reverts to you." Another priest brought a hefty bag and handed it to Odel. "And here are your payments for the granite we have taken. Minus your taxes, of course."

Odel couldn't believe his eyes or his ears. The heavy bag of coppers would support any number of people for half a year; they wouldn't have to work elsewhere to buy food or supplies. Plying the priests with more wine and food, he encouraged them stay the night, and had his people set up a tent for their most welcome guests.

As a spontaneous party evolved that night, Odel inquired of Preesen, "I don't want to sound ungrateful for your visit and resolving this situation, but—I hate to say it—you all seem to be much more, er, *forgiving*, than I recall. I am very glad that it has worked out so well"—*because I was dreading having to have my people fight your Priests' Men*, he thought—"but would you mind telling me what has changed in the time I've been gone?"

Preesen laughed at the question, as did his fellow priests. "Mr. M'ridge, a lot has happened, and we are the happier for it." After yet another deep draught of wine, he said, "It all began last year when a big green cylinder came out of the sky right on the plaza in front of our temple in God's Port. Out stepped a dark little man, like some of your folks here. And then..." Told in a rollicking, humorous tone, Preesen's tale was the stuff of legends. "So after a day of being trapped in a godscloth web, the damned green thing grew big old insect legs, eight of them, and walked out of town, dragging rocks and banners and kiosks and storefronts with it. And all the time, a weird big white man-thing with huge black eyes was yelling from the top of it."

The priest grew silent. "When that big green bug jumped off a pier and sank, some of that crowd that followed it were afraid it would come back and harm them. But more importantly—when that bug was walking away, the white man-thing on top of it had been shouting that our priesthood was at fault. Or something to that effect; I wasn't there, was on a pilgrimage out west." Preesen went on, his speech slurred from the effects of the wine. "But anyways, that mob went back to the plaza and in a frenzy of fear, attacked the priests who were still standing there cursing the green thing." He stopped, wiped his mouth. "It apparently was not a pretty sight; they eliminated a contingent of Priests' Men as well. Missing ten or so of our calling, and the guards who enforced their rules, the temple essentially shut down. As some of us who were out of town when that all happened returned, tempers had cooled down by the time we returned. We were allowed to reoccupy the temple. But listening to the citizens' reports of the tragedy, we decided to institute new practices. In order to survive, we disbanded the Priests' Men for good, and began to sell off properties and businesses that priests should never have owned.

"And so it is in good faith that we few visit here now and bring you all our blessings and that bag of coppers. God's Country is a new place now, thanks to that dark little man, his strange white man-thing, and that big green bug." Looking at Odel's grin, he asked, "Do you know any more about them? Did they drown in the harbor? Tales are told, but nobody really knows. I do wish they would come back. They changed our land for the best."

Odel waved solemnly as the wagonload of Solar

Priests pulled away down the gravel access road toward the highway, returning to God's Port. "Glad they are gone, Mox," he said to his wife, looking down at her swelling belly. He had asked the priests about medical facilities back in their city or their temple, and was assured that healers there were the best to be found. But compared to the more sophisticated culture of Mother's City, he wasn't so sure.

To his credit, Odel had summoned all of the local healers within fifty miles to monitor Mox's pregnancy from time to time, so it seemed to be proceeding normally. "Back in my homeland," his wife said, "nine months or more is normal. You big people take ten or eleven months, which seems strange to me, dear." Odel agreed, but having lived next door in his homeland, The Woodlands, and here in God's Country, and lately down in Motherland, he had seen many strange things and many strange people, so that different gestation periods for different-looking little people like Mox and most of his refugee camp were just one more inexplicable factor. *I am certainly glad that I got to know Mox intimately,* he thought with a grin, blushing at his memories. *I guess she and her kind are just special in that tasteful way.*

CHAPTER TWENTY-SEVEN

Captain Lork stood on deck as his crew came aboard carrying their gunnysacks, the heat of the bright sun providing a bit of welcome warmth against the slow but steady eastern wind. In the distance, Hillmork, the volcano goddess, was belching up an intermittent column of black smoke. *Look like she's going to spew out more lava,* he thought. *I hope the metalsmiths are already up there and prepared.*

Centuries of lava-capture techniques, dipping godsmetal into the flowing molten rock, were the basis of Stonehaven's trade in metals; its smiths took remnants of abundant ancient alloys—most often found in springlike coils that would fit on your arm, or as yard-long arcs of thin beams—and utilized the heat of lava to work a kind of magic with them, crafting iceboat skids and tillers, camshafts and skritchers, *And my godspring harpoons, too!* He smiled, rubbing his hand over the smooth barrels of the new ten-foot-long tubes. Six of the cylinders held godsmetal-tipped pronged spears, *Big enough to bring down those huge sorihan and ice-bears,* he recalled. *Those tons of ice-bear meat we brought after the raid last month saved my skin, for sure! These new long-range harpoons will kill them even farther away.* He shivered at the memory of that biggest ice-bear, tall enough to swipe above the gunwale, knocking the head off one of his icers.

Talking to himself out loud, he said, "But bringing that Kech guy in too, that helped." The tall exotic stranger from some unknown foreign land out beyond Ice-End had proven such a novelty that Lork's failed raid on the Dvora valley was all but forgotten. Not only did Alty-Moon tell tall tales of faraway places, but the man said he had traveled on huge ships that sailed on melt, "Five to ten times the size of your iceboats," he said, "and on *water*—what you call 'melt'—that can get wind-blown in waves up to ten to twenty feet high."

After seeing that incredibly large melt-sea for himself when they had rescued Alty-Moon, Lork believed the rest of the stranger's stories, too, as incredible as they were. In explaining what he had seen at Ice-End, Lork tried to have his fellow Stonehaveners imagine that their fresh-melt Lake Perido—measuring three miles wide by twenty long, all the way to the foot of Hillmork—was stretched from horizon to horizon, and that it was *salty*! Laughing at Lork and the crews who had been there with him, the townspeople dismissed such wild claims as just more icers' wild ice-sea tales. They had no trouble believing stories of giant ice-bears and sorihan birds, since Lork had brought back pelts and leg bones. But a huge, salty ice-melt *sea*, that was just too much! Lork figured that someday he might bring back a jug of that melt, but knew the laughers would think he had salted it himself.

Even First Mate Attuk's verification of finding Ice-End and the crevasse valley ("Attuk's Valley," the geographer had modestly named it, to Lork's chagrin), and the new maps he had created from the discoveries, had not fully convinced the populace that Lork was a truly legendary explorer. *I should already be a celebrated hero now*, he thought. *Ice-End was only a folktale until I found it, and the melt-sea was not even thought of!*

Though his failed raid was no longer a worry, he knew that the Ice Hall Council had granted him not a full pardon, but a conditional one. *I have to bring back loot this time*, he thought, *or at least a lot of food. The*

Council wants a return on investment, and the people want silver or food. These citizens don't prize discoveries of knowledge. If you can't touch it, or eat it, their little minds can't grasp it!

As the last of the crew stumbled aboard, these being somewhat tipsy and pushed by Attuk, Lork examined the other godspring-harpoon installations, three fore and three aft. Capped with iron disks on the open firing ends to prevent ice buildup, bolted onto turrets with full 360-degree swivels horizontally and 90-degree upward swings, he thought, *With these babies I can take down any flying sorihan as well as ice-bears and seals and any other living thing. And with the extended ranges the smiths promised, I can hit targets a quarter mile away. Not enough yet for taking out Dvora, but one day... And if we meet any unidentified boats out on the Ice Sea, well....* He knew that a rare foreign ice ship would show up within his raiding area from time to time. *Probably they get blown off course from far east of here, as was I when we almost went over Ice-End. If so, then too bad for them; lucky pickings for me!* He patted the harpoon launchers again, for good luck.

The morning breeze from the north began flapping the topmast banners, telling Lork that he should shove off soon. Attuk reported, "All set, Cap'n. Instruments, crew, sails, skritchers, 'poons. Whenever you say, sir." Lork looked over his fleet, the same three ships again for this trip; by affirmative hand signals from the other captains, he and his flagship *Ice God* were all set to sail.

Smiling and ready for the adventure, Lork raised his hand to order "Slide out!", when the unbelievable happened.

ABOARD UNA, THIST, THUSK, AND THE TWO Mothersmen were staring at the view before them: out of the sea of glacial ice rose a chain of stony mountains stretching hundreds of kilometers east and west of them, flecks of clouds scudding in and out around snowcapped peaks. Flying north for hours at an altitude of a two thousand meters, Una's scanners so far had picked up only scattered packs of huge white bears, flocks of gargantuan birds, and varieties of seals and similar creatures. "Interesting species of wildlife down there, but no evidence of human activity," Una announced, repeatedly.

"I think she is bored, Thist," Thusk said, munching a sweet tropical fruit from the Noorstown market, "After all, she thinks infinitely faster than we do, so each day for us is probably like a year to her."

Thist sniffed. "If she thinks at all. I think an intelligent creature needs a brain of meat to think. These qomps she talks about are tiny specks of semi-somethings or other, like sand or iron. Hard to believe that nonliving stuff can think." He looked at the front screen for a rebuke, but the Anklya-image was sitting on a wooden stool, sulking.

"I sulk, therefore I am," Thusk laughed.

Una then spoke, the woman's image acting excited. "One hundred kilometers north of here a mountain range protrudes from the glacier below, extending far into the distance east and west. My sensors detect moving iron on the northeast horizon." The front view screen zoomed in on the rugged peaks completely covering the width of the view. "And thirty kilometers away now, moving iron sources are converging toward one point. Here is a close-up; they appear to be more of those ice-sailing vessels, all heading for the human settlement."

Thist had no reply, but said, "Una, drop to a hundred meters so we can have a better look. Stay invisible, but let's follow them to their destination."

Within minutes, Una arrived and hovered motionless above a harbor of sorts, where the iceboats slid in next to piers, unloading people and cargo. Immediately to the north of the ice ships lay a town of apparently twenty to thirty thousand people, mostly nondescript one-story graystone buildings with thatched roofs, their chimneys puffing out thick smoke. The town's skyline was dominated by a tall, spired building with a plus sign atop it and spacious walled-in grounds around it. In the distance a sparkling rectangular lake stretched toward an active volcano, now presenting a sky-high column of roiling smoke. A few small sailboats dotted the lake's near-mirror flat surface.

"Looks like a fishing town to me," Thusk said. "But on ice instead of water."

Thist nodded. "People adapt to their conditions. They might be interesting to visit, but Altamun Kech and Captain Noor are my primary concerns now. I think we should land and try to talk to these folk. Think we're safe here? Thusk? Una?" The guards, he saw, were already checking their gear. "No weapons when we walk out, men. But do keep them handy inside the door."

"Looks peaceful enough to me," Thusk agreed. "I don't see any catapults around the ice harbor, and no defensive walls or fortresses, so they must not get attacked."

Una concurred: "Though godsmetal is in ubiquitous use in the ships and all throughout this city, I detect no borophene weaponry to which I am vulnerable."

"All right, then, Una, go visible here and take us down to the open space down there away from the docks in front of that big spired building. It must be an important place, where their leaders might be. Let them see us before we land, give them time to see we are not a threat."

<hr>

At first, Lork couldn't believe his eyes: high above Stonehaven's ice port, a giant bird suddenly appeared out of nowhere, big and green with a black bubble or eye on top of it, angling slowly down toward the marketplace in front of the Tag Temple!

"Cap'n! What is it?" Attuk screamed.

"Shoot it, men!" Lork yelled. "Uncap and fire at will!" Confused harpooners quickly reacted to their captain's command, screwing off the iron caps from their launchers and immediately swinging their new weapons toward the descending green flying cylinder.

"*Fire! Fire!*" the crew chief commands echoed off the walls of the dock buildings; "*Fire! Fire! Fire!*" all three ships responding.

As Lork watched, six of his new long-range harpoons hit the strange bird while it was still fifty feet from landing; he saw it wobble, shake violently, jerk strangely, then slowly fall toward the spire of the temple. Intervening buildings blocked his view, but he heard the loud crash; to his horror, the spire of the temple tilted sideways and disappeared from his sight.

CHAPTER TWENTY-EIGHT

Una shouted, "Borophene-tipped projectiles! Warning! I…"

With no more warning, the craft jerked to one side, slinging Thusk against a far wall. To his horror, a sharp-pointed spear penetrated Una's hull, skewering a Mothersman through his neck, a torrent of arterial blood spewing over the cabin walls. The other guard, thrown off balance, was hanging onto a seat, where yet another penetration narrowly missed him. In slow-motion vision brought on by shock, Thusk observed four more spears coming through Una's hull, several barely missing him and his twin. His mind casually dismissed the impossible scene.

Thist, who had been holding onto a seat back when Una moved violently, now had his feet in the air. "We're falling! Hold on! Get a cushion!" Without waiting, with one hand he grabbed Thusk, pulling both of them onto the cushions of the two front seats. The Mothersman, in shock at the instantaneous bloody death of his comrade, just hung on without finding a place to prepare for a hard landing.

Una fell slowly at first, seemingly to attempt a controlled descent, then as all systems failed, the god-machine smashed into something with a loud crash, finally dropping the last ten meters, hitting hard.

Trying to absorb the fantastic sights he had just witnessed, Lork yelled out commands: "All crews, to land! Bring weapons to the Tag Temple! Now!" Infuriating minutes of delay occurred as the crews quickly tossed back the ropes and brought their ships to the docks. Lork and Attuk leaped off *Ice God* before it was made fast, running toward the site of the sky-thing's crash.

"It wasn't no bird, Cap'n," Attuk yelled as they ran, "but I couldn't tell what it was!" Lork didn't take time or breath to respond, having his sword in hand as they approached the marketplace. Luckily, the morning shoppers and vendors had dispersed before the thing crashed, so there appeared to be no deaths, only a few colorful tents blown over by the impact of the thing and by the fallen temple spire.

As he drew closer, Lork saw another unbelievable sight: the huge green cylinder—*Not a bird, Attuk was right!*—lay tilted up against the stone wall of the temple grounds, one end atop the wall, where it had gouged out several courses. The other end, with a black bubble atop, lay on the cobblestones of the marketplace. Along the length of the slanted cylinder lay a long section of the demolished temple spire, bricks and stones piled up almost to the height of the temple wall. Dust from the toppled spire was still rising, but Lork saw nothing emanating from the green cylinder.

"Ten-foot diameter," Attuk was saying, "thirty-foot long. And a big black blister atop it. What in Hel is it?"

"I don't know," Lork said, running his hand over the smooth outer surface that was free of debris. "But it's not a bird, but a made-thing. And look, this rubble of the spire, all this weight, didn't even scratch it. Not a dent!" His respect for whoever—or *whatever*—produced the thing, increased by the minute, as did his fear.

Attuk walked around the scene as hundreds of townspeople gathered, some close in but most staying farther away, as curiosity and caution battled. "Cap'n, over here!" he shouted.

When Lork walked to the other side, he saw Attuk holding on to one of the harpoon shafts that had penetrated the green hull. "Our harpoons stuck it good. I count six of 'em, all with pointed ends deep inside." From his smile, the first mate was happy with his crew's performance.

Lork was not so inclined. "Attuk, so our harpoons killed it? How could such a made-thing, a giant flying machine of some kind, be shot down by our weapons? Makes no sense!" *Attuk is right about one thing, though,* he thought, inspecting all of the machine's outer surface that was visible under the debris. *If any more things like this come into our sky, we can shoot them down.* Then the chilling realization hit: *But only if we see them and they're not too high up...*

INSIDE UNA'S CABIN, AFTER THE FALL, THIST SLOWLY became conscious. In the dim luminescence of the craft's default emergency lighting system—*Not controlled by Una's qomps,* he vaguely recalled, *but just an automatic response of the wall material itself*—he became aware that he was lying on the cushion of his usual seat. His head, overhanging the seat, had hit a stanchion, and his neck hurt like blazes. Gradually cognizant of a heavy weight on his chest, he realized it was Thusk, whom he had grabbed as Una fell. Groaning with the pain of a severe headache, he pushed up against his twin, who did not respond.

"Thusk," Thist whispered, his voice weak and his breath gone, "are you awake?" No response, but his twin was still breathing. He pushed Thusk off of himself, gently moving him onto the floor. Fortunately, Una had landed floor-down, though pitched at about a 30-degree angle. Sitting up with his back against his seatback, he looked around inside the cabin.

"Una," he whispered, praying for a response. There

was none. Recalling her last message, a warning about borophene weapons, he wondered how she had not sensed the danger before attempting to land in the ice-port town. *We'll know later. I hope.*

A grotesque scene played out in the rear of the cabin, the dim lighting revealing one Mothersman guard shot through the neck by a spear, its wrist-sized shaft having penetrated one wall, its point stuck in the other wall. The second guard had not been any luckier; having been missed by the spears, apparently his head had fallen against another spear point that protruded from the same wall where four more projectiles entered. *I hope it was quick,* Thist thought, *bleeding out hurts a lot.* At that, he realized that he had injuries other than his head and neck—his ivory foot was gone, ripped from its bindings.

"And bleeding, of all the damned luck!" On closer examination he recalled that curse: his ivory foot had been sheared off by one of those spears. "A real foot," he whispered to no one, "would have been the death of me."

Consciousness faded, the darkness a welcome relief.

"CAP'N, LOOKIT HERE," ATTUK SAID, POINTING TO A series of slight depressions immediately below the black bubble atop the green cylinder. Crawling up the piled bricks and stones that just minutes before had constituted the Tag Temple spire, the first mate reached the top of the thing, searching for a way in. "I figger this thing oughta be carryin' somethin', elsewise why would anybody—gods or no gods—ever build it in the first place?"

Lork scrambled up beside Attuk, taking his proffered hand. "You're right again, Attuk. I don't see any weapons; no springbows, no harpoons, no arrows. But the way this thing just appeared out of the air, that's enough to scare you to death, right there." Looking over to where Attuk had his hand on the green surface, he said, "So, show me those holes you found. Think there is a key somewhere?"

"Dunno, Cap'n, but they seem to fit a man's hand."

"Let me try to feel them, see if anything works."

As Lork placed four fingers in the depressions, he felt a slight tingle; the green cylinder let out what sounded like a groan. And yet another unexpected incident appeared before the two astonished men and the hundreds of onlookers: the black bubble, a meter in length and half that in height, began to swivel backwards as if on a hinge. Shocked, Lork and Attuk both jumped backwards, falling off the cylinder and onto the pile of brick and stones.

As the two men dusted themselves off, ignoring superficial bruises and scratches, the black bubble was standing vertically. Inside a cavity of the green cylinder sat a white humanlike figure, featureless save two large black circles resembling eyes and another one for a mouth. Rotating slowly as if from its waist, the man-thing appeared to look straight at Lork and Attuk. Then it made sounds, loud, unhuman, meaningless croaks: "Where is this? Passengers inside. Need help."

"Is it…*talkin'*, Cap'n?" Attuk could barely speak. "Don't make no sense."

Lork shrugged, retrieving his sword from the pile of debris, where he had fallen. "Sounds like words of some kind, but mostly grunts and whistles."

The white creature, whatever it was, kept on making unintelligible noises: "Emergency power interrupted. Qomps override. Opening door. Please assist humans."

Lork and Attuk just stared as the black bubble slowly closed, leaving not so much as a seam where it joined the green surface.

Just then they heard the crowd yelling, "It's coming out!" "Help!" "Run for your lives!"

Clambering down from the top of the cylinder, the two men again watched in wonder as a doorway opened on the other side of the cylinder, hinging from the top and providing a first look into the strange object from the sky.

By this time, in addition to the townspeople and tradesmen who had gathered round, Lork saw Tag priests, a few men that he recognized as Council members, and more of his own ice ship crews—all with swords, springbows, or spears. *I hope we don't need any of that*, Lork thought, *but it's best to be ready*. As the others looked at him, he knew that he was the ostensible leader of the investigators, and stepped up to the open doorway to peer inside the crashed machine.

CHAPTER TWENTY-NINE

With a pounding headache and agonizing pain in his neck, Thist was standing, trying to lift up the unconscious Thusk to place him on a cushioned seat, when Una's door opened up, letting bright light flood in from outside. With Thusk safely seat-belted, leaning back on the tilted seat, Thusk made his way to the doorway, squinting his eyes at the sunlight.

Suddenly a silhouette appeared: a large man—with a sword aloft! Thist tried to speak out but could only mutter; his throat was bruised from the fall and he could only grunt. Trusting that the big man was not hostile, regardless of his raised sword, Thist bowed and laid his own weapon at the man's feet. As he rose again, the man swatted him across the head with the flat of his blade. Darkness fell.

LORK'S FIRST IMPRESSION OF THE INTERIOR OF THE crashed cylinder was of a small cavern with luminescent walls, similar to ancient underground sites near Hillmork's foothills that he had visited with metalsmiths years ago. But as his eyes adjusted to the dimness within, he saw motion—*An animal!* he thought. *Wearing clothes?! Carrying a little sword!* As the dark little creature bent toward him and laid down that pigsticker of a weapon, Lork reacted as would any fighter, slamming the thing upside the head with the flat of his blade.

"Attuk, get in here," Lork yelled as he stepped inside the cylinder. "Take this critter, and its twin on that chair, and give them to the Tag priest. I'm going to look after the two men in the back of this, this, this, *flying machine.*"

Attuk and other icers removed the two dark animals as commanded, while Lork inspected the remains of the dead humans. *My harpoons killed these men,* he thought. *Warriors by the looks of them, with springbows and armored vests. What were they doing with little animals?* Looking around inside the cabin, the realization hit him: *How did this cylinder fly? Is it dead? And why were they flying over Stonehaven?* He feared he might never know any answers.

An hour later, with the dead strangers removed and their machine inspected, Attuk came in report to Lork, who now sat at a large oaken table in the Tag Temple with a dozen members of the Council, a few rich traders, and three Tag priests. The first mate wrinkled his nose at the plethora of odors that permeated the room—the wax candles, the long pipes of the smoking Council members, the perfumes of the traders, and the ever-present aroma of mustiness of the priests' unwashed woolen robes.

"Damages to our spire," the chief priest was complaining, his woolen robes dirty and wet with sweat, "caused by this green flying thing. We have to rebuild. I propose we dismantle the object and sell it off in pieces, as appropriate compensation." Angry shouts and murmurs from the other men around the table caused him to sit and quietly simmer in his outrage.

Lork stood to be recognized; the leading Council member, Lord Montrea, gave him the floor. "All gathered here, first we have to realize that the 'green flying thing' is indeed a made-thing, not bird or animal or spiritual; it is just something made by men, in ways that we do not yet understand. Our legends tell us that the ancients once flew, so perhaps this was of their doing." A sidelong glance at the Tag priest showed that the wool-robed graybeard was nodding; the Tag religion indirectly alluded to winged beings in the sky.

"As the one whose harpoons brought down this *flying machine,* I have asked Attuk, first mate on my ice ship, *Ice God*, to tell us what he found aboard the, the crashed *sky-ship*." That term caught the attention of the others around the table, as Lork had known it would. *Ship* always meant *purpose-built*, and *that* implied purposeful people and civilizations and possible enemies or targets. The concept of sky-ships bought with it unimaginable means of construction, unknown people, different civilizations—and terrifying enemies.

"Lords, Priests, Cap'n," Attuk said haltingly, "other than four cushioned seats—two little ones in front and two regular ones in back—there is not much inside the ship. In the far back is a door and a small room with what looks like a basin and a chamber pot. The inside walls, floor and ceiling all, are glossy but of a material we can't even scratch. No markings. A tilted panel at the front has depressions that look like they's for fingers, but they make no sense. There was some bluish glow to the whole inside for a while, but it died down to just darkness."

Laying out a sheet of paper with markings, he said, "I done measured it all, outside and in, and here's my sketch of it." Spreading his arms in puzzlement, he shook his head. "*How* it could fly, and why our harpoons made it crash, if they did, I got no idea."

Before the others could ask questions, Lork took command again. "Priest, tell us—what about those two little animals Attuk gave you? They were wearing some kind of clothes, and one had a little knife or sword, seemed to be trained to do tricks. I knocked him out before he could do anything dangerous, though. Have you seen anything like them before?"

The priest did not rise, pointedly disregarding Lork's authority. In a disgusted voice he said, "They are safely chained up and locked away in a secure cell. One is unconscious, perhaps dying. The other had to be manacled and gagged to keep it from hurting anybody. It's almost like it's trying to talk, if you can believe that.

"As part of the compensation we are due to damages, caused by *your* harpoons, as you just admitted, our priesthood demands permanent possession of the two creatures. They may be useful as pets, or for novelty presentations, to show how pitiful some of Tag's creations might be—as a lesson to those who might think they are above His laws." After a huff, he added, "One of them is near dead, anyway. Knocked out by that crash, I'd warrant. And the other one just made gargling noises, most probably like some birds that try to imitate human speech."

The priest's statement about Tag's creations made no sense to Lork, but he didn't want to fight about it just yet. What he wanted was to take the green cylinder and see what he could learn from it, what it was made of, what that white man-thing was, and above all—how did it *fly*? He said gently, "Priest, I have no issue with you keeping those animals. But I would like for you to ask that captive of mine, Alty-Moon, to inspect their clothing. I think their masters may have used materials like those he was dressed in when we found him in, in Attuk's Valley."

Lork left unspoken a conclusion he didn't want to share with the important men around the table: *Maybe Alty-Moon came from the same land as that sky-ship? But if they could fly, why was one of theirs left to die in an ice valley? Why would he claim to have been shipwrecked on the big Melt Sea?* He knew those little manlike things would hold the key to many mysteries but he would have to wait for an opportunity to try to investigate them more closely.

Hours later, toward evening, Lork and his crews were allowed to dig out the machine from the rubble of the spire, and to load it up spanning multiple wagons for removal to the Ice Hall, there to be inspected by himself, the Council, the priests, the metalsmiths, and interested citizens. Their exploration and hunting schedule now delayed indefinitely, the crews eagerly accepted the wages for the unusual task. It took them three days to uncover the cylinder, pull it with horses to the horizontal, and leverage it up to fit onto low-slung specialty wagons. Finding the harpoons difficult to remove, their shafts were cut by smiths, leaving the spear points embedded.

Not knowing the religious customs of the two dead masters, their leather armor vests, short coats and boots were removed for further study, and their bodies given a pyre funeral at the crash site, two Tag priests presiding over a short ceremony prior to the burning.

***

As the junior Tag priest visited the two little creatures in their locked cell, he was gratified to see that at least one of them was trained well enough to use the waste hole. The other lay still, occasionally groaning, his wastes now staining the thin straw bedding. The other—a twin?—sat manacled, glaring at his captor.

"I wish you could talk, little one," the priest murmured. "What wonders you could tell of your masters and their flying machine. But all I can do is try to find clues that my chief and Captain Lork and the Council might use. Starting with your costumes." Approaching the active animal, he took out of his pouch a pair of scissors and pulled a section of the costume's yellow cloth to cut.

As the creature drew away from him, the priest slapped him hard, knocking him on his back. Angry at the resistance, the priest closed the scissors handle. To his surprise, the thin fine weave did not separate, the scissors not closing. Again and again he squeezed but his scissors would not work. The creature grinned at him as if it were intelligent, infuriating the priest even more. As the frustrated priest drew back his fist for another blow, the animal got to its feet and jumped at him, both feet forward, tumbling the man backwards, then grabbing the scissors. Only the short chain holding its manacles close to the wall kept the creature from stabbing the priest in the chest. As it was, the plunging implement stuck in the calf of his right leg, which he quickly pulled back, bleeding. The dark creature stood defiantly, a sneer on its face, bloody scissors in hand, screeching out animal noises.

Sobbing, the priest crawled to his feet and backed out of the cell. With a bleeding leg, he hobbled down the hallway, calling for help.

"ALTY-MOON!" JUNIOR PRIEST EKI CRIED, POUNDING on the door of the dungeon library. "Come quick!"

Interrupted from his studies of Na Saam's ancient manuscripts in a subterranean vault far beneath the Tag Temple, the Kech wearily arose and stretched. He looked forward for something else to do, rather than spend more hours in dim candlelight, poring over faded parchments and books. Since being released from captivity at the Ice Hall weeks ago, he had been allowed —*encouraged*—to study the mysterious books and other artifacts kept by the Tag priests for centuries. Unable to translate any of them, the priests had made it customary that any newcomer be required to peruse the documents and devices, on the off chance that a stranger's culture might know details. Over the years this strategy had paid off, with some books translated, many useful, many not.

Because the Kech captive was unlike any foreigner ever found in Na Saam history, the Tag priests had insisted on his participation. Not having any alternative, Altamun had readily agreed. But when he had found a godsphere, something he was familiar with, he was forbidden to remove it from its dark chamber.

As the chief archivist told him, "It is foretold that such indestructible globes, if brought into the light of the sun, would lead to the End of All Things. They are instruments of Darkness, the fate that befell the ancients, destroying their evil world. Therefore, this one must remain in darkness forever." In his research of the temple archives, Altamun learned later that many such globes had been uncovered from The Ice over the years, especially with the recent warmth, and that the accursed things were thrown into Lake Perdis as a matter of course. "It is only that this particular globe was damned to eternal darkness that it remains down here. Were it taken to the surface, it might draw light unto itself and cause the destruction of Na Saam." Altamun did not point out the obvious fallacy that the godspheres thrown into the lake must have encountered daylight themselves at some point or other, but Na Saam still survived. But he knew there was no arguing with religion.

Altamun Kech accompanied the insistent priest, first stopping by his modest room adjacent to the archives to put on a decent robe. *I wish they would let me have back my godscloth robes,* he thought. *But I think they are trying to figure out how to make the weave. They didn't believe me when I said I didn't know; as traders and raiders, they don't trust anybody. And I don't really blame them. Still, I look my best in my yellow billowys. Better than all of the locals!* If nothing else, he knew, that was reason enough for the priests to keep him clad in drab woolen robes.

"What is the problem, Priest?" he asked almost out of breath as he tried to keep up with the short man. "Why do you need me?" But the priest kept up a fast pace, up spiral flights of steps through damp, dark underground passageways, up a hundred meters. Altamun was grateful when, heart pounding and out of breath, he staggered through an archway and into daylight.

Leaning against a courtyard wall, the priest said, "When I catch my breath, follow me. I want you to look at the animals we caught in the crash last week. One of them near killed a brother."

"Crash? Last week?" Altamun exclaimed. "Of *what*? Wagons? Ice ships? And *animals*? What kind?"

Shaking his head, the priest said, "Of course. You have been below all these weeks. The brothers who serve you food do not speak, so you are unaware of the big green flying thing that crashed into our sacred spire, knocking it to the ground."

Open-mouthed, Altamun only gasped. "Flying machine? *Here?* Where is it?"

"And the little dark animals inside of it. With clothes and swords. So strange!"

With both apprehension and a rising sense of hope, the Kech said, "Take me to these—*animals*—right now!" *Please, Mother, let them be who I think they are!*

CHAPTER THIRTY

Thist's headache was throbbing, a pain almost beyond belief. *In a place almost beyond belief,* his foggy mind reminded him. *In a cold, dark room, scissors in my hand.* Flashes of strange activity reeled in his mind. *Did I just stab a tall stinking guy in a filthy robe? A man trying to cut my clothing?* In the slices of dim light trickling around the ill-fitting metal door, he could make out almost nothing. The man had come in through that door, fought with him, and left through it. *With my cut in his leg!*

How did I get here? He remembered being broadsided by a large man with a big sword as he was walking out of Una. *Una? I remember now; Una started falling, and Thusk and I—* At the thought of his twin, he turned quickly, in the dimness seeing the dark lump sprawled on the floor beside him.

"Thusk!" he tried to yell, but his voice only croaked. His throat was bruised, sound only emanating with strenuous effort. Falling to his knees, he quickly felt his twin's chest. Thusk was alive, breathing, but unresponsive and not awake. Lifting up his twin's head gently, he rubbed Thusk's face in the dim light, hoping not to find an injury. "Damn!" he breathed. "A lump on his forehead, the size of an egg!" Arranging a thin blanket under Thusk's head, he felt the rest of his twin's body and found no evidence of bleeding or broken bones. *But who knows what internal injuries he might have?* he thought. *A healer needs to see him, quickly, before that swelling does permanent damage. But how do I get anybody to look at him? I don't even know where we are!*

As he sat next to the motionless Thusk, Thist felt around the floor and found the scissors. Trying to piece together his situation, he forced himself to recall his most recent actions. "Let's start with these scissors," he whispered, attempting to recover his voice. "These belong to that stinky man who tried to cut my clothes. He slapped me. I grabbed these and stabbed him in the leg. If I wasn't manacled and chained to the wall, I would have cut his throat." His face still stung from that vicious slap, so that memory was real.

"Una fell. I remember that." Talking as loud as he could, he found that the vocalization spurred recollection. "Thusk and I were on a seat cushion when we hit, but I think that he hit his head when we crashed. I laid him down, then got up and left through Una's door, and a tall man in outlandish clothes slapped my temple with the flat of his blade."

And that was all he remembered, until he awoke much later in complete darkness, crawling on a cold stone floor to find a hole where he relieved his bowels. And then more darkness, and a coldness only mitigated by the warmth of a body next to his—*Thusk!* Finally, hunger and thirst alleviated by a pan of water and crusts of moldy bread magically placed next to him while he slept, his vision improved. At last he could barely make out a thin line of light around the door to his—their— cell. Was that a day ago? Longer? He had used that hole in the floor numerous times, he knew, his chains barely reaching the spot. Only some kind of cloth available to clean himself. *Like an animal!* he thought. *A damned animal!* Anger, he found, helped him remember. *Wakan always said that passion etches memories into our brains. I think he was right about that, as he was in so many things.*

And finally, lastly, he remembered his fight with the

stinky man trying to cut his clothing. He could not imagine what that was all about, but with that leg injury Thist gave him, he was sure his injured antagonist would be returning, and probably not in a good mood. Thist held the scissors tight; at least he had a weapon of sorts!

Speaking more loudly now, he said, "So I now remember that we crashed into that tall pointed building in the city where we were looking for Altamun Kech. And our two Mothersmen guards were killed by spears that shot through Una's walls. After we fell, with my head killing me and my throat hurting, I couldn't speak very loud, and I didn't know the language anyhow." Closely examining the scene in memory, he concluded, "So that big guy hit me without provocation. But at least he didn't cut off my head with that huge sword, either. I just wonder who these people are and what they want. And what they'll do with us. *To* us!"

THIST DIDN'T HAVE LONG TO WAIT; THE METAL DOOR clanged open, revealing two tall silhouettes. "*Two* of them?" Thist whispered, pointing the scissors toward the figures. "Come and take it!" he yelled, getting to his feet, trying to position himself in front of his unconscious twin. Knowing that he had no chance against two large opponents, he nevertheless was ready to hurt the attackers rather than submit meekly. Already he could smell their stench. *Stinky men again?* "I'll kill you!" he shouted again, defiantly. To his surprise the dark figures halted, one man holding the other back with an outstretched arm. As his eyes adjusted to the light, Thist saw that the man in front was of a familiar type: tall, thin-faced, black hair and eyes, olive skin. The man's soiled woolen robe could not hide the athletic build, the certain poise, all the features characteristic of his old friend, Wakan Kech.

"Are you a Kech?" Thist asked in astonishment.

The man sputtered, bowing slightly, still holding

back the second man, the one carrying a raised spear-like pole. "Yes," came the hesitant response, spoken in a perfect Motherland tongue, "I am Altamun Kech. And you, little man—you are from Motherland? That flying machine—yours?"

Thist laid down the scissors and stood erect, rigidly. Speaking as loud as his injured voice allowed, he raised his face toward the Kech and said firmly, "I am *General* Thist, commander of Mother Perneptheranam's army." Pointing to the recumbent form on the floor beside him, he said, "And this is Thusk, special advisor to our Mother, who is in need of a healer." In anger he snarled, "Why are we being treated so, like animals? Who ordered this?"

Kneeling in front of Thist, the Kech hugged him, turning to the spearman and speaking in the local language. "At once! Release these men—they have important positions in my homeland, and must be treated like the dignitaries they are! *At once!*" The other man fled. Within minutes another man appeared—Thist noted that, unlike the Kech and the others in dirty robes, this man had no offensive odor about him. Jangling a set of keys, the presumed jailer unlocked the manacles of both released prisoners. But Thusk remained unconscious as yet two other men came in and carried him from the room.

Taken to more comfortable quarters, with Thusk now lying in a soft bed being attended to by a healer of some kind, Thist bathed in hot water, dressing himself again in his blue godscloth clothing. Feeling refreshed, his headache gone, Thist sat on a padded chair in front of his rescuer, Altamun Kech. He munched on slabs of juicy meat and cheeses, enjoying the flagon of honeyed wine his unknown hosts had provided.

"I thank you, Altamun Kech, for saving my twin and me from that ghastly cell. But why was I attacked and why were we imprisoned? Did you know that we came all this way, thousands of kilometers, to find *you*, to bring you home to WaterEdge? And yet *you* wind up rescuing *us*."

The Kech shook his head. "I was shipwrecked with Captain Noor. An ice ship captain, one Lork—whom I believe to be a pirate, in truth, a pirate on ice instead of the sea—rescued me and brought me here, where I have learned their language. The priests of Tag—the one you stuck with the scissors"—Altamun smiled at the imagined scene—"and others, they now own me in some sense. I am not a slave, but they are my only support for food and shelter." Rubbing his hands on his robes, he added, "Not much in the way of clothing, though. I think they took my Motherland robes and are trying to figure out how to weave godscloth."

Thist laughed at that. "So the one I stabbed, he was trying to take a sample with ordinary scissors?" He kept smiling as he recalled the brief fight. Gesturing toward his twin on the bed, he said, "Were it not for Thusk's injuries and my two dead Mothersmen, this would have been a most interesting experience; a rescue, discovery of a new civilization, and those ice ships. What a concept.

"Speaking of which, where is my flying craft, Una? We crashed and she fell. What's happened since then? Where is she?" Standing and stretching, he yawned. "We need to get back to Motherland with you, as ordered by our Mother Pernie and Wakan Kech. But first I want this healer to tell me how Thusk is doing."

The healer was leaning over the bare chest of Thusk, poking the skin with a metal disk connected by thin hoses to his ears. Altamun translated the healer's speech: "His signs are normal—heart rate, blood pressure, and so forth." Gently rubbing Thusk's swollen forehead, the healer sighed. "But this dark lump on his head, that bothers me. He is not able to be awakened, and when I pull back his eyelids, there is a lot of black around his eyes. I fear damage to his brain.

"All I can do now is to keep ice packs on that lump, hoping it will go down. We just keep him warm, clean his bodily emissions, and give him only soft foods and liquids. Thankfully he can still swallow without effort."

Spreading his hands out, palms up, the healer said, "He is in the hands of Tag now, and Goddess Hillmork."

Thist snorted at that; he had little truck with gods. Only the god Shining One had ever helped him—back when he was fleeing the God's Country priests before his fall into Motherland—but being shown later that the bright sky-disk was just a burning ball of fire had taken away any notion that such an object ever really listened to him, much less helped him. But being in a strange land, with people sincerely trying to help his twin, Thist did not let his own opinions interfere with the healer's beliefs. *Whatever works, works, as my Sire, Reader Thess, used to say.*

AS ALTAMUN KECH AND THIST RODE ON AN OX-DRAWN carriage to a place the priest called the Ice Hall —"Where they have taken your Una machine, Thist," Altamun said—Thist took notice of the settlement through which they traveled—"Stonehaven, it's called; it is the chief ice port of this land called Na Saam. I believe these people number only a few hundred thousand in all, spread over a dozen towns. Much smaller than Motherland, and much more primitive."

Thist agreed; from the looks of it, Stonehaven was a bit larger than his home town, originally The Tharn's Town, now—he didn't know what his people called it, since Thusk had killed The Tharn in instant revenge for the murder of Sire Thess. The streets over which their vehicle bounced were cobblestoned, which Thist thought were an improvement over the mud and dirt streets he grew up around, though nowhere near as smooth as the stone pavements of Mother's City and other civilized population centers in his adopted homeland. The stone buildings were rough-hewn but sturdy, better than in his birth nation, but again poor in appearance as contrasted to Motherland's polished structures—or even the massive stone temples in the upriver cities of the place its priests called God's Country.

Thist concluded to Altamun, "This country is primitive, I agree, but they have done quite a bit in such a cold and desolate environment. One thing I want to inspect more closely is the spears that made Una crash." Without telling his Kech companion, Thist knew that only borophene projectiles could interfere with Una's own qomps, the untold quadrillions of quantum computers comprising her entire structure. The craft had been shot down when Thusk first flew her to ShadowFall, but then by arrows of Princess Pernie's guardsmen. Una later explained that rather than physical damage, it had been the intimate connection of the borophene materials originally from the global SKY web, adjacent to her hull, which triggered software interactions that terminated all qomp activity. Those qomps controlled Una's power source, its digital features, its hull opacity, and its flight systems.

Thist knew that removing those spear materials would rejuvenate Una, as had occurred in ShadowFall, but he did not want to share that information with anyone. Even though Una would only respond to himself and Thusk, the temptation for others, especially this new and unknown society, would be too great. He didn't think Una would respond to any of his own commands give under torture, but he didn't want to test that idea, either.

CHAPTER THIRTY-ONE

The huge Ice Hall impressed Thist. "Altamun, this one big building is half the size of Mother's Palace itself." Seeing the curved arch that defined the front of the structure, at least fifty meters high, was only his first surprise; the building stretched at least two kilometers in length, its entire exterior surface a smooth arc a hundred meters wide. "Who made it? What is it made of?"

"The Na Saam say it is an ancient temple, left behind when the gods departed," Altamun said. "Back before The Ice came. Nobody knows how it was built; they can't even scratch the surface. And unfortunately, the gods did not leave any written inscriptions, either."

Inside, the high arc of the ceiling was dark with the soot of centuries, sunlight breaking through in large transparent rectangular panels evenly spaced at the apex over the entire length. As far as Thist could see in the spacious hall, a long series of small rooms on either side were the only interior features, other than empty overhead niche-like depressions every hundred meters or so.

Altamun pointed upward, "Those big niches may have been for hanging lamps, but because the material can't be chipped or rods inserted, the Na Saam use torches when it is dark outside. The small rooms at the bottom have a lot of empty niches, too, but nobody knows what they were for, either. And as far as those clear skylight panels, they are impenetrable, too."

As they walked on the smoothly textured floor of that same unknown material, Thist saw Una in the distance, a wooden framework built around her, and a dozen Na Saam men on walkways at various levels around her. As they approached, one bearded man called out, "Hey, Alty-Moon. Why'd you bring that animal with you? Think he can fly this damned big vegetable?"

Thist tensed, clenching his fists; this was the man who had knocked him out! Stopping where he was, he told Altamun, "This ruffian is the one who hit me with his sword. If he doesn't apologize, I will kill him!"

Both Altamun and Thist knew the little man had no sword, so his threat was just bluster. However, beholden to both antagonists, the Kech made an appeal: "Captain Lork, meet General Thist, commander of the Mothersman Army of Motherland, leader of fifty thousand troops back in our common homeland."

Shocked, Lork jerked back, confused. The other men working about Una stopped to hear more. Lork said, "He's a *man*? That little? And the color of a narwhal?" He stuttered, trying to regain his composure in front of his crew. "I, er, I, did not know. I thought the two normal men, the dead ones inside this thing, I thought they were the masters, and this one"—pointing at Thist—"and the other one, they were pets or mascots, or whatever."

Seeing the fierce scowl on Thist's face and watching Altamun shaking his head, Lork stopped talking and climbed down from the wooden framework around Una. He strode confidently toward the newcomers, bowed respectfully before Thist, then bent down to offer his hand. To Altamun he said, "Tell General Thist that I offer my apologies to him. I only have my ignorance as an excuse." *Fifty thousand warriors?* the icer captain was thinking. *I don't want this one mad at me, even if he is from the other side of The Ice!*

Altamun relayed Lork's apologies, though the interpretation was not needed; the icer's body language demonstrated repentance. Thist thought, *If this man can afford to lose face like this, in front of his own men here, he must be sincere.* He said as much to his Kech companion, who relayed it to the icer. Thist relaxed, smiled, and nodded his head at Lork. *I respect his admission,* he thought, *but I don't trust him—yet.* It was Thist's understanding that Lork had ordered the harpoons fired at Una, so he was responsible for the crash. Thist wanted to know more about those weapons; at ShadowFall, Una had fallen less than a third of a meter; in Stonehaven, it was ten times that. *If it had been fifty meters, we could have been killed—by this man in front of me.* No, this Lork would have to go a long way to be trustworthy.

Smiling, Lork stood up and escorted Thist and Altamun over to the inert Una. "The door is open," Lork said as the Kech translated for Thist, "but everything inside is dark. When I first went in, after, er"—the icer hesitated, thinking, *After I knocked you out with my sword!*—"the place had a glow about it, like sometimes in an ice cave, when the walls shimmer. But then it went dark and stayed."

Thist saw that the harpoons or spear shafts were still in place from Lork's attack, several in the cabin volume and two beneath the toilet room aft. He asked Altamun to order them removed. Following Lork's barked orders, of which Thist did not understand a word, his crew set up block-and-tackle arrangements and with some effort, removed those that penetrated the cabin. But when attempting to pull out the two projectiles from below the floor, only the shafts came out, their pointed ends remaining deep inside Una's rear compartment.

At once, Una's interior lights reactivated, her display screens showing kaleidoscopic patterns. Stepping inside with the icer and the Kech, Thist asked, "Una! Are you there?" No answer. After trying the finger depressions of the tilted keyboard under the front screen, Thist asked again. "Una, if any qomps hear this, I command a response—now! In my homeland's language, please."

"Thist, I hear you," came the voice of Una from

within the cabin, at which Lork looked around for the person speaking.

Laughing, Altamun swept his hand around through the air. "Captain, it comes from everywhere. It is the voice of the flying machine—Una." Wide-eyed, Lork gulped and stared at the front screen of the cabin, now exhibiting a three-dimensional digital figure of a beautiful blonde woman, outfitted in tight-fitting white godscloth. "And, that is how she prefers to be seen."

Seeing the familiar image of his former companion Anklya, Thist smiled. "All right, Una. So happy to see you come alive again." He looked around to see Lork slack-jawed as the little "animal" conversed with the "big green vegetable." "What happened three days ago? Why did you crash? When can you"—he looked around again, seeing that Altamun could not translate his and Una's conversation, thereby ensuring that neither the Kech nor Lork would not understand his intentions —"get us out of here?"

"Thist, in answer to your questions. First, the borophene projectiles were in iron cylinders and capped with iron disks, so that I only sensed them seconds before they hit. Unfortunately, not only did I suffer the programming interference caused by those harpoons, two of them physically damaged the microfusion generators that provide my propulsion power."

At first, Thist's mind did not register the unbelievable news that Una was relating. When it did sink in, he whispered, "You mean, you can't—*fly*?"

"That is correct, Thist. Both of the redundant fusion systems in the lower rear panel are physically damaged beyond repair. It would require the specialized facilities of a UNA depot to replace the units. I fear that such installations no longer exist, as I am not able to establish communications with any.

"With solar power input, such as comes through the skylights here, I am able to maintain higher-order cyber functions such as consensual consciousness, a fraction of the sensor arrays, some of the digital displays, and a modicum of temperature controls. But the power source required for my flight systems is permanently disabled."

Thist's first thoughts were, *We're thousands of kilometers from Motherland, Thusk needs medical care, we may be surrounded by enemies—and Una can't fly!* His second thoughts were, *Una's scientific knowledge and technological information archives could lift this icebound country out of its primitive state—and they may know it shortly. I can't let that happen. I need bargaining points.*

"Una," Thist said after a minute's silent reflection, "you are to answer only to me. Do not reveal any information to any person other than myself; do not use any language except Peoplespeak. Do you understand?"

"Yes, Thist."

Thist turned to Altamun. "Do not relay any of Una's answers to these, these, Na Saam people—especially that Captain Lork. I still don't trust him."

"Thist," the Kech said plaintively, in Motherland language, "I don't know your native tongue. I don't know what your Una machine is saying. But—" He paused. "I share your doubts about our big captain. We had best look out for ourselves. Er, when can we fly out of here?"

"Altamun," Thist said quietly, "Una says we can't. She will never fly again." Nodding toward Lork and the others—pirates all, as far as he could tell—he told the Kech to say that they had damaged Motherland's flying machine beyond repair and would have to compensate for the trouble. "And don't forget to mention that I can raise one hundred thousand troops if I have to." He smiled. "But you don't have to add the detail that they are all four or five thousand kilometers away with no means of getting here."

Altamun spoke excitedly to Lork, who acted appropriately surprised, apparently taking both the damage report and the strength of Motherland very seriously. The pirate conferred with a particularly ugly big brute—"Attuk" by name—and then reeled off sentence after sentence to Altamun, who then summarized them for Thist.

"Captain Lork says," Altamun translated, "that he apologizes for the damage. But all he can offer in the way of compensation must be judged by the Na Saam Council of Elders. He proposes convening the Council as soon as possible."

"Tell him I approve," Thist said. "Meanwhile, let's think about how to get us all back to Motherland without flying at over a thousand kilometers per hour."

***

THIST AND ALTAMUN REMAINED IN THE ICE HALL WITH Una after all the Na Saamese had left, save two silent guards. "They want to make sure we don't fly away, I suppose," the general said. "I don't blame them. We must seem like magicians to them, with our Una that flies and talks.

Altamun leaned back on one of the large seats in Una's cabin. "Where are we anyhow? Does your Una know? Does she know the way back?"

"Let's ask," Thist replied, switching to his native Peoplespeak language so that Altamun could not hear the answer; he wasn't completely convinced of the Kech's loyalty to Motherland, not after all the time the priest had spent with the pirate Captain Noor and more recently with the Na Saamese. He guessed that Altamun would probably like to return to a position of authority in Motherland, but the princess Sathronin whom he had served was now in the dungeon beneath Mother's Palace and an interim leader, Awhalpa Kech, was currently serving as administrator at WaterEdge until its transition to a republic was complete. Not everyone in Motherland wanted to give up the matriarchy and their privileged sinecures in it, and yield to the will of the citizens to become a democratic republic; two insurrections in one year had proved that.

And, knowing that the previous Kech advisor, Loranthip Kech, had stimulated WaterEdge's rebellion

—Which I crushed with much destruction, he reminded himself—Thist could not be certain that Altamun would not prefer the free and easy life of the Lordship Isles, or even in the cold of Na Saam, to an uncertain future in a turbulent Motherland. He did not yet consider Altamun a friend, merely as a possible ally with a mutual interest in getting back home. *I have no friends but Thusk and Wakan,* he thought. *But Thusk is in a coma and Wakan is thousands of kilometers away. I have to do something drastic on my own, to get us out of here.*

Having followed Thist's conversation, using Peoplespeak Una answered the unspoken query: "Thist, I estimate our present location as approximately five thousand and two hundred kilometers due east of the site where I was retrieved from the glacier by Thusk and the Ice People nearly two years ago. This area appears to be glacial ice. I have no information on the topography between here and there, whether there are voids, or lakes, or thin sea ice.

"An easier route may be to retrace my path here from the Lordship Isles. We are two thousand kilometers northeast of the valley where Altamun Kech was rescued by Captain Lork. From the edge of the glacier there, to WaterEdge, is another three thousand kilometers by sea."

Thist whistled at the distances involved. He had been envisioning methods of ice transport. Any chance of getting Una away from Stonehaven would require outfitting two ice ships to sandwich Una on either side, then using their sails and skritchers, escorting her and her passengers over the ice to—somewhere. Then other ships and mechanical means would be required for some kind of pulley arrangement to lower Una down a thousand meters. And only then, there had to be some means of sailing her back to WaterEdge.

But which way should he choose? What would be the safest route, and how long would it take? He worried that Thusk's condition might worsen if the expert healers in Motherland didn't get their hands on him soon. The Motherland healer, Fyth, had expertly outfitted Thist with his ivory foot after his injury at the Motherland Game, and he had other healers on call there as well. *If we can get back to them soon!*

Evaluating his situation, Thist appeared to have two choices, neither of them without risk. They could attempt to drag Una directly west over uncharted glacial ice, with its possible unknown cracks, crevasses, valleys, mountains, rivers, hostile tribes, all the way back to The People's Lands. There they would face the challenge of lowering themselves and Una down over the kilometers-high glacier and getting to the New River. The prospect of returning via The People's Lands —*And my beautiful Anklya, of course*—was tempting, but then floating down the length of the New River would be a challenge in itself, what with the Solar Priests of God's Port controlling passage at that place. *And then that waterfall drop down to ShadowFall?* Although at any other time such a trek would be a welcome adventure, Thist could not imagine transporting the bulk of Una over all of those obstacles, any one of which might prove impassable or impossible. Not to mention subjecting the fragile Thusk to such rigors. *And I still have responsibilities to Pernie and Wakan; there may be other troubles brewing in Motherland. I have no reliable second-in-command, so my very absence, and that of Una, might be incentive enough for another Sister princess to try her luck.* Sighing, he thought, *There is no time to waste. I have to take the quickest route back!*

The better alternative—going southwest down to Ice-End, lowering Una down off the glacier there, and into the sea to sail back to WaterEdge—seemed to present fewer problems. He knew that Una could float, but providing her with power—sails? Noor's pirates had those, but could he contact them? Could he trust them? And thinking of trust, would Lork and his crew willingly give up Una's potential, even if they couldn't yet use it?

As Thist was considering all the ramifications of his possible choices in silence, Altamun Kech was looking at him, puzzled. "Thist, what is it? What did your Una tell you?"

"We are thousands of kilometers away from anywhere, Altamun," he said. "We are going to have to get these Na Saam people to provide at least two iceboats and hold Una between them, and sail us down south to the glacier's edge." Smiling, he added, "Possibly several other boats with provisions and pulleys for going down over the edge of the glacier. And then a way to sail home. That's all. Think we can do it?"

Altamun laughed ironically. "Thist, we are powerless here. Your twin is unconscious, your flying machine can't fly, your guards are dead, and you and I are even without swords. You think these people are going to give up a treasure like Una?"

"My Sire Thess used to say, 'Knowledge is important, especially if others don't have it.' That's what I think. Now listen, here is what we are going to do." Looking straight into the Kech's dark eyes, he said, "That is, if you want to return to Motherland."

Altamun relaxed, tension fading from his face. Looking around at the grim-faced guards, he said, "I will do anything to return home, Thist. *Anything.*"

CHAPTER THIRTY-TWO

In the Ice Hall at noontime the next day, Thist stood before a hastily called meeting of the Council of Elders, Altamun Kech interpreting for him. The little man stood in front of Una's raised door, so that a large video screen was visible through the opening. To Thist, the place reeked of unfamiliar and unpleasant odors: fish-oil lamps on the walls wafting their acrid compounds, a haze of foul-smelling smoke from the carved walrus-tusk pipes that the Council Elders were puffing. *And maybe the odors of the Na Saamese themselves?* he thought. All of Stonehaven seemed to be replete with olfactory irritants. *Not like the fragrant gardens of Mother's City. Not like Pernie's perfumes...*

Dismissing such thoughts, Thist looked over his audience; seated behind their large curved oaken table, over a dozen Na Saamese elders—and that Captain Lork, *the ice pirate*, Thist thought of him—all stared at him with open disdain. They had no idea why they were meeting, only that the Tag priests had said it was important, and to do with the crashed flying machine. Most of the men were hoping to hear that the green flying thing could get back into the sky so they could use it, their wild imaginings ranging from raiding farther away to towing iceboats without sails. Surprised that the small dark man—whom they viewed as little more than an animal—was leading the presentation, and not as they had expected, the acclaimed Captain Lork, the man who had shot it down, they were grumpy and disbelieving, muttering curses among themselves.

Until the little general spoke; then they suddenly became silent. After the man said some gibberish words, a miracle occurred: on the cabin wall as viewed through the doorway to the flying machine, something like a window appeared, showing realistic, three-dimensional colored pictures that began to move—tiny but recognizable images of Lork's small fleet of ice ships, skittering across the Ice Sea, then a view of approaching Stonehaven's ice harbor as seen from hundreds of meters up, the docks and ships like toys—even flying over Lork's unmistakable ice craft, *Ice God*. And finally, the approaching spire of the Temple of Tag; then, jerking, spinning, and darkness. Having never seen video of any kind, never having had even the concept of such pictures or moving images, the Council was shocked into silence.

Attempting to establish leadership among his amazed countrymen, Lork stood and shouted, "Alty-Moon, what kind of man-made magic is this? It was as if a bird were flying above ice ships. But your flying machine is on the ground now. What is happening?" He sat down, obviously disturbed and confused for all his bravado.

Altamun Kech was once again dressed in his finest yellow godscloth robes, the locals having given up hope of even cutting it. "My Lords," he said, as the stunned Elders were shaking their heads. "What you have seen is called 'video'; it is an ancient technology that mimics our eyes. It preserves images of actual activities and retrieves them when desired. Those scenes you just saw were taken by the Una machine here as it and its crew— including *General* Thist here—flew above the ice ships, Captain. You all saw what Thist's crew saw, flying a hundred meters above Stonehaven, until it was, er, penetrated by harpoons." Glowering, Lork crossed his arms and said something under his breath. The Kech motioned for Thist to continue.

As Thist went on, Altamun translated. "The engines of my flying machine have been damaged beyond repair, by the harpoons fired by your Captain Lork, in an attack both unprovoked and unacceptable. In normal circumstances this would be considered an act of war." As Altamun repeated those words, Thist could see the tension building up in the Council members. Thist thought, *They don't know if I have weapons here on Una that I can use against them now, or whether I can bring down a hundred thousand Motherland troops on them later. What they don't know, I do. Time to play on their ignorance—and their awe.*

"But Captain Lork has apologized for his actions. Because the harpooning was an accident, no offense is taken. However, we will require assistance in returning to our home in Motherland. I will accept an apology in return for your help." Again, confusion reigned among the Council. Thist sensed relief but uncertainty in the crowd of Na Saamese still overawed by the Una-image now appearing on the screen. Una had switched to the Anklya-image in full color and three dimensions, dressed as no woman in Stonehaven would dare. *Outside the brothel,* Thist recalled with a smile; a local visit with Altamun had proven most enlightening.

Thist said, "In addition to gratitude, I can offer you information—maps of the Ice Sea from here to IceEdge, and more, much more. And—would you like to know *who* the ancients were, *why* they left, and *how* The Ice came to be? Please view the screen again." Thist hoped that Altamun was stressing his words in the same way he was; he wanted to excite the curiosity of these strange people. At this invitation, the table emptied as the Council gathered around Una's doorway to get a closer look at the magical 'video' screen.

"Here are speeded-up pictures of our trip of over five thousand kilometers, leaving Motherland, flying to the Lordship Isles, to the Ice Valley, and finally here to

Stonehaven." As he narrated the pictures, the Na Saamese saw the world outside the Ice Sea for the first time, beginning with a liftoff from WaterEdge, with a carefully edited pre-war view of the spectacular Pink Palace. Here, Altamun gasped at the remembered beauty of his former posting, the site from which the pirate Noor had kidnapped him; Thist had not brought him up to date on its destruction—*By me!* Followed by representative overflights of large island cities, a brief glimpse of the colorful tropical nightlife of Noor's Town; and the final flight to Stonehaven with a view of the Ice Valley, showing the true height of the glacier that formed Na Saam's raiding territory. *And its concept of the whole world,* thought Thist.

Thist deliberately left out video of the widespread terror Una had stirred up within Thornveld, the aggressor island that had been preparing to invade Noor's Town. *I've shown them what Una can do peacefully; let them only imagine what she can do when at war!*

"You can have your scribes draw up the maps from these picture screens; Una will even provide bearings, distances, and ancient coordinates. Furthermore, she can give you estimates for the locations of other mountains that may protrude above the Ice Sea and beyond to the east. These are projections based on the presumed locations of sea mounts and other ocean floor topography back before The Ice came."

Lork tried to hide his excitement; any one of these maps was worth many a hundredweight of any metal he could name. He could envision many years' worth of exploration and raiding in all of those new targets far to the east. He was content to let these foreigners ply their trade on the Melt Sea—*Or in the sky if they can!* he thought—but with the information on those "screens," however it was recorded, the whole Ice Sea could belong to Na Saam alone. *Or maybe just* me *alone, if I play this right!* His ambition burned brightly, raising possibilities he had never considered.

And then the little Thist-man showed them all how

the old world had ended, the Sun reaching out and burning Earth and Moon, the decades of worldwide rain, and how The Ice came rapidly, covering so much of the whole round world. Then, who the ancients had been, and why they had disappeared. After that, nobody spoke for several minutes, trying to absorb the truth of the ancient cataclysm that had produced their world.

Lork himself was thinking, *These Elders and the priests here find it hard to believe that all of us, everybody, descended from the ancients who lived before The Ice came. Even harder to accept was that those legendary folk never left us; we are them! For myself, the past matters not at all. I don't live there, I can't raid there.* He sneered at those who worried about myths and legends; all he wanted was those maps.

The Tag priests, in particular, sat in stunned silence. Although Una's videos, as recorded from Mienne's Control Room simulations on the Moon, confirmed many of Na Saam's legends, and to an extent, the most important aspects of the priests' own teachings, the holy men were visibly uncomfortable. Closely watching their reactions, Thist thought, *Maybe it is better to have your faith remain intangible, ineffable, than to have it revealed to all the world as hard facts?*

Escaping from his thoughts and eager to advance his cause, Lork was first to respond publicly. "So, Thist and Alty-Moon, these *videos* might be impressive, but how do we know they are true? I can believe the pictures of you flying over our ships and our city, but—pictures from the *Moon*? Are you serious? And I can't believe all that about Earth and Moon being big round rocks just floating in something called 'space.' Or the Sun as a big burning ball of gas!"

Thist said softly, "Una, show them the pictures from ShadowFall, when Mienne made the necklace of Moonlights flash off and on." As the Council grew silent, the screen's realistic image of the Moon appeared above the battleground near Pernie's palace. Upon an unknown command given by a tall woman in white godscloth robes, the colored lights across the face of the

Moon flickered and died. Then they turned on again, each time after the tall woman raised her hand and spoke.

As the image faded away, Altamun asked the Council members, "Did you not see this same phenomenon across the mottled face of the Moon, a year ago?" Nods and gasps told him that Na Saam had indeed witnessed Mother Messinex's powers; the priest rightly assumed the whole world had. "Now you all know who caused that to happen." Pointing at Thist, he said, "And that man there, *General* Thist of Motherland, he also has such powers. And more. I suggest you listen to his requests."

As the Council members returned to their seats behind the curved table, they conferred among themselves; more than one argument was loud enough to be heard by Altamun, who told Thist, "They believe in your powers; they saw the videos of the Ice Sea and very much want to copy those maps. They are not so sure about all the ancient history, and the Tag priests are concerned that everybody will soon know all their secret lore. They saw Una fly, but also saw Lork shoot her down. Some want Una gone; others want to seize her and try to use her. You are not invincible, yet you command an army the size of their whole population. Some want Lork to help you leave; others are afraid that you may return. Some would as soon have Lork go away permanently; local politics overlays every decision, it seems." The Kech sighed. "These are the discussions I'm overhearing. They act just like people everywhere, putting their private concerns ahead of the good of the community. Unfortunately."

Thist thought over Altamun's report. "Very well, tell them that Una responds to me alone, and I control the power that made her fly. Although she is temporarily disabled, that power is still there, and if there is any attempt to force me to command her, I need only say a certain signal word or give a particular gesture and she will destroy herself and everything within several kilometers—in an explosion like the Sun itself." He swung his right arm to encompass the entire Council, and then the extent of the Ice Hall itself, from one end to the other, from one side to the other, to make sure they knew he was saying something about them and the Ice Hall. "Tell them their Ice Hall would be as melt mist, just vapor, hotter than their Hillmork. That Motherland is always prepared to obliterate its enemies—but to generously reward its friends!"

***

"I won't tell these people, Altamun, but I am surprised at their advanced metalworking," Thist said early the next morning as Na Saam workmen swarmed all over Una, working at a frantic pace. "They can do things with godsmetal that even Wakan Kech cannot. I mean, they are fabricating those thin runners and gears and interlocking pieces and skritchers and harpoon launchers; things a lot more complicated than our simple springbows, wouldn't you agree? Lork mentioned in passing that they combine local minerals with godsmetal using fresh lava from the volcano they worship, that Hillmork. I would like to find out more about that."

Already, Thist was envisioning a Mothersman army outfitted with newly fashioned godsmetal weapons, so powerful they could quickly overcome any rebellious Sisters. Or any foreigners who might threaten Motherland. *Even foreigners like these?* He frowned. Na Saam's expertise with godsmetal had surprised him. *I don't like others knowing things we don't. With our Una here, we should know more than any other nation, anywhere. If we don't, there is a potential threat. Damn, but I wish Una could fly again!*

Becoming more distrustful as he grew more experienced in the ways of the world, Thist didn't share his grimmer thoughts with Altamun, choosing to focus solely on their upcoming trek across ice and sea. "And I am equally surprised by that pirate Lork. I mean, he had the idea of building a carriage underneath Una, outfitting it with their godsmetal skids and those skritcher wheels. With his sail-driven ice ships on either side, we should be able to make good time over the Ice Sea."

Altamun nodded. "Seventeen hundred kilometers at better than thirty kilometers per hour in decent winds, and we could make it in two to three days, eight to ten hours a day not including any detours for melt ponds or rough ice or even if we meet those big animals and birds out there." Lork had spoken to them about his precipitous and mistaken attack on Una, thinking it was one of those sorihan birds that had attacked his fleet earlier when he was returning to the Stonehaven ice port. But Thist was more concerned with the ice-bears; a vicious two-ton creature standing four meters tall was worse than any velk he had killed as an emu-rider back home. *An ice-bear swiped off the head of one of Lork's icer crew, above the eighteen-foot-high gunwale,* he thought. *Thank Mother that Una's hull can't be breached. Unless the critter has borophene claws,* the unwelcome thought surfaced.

"THUSK'S CONDITION HASN'T CHANGED," THE PORTLY Na Saam healer said, shaking his bald head. "But at least he doesn't seem to be getting worse, either. His breathing is normal, his blood pressure a bit low, but nothing of concern. That knot on his head is going down slowly." The healer smiled. "So in answer to General Thist's question, Alty-Moon, his twin brother is as ready to travel as he will ever be. Just no jolts or jerks, no falls or fights, no undue stresses on his body. He is still very fragile, given the unknown effects of that concussion, so he must be kept warm and as still as possible. You have to consider the possibility of a blood clot coming loose from that bump, which could cause a stroke or worse." The healer bowed to Thist and Altamun, picking up his little black bag and bidding them farewell as he left Thusk's bedside.

Thist listened as the Kech passed on the healer's

report. *So we will have to go slower, try to avoid bumps and rapid changes of course, and any quick stops. Traveling by daylight only, we'll be at least a whole week, maybe more, getting back to that ice valley, and then three thousand kilometers of sailing west—how?*

Confronted with Thist's concerns, Captain Lork proved resourceful once again. "Look, gents, I know your—*brother?*—is not well and cannot endure the rigors of our usual journey across the Ice Sea. So I am providing soft springs under your Una machine between the runners and its cradle. These will dampen out any rough ice we encounter. And the lateral frameworks between it and my ice ships on either side can slide a bit, too, so no jerking."

Though impressed with the pirate's forethought and ingenuity, Thist only nodded approval. *I can't let him know that Na Saam is so far ahead of Motherland's inventors,* he thought. *But maybe I can convince him— or coerce him?—to come home with us and stay, and teach us his skills?*

Lork answered Thist's unasked question. "As far as getting down from The Ice to the Melt Sea, I propose to bring along two more ice ships that will use chains and pulleys to let your Una gently slide down the ramped sides we saw there. Because you said she can float, we will then outfit the metal framework with sails and tiller so that you can take her home by the wind."

Earlier, Thist and Lork had discussed making Una into a sea craft, a reasonable solution easily implemented. Thist had suggested the solution, recalling that Thusk had transported Una down the New River from where she was extracted from The Ice at the End of the World all the way to The Tharn's Town. *Only two years ago?* he realized. *Seems like a lifetime.*

Then Lork added, "And I propose using the same equipment to lower down one of my ice ships as well." At the quizzical looks, first from Altamun and then Thist, he smiled and said, "For I propose to bring along two new hulls, fit for travel on the Melt Sea, then use it to convert my *Ice God* and the *Hillmork* to melt-ships and sail back to your Motherland with you!"

Upon hearing the Kech's translation of Lork's nasal squeaks and squeals, Thist just nodded grimly. He couldn't have planned it any better.

CHAPTER THIRTY-THREE

Thist had little to do in the days during which Lork's ice fleet shepherded Una and her crew across the Ice Sea, with Una's green fuselage resting on runners, sandwiched between two ice craft. Most of the time he kept the craft's walls transparent-out so they could watch their progress, but after unending kilometers of blinding whiteness, only occasionally interrupted by a welcome colorful flash of blue water —"melt" in Na Saamese—captured in a pond or lake formed by a depression in the ice, his thoughts turned to Motherland, Mother Pernie, and Wakan Kech. In the weeks since his departure for what was planned to take no more than a few days, almost anything could have happened.

Or am I thinking of myself as indispensable? Motherland got along without me for thousands of years. But realism told him that the ancient matriarchy had been corrupt, ossified, and that he himself had helped bring about needed change. *By lots of killing!* his conscience reminded him. Thinking back on the flashing of the Moonlights, he wished that he could communicate with Mother's Palace as easily as he had with that Mienne girl during the Battle of ShadowFall. Surprised that he had not thought of that possibility before, he asked Una if there was some way.

"Thist, of course. The Crystal Throne is a receiver,

and I am a transmitter/receiver. From the throne, any of the godspheres in Mother's Palace may be accessed and used for two-way communication."

"Don't tell me this now, Una," he groaned. "But why didn't you volunteer this information a year ago?" He already knew the answer of course: *You didn't ask.*

Suppressing a sigh, he said softly, "Una, will you please establish communications with anyone in Mother's Palace. Preferably Wakan Kech."

In an instant, it was done. "Thist! Thist!" Wakan's voice came through Una's speakers, "This godsphere tells me you are alive! Where are you? Do you need help? Where have you been?"

Thist gulped. This unrevealed feature of Una's and the godspheres' would change everything. *I can command all across Motherland. I can—* He cut off that enormous range of possibilities and focused on immediate needs. "Wakan, listen, Una can talk through the Crystal Throne to any godsphere. This means we can talk anywhere, anytime." Catching his breath he went on, "Wakan, you're not going to believe everything that has happened to us."

Two long weeks after departing Stonehaven, a wearied crew painfully and slowly lowered Una, minus her rails and harnesses, from the top of the Ice Sea down into the muddy floor of Attuk's Crack. It took half a day, the cable drums on two ice ships ratcheting out measured lengths of godsmetal chain a gear tooth at a time under the watchful eye of First Mate Attuk. Once down, Lork's men swarmed over the flying machine, attaching masts and tiller to outfit her for sailing on melt.

Another half day passed as the crews manually dragged the Una sailing ship contraption from its construction site in the mud, across the kilometer of rocky shore, and over to the moderate surf where the Cold Sea began. The next day's task had been to lower down the converted *Ice God*, a much heavier configuration, from the Ice Sea and then drag it over the same route of rocks and pebbles to the surf and even farther out. At present, however, Lork's ship was stuck in the mud where it had lodged when sliding down the thousand meters from the glacier surface to the valley floor. Thist and Altamun were impatiently waiting to get underway to take Thusk home for healing. Una was now safely anchored a short way out past the surf, but Lork had to convert his own ships first. Both of those vessels were needed to escort Una sandwiched between them.

Lork was standing on dry rocks on the valley floor, overseeing the lowering of provisions and equipment down to his ships. As Thist and Altamun approached, he said in disgust, "I didn't know we would come across so many melt ponds in the Ice Sea, so many detours, taking so long. But those warm and strong easterly winds seem to be melting more ice than usual. And then"—he gestured at his crews laboring in ankle-deep mud, pulling *Ice God* slowly toward the surf—"I didn't know the wind gods would be bringing the rainy season upon us so soon, causing all this mud. We can do the job, but it's a lot more work than my men are used to."

Thist smiled at the translation. *Sure, pirates like to sail and fight and plunder; no real physical work. But digging out a causeway for ships twice their usual hull size is a real challenge. I hope your ice-skating boat skills will be up to commanding real ships in the open waters of the Cold Sea.* As usual, he didn't reveal his thoughts. Lork wouldn't like them, and Altamun wouldn't understand.

MAKING HEADWAY OVER THE COLD SEA TOWARD Motherland was slower than Thist wanted, but Captain Lork, too, was finding liquid water more difficult to sail over than frozen water, especially with the three boats loosely hooked together like a trimaran, Una in the center. Getting used to a sailing medium that resisted motion on all sides of his ship rather than the slight but constant friction of rails over smooth ice, Lork was only slowly becoming conditioned to the new situation. "It's a lot like going over rough ice," he told the helmsman. "You don't know exactly which way the force is going to hit you." The hourglass and compass told him that they were not making the speed or distance that the Ice Sea would have offered them.

Looking over the map sketch that Attuk had made, based on the strange picture-making glass screen in that Una flying machine, Lork saw that their course avoided all the islands in this Cold Sea they were traveling on, sailing between Ice-End some hundreds of kilometers to their north, and the nearest land protrusions eighty kilometers or more south. He wondered whether being a pirate on melt—"water," the little General Thist called it —would be more profitable than it had been on the Ice Sea. "There are a lot more people and a lot more places down here," he said aloud to himself. "Alty-Moon said that the melt pirate ships were a lot bigger than mine. But maybe they are not as smart as me?" He determined to hold off on any unfriendly behavior until he had successfully brought the Motherlanders and their big green vegetable ship safely home. *I'll see how these melt sailors defend their ships and their harbors, and if these people have anything worth raiding for.* If Attuk's maps were correct, they should be arriving in WaterEdge in two or three more days. Thinking of the stash of weapons in the hold below and of the twenty icers he had as crew on each of his ships, trained fighters all, he smiled. *I will take a look around, see the lay of the ice, and go from there.*

"*Land*," he corrected himself, "not ice."

LORK'S FIRST MATE, ATTUK, WAS HELMING THE UNA trimaran lash-up from a makeshift platform that ran fore and aft, astutely avoiding the black bubble and its unpredictable white-pilot creature. Attuk and his small crew, too, were finding it harder to sail *through* water than skate on top of it, even with Lork's shouted encouragements from *Ice God*. Since neither Thist nor Altamun had much sailing experience, neither could help.

"My major sailing journey," Thist told the Kech as they sat in Una's gently rocking cabin, "was to take a twenty-footer from God's Port down the New River, until it fell over a huge waterfall." Laughing, he said, "And without the miles of godscloth I stole from those damnable Solar Priests, I wouldn't have survived getting down to ShadowFall and meeting the Princess. And Wakan." He didn't add, *And losing my damned foot in a stupid bloody game!* As usual, that memory was accompanied by an unwelcome stabbing pain at the stub of his left ankle. He squelched the other unwanted recollections, those of killing other men. However, his entire reputation since that fateful day had been built on war and killing, so combat was no longer a traumatic event. *But still, that first time...*

Thusk was lying in a makeshift bed in the rear seats of Una's cabin, occasionally groaning or moving around restlessly but still comatose. Thist monitored his twin's vitals as Una's videos showed him how, but nothing had changed since their departure from Stonehaven. When asked to use sensors to help with his injured twin, Una replied as requested, in Peoplespeak, "Thist, Thusk's body temperature I can surface scan—his heart rate by scanning surface blood vessels. But nothing internal. Yet based on comparison with available medical records his condition appears to be stable, neither worsening nor improving."

CHAPTER THIRTY-FOUR

Days passed, unending hours of open sea, clear skies, constant east winds pushing Lork's *Ice God*, the *Hillmork*, and Thist's Una-ship, now named half-jokingly by the icers *The Motherland Express,* ever westward. Una kept updating Thist on their coordinate position, illustrating it by color video. Lork came to visit several times a day, still marveling at the digital displays. "Having that feature on my iceboats would be a godsend," he said admiringly. "Knowing where you were without sighting the sun or stars, and all about those islands out there."

Thist suspected that the flashy captain was formulating plans for raids. *How could he think any differently? The man is a born predator. But maybe we can show him a better way.* Part of Thist's mind silently laughed sarcastically at that thought. Thist was also concerned that with Una's language lesson displays, Lork was learning Motherspeak during his visits, surprised at how fast the pirate was picking up the language. *At the rate he is going, Lork will be fluent in a matter of weeks. His people must be very adaptable to learning new languages. Of course a predatory society has to learn to talk to its victims.* He had no way to prevent Lork's lessons, needing the pirate's ships and crews to get him and Thusk back home safely. *I just wish he didn't know so much about us.*

"General Thist," Altamun Kech asked after Lork returned to the *Ice God*, "your Una only speaks to you in a language I don't know. Is it capable of Motherspeak? Is it permissible for me to hear her, to talk with her?"

Thist nodded. "Altamun, I will let her speak to you. Una, talk to us in Motherspeak, please." At once, the figure of Anklya—Una's chosen means of representing itself—appeared on the front screen of the cabin, a tall, voluptuous figure of a blonde woman, stirring certain familiar feelings in Thist. *I have got to get back home and see her. But when and how? There is so much to do in Motherland. Unless I decide to leave…*

"Of course, Thist. How are you, Altamun Kech?"

Flattered and grateful, Altamun said, "I am well, Una. And hope you are, as well." Immediately he felt somewhat embarrassed; of course, the machine was not well—it was disabled, could not fly.

"Though unable to utilize my damaged microfusion power supplies for flight, I am otherwise functional. Thank you, Altamun Kech."

"May I ask Una questions?" the Kech inquired of Thist.

"Certainly. Just not on military matters or national security."

Altamun nodded, but did not understand his general's meaning. *What could I know about that?* he thought. *What does it even mean?* Aloud, he said, "Certainly, General." To the Anklya figure on Una's screen he asked, "Una, though I was able to read some of Na Saam's history while I was a, er, a *captive* of the Tag priests in that temple in Stonehaven, I still don't know a lot about Na Saam or its people. Do you have any knowledge? Could you sense details that might help us—General Thist and me—understand those people? For example, will they ever be a threat to us?"

Listening to the Kech's questions, Thist was impressed by the priest's strategic thinking. Why hadn't he himself thought of asking Una those things? *Because I had other things on my mind,* he comforted himself. *Things like survival!*

"Altamun Kech, based on the bathymetric maps in my archives and the coordinates of Stonehaven, the region now called Na Saam was once a series of undersea mounts. I conjecture that when sea levels lowered by hundreds of meters as the ice came, thick glaciers flowed over the newly exposed terrain. As well, tectonic shifts caused by the weight of the glaciers caused uplifts of crust to form the high mountain valleys to the southeast of Stonehaven." Una paused; dramatically, Thist thought. *Na Saam's traditional raiding targets.*

"Vulcanism, also most likely stimulated by the tectonic shifts, ameliorated the frigid climate where Na Saam is now located, providing freshwater lakes, ice valleys, and fertile volcanic soil farmlands."

Altamun opened his mouth in wonder at the unexpected geological history of Na Saam, then said, "Thank you, Una, but, but, can you tell us about the *now* there?" Thist smiled at the Kech's reaction. The man was getting a lesson in how to talk with a DI!

Una continued. "The information globe in the library below the Temple of Tag in Stonehaven recorded the conversations of Tag priests for millennia. I accessed it while we were in Stonehaven, providing it with power to respond. What do you wish to know?"

At that, both Altamun and Thist sat back in their respective seats. What a treasure trove! Thist said, "Una, please analyze all of those conversations for content, add a timeline, and then summarize for us the important, transitional, and 'tipping point' events so revealed."

The next few hours were amazing. The godsphere itself had been in possession of an underground facility of sorts during The Day the Sun Raped Earth. Thist and Altamun were enthralled; this was looking back in time thirty thousand years, they knew. Una quickly presented graphical simulations of what the godsphere revealed: a group of several dozen individuals in a large underground room, surrounded by unknown objects, flashing lights. Discussions of how their world was ending, in a language vaguely resembling Motherspeak in cadence and tone, but totally unintelligible. To Una, though, it had been a contemporary tongue called *Spanglish.*

Various scenes quickly appeared, apparent violence among people that made no sense to either watcher. The survivors growing older as the pictures flickered by rapidly. Then centuries of darkness. The godsphere being excavated by hairy, animal-skin-wearing men and carried over vast landscapes of ice and snow. The godsphere as the center of rituals in a circle of standing stones, eventually replaced by a temple of cut stones. Volcanic eruptions, ice-tsunamis, warring tribes. A warmer climate, a larger temple, ice ships. Tag priests, century after century, talking about mundane affairs, discussing wars, raids, slaves, sacrifices, taxes, theology. More and different civilized people. Melting ice revealing the mysterious, gargantuan Ice Hall. And on and on, ad infinitum.

When Una's presentation ended, Thist said, "So we still don't know where the Na Saam came from or if they were descendants of those few people who were in the underground facility when The Ice came." But the whole story of Na Saam sounded ancestrally familiar, much like that of his own people back in the former Tharn's Lands. *Unfortunately,* Thist thought, *the priests did not talk about the wonderful godsmetal workers and their craft, or the marvelous ice ships and their skritchers. Nothing really useful in thirty thousand years of jabbering!* As far as he was concerned, the contents of that globe were all but useless. *Too bad that globe hadn't been kept in a blacksmith's shop!*

Una's compass and digital map kept the fleet of three strange ships on course during a week of smooth sailing, day and night. They saw no pirates from the Lordship Isles or even traders from the archipelago of other islands. Thist figured that news of the possible war between Noor's people and the disaster visited upon Thornveld had probably reached every other sailing fleet and harbor city by now. Possibly with deliberate rumors of a big green flying warship wreaking destruction from the sky. The safest bet in such a violent environment was always just to stay home. Thist was happy with that; Thusk was still in a coma after a month now and the general was afraid that his twin might never recover. Una's constant physiological monitoring was a comfort, but nothing could be done medically.

To his own disgust with himself, Thist could not help but think about what might have happened in their absence. In his daily talks with Wakan via Una's screens, he felt that his Kech friend was too reticent, not being totally forthcoming, that he was holding back some news. *If I can't be told, it must not involve me. But if it is a security or war issue, then it would be my concern, so it must not be important to all of Motherland.* Again, Thist hoped that he was not inflating his own importance. *Things do happen that don't concern me.* He knew Wakan better than to directly address those concerns. *Whatever happens in a vast nation of millions of people, not every event is something that I can address. Nor even Pernie, for that matter. Or Wakan.* Still he wondered, then put his mind to arriving at WaterEdge and getting both Thusk and Una back to Mother's Palace. Whatever he faced there could be no worse than the last month.

Late one night, unable to sleep, Thist quietly asked Una if there might be anything else he should know about the Na Saam nation, their one-time captors, things that might have escaped his attention because of his concentration on survival for himself and Thusk after Lork's attack shot them down. "Are there details, weaknesses, strengths, about Na Saam that you are aware of, that I need to know?'

Una's answer shocked him.

"Thist, be aware that while in the Ice Hall I overheard Captain Lork and some of the Elders discussing ways to betray you and seize me for their own purposes. They trust no one who is not of their own clan, and not even all of them."

Whistling softly, Thist was once again thankful that he himself was likewise distrustful of foreigners. "But, Una, I suspected as much from what Altamun overheard. And my bluff about you blowing up like the Sun, melting their town, that appears to have stopped that plan. Right?"

Una said in reply, "You were bluffing? I thought you knew of my emergency features."

Shocked again, Thist gulped. "You mean you could—?"

"That option has always been available. My designers wanted ultimate flexibility when the ice was advancing. Who knows what scenarios they envisioned? Perhaps melting a dangerous glacier?

"But yes. On your command. At any time."

Thist squeezed his eyes shut, trying to dis-remember some of Una's history videos of such explosions occurring over ancient cities, their names long forgotten but once prominent in the documentaries of the late twenty-first century—*Beijing, Tehran, Moscow, Houston, Hiroshima.* Millions killed in a flash. His mind could barely fathom having such destructive power at his fingertips. *And located just a few meters behind us, under the floor!*

Sleep came hard that night.

ENJOYING THE EARLY-MORNING SUN AND THE SALTWATER tang of the sea spray, Thist was lounging in a hammock over the wooden platform atop Una, observing how Attuk commanded the three men who kept the sails trimmed. The first mate was Lork's height, a ruddy light-haired man with numerous dark blue and red drawings on his massive biceps, some even showing on his chest as his thin blouse ruffled in the breeze. Thist noted that all of the ice pirates had shed their cold weather clothing for light, silklike blouses and pantaloons. He briefly wondered how Stonehaven could produce such clothing, and why. But he dropped that line of thought and turned his attention to the icer-turned-sailor who was guiding Una back home.

"*Tattoos*, Mr. Thist," Attuk said when asked, "they tells my story, what I want people to see. Here, for instance"—he rolled up his right sleeve to show what looked like an ice ship and some kind of dragon—"is when the cap'n and I met; we's on an iceboat and come accrost a critter what emerged from a deep crevasse during a raid we's both on. We killed it, him and me, with just our handheld harpoons." Smiling broadly, waving that decorated right arm while keeping the tiller tight with his left hand, he said, "Cap'n made captain right after that, and I's his first mate." Looking straight down into Thist's eyes, he said softly, "That's why we's together, and always will be."

Back down inside Una to feed mush to his comatose twin and take care of his bodily emissions pan, Thist asked Una if she had any analysis of Wakan Kech's conversation, any intimation of trouble.

"Thist, from the recorded conversations I have made and analyzed, Wakan Kech appears to be becoming more and more nervous as we approach WaterEdge. I detected your interest in his mien after your first talk when we established open communications. Anticipating your requirements, I have recorded Wakan's conversations that occurred in the proximity of the information globe. I did not think it appropriate to access all of the globes in Mother's Palace and violate the privacy of every person there who is near a globe."

"You mean you can—you can—yes, of course you can." Thist had thought he was beyond ever being surprised again, but Una's bland statement opened up entirely new possibilities. Sighing, he said, "Please summarize Wakan's conversations, and only those that mention me." With a hand motion, he added, "And Pernie. Anything with her or me."

Una complied. The first voice Thist heard was Wakan's: "Mother, Thist had disastrous news—their

Una is damaged; it can no longer fly! And little Thusk suffered a head injury when the Una crashed and has been unconscious ever since! Not only that, it will take them a week or more to sail their Una here on the Cold Sea." Thist could hear Wakan growing more concerned, if not completely dismayed. "And that's just to WaterEdge, eight hundred kilometers from here."

Thist welcomed the sound of Pernie's voice, but not her words. "Damn, Wakan! I never should have let those two go exploring together, not and take that Una with them. You know what happens if the Una can't fly, if we can't do what we promised Odel and his little People."

Wakan again: "Mother, I propose to take a fast carriage, using Creesile's relay method, and be at WaterEdge when they arrive. I need to work things out with the general. And if you permit, I will take along our best healer, Fyth, to attend to poor Thusk."

The rest of the conversation switched to other affairs, some involving Odel M'ridge and incidents at the Republic of ShadowFall and elsewhere. Thist ignored these, asking Una just to stop; he already recognized that running the limitless daily affairs of a great nation was not something he wanted to be involved in. But what was up with Odel? I can't imagine him causing any trouble. *Ever since Thusk and I met him at his quarry in God's Country, he has been a most interesting and loyal fellow, a stonecutter using godscloth wire, an inventor of his own flying machines. And when he flew down from God's Country to help us at ShadowFall fight Miran Kech's and Creesile's army of Mothersmen, he was a savior!*

Thinking over Odel's military use of godscloth wire to cut down Creesile's troops on their riverboats, then during the battle of ShadowFall, Thist thought, *His wire traps killed hundreds of Mothersmen invaders, his bombardments from the sky hundreds more.* Recalling the performance of M'ridge's aerial force in putting down the last two rebellions, the little general concluded, *Whatever trouble Odel is causing, I would love to have a hundred more like him!*

CHAPTER THIRTY-FIVE

"What is that huge building?" Odel M'ridge asked his driver, pointing at a pinkish granite structure spanning half the width of the Solar Temple plaza, its shape half hidden by a cloud of dust coming from the workmen swarming over it. "And what does it mean, that strange shape?" Wiping the dust from his eyes, Odel could taste the granite particles in the air, the ever-present dust cloud evidence of the ongoing handiwork of the dozen or more sculptors and stonemasons busily applying stone-finishing tools over a forty-foot-high by hundred-foot-long representation of—*what?*

To Odel it appeared to be a near-cylindrical shape, roughly hemispherical at each end, topped by a dark ovoid at one end. And extending from the underside of the curved surface, emerged what appeared to be thin, bug-like legs. "Legs twenty feet long, four feet thick," Odel said in awe.

"Some kind of bug, ya ask me," said his driver. "Never seen nothin' like it."

As his wagon drew closer Odel could tell that the eight legs, massive as they were, were not holding up the huge mass of the stone cylinder; that was done by cleverly hidden cantilever supports behind the main body, not visible from the vantage point of anyone looking at the structure from any distance. "But it still looks like a stone cylinder," Odel said to his disinterested driver, "and it reminds me of...of...that *Una!*" Telling the driver to stop, he jumped out of the wagon and ran farther back to view the construction from several angles. Laughing out loud, he shouted to the work crew and others passing through the plaza, "They are building a shrine to that Una, the flying god-machine! Ho, ho! I wonder if it will be painted green?"

Just then, a white-robed young Solar Priest strode up to Odel, red-faced, saying, "Of *course* it will be green. You don't think a heavenly messenger would be arriving in a, a, *pink* cosmic creature, do you?"

At that, Odel continued laughing until his breath left him. Regaining his composure, he asked the startled priest, "Where is Priest Preesen? I want to see him."

Shaking his head, the young man pointed toward the main temple building and walked off in a huff, stomping his feet as he departed. Odel just laughed again. *So what old Preesen told me was true—the people here did think Thusk and Una were sent from the gods above. You know, I guess, in one sense, they really were.* Quickly estimating the volume of pink granite the Una shrine occupied, Odel concluded: "Yep, this is where my stone has gone. To build another Una, a giant one. Boy, if I ever get to see Thist or Thusk again, what a story I'll be telling them!"

"Too bad that thing won't fly," Odel said as the priest Preesen walked down the wide steps of the Solar Temple, smiling and holding his hand out.

"Ah, but it will, Mr. M'ridge," Preesen said, pointing out an array of niches and depressions around the circumference of the Una shrine. "When you see what we can do soon, at night, with shadows and mirrors, firelight and reflectors, you will believe it is flying yourself."

"And that is where my granite went, Priest? Not a bad use, really. It is impressive."

"Well, after that big green bug or machine or whatever it was, with the white man-thing on top and the little dark man coming out of it, after it came out of the sky right here onto the plaza, our whole city was shocked." He took Odel by the arm and walked him around the shrine, pointing out various details as he spoke, coughing at the falling dust. "I told you how the crowds reacted when the thing sprouted legs and strode out of town, shouting heresies."

"I do recall that, Preesen. You told quite the funny story. Must have been something to see."

"As I said before, the people didn't think it was funny at all. And you recall I said they returned here to the plaza and the temple, and in their fury killed many of my brethren. When we returned a few days later, those of us who were out of town at the time, tempers were cooled off a bit and we were not harmed. But to assuage the turbulence, we offered to build a shrine, this one, to commemorate that visit and that event. We went to your quarry for the stone, but it was deserted. You know the rest."

Odel smiled to hear of the fates of the ignorant priests who had fried his friend Razzo on this very plaza. But he said nothing, only nodded, wiping stone dust from his eyes and beard. He hadn't tasted or smelled such material for a long time; it was not unpleasant, bringing back old memories of quarrying back in his homeland of The Woodlands. *Someday...*

Inside the temple, over welcome cold wine, Odel told Preesen, "Priest, in addition to taking your order for more granite, I need to ask about finding a healer, one that can deliver my baby." Preesen looked puzzled. "I mean, my wife's baby. You see, she is one of the little dark women from the far north, where your icebergs come from. We are concerned about the size of the baby and her ability to deliver it."

Waving off the priest's barrage of questions, Odel said, "Long story about Mox and me. No time to tell you now. I have business down at the docks." *And I won't be telling you the truth about that Una and Thusk and Thist. No use in spoiling your little game here. Yet.*

THE DAY WAS COOL, THE SKY CLOUDLESS AS ODEL walked up to the dockmaster's kiosk. The harbor of God's Port was busy with ships of all sizes, flying banners he had never seen before. *I hope there are no warships of any kind here*, he thought. But they all appeared to be merchants of various kinds, unloading bags and bales and skids of colorful cargo. He asked about any crews from The People's Lands, the berg sellers. "I'm sorry, but all them little guys look alike to me," the dockmaster said to Odel, "but they do shepherd those bergs down here, and we all benefit. Bergs is bergs, though, and I think they all come from the same place, way north upriver somewheres. One's coming in now, over there." Odel followed the man's pointing finger, seeing the iceberg and its crew emerging from behind a larger merchant vessel that had blocked his view until then. He watched patiently as the crew of small men used poles and grappling hooks to keep their iceberg from colliding with the wooden dock, opposing the force of the godscloth netting that had pulled them in from the New River.

Odel thought, *This same kind of godscloth got my friend Razzo fried.* Shutting off that regret, he went to talk to the iceberg crew.

THE LITTLE BERG-CREW CHIEF WAS SWEATY, WHICH seemed peculiar to Odel. "Sweating? And you just came off of an iceberg?" he laughed, as the little man took off his work tunic and put on a dark blue shirt and matching short pants. Odel marveled at the intricate boot-shoes he slipped on. He couldn't tell exactly how they fit those little feet, but it was quick and easy. *I'd like to have some of those, my size. But later.*

The little man laughed, too. "Big guy, work is work. Ice ain't going to warm you all over unless you bathe in it. I guess you're wanting to buy ice?" he said, thumbing toward the berg he had just brought in. "But that lot's already sold. I can make you a deal on another one, a month from now, though. I'm Cruthar, by the way."

Odel looked at Cruthar closely. "I'm Odel M'ridge. Didn't we meet right here, years ago? I gave you a note to take up to—Tharn's Land, was it? To a fellow name of Rusk?"

Cruthar's eyes grew wide. "Ah so, you did. Should've remembered a big lug like you.

I gave him the note, right before they both took off for a place he called Motherland, but nobody's heard from them for a long time now, not since Rusk—he's called *Thusk* now, that's his earned man-name—came back and flew a lot of our people down there to fight wars or something. Have you heard from them lately? What they are doing?"

Odel shook his head and pointed toward a pub. "Let me buy you a drink, sweaty Cruthar, and we can catch up. There's a lot of news about those two."

THE PUB WAS CROWDED AND NOISY, AS ODEL EXPECTED. *Stinky people, too*, he thought. *Smoking pipes and cigars, drinking watered wine. Women of all sizes serving the crowd of little guys. These berg-boys do know how to spend money!* He ordered an iced pail of dark beer for himself, a flagon of cold honeyed wine for Cruthar.

"So Cruthar, the last time you saw our twin adventurers, they were flying down to Motherland?" Odel liked the taste of his beer; nothing in Pernie's country could match it. He'd have to take some barrels of it back home to the quarry.

Cruthar wiped wine from his lips. "Well, I gave Thusk the note, like I said. They was gone a while, then come back and recruited a bunch o' our folks and flew them back down south. A couple dozen times they did; maybe took a thousand or more with 'em." Swallowing another swig, he said, "Been near on a year and a half now. No word back from any of 'em." Looking at Odel, his demeanor changed; with a frown he asked, "You know, my crew, we heard the locals was building a statue in this town here and it sounded like a bigger version of that green flying machine them boys used. We ain't said nothin' 'bout it, 'cause these priests are sensitive 'bout their worship." After another drink, he said, "Thist and me, we even seen 'em roast a fella here, blamin' him for stealing godscloth or somethin'."

Odel cringed. "Yeah, that fellow they killed was my friend Razzo. Never knew what he was up to, but he didn't deserve being fried like that." He took a long draught of beer and shook his head.

Cruthar picked up on Odel's sadness and anger, and decided not to confess that it was his and Thist's theft of godscloth from that Razzo's warehouse that resulted in the man's horrible death. *Some things are better left unsaid*, he thought, not wanting to incur the big man's wrath. *I sure hope Thist don't tell him anything!* Aloud, he said, "Somethin' happen to those boys? To all them other folks what went with 'em?"

Odel laughed ironically, brushing away flies that seemed to think they owned the pub. "Let me tell you what happened, little friend. See, they brought down your people and they all got trained on those fighting birds…"

HOURS PASSED AS CRUTHAR SAT, EYES WIDE, marveling at the tales that Odel spun—the Battle of ShadowFall, trips to the Moon on the Crystal Throne, other rebellions, and more. "Last we heard of them, the boys were flying that Una machine out to the Cold Sea, looking for a pirate and a hostage priest. Another adventure. But the original ShadowFall people, big ones like those here in God's Country—like me—they couldn't get along with you all, even though y'all helped them fight off that General Creesile. You lot are smarter, work harder, fight on war-birds like nobody's ever seen; I mean, vicious, quick, berserker, violent, unstoppable."

Cruthar was surprised but excited to hear of his countrymen's and women's bravery and valor in fighting the wars of rebellion in Motherland. "Hundreds of us riding two-legs, fighting with bolos and swords— What is that *springbow*-thing, anyway?" he said in awe. "Charging a line of big Warmlander enemies, armed to the teeth. Must have been an awesome sight!"

Cruthar didn't ask about casualties, losses, and Odel didn't volunteer. *Hundreds,* the big man recalled with a frown. *And no gratitude from the Originals.*

Odel quickly switched topics, to talk about his AFORS tri-wings. "Rocket-propelled gliders, Cruthar. You shoulda seen them. Like birds of prey we were, and because of your people's size, natural pilots for them."

Cruthar sputtered out wine. "You can *fly*? My people flew? Like birds? Without that Una-thing?"

Odel enthusiastically talked more about his flying, with Cruthar and eventually other barflies listening intently. One asked, "We all seen that big green flying bug long time back, and one of us dark people was in it. That's what the priests here in town are building a statue of. They's hoping it comes back."

Odel laughed again, the potent beer taking effect. "These priests today, boys, they are not the same ones roasted my friend Razzo. When that big green flying machine was leaving, it badmouthed those other priests pretty good, so the locals took out the ones that had tried to capture it. The new priests, they learned from that Una machine and its pilot, my friend—*our* friend— Thusk. So, no more executions, a lot lower taxes, and they gave back lots of buildings and lands to help the poor. A different bunch now. Better ones."

Nods and grunts from the onlookers told Odel that most of them agreed with him; some had not known about the changes. Cruthar offered, "Then our old friend Thusk made some good changes here, didn't he? I sure hope he flies back here again. Hope they both do. Folks here'll be overjoyed to see 'em."

Odel wasn't so sure. Seeing the twins in the flesh and Una as she really was might not match their memories or their expectations. *Oh well, that may never happen anyhow. I'll worry about that if and when it does.* Thinking of his two friends, he wondered how they were doing out over the Cold Sea. *If I had a way to communicate with them, I'm sure they'd like to hear about the changes they caused here in God's Port.*

"But what about you, Cruthar? And The People's Lands? And that Anklya that Una presents herself as?"

Cruthar stared at Odel. "Una does *what*?"

"When Una talks to Thist or Thusk, she shows a lifelike moving picture of Anklya on her front screen for them to talk to. Better than speaking to a bare wall. Very realistic, and quite a good-looking woman, I have to say."

Cruthar coughed. "Well, she is that. Our Anklya is a member of the Council of Electors in People's Town. A powerful woman in a very important position. And she is also on the board of directors of my berg company, the one deeded to me by Reader Thess before he, before he, *died*." Odel nodded solemnly; he had heard of Sire Thess' murder by The Tharn, of Thusk's killing of that chief in return.

"She's on your board?" Odel was confused. "Politics I can understand; she would be good at that, her being at Pernie's court in ShadowFall for so many years. But—is she that good at business, too?"

Cruthar smiled broadly, slamming his flagon down on the table with a *thump!* "Damn, man, but she is good at *everything*. She is also a good *mother*!" At Odel's dropped jaw, the berg-man laughed. "Mr. Odel, Anklya is my *wife*!"

CHAPTER THIRTY-SIX

Captain Lork was all smiles as he spotted the towers of WaterEdge on the western horizon. "Land, ho!" he shouted, pointing at the spires. "We have arrived!" His delight stemmed from the obvious grandeur of the city they were approaching—the towers, the majestic white buildings that peppered the green hillsides overlooking the harbor—and from the wealth all of that represented. *Wealth that can be taken if we're clever enough*, he thought. His mind was already assessing the possibility of melt-sea raids, assuming he could train enough Na Saamese to sail on the strange new liquid medium rather than on the unyielding solidity of the Ice Sea.

Ten meters away from Lork, atop Una at the center of the trimaran fleet of boats, Thist and Altamun Kech were likewise smiling, shaking hands. Thist had been watching Lork's reactions as they approached WaterEdge. He said in a low voice, "Altamun, once we arrive have your local spies keep tabs on this pirate, Lork. I still don't trust him."

The Kech answered in a hoarse whisper, "General, I'm not sure I have any contacts after being gone so long. Who is in charge now since you had to put down a rebellion here?" Thist could tell that the Kech was hoping the new fellow would be one of his old friends.

"Awhalpa Kech," said Thist. "Know him?"

"Yes, General, he was one of my subordinates before…before I was kidnapped by Captain Noor. A good man." Altamun was wondering what his own status would be, returning to his post after his absence.

"Good," Thist remarked. "For the time being, you will report to him, until we can figure out something more suitable." Altamun gave a weak smile at that, as if not in agreement, but Thist quickly dropped the subject; to him, once a decision was made there was little reason to discuss it. Avoiding Lork's stare, he turned his attention toward WaterEdge, hoping Wakan would be arriving as his godsphere messages had indicated.

Meanwhile, as the fleet of three unusual ships passed into the WaterEdge harbor, Lork paid even closer attention to the layout of the piers and docks, and in particular to the trebuchets and catapults entrenched, all but concealed, in revetments protecting the approaches. *These people have been raided before*, he thought, *and have decided to not let that happen again.* Still, he memorized the defensive features, trusting to another observer, a skilled crewman of his on the *Hillmork*, who would be sketching up the harbor's defense information unobtrusively. *You never can tell when it's good to know things.*

Crowds of people now clogged the harbor front, looking for a chance to see the three strange lashed-up boats, or two boats with a green cylinder between them. A shout soon arose from thousands of voices: "It's the Una!" "It must be General Thist returning!" Cheers and shouting erupted, punctuated by a few boos. "He destroyed WaterEdge," one yelled, "and took our princess!"

Altamun Kech dropped his jaw at the shouts. "What do they mean, Thist, *destroyed*? You said you had to put down a rebellion here, but—" He stopped talking as Thist pointed to the top of the hill overlooking the harbor. There, where once stood the legendary Pink Palace, was only desolation: a pile of stones, some scattered down the hillside, from this distance looking like a ragged field of pink clover. "You—you—did *that*? To our palace? A thousand years of history?"

Thist shrugged. "Rebellion, resistance, they have a price," he said. "If Princess Sathronin or Loranthip Kech had surrendered outright, there would have been little or no destruction. But they didn't, and so my catapults and trebuchets had to pound down their army. And that palace. My aerial force and the bird-riders took out most of their foot soldiers." Thist was firm, his jaw set. He wanted this Kech to understand that new republics were going to replace all of the matriarchal Sisterdoms, period. He would wait until later to tell Altamun about the one Sisterdom that had been vanquished and erased from history, being divided among its neighboring princesses. *Pernie can be vengeful*, he reminded himself. *Sometimes a bit too much.* He was not proud of that fight, nor of what he had been ordered to do to the survivors. *But freedom has a price, too!* He reminded himself. And he was not oblivious to the fact that Motherland had a millennia-old tradition of subversion, treachery, and even assassination. *Maybe Pernie has to be cruel to be thorough? I still shudder, though. How could I order such cruelty? What have I become?* Shaking his head to clear such thoughts, he concentrated on problems already at hand. Rebellions, for one.

Thist realized that establishing the new version of Motherland was becoming as bloody a fight as the old inter-Sisterine wars of the past. *And I am the one who has to fight for it*, he thought. *Do I want to do it? Can I do it?* As his mind wandered from immediate concerns, just enjoying the familiar sight of the coast of Motherland, he wondered, *Could I just leave? Could I really make a life somewhere else, without all this killing, this responsibility?* The memory of the one warm night in Noor's Town, with its joyous people, its street music, its fantastic aromas and sweet foods, kept haunting him. *Could I do it? Give up Pernie, Anklya, and just disappear in the Lordship Isles?* He tried not to think of a Pernie angry at him for leaving Motherland.

But she has no navy, no flying Una, so could never reach me if she wanted to.

Thist's treasonous thoughts, once allowed, would not cease. *Or would I want to return to my homeland, try to make a life there?* At the thought of Anklya up in his homeland, now The People's Lands, he realized that without Una flying him there, he most likely could never return. Over twenty-five hundred kilometers distant, he would first face that six hundred meter cliff, then have to traverse through a large country of hostile Solar Priests where he was wanted for theft, then find his way up many kilometers of raging rapids north of God's Port. *Or find the secret lift that Cruthar told me about.* But lacking knowledge of where that access point even was, that was not an option. He could think of no way ever to get back home, not without the flying god-machine that had made his journeys so easy. *The ancients did this kind of travel as a matter of daily life,* he thought. *What must their lives have been like?*

Whispering to himself, arguing with his concerns, Thist said, "But home is where you make it, my Sire Thess used to say, and Mother's Palace with Pernie is not the worst home." Altamun Kech paid him no attention; the priest was in tears as the extent of the Pink Palace damage became more apparent as they docked.

"Obliterated," Altamun groaned. "Totally gone."

"Thist," Wakan Kech shouted, striding up the dock and looking over *Ice God* toward Una in the middle of the lash-up of ships. "Are you all right? Are you captured?" Then, as Thist waved back, Wakan said, appraising the strange configuration of boats, "What is this arrangement, anyhow? I've never seen any ships like these other two."

By now Lork had had enough of being ignored and jumped down from his ship to greet Wakan and the others who were with him. To Lork, having never seen but one other native of the High Antis, Wakan looked like a close relative of Alty-Moon: tall, dignified, olive-skinned, and dressed in that incredibly beautiful material, that godscloth. Dark red in this case, serving to set off the distinctive and dignified features of the impressive Kech priest.

"Alty-Moon"—Lork waved at Thist and his companion—"will you introduce me?" Wakan waited while Thist and Altamun clambered over gangplanks laid across Una and *Ice God* to reach the dock. After an embrace with the little general, Wakan said to his Kech countryman, "What is this flamboyant red-haired fellow saying, Altamun? Anything worth hearing? He's the pirate you spoke of?"

Within a few minutes, Altamun interpreting for them as Lork stumbled over some words, Wakan and Lork shook hands, followed by First Mate Attuk and other crew. Wakan turned to Thist. "Where is Thusk? I have brought our best healer, Insart Fyth, to attend to him." Fyth was a stooped and wizened old man, probably the oldest person Thist had ever met, judging by the curtain of facial wrinkles, the paleness of the sticklike, heavily veined arms protruding from his dark robes like white serpents. But the healer's voice was deep, calm, and assured. Thist could only hope that with his age had come knowledge. If not, Una could certainly guide him.

THAT EVENING, WAKAN AND THIST SAT ALONE IN A private room in what had been the palace of a now-deposed (and decapitated) WaterEdge noble. Wakan puffed on his ivory pipe and said, "Fyth tells me that your Una and he agree that Thusk's condition is stable but serious. There is a possibility that blood clots could travel from that injury into his heart, and kill him. I am at a loss, Thist."

Thist replied, "Wakan, I was worried about this. If I do nothing, he may die. If I do anything at all, he may die. There is no safe way of cutting into his injured brain, and even if there were, no way to take away only the damaged part. If we did, who knows then what would be left of our Thusk?" Una's video archives had brought up case after case of brain injuries that resulted in epileptic seizures, a loss of awareness, or diminished intellectual ability, even catatonic states. "So I have thought of one last resort. But it means transporting Thusk safely carefully, back to Mother's Palace."

Wakan listened in disbelief as Thist outlined his plan. "You really think this could work, Thist?"

"I know of no other way to bring my twin back to a real life." *Or even one that's not quite real*, he concluded.

———

BASED ON THIST'S VERBAL SPECIFICATIONS, WaterEdge carpenters were busily constructing a large, articulated horse-drawn carriage on which Una would rest. Wakan was still doubtful of Thist's plan. "I have sent for more horses, Thist. I think it will take at least eight of them to pull your Una across our miserable roads. Once things settle down, we really need to devote resources to pave our main highways with smooth stones; what we have is not good for transporting people or cargo quickly."

Thist nodded; he had entertained similar thoughts of wide, smooth, paved roads. *But not only for commercial purposes, my friend. I want to give my Mothersmen and their carts and wagons good roads for rapid deployment anywhere in Motherland, to put down other rebellions. And horses, we need hundreds or thousands of horses for those carriages; I want to start a breeding program.* He didn't know if the small number of such animals existing in Motherland was because of some natural problem like infertility, but suspected they may have been deliberately kept low in numbers for use by nobles only. *There are so many things in Motherland that need correcting! Why did all of this go on for so long?* But he already knew the answers: power, control, tradition, ignorance—the usual suspects.

AT TABLES IN THE SERVING HALL OF A HARBORSIDE INN, Lork and Attuk and the Na Saamese crewmen were enjoying the hospitality of Motherland. Wakan had made arrangements for a good hostel, fine provisions, and other delights to be made available to their guests as reward for bringing Una and her surviving crew safely back to WaterEdge. The matter of the two Mothersman guards killed by Lork's own harpoons, as well as the loss of Una's ability to fly, were not discussed by anyone but Thist and Wakan. Altamun Kech, for other reasons, was told not to talk about Na Saam or any of the unfortunate events that happened there. He was made to know that his future career—and perhaps his life—depended upon his silence.

Though none of the Na Saamese, save Lork, understood Motherspeak or any of the several other languages encountered along the WaterEdge harbor, all of Lork's fellow icers were alert to finding and recording possible stores of treasure, of resources, or any other potentially valuable plunder, should their captain give the word to seize it. Amidst the bragging and laughing and smoking and drinking, groups around each table were comparing notes on their findings.

"Lots of grain in warehouses," one icer said loudly. "'Nuff to feed hundreds back home." "We seen bolts of that godscloth stuff, all colors, too." "I'd like to take back one of them catapults," another said, "and go pound that stone fort of Dvora to dust." Other suggestions floated through conversations, becoming louder as the beer and ale flowed freely.

"Cap'n," Attuk offered, over a flagon of a very good beer, "Mebbe we should just offer to trade with these people, 'stead of thinkin' of smash-and-grab? I mean, they's treatin' us better'n we get at home. 'Sides, they's all livin' better than us 'round here, seems t' me."

Lork snorted. "*Trade?* What do we have to offer anybody? On our melt-ships we got nothing. Even if we went home, what could we bring back that they might want? Ice-bear skins? In this hot weather? Walrus tusks? Sealskins?" He took a swig of beer and grew silent. "Even their beer's better than ours. Nope, nothing. Hel, that's why we raid over the Ice Sea. We have nothing anybody wants, so we raid to feed our families." A thought struck him as he said that. *I guess we're no different than the ice-bears and the sorihan birds, then, are we?* Not liking that train of new thought, he dismissed it.

Attuk sat and thought, occasionally sipping his beer. "Cap'n, while we was building that cradle for their big green Una, I overheard that Alty-Moon translatin' some information from one of our smiths back to that little Thist. They was very interested in how our skritchers was built, how our smiths was able to bend and stretch and flatten and weld together the godsmetal." As Lork bent over to hear better, the first mate continued, "I don't think they knows how to do what our smiths can do. I mean, the only weapons they had aboard that Una of theirs, besides just knives and spears, was just two little bows made out of regular curved godsmetal arc pieces, and we got tons of those. We find 'em just like that. Didn't take much to make those 'springbows,' they call 'em.

"What I'm sayin', Cap'n, is, a few of our crew is smiths I brung along in case we was needin' repairs or somethin' built. We can give these Mothers a good smith, not the best, just one who can do a little somethin' with godsmetal that they cain't. He can stay and teach them. In return, we can prob'ly name a price —in metals, or grain, or that there godscloth of theirs. We'd be rich, back home."

Realization dawned on Lork and he laughed so loud that his crew in the pub stopped talking and stared at him. "Boys!" he yelled. "Ol' Attuk here is a blooming genius! He just told me how to trade with these Mothers!" Rousing cheers started up, calming down only when a bevy of smiling young women swarmed in through several doors to meet and greet the exotic foreigners. Wakan had rightly figured that sailors of any nation, away from home for weeks, would welcome compliant feminine companionship. At Thist's objection to subjecting Motherland women to such a practice, Wakan had just laughed. "Thist, Thist, for a man of the world you are too naive. WaterEdge has always had a ready supply of these willing women. Just because Mother's City is prudish and reserved, not all of our country is so, so, shall we say, 'uptight'?"

TWO DAYS LATER WAKAN AND THIST WERE RIDING IN Una's cabin with the comatose Thusk, the gentle swaying of the horse-drawn conveyance making it difficult for both of them to stay awake during the long hours every day on the main road to Mother's City. The Kech said, "I have established the Creesile relay system for this trip, Thist. We change horses and drivers at a station, take on provisions, then keep on going without further delay. It took some doing but I was able to convince Pernie to let me use all of her horses and distribute them along this road for the sole purpose of getting you and Thusk back to the palace as fast as possible." Pointing upwards, he said, "I didn't plan on bringing that pirate captain up there and one of his crew with us. But that superstructure on top, it makes for easy surveillance and control of our…guests."

Thist said, "Wakan, I didn't tell Captain Lork and the godsmetal smith, Zeerance Kleete, that Una was recording their every word. Which is why I don't worry about them trying anything against us." He smiled. "And the farther we get into Motherland, the less likely they are to try escaping." Wakan laughed. Thist didn't know that the Kech had ordered guardsman springbow snipers to kill either of the two pirates if they did try to get away from the caravan.

Atop Una, in the wooden superstructure left attached after the ship hull was removed, Lork and Kleete sat, enjoying their open-air view of the rolling hills and croplands of Motherland. As overloaded ox-drawn wagons of fragrant green produce, bound for the markets at WaterEdge, passed beside them, Lork looked down on them approvingly. "A lot of room here in this big country, Zeerance," he said. "A lot of people, and a lot of food."

"A lot of everything, Cap'n," the smith replied, spreading his muscled arms wide. "You think they wouldn't miss it if we took a little bit for ourselves?" Both men laughed, but nervously. Behind them rode six large Mothersmen guards, outfitted in black-leather armor and carrying both spears and springbows.

Lork was convinced that they would kill him if he tried anything, so he was on his best behavior. He felt uneasy being so outnumbered by the foreigners, but when he had insisted upon traveling to Mother's City to meet Mother Perneptheranam, he was forced to leave his crew, save Kleete, at WaterEdge, with Attuk in command. "Not as hostages, Lork," Thist had explained through Altamun's translation, "but as guests. *You* are the hostage." Besides, Thist had already given orders to keep those crews away from the harbor; they would be transported out in the country to a safe farmstead until Lork returned. With plenty of food, beer, and women, he was certain the icers would not complain. Meanwhile, Motherland Army engineers were going to study those converted iceboats, to strip apart the skritcher mechanisms and the harpoon launchers to see how they worked.

And with the smith, Kleete, teaching my other engineers and smiths how to work godsmetal, we will soon have enough knowledge to reproduce their devices and machines and to build our own. Then we won't need Lork or his stinky people. Na Saam has nothing we need, and so far away over the Ice Sea, with so few people, can never be a threat to us. He didn't want to think of the eventual fate of the two pirates. *Pernie has not shown a lot of mercy since becoming Mother, but maybe these two might at least get quick deaths.*

Even as the horse-and-Una procession continued toward Mother's City, Thist was talking to Wakan about the Lork situation, trying to decide the fate of the forty-two foreign "guests" who had rescued Altamun Kech and Thusk and himself. Wakan, as usual, had the practical solution: "Keep them, Thist. Disassemble their ships and transport the crews deep inland, to the far western high country. They might even choose to stay voluntarily if it's as cold and barren in their Na Saam as you say. Let them harvest crops, tend sheep, or send them to fight barbarians in the Southern Highlands. "

Thist nodded. "Or just execute them all, but keep the smith?"

Wakan nodded grimly; his once-naive little charge, two years ago just a near-naked refugee from the Dark Highlands, was now a famed and hardened warrior, to whom betrayal and murder were only impersonal tools. *You'll make a great commander in chief, Thist, when Pernie decides for Motherland to expand out of our basin, to conquer others.* The Kech didn't care for that new direction of Motherland, but felt powerless to do anything other than try to moderate Pernie's increasingly harsh practices. He thought, *She has been unnecessarily brutal, and is no longer pressing for more Sisterdoms to be liberated as republics. Where is that young girl who was so receptive to ideas of freedom and equality?* He was afraid that he already knew the answer: *Genetics, tradition, and the addiction to power. The three legs of tyranny.*

Zeerance Kleete sat atop the stopped Una, his mouth open in amazement. "Cap'n," he said in hushed tones, "I never seen anything like this. I thought the WaterEdge place had big buildings, twice as big as ours, even bigger'n our Tag Temple, but this"—he pointed toward the enormous white dome of Mother's Palace in the distance, standing astride the city—"like a, a, a *breast,* that's what it is, Cap'n. A big white tit, for all to see. No wonder they call it Mother's Palace!" His laughter betrayed nervousness; Motherland was an invincible country, by comparison to Na Saam an ice-bear to an insect.

"Four hundred feet high, if it's an inch," Lork replied, marveling at the sight, a building large enough to hold all of Stonehaven. It did not escape his attention that another half dozen smaller domes surrounded it, each half the size of that largest one. "So much wealth," he muttered, "so much knowledge, so many resources, so many people, to be able to build such things." To his mind, Na Saam's largest structure, the Ice Hall, would not reach even halfway up one of the small domes there. And as their procession entered the metropolitan area itself, Mother's City itself was equally spectacular to the icers, with its thousands of colorful buildings —*Individual houses for ordinary people?* he marveled —its broad, paved streets, its flowered avenues, palm trees, gilt facades, white marble everywhere. Even streets paved with smooth stones, which would be an unimaginable extravagance in Na Saam but ubiquitous here.

"Beyond belief," Lork said aloud, "I never imagined anybody could live so well, could have so much." A glance at Zeerance showed that he was thinking the same thing, each man realizing that they had best not try to steal from these people, but to learn from them. Being faced with such a choice, such feelings, for a pirate accustomed to seizing valuables and food, this reality they had never even dreamed of was disheartening. *We've been wrong all our lives,* they thought as one. *There are better ways to get wealth, much more of it, and many more ways to enjoy it.* As they neared Mother's Palace, the contrasts between their homeland's soul-rending poverty and Motherland's incredible wealth grew more pronounced. This noble and that rich merchant had built and shown off their wealth and power through architecture; some of their palaces would have compared in height almost to the Ice Hall itself.

It was in this despondent state of emotion that Captain Lork, one-time notorious ice pirate, and Zeerance Kleete, godsmetal smith, rode atop Una on a wagon pulled by eight white horses, down the broad tiled avenue to the immaculately landscaped grounds of Mother's Palace, while puzzled crowds alternately cheered and shook their heads at the strangely dressed foreigners.

CHAPTER THIRTY-SEVEN

Led by mounted Mothersman Guards, the coterie of returnees from Na Saam made their separate ways to luxury apartments in a white-marble building adjacent to Mother's Palace. There, multiple servants of both sexes attended to their baths, changes of clothes, and meals. Healer Fyth had the comatose Thusk carried to a treatment room where the aromas of herbs and incenses were so strong that Thist and Wakan had to leave.

"I think those odors might be strong enough to awaken the dead!" Thist said, immediately regretting making the statement, but Wakan just smiled. The Kech escorted his High Antis countryman Altamun to guest quarters, and stayed for an hour to debrief him on his capture, the whereabouts of his kidnapper, Noor, and an assessment of Stonehaven's society.

Meanwhile, Lork and Kleete luxuriated in warm soapy baths, followed by deep massages given by attractive young women in tight-fitting shift dresses. "This is like the paradise the Tag priests promise us, Cap'n," Kleete said as a maiden wiped oils off of him with a hot towel. "Except, we're still alive. I always heard that their paradise was way beyond the Ice Sea, and here we are sure enough!"

Lork just laughed, thinking. *Nothing in Na Saam has anything like this. I could get used to it!*

SETTLED INTO HIS OWN QUARTERS, THIST CALLED FOR A scribe, who took down his quick summary of recent events including the crash of Una and Thusk's resulting injury and coma. He knew than Una would not have a record of events from the time of the crash until the arrowheads were removed, and in any event he wanted to record his own personal memories of his captivity. Wakan said earlier, "I have already given Pernie a synopsis of what you told me by godsphere, but your own words to her will be more important, part of the official record of your experiences." Thist agreed. He began his dictation with a brief description of the islands in the Cold Sea, followed by the intimidation of Thornveld and the gratitude of Noorstown. *I don't want to make any of those islands seem too attractive*, he thought. *Not if I should ever want to…to go live there.* The bulk of his report was about what happened at Stonehaven. Here, he didn't want the story of Lork's remarkable rescue of the exploration party to stand alone, not without an equal stress on just how and why Una and his Thusk were in such conditions to start with. *I still don't trust the man,* he thought, *so* my *words have to get to Pernie first.*

Reviewing the scribe's written report, he sent it off to be delivered to Pernie. Later that evening, he was disappointed that she had not sent for him; after all the time away, he had thought for certain that he would be spending his first night home, together. *Is she upset? Has something changed?* His sleep that night was troubled, not at all what he had expected upon returning from the barbarians on the Ice Sea.

AT COURT THE NEXT MORNING, MOTHER Pernepptheranam rose regally from her blue throne to greet Thist and Altamun Kech. As Thist approached her, bowing, she gave him a nod and a broad smile. "I am happy you have returned, General Thist, well and whole, after all these weeks away. Your report was most enlightening and I look forward to discussing it—and other matters—in greater detail, soon." Thist smiled in return; he was hoping Pernie would be receptive tonight; after his time away he was missing her in many ways, both emotionally and physically. Being in her presence made the pressure almost unbearable. Pernie continued, "I am most saddened by the injury to our Thusk, but my healers, led by the able Healer Fyth, will provide every assistance for his full recovery." Thist saw in Pernie's face that she seemed more concerned than her haughty tone conveyed.

The Mother then acknowledged the returned Kech priest with a formal but dispassionate statement: "Altamun Kech, we are sorry that you were subjected to kidnapping by the late pirate, Noor. It is our pleasure to welcome you home. You will receive back pay for your time away, and Wakan, here, will discuss your new assignment with you. You may leave."

As the Kech departed, backing away and bowing, Wakan motioned for the guards to bring in two more guests for an audience with the Mother. "Mother," he said, "let me introduce to you two of the men of the nation of Na Saam who rescued General Thist and his twin, and facilitated their return here—ice captain Lork and godsmetal smith Zeerance Kleete. Gentlemen, Mother Perneptheranam, ruler of Motherland."

With that, a freshly dressed Lork, clothed in sky-blue godscloth robes with a white sash and striking black boots, stood at attention, then bowed very low. Lork had talked Wakan into letting him don the godscloth robe to replace his rough icer outfit. The smaller and less well-dressed man beside him tried to genuflect as well, but almost fell over, eliciting an embarrassing chuckle from Mother Pernie. Flushed, Kleete stood erect, trembling.

What the Mother saw in Lork took her breath, but she recovered immediately, having had much practice in the daily court for over a year now. To her, Lork was a man-god: tall, well-built, with massive chest and muscled arms, and a slender body that the godscloth clung to in all the right places. His long, bright red hair, coils of spun copper, was braided in back, falling over his left shoulder like a wanton invitation; his immaculate beard framed features seemingly carved out of the very granite of the far mountains. His eyes—the palest blue she had ever seen, inviting her to dive into his soul. And something else, what was it? A unique body odor, a combination of manly sweat and a light touch of a lavender perfume, wafted toward her across the distance between them like an intimate caress, causing an immediate trembling response over her entire body, but especially—*specifically!*—in her warmest regions. *An amazing man, unlike any I've ever seen*, she realized in mild shock. Pernie felt as if she had fallen through a trap door, an emotional depth from which she would never escape. *Nor do I want to*, she thought feverishly. *I will have this man!*

Glancing quickly at a frowning Thist, then over to a smiling Wakan, she froze her face and tried to act the uninterested Mother. "Captain Lork of Na Saam, Smith Kleete, we welcome you to our court. We thank you for your courage and skill in returning our citizens—and our flying machine, Una—to us." She allowed a slight hint of displeasure to show; she was aware that it was Lork's harpoons that had injured Thusk and damaged Una, so her pleasure could not be seen to be complete. Nevertheless—all other aspects aside, she wanted this man. *Tonight! I don't know what Thist or Thusk will say, or what Wakan will think, but...but I am Mother, and this Lork will spend tonight with me!*

As if reading her mind—*And sometimes I think he does, that Wakan!* she thought—her priest took Lork's arm and led him and the smith to a copper chest located next to a wall with a surly-looking Mothersman guard, who opened it. "Inside this chest are twenty pounds of gold coin," Wakan said as Lork and Kleete looked on with astonishment. "This is your reward for your heroic actions. You may share it among yourselves and your crew as you see fit."

Lork gasped. The shining coins before him represented more wealth than all of Stonehaven together possessed, he guessed. "My men will be very pleased, as will I," he finally said, in near-perfect Motherspeak. "Thank you, Mother *Per-nep-ther-an-am*," he said slowly, carefully pronouncing each syllable. Wakan had the guard carry the treasure out as the Na Saamese bowed and left.

Before Thist could say anything, the Mother announced, "Tonight, we will have a feast for our returned heroes, and honor their brave rescuers. That is all for now." An astonished Thist stepped back as she departed, a puzzled look on his face. Wakan then came over to him and said, "Thist, she is a passionate young woman, and now the Mother. She chooses who she wants, you do understand? And you have been away for some time now."

At Thist's clenched jaw and fierce eyes, Wakan said, "General, I will provide you with more women than you can handle, tonight. And *every* night if you wish. As the hero of the Games and general of the Mothersman Army, you have an unlimited number of willing and anxious young women at your beck and call." The Kech chuckled. "Older ones, too."

AWAKENINGS

CHAPTER THIRTY-EIGHT

Thist sat in his seat in Una's cabin, his attention focused on the image of Anklya on the front wall screen. He wished he could speak to the real woman herself, but settled on talking to the image. "Una, will you please set up communication with that Mienne, on the Moon?"

Una replied, "Thist, I am attempting to establish the qomp communication link, but at present there is no response from Mienne at her device. I will continue to try." Thist felt that Una was almost evolving sympathy, realizing that he wanted urgently to talk with Mienne to attempt Thusk's recovery.

Standing beside Thist, Wakan Kech said gravely, "Thist, do you really think that this will help Thusk? His condition seems stable, he's not getting any worse, and he might recover. What you're proposing is risky, don't you think?"

Thist stood, waving his arm at the Anklya figure. "If Una can set up a talk with Mienne, I want to discuss it with her. Before his accident and injury at Stonehaven, Thusk told me about his last trip up there." Thist went on to relate how Thusk had essentially entered into an artificial body there on the Moon the last time, not just the weird mind-mixing that Thist himself had experienced.

At Wakan's shocked reaction, Thist said, "Yes. The ancient machines on the Moon, some of them still operate after all of this time. They were able to assemble some kind of qomp creation, rather like Una here, I would guess, but in human form. And instead of just making a digital image like Anklya's here, it allowed Thusk himself to occupy its physical body."Wakan's mouth formed an O, still unbelieving.

"Who knows why the ancients built such a thing, or what they used it for?" Thist said, smiling. "Thusk told me it could do everything our bodies can do. *Everything,* understand?" Wakan nodded, still in disbelief. "So, Wakan, I want to place Thusk's unconscious body on the Mother's Crystal Throne, and—"

"And have him wake up on the Moon, in that made-body?" Wakan said in a raspy whisper.

"Yes, and then when he's awake there, to return here, Wakan, back into his real body. Maybe it will start this one up again. Maybe being awake during that transfer will mean he will be awake when he comes back."

"How did you think of such a thing, Thist? The whole idea is just, just, *incredible!*"

Thist smiled without humor. "Wakan, old friend, we little people who evolved in the land of The Ice, we had to adapt or die. Our ancestors had to be smart to survive at all in that harshness. Because of lack of food, our bodies shrank over those thousands of years, but our brains didn't, and our minds didn't. You big people down here in the Warm Lands, you just had it too easy."

WITH PERNIE OCCUPIED WITH HER NEWFOUND LOVER Lork for the entire night and next day, Wakan and Thist were unable to contact her, so used their own status and authority to have Healer Fyth deliver the unconscious Thusk to Mother's Auditorium on a stretcher. Thist explained his proposed treatment to the healer, who agreed that something extraordinary needed to be done for his brain-injured patient. "He could experience a dislodged blood clot at any time, and die of a stroke or seizure. The sooner you try something, the better chance he may have."

The huge space of the auditorium was now a vast and silent void, empty of the thousands who periodically witnessed Mother's rituals there. Situated under the arching sky-painted dome high above, the Crystal Throne sat in magnificent silence atop its pyramidal pedestal, illuminated by a stiletto of bright light that stabbed down through a hidden aperture.

"This is a place of awesomeness, Thist," the Kech priest said reverently. "I never tire of seeing it. Almost a living thing." As if in reply, as soon as Thist approached the first of the thirteen steps up to the transparent chair itself, streams of bright colors lit up each riser in turn, an invitation to follow. "So sad to learn that it is only a machine, a qomp communicator."

Thist explained the throne's operation to Healer Fyth, who stood in awe of the throne and of Thist. He had never seen anyone but a Mother touch the transparent steps and chair. Thist said, "I accidentally operated the throne last year when searching for the missing Mother Messinex, an experience I do not want to repeat. I felt that my mind was being stirred, mixed, separated from my body. And then swirled together with the mind of that Mienne up there on the Moon. It was marginally erotic in a sense, stimulating, but just too weird for words. Literally." This time, he was careful not to have any skin contact with the big crystal. That would be for Thusk alone.

The guards dismissed—for they did not want anyone other than the healer to witness them violating the Crystal Throne's no-touch taboo—Thist and Wakan carried the unconscious Thusk all the way up the thirteen stairs, avoiding touching the crystal itself with any bare skin. The cascades of colors increased in frequency as they approached the top level. Once there, they stripped Thusk's undergarment, ensuring that his bare bottom was situated on the transparent seat. Below them, the rainbow of colors became a frenzy, escalating up and down the staircase, finally swirling around and into the Crystal Throne itself. The maelstrom of hues and brightness continued for several minutes, as if hesitant to make a connection, a commitment.

As the three men stood back watching Thusk, they saw his body suddenly stiffen, jerk, and finally collapse, falling forward off the throne, all the former illuminating colors fading to darkness. In panic, Thist ran to pick up his twin, feeling his neck for a pulse. There was none. Healer Fyth likewise tried and failed to find any signs of life.

Sobbing, Thist held Thusk close. "Wakan, I have killed him. What have I done?"

WAKAN KECH CARRIED THE SMALL, LIFELESS BODY OF Thusk down the dark stairs from the Crystal Throne and placed it on the stretcher that had borne him into Mother's Auditorium. Thist followed behind, numbed by the death of his twin, in absolute despair as his world was disintegrating.

First, Pernie's dismissal of their relationship for the pirate from Na Saam—*Who I brought to Motherland with me, stupidly!* he thought. And now, much, much worse, infinitely so—Thusk's death, a void that could never be filled. Rage began to fill that void—*It was Lork's harpoons that brought down Una and injured Thusk in the first place. And now, Lork has killed him!*

Calming himself as he descended the stairs, Thist decided there and then that he would kill Lork. *But how?* As Pernie's favorite, the pirate couldn't be touched by Thist or his soldiers. *I'll think of something,* he thought, trying to assuage his own guilt for attempting to awaken Thusk via the Crystal Throne.

Wakan summoned the stretcher-bearers to return and take Thusk's remains to Healer Fyth's clinic for further examination. With a hand on Thist's shoulder, he accompanied the general in following the body of his dead twin as Healer Fyth led the way.

CHAPTER THIRTY-NINE

With a shock, Thusk felt the familiar physical and mental effects of a qomp trip returning: *the Universe swirled around him, jerking him this way and that, roiling his mind with images from his past life, from his childhood, from his travels, his lovers, his Sire and birther, his twin Thist, times with his Moon lover, that Mienne, then falling inside Una, and finally, descending darkness and myriad dreams, repeated dreams, nightmares and images.* But unlike that ongoing eternity of repeated memories, things suddenly became more realistic now, he sensed, as if life was returning to order, no longer surreal. He felt as though a thick dark mist was clearing...

"Mr. Thusk, is that you? Have you arrived?" The soft voice was familiar, yet mysterious. *Who is that? Where am I? Is that*—"Mienne? Is that you? I don't... how did I get here? I was flying in Una—" Suddenly Thusk felt overwhelming fatigue, something draining all of his energy, all of his *everything. Am I shrinking? Am I dying? Am I*— Blackness absorbed him once again.

This is not a dream! This is real! A fully conscious Thusk opened his eyes, this time seeing clearly. Above him was a dark ceiling, around him a huge, softly lit room of indistinguishable shadows. To his left a high wall of dark metal punctuated by small doors rose up at least thirty meters, reminding him of a hutch for pigeons, but obviously for something much larger than those birds. He was having trouble understanding where he was, so looked around as much as his throbbing head would allow. To his right, a familiar face! "Is this the Moon?" he whispered. "Am I back with—*Mienne!*" In alternate disbelief and happiness, he made out the tall girl's features, her face now close to his, suddenly kissing him. Barely able to speak, he said, "Mienne, I remember Una being hit with something, hard, and then I was falling, and then only dreams. Wild dream, crazy ones. Was I here before? Was I on the Crystal Throne again? Into this avvy body again? What happened to me?"

"Oh, Thusk," she cried, embracing him where he lay on a gurney, clothed only in shorts. "You have been away for so long, but now you're back. In your avvy body!"

Trembling, uncertain of his control of the avvy's functions, Thusk felt a coldness, an emptiness that he had never before experienced. *Something is missing,* he thought. But checking his memories, he concluded, *It's not my memory.* Forcing himself—or the avvy body— off the gurney and barefooted onto the warm floor, he thought, *And it's not my body, either. This one feels fine again, just—an unknown I can't place at the moment.* "Where are we, Mienne?" he said shakily, "I don't recognize this place, this room."

Mienne appeared to be concerned about Thusk's uncertainties. "Thusk, we are down in the deepest level of the complex, down where we first discovered this avvy body." She pointed to the nearby metal wall, which contained dozens of doors, the one closest to them now open, revealing a dark chamber just big enough for his gurney and a body to fit inside, and a series of blinking colored lights inside it.

Like a storage vault, a mausoleum, Thusk thought. *What are all those other ones for?* "Did I come out of that? Was I in *there*?" He shivered at the vision of himself locked up in a metal box in that dark wall.

Mienne said, "Thusk, after you were here last, Jolan thought the avvy should be brought back down here so that the DI could communicate with the consoles here, to find out if the avvy needed any maintenance. He was worried that after such a long time, some of its parts may have worn or been corrupted. He was concerned that inhabiting the avvy might harm its user. He had worn it himself with no problems and you did, too, the last time." Mienne blushed; Thusk remembered *that* visit with great pleasure. "The DI worked with the systems down here and discovered that some fixes *were* necessary, some tuning needed to be made, and even updates." Pointing directly to the open chamber, she added, "So yes, the avvy has been in there since right after you left, months ago."

Thusk laughed. "I sound like a machine that needs oiling and new parts, huh?" He wasn't certain that he liked being a machine of any kind, but alive was alive. *But what happened to me? We were flying in Una over a harbor, over ships that sailed on ice.* Slowly his memories surfaced. *The Lordship Islands, the Thornveld attack, that crevasse valley, then following above the ice ships.*

Before he could ask her anything, Mienne took Thusk's arm as, still weak, he walked over to a table and sat. Already seated and eating through a straw-like tube, Wayer smiled. "Hello, Mr. Earthman. Welcome back to Moon."

THUSK WAS ANXIOUS TO FIND OUT WHY HE WAS BACK ON the Moon, in the avvy body. "I don't know how I got here, Mienne, I really don't. You say that down here you've been cut off from qomp communication with the Crystal Throne or Una back on Earth. Can we get back to your Control Room and contact Thist? Maybe he can tell me?"

Mienne gave him a hug and kissed him again, at which Thusk felt the familiar erotic stimulation last experienced during his first avvy body visit. She said, "Yes, Thusk, my love. We can go up there but it will take a few hours. Jolan and Ledd have been trying to excavate and repair the old elevator system, but it will take them a long time to fix because of all the cave-ins and destruction. In the meantime, we have to trek a few kilometers out and then take the new digger tunnels and cavities upward. That's why Wayer and I have stayed down here for weeks now, watching over the avvy's recovery, and exploring other hallways and rooms in the meantime. We were cut off from Motherth, but I didn't care; I wanted this avvy to be ready for you if you came back—*when* you came back. And here you are!"

Mienne smiled again, blushing, responding to their kiss herself. "Knowing you, how curious you are, when you are fully able, you will want to see some of the strange things we have found down here." Hoisting a full backpack and helping Wayer put on her smaller one, she took Thusk by the hand. "Come on, love. We've got a long hike ahead of us."

Afterward, Thusk and Mienne lay arm in arm, the thin blanket pulled up over them. Mienne's long dark hair was spread back across the pillow they shared. Still amazed at his situation, Thusk said, "Mienne, you were great. But I wonder, this body. Why would the ancients make it so that it can, er, *perform* this way?" As Mienne brought up her head and propped herself on an elbow, a look of disapproval on her face, he said, "I am not complaining, not at all. I was only trying to think of why —not to mention *how*—they did it." Smiling and taking her in his arms, he kissed her and said, "We may never know, but I am glad they did!"

THE NEXT WAKE PERIOD MIENNE AND WAYER SHOWED Thusk around the areas of the complex that the two women had explored during the last year. One room of particular interest featured a three-dimensional image of the Moon that appeared as they stepped inside, a globe some three meters in diameter. Within the image and on its surface ran numerous colored lines that interconnected colored dots, a three-dimensional spiderweb of colors with a nexus at each dot.

Mienne pointed to a blue dot on the northern hemisphere. "This is where we are, always facing Motherth, er, *Earth.* The colored disks are, or were, cities on the surface, the ones that your twin, Thist, had me flash off and on last year. Not very many people live in them anymore, but the quantum electronics and nanobots keep them mostly in good shape. Only a few on this side facing Motherth were destroyed by the Sun." She turned suddenly grim. "And the qomps can't tell us where all those people went, or if they died, or what. A few thousand still live in Tycho City, I know, but they don't answer any queries and won't talk to me." She explained to Thusk that apparently religions and superstitions in those cities kept them from accepting the truth she had revealed about the solar eruption that ended the ancient world, refusing even to watch videos of The Day.

Walking around to the other side of the model Moon, Thist saw numerous lights there, too. "And these are cities, too? I thought the Sun scoured them all away," he said.

"The lights are there because this is an ancient representation, a model of what used to be. Many are now unresponsive. The qomps can't access them." As she touched one particular disk, the image zoomed in, as if the trio were approaching the lunar surface, craters suddenly rising up at them as they "landed."

"Here is a mystery that we don't understand," Mienne said, pointing to a latticework of metal structures that spanned across an entire crater, horizon to horizon. "The qomps can't or won't say what this massive installation was, why it was built, what it was supposed to do. These metal constructions span this depression, which the DI calls 'Parson's Crater,' forty kilometers across. An enormous place, but we have no information about it. Any ideas from Motherth, Thusk? Can your Una possibly help?"

"That place is thousands of kilometers away, Mienne, on the other side of your Moon. Doesn't this big globe show other interesting places closer by, other abandoned complexes, those empty cities and all? I mean, if that side of the Moon was destroyed, why even bother?" Touching the globe image nearer to the blue dot that was their own location, Thusk said, "Here, the sphere shows other tubes going down from Community in all directions. Has anybody ever been to those?"

Mienne and Wayer stared at Thusk. "We like to explore mysterious things that the qomps don't even know about. All of these dozens of tubes, these lighted-up cities, they can tell us all about them." Mienne hesitated. "Except what happened all over Moon at the End of the World. And, and, a place that I want to go visit, a particular city."

"Which one is that, Mienne?" Thusk asked with some frustration, thinking, *Here is a whole new world, one that will take lifetimes to explore, discoveries to be made. Why does she want to go to any one place over another?*

Mienne pointed to a green light adjacent to their blue dot. "Here, Thusk. I have been waiting for you to arrive in the avvy to go exploring with me. None of the Community men will, not even Jolan or Ledd." As she touched the location, the zoom feature made it appear as if they were approaching the domed city, its green coloration evidence of a small forest of Earthlike trees visible through the transparent hemisphere. As they neared, small lakes appeared, scattered among villages of small houses and a large city of tall brown buildings; Thusk recognized the architecture from one of Una's videos of ancient lunar settlements: three-dimensional printed blocks of local dust, replicating the appearance of desert towns in what had once been North and Central America.

"This is just an archived image of a city now destroyed, too, Thusk," Mienne said with a sob. "It was called Zhee. I was born there." Holding both of his hands, she asked, "By this map, it's less than twenty kilometers from here. Will you take me there, please? I want to go home. To UpTop."

CHAPTER FORTY

Mother Perneptheranam, absolute monarch of Motherland, sat up in her bed, exhausted but satisfied, smiling at the sleeping figure of the Na Saam icer, Captain Lork, next to her. "I can't believe we've been at this for two whole days," she whispered lowly, "but I'm ready for a third day. If he is." Nuzzling the big man's neck, she kissed him full on his mouth and put her hand in a sensitive place. Lork jerked awake, pulled back his head, and smiled. It was apparent to Pernie that her new lover was rising to the task once again. He kissed her lips passionately, then lowered his head to taste her more fully.

With a quick intake of breath, Pernie gasped, "Lork, you are incredible, you know?"

"Yes, Pernie, I do know," he whispered, and set out to prove it again.

Later, as handmaidens brought in golden and silver trays of food and drink and placed them on low tables, Pernie watched Lork wolf down the expansive morning meal, amazed at his appetite and his omnivorous tastes: beef, bacon, goose eggs, dark and light breads, cheeses, and Motherland's variety of sweet fruits, washed down by cold honeyed wine and hot chai.

He is not used to our variety and plenty, she thought admiringly. *Nor has he met a woman like me, I believe.* "Variety and plenty," she whispered, catching his eye. With a smile and a nod, Lork continued his repast.

After the meal Pernie and her icer captain relaxed on soft godscloth-covered divans, Lork still sampling grapes and oranges from the dishes on the tables around them. *Fun is fun—and was it ever fun!—but now it's time for serious business now,* she thought. Although circumstances would not allow, she truly needed and wanted the advice and consultation of Wakan Kech. *And even Thist,* she sighed. *But I'm afraid he won't relate to me anymore, not the way we were before...before Lork!* The memory of her twin lovers from the Dark Highlands, up near the glacier, was all but displaced by the fierce passion that Lork had aroused in her in some mysterious fashion she did not understand. *Wakan used to say that pheromones—little smells—were responsible for sexual attraction.* Looking over Lork's face and physique, she wondered, *Do looks smell? Do smells see?* She concluded, *Sometimes my Kech priest is a bit too mysterious.*

"Lork," Pernie said, waiting until the icer was between bites of fruit, "I think you can contribute to Motherland's well-being. I want you to stay."

The icer stopped eating, and put down the unbitten apple. "Pernie, I, I, I don't know what to say. My people are expecting me back home. My crews have families, too."

"You may send back a ship with those who wish to return. But you *will* stay, as will your godsmetal smith. From what you have told me these last few days, the man works a kind of magic with godsmetal, far beyond anything my own smiths can do."

Seeing that the Mother's mind was made up, and that she was commanding him to do what he had been trying to arrange all along, he replied, "Your wish is my command, Dear Mother," while thinking, *And your command is my wish!*

Pernie nodded; she had not expected any different

answer. Still, it was always better to have compliance than resistance. "I am impressed that you were able to convert your iceboats to seagoing vessels and then sail them and the Una machine over three thousand kilometers of the Cold Sea." Those were details she was going to make use of, if her plans were to succeed.

Between lovemaking sessions the last two days, Lork had talked and talked and talked about his life—sailing over the Ice Sea, pirating. When she had condemned piracy as criminal, Lork defended his past. "Look, Pernie, Na Saam has little to offer to others. Some furs, fish, or seal skins. But there are many thousands to feed in each of our cities. Sometimes we do trade in copper or silver or gold with a few more powerful kingdoms to our southeast, people who have condiments, fruits, things we can't grow, and are too strong to raid. But the weaker places, we do raid and take what we need." At Pernie's objection to that, he said, "But you yourself, here in Motherland, you tax your citizens, do you not?"

"Of course. Motherland needs the funds for, for, our army. And for maintaining roads and, and—"

"And palaces, like this one?" He waved his arms at the spacious room, its painted walls and ceiling, its light panels. "And what do you do if a citizen refuses to pay those taxes?"

"Why, my guardsmen will confiscate that amount in property—lands, houses, furnishing."

"And if that citizen resists?"

"Then my guardsmen will use force, they will—" Pernie stopped, blushing, realizing what she was admitting to the pirate.

"Of course. You use force to take what you need. My crews and I just do that directly, without any pretense of serving a greater good." Lork smiled that attractive crooked grin again, a sparkle in his eyes.

In a sober tone, he added, "Pernie, in all of Nature, creatures take what they need for themselves and their families. No less than the sorihan and the bears, we Na Saamese do the same, just like your Motherland does. I admit, we do enjoy the physical thrills of our raids. Cooped up in this palace of yours with all its luxuries, you have not experienced life in the wild—the wind in your hair, the ice spray on your face, the shared exhilaration of a crew of ten strong men, driving their craft across the Ice Sea looking for prey. We raid for food for our women and children, we take iron tools and weapons that we need, and we plunder for gold and silver and copper.

"And, though we don't talk about it, we raid for *glory*—for the songs the people sing about our exploits, the stories they tell about us." He didn't add, *And the women who lay down for us!*

Pernie's eyes lit up as her new lover regaled her with detailed descriptions of life on the Ice Sea, free of all social restraints and obligations. He spellbound her, relating his fights with other pirate craft, wrecking ships in deep crevasses and against perilous rocks, spending desperate nights and days fighting off bears and sorihan birds and other denizens unknown even in legends in Motherland.

Pernie finally asked in a quiet voice, "But what of those you raid? What about *their* women and children, *their* food?"

Lowering his eyes, Lork said, "We never take *every*thing; like a shepherd and his flock, we have to leave enough behind so that they can recover. We space our ventures over the years, like leaving fields fallow for regrowth. And we try not to kill any more men than we have to."

Alternately excited and disgusted by Lork's wild stories and adventurous lifestyle, Pernie still sensed the pirate's sincerity and honesty about the brutal necessity of his actions. She could understand his comparison of her taxes to his raids, a viewpoint very different from what Wakan Kech had taught. And she had never considered the philosophy of comparing her government to Nature in the wild, or to pirate raids. *Am I really that predatory? Here I am, trying to bring Wakan's ideals of freedom and democracy into practice, but it is difficult;*

Sisters and their people fight against it. Is there another way? The pirate way? Is piracy, raiding, what I am doing myself, in wanting to annex those islands in the Cold Sea?

While she was musing, Lork asked, "Pernie, why is it that you are trying to change the way your country is run? Giving up all your personal power? Back home, I admit, we don't have one person who rules absolutely over everybody; we have a Council of Elders that makes the decisions. But, seeing that your country is so big, with so many people and so much land and wealth, it only makes sense that one person—*you*—should be in charge. I mean, Mother's City here alone, has more people than all of our Na Saam towns. I can't imagine everybody here trying to run things individually, doing it all their own way. Nothing would ever get done."

"But Lork, Wakan has taught me that people being free is the natural way. In his own land, way down south in the High Antis, they are free. They elect Elders, like you do at home."

"Pernie, I'll bet you that your Wakan's homeland is small, like mine. What works for small tribes like ours doesn't seem feasible for your millions of people. And hasn't Motherland always been ruled by one Mother, with the princesses administering over their smaller Sisterdoms, for thousands of years? Seems to me that having strong leaders like that makes for a strong nation."

"Lork, you have given me a lot to think about," Pernie said, reflecting on her problems. "You are correct that giving people freedom can lead to troubles. Even we in ShadowFall had to fight for ours. Then there was"—she wouldn't mention the Sisterdom she had erased from history—"one rebellion last year, and the other one at WaterEdge that Thist put down. And Wakan's spies tell of rumblings in other Sisterdoms. My strong hand was necessary to squelch those two and might be again, if more rebellions break out." She looked Lork straight in the eyes. "You know, lover, you might be right. It does seem more efficient to me, just to give an order and have it done, not have to argue with anybody, to get things done.

"But I may have to go slower, keep my foot on the neck of some Sisters until their people can learn to be free. Gradually. After all, I am young yet, and should have a long time, years, to do it. So I think—no new republics for a while."

Lork smiled and put down his snack, pulling Pernie to him, kissing her passionately, while thinking. *Raiding is not the only thing I'm good at. And this is a lot more fun than freezing my ass off in an ice ship!*

SOMETIME LATER, PERNIE ASKED LORK FOR DETAILS about what had happened to Una and Thusk and Thist at his city of Stonehaven. "Thist's report has his viewpoint, but I would like to hear yours. I want to understand fully why my Una machine can't fly anymore and why little Thusk is unconscious."

Once again, an enthusiastic Lork spun his story, this time about everything that occurred when Una crashed —"Shot down, actually, when my crews thought it was a big sorihan killer bird!" From there, he told her about Thist's and his presentations at the Ice Hall, of his surprise at Una's talking DI and its digital display capabilities and the archives of the ancient world. Becoming more animated as the story continued, he told of his own heroic transport of the god-machine and his own ships over the Ice Sea, down into the crevasse valley, and then sailing them, trimaran style, all the way to WaterEdge.

As she listened, Pernie thought, *He talks entirely too much, but it is very useful information. He may fit into my plans. I need to find out more.* "How were you able to transform your ice ships into ocean-going vessels, Lork? Did your people have such shipbuilding skills back in Na Saam?"

"They do now, Mother," Lork said, munching on an apple. "That Una machine of General Thist's revealed much useful information. Given the melt-sea environment we were going to have to travel through, looking at the pictures and construction details of ancient wooden ships, we were able to modify the iceboats to melt-boats—*sea* boats—and we made conversion parts that we took along with us."

Pernie sat up straight and pushed Lork back. "Good. Because I want you to build me a big navy. And I want that godsmetal genius of yours to put your harpoons on all those ships, and any other weapons he can build. Motherland is going to annex all those islands in the Cold Sea."

As Lork laid back, open-mouthed yet smiling, Pernie added, "You will be admiral of the first Motherland Fleet."

SEVERAL HOURS LATER, AT WAKAN'S CONTINUED insistence from her blocked doorway, Pernie and Lork emerged, fully dressed and ready to greet the public. Wakan was desperately trying to get her attention to tell her something, but Pernie sternly motioned him to stay behind her back. Lork followed behind the crestfallen Kech, as Pernie led the procession of handmaids and guards to her throne room. Her little lover, Thist, looking dejected, stood at attention as the Mother and those trailing her entered and took their places, all standing. Only Pernie ever sat in this room, and then only on the blue stone throne situated on its raised dais.

As Pernie made herself comfortable on the throne, she looked around the room, assessing the states of her court. *Thist is here, and so is Wakan. Good! They need to hear me now. When little Thusk awakens, he will have to know, too.* She felt a slight twinge of guilt in changing companions, lovers, but *As Mother, I have the right to choose whomever I want. And should I tire of Lork, then I may have my little men come to visit occasionally. But for now, Lork is most satisfactory!*

Speaking in the authoritative voice that Wakan had

coached her in, Pernie said, "All you present here, be it known that as your Mother, I have obligations to our Motherland. Among these are the defense of our nation, the protection of its citizens, and the perpetuation of our commerce and trade.

"Be it known that as of this day, Captain Lork is made a citizen of our nation, as is the godsmetal smith, Zeerance Kleete."

Still devastated by Thusk's death, Thist was at first numb to Pernie's announcement. As it sank in, it appeared to him that Pernie was issuing him a challenge of some kind. From her open invitation to the Na Saamese captain at the welcoming feast two nights before to stay in her chambers, the general had known that he and his twin were no longer her favorites. Ever since then he had been thinking, *Why is Pernie acting this way? Did I do something wrong?* He had contemplated asking her those questions in private, but not dared interrupt her new dalliance with the icer pirate; the remembered threat of a Mother's irrationality kept him quiet, if disturbed. He knew that, regardless of the twins' service to Motherland in wars, and to Pernie in bed, their very lives were forfeit at any time she should so decide; even their friend Wakan could not countermand a Mother's orders. *Motherland has not yet become the nation of laws that Wakan is hoping for,* Thist realized. *Far from it!*

And finally, Thist recognized, as he was sure that Pernie did, that with their Una unable to fly, the twins were effectively trapped in Motherland. Even horse relays, should they try, would not save them from the very systems they themselves had established in their adopted land. So without expression and with disappearing hope, Thist stood silently, awaiting whatever fate Mother Perneptheranam might declare.

"I HAVE FURTHERMORE DECLARED THAT CAPTAIN LORK shall be promoted to the new position of Admiral of the

Fleet." Looking around at her advisor and the general from the Dark Highlands, Pernie smiled. "Admiral Lork will be of equal rank with General Thist." At which, she observed with satisfaction, the little man flinched. "The Admiral will have as his responsibility the design and construction of a fleet of naval vessels, ships capable of transporting both soldiers and war machines to the Lordship Isles and other pirate dens that infest the Cold Sea over the horizon. We will no longer have to suffer piratical raids against our WaterEdge."

At that unexpected condemnation of piracy, Thist noticed Lork's sudden forced grin. *Pirates to fight pirates?* he sniffed. *Ironic!* Already he was trying to think of ways to counteract Lork's new position; sharing military command was never feasible; his study of Una's ancient warfare archives proved that over and over again.

Gazing at Thist, Wakan, Lork and her guards, Pernie declared, "To prevent any further depredations, Motherland shall annex all of the islands that our Una machine recently flew over. Peaceful terms will be offered to any inhabitants, generous agreements with all the benefits accruing to our other citizens. Admiral Lork will ensure that, should our peaceful overtures be rebuffed, appropriate military action will be taken to force compliance.

"I expect all of the Sisterdoms and republics of Motherland to fully support this national effort. To that end I shall transmit the necessary financial and manpower requisitions to each Sister and Governing Council." She motioned to Wakan. "You may admit the representatives now. They will need to take back the appropriate documents to begin the mobilization efforts in each of their domains."

After court business was finished, Pernie wanted Wakan and Thist to leave with the rest of the attendees; she didn't feel a need to explain her provocative actions to either of her advisors. *And most certainly I will not listen to any objections about Lork from either of them!* But because she had never seen either of them looking quite so despondent, she invited them to her chambers to discover their concerns, motioning Lork to remain outside.

Lork nodded, apparently understanding Mother Pernie's need to assuage the suspicions and possible antagonism arising from her pronouncements of his promotion, the new taxes, and possible wars on the sea. Thinking of his rapid advancement in ancient Motherland, the pirate could not help but grin. *I am glad we shot down that big green bug. If it could still fly, I'd still be just a thief skating on the Ice Sea. But now? Now, I've got entrée into a whole country, and more wealth than all of Na Saam combined!*

CHAPTER FORTY-ONE

Dismissing her guards with a wave, Mother Pernie sat on a divan and invited Wakan and Thist to sit opposite her. "So what were you wanting to say, Wakan, even before we had court? Something that couldn't wait until I had made my most important announcements? About Lork and Kleete, and my plans for a navy and taking those islands you, Thist, discovered on the Cold Sea?" She wanted their support on these new ventures, the first expansion of Motherland in over a century. But supportive or not, she would have their compliance, their work, to make it a reality.

Holding up a hand, Pernie continued, "Before you object to those decisions, remember that I, and I alone, have the power to so decide and so order. I value the opinions of you both but by now I know you well enough to understand your reluctance. It is so noted, so there is no need to state it. Now, what *other* urgent matter did you want to bring to me? Thist?" She picked up a handful of grapes and nibbled on them as Thist stood up before her and bowed.

"Mother Perneptheranam," he said, tears in his eyes "My twin, Thusk, is dead."

Pernie dropped the grapes from her hand, put the hand to her mouth, and moaned. "Thusk, my little Thusk? But, but, Fyth and his fellow healers thought he would recover! What happened to him? This is terrible!"

The shock of the news brought not only tears to her eyes, but an instant flash of anger. Anger at Lork's shooting down of Una, even if it was an error; anger with herself for suddenly thinking of revenge against the very man whom she had just promoted to a stellar position in her government. Then anger at her healers and anybody else who had misled her about Thusk's condition.

"I can't believe my little man is gone!" she sobbed. Gathering her composure, she asked, "What exactly happened? Who is to blame, other than—" She didn't finish the question.

Thist interrupted. "I hate to say it, but *I* did, Pernie. I placed Thusk on the Crystal Throne, hoping that the journey to that Mienne on the Moon, then back here, would bring him back to us. I am so sorry."

As Pernie's eyes widened and her mouth opened, Wakan jumped up to defend Thist. "Pernie, Thist had my blessing to try. On his last visit to that Mienne, Thusk awoke in a body—an artificial one—up there. It seemed to us that Thusk might awaken up there and then be able to return here, but awake and in good health." Spreading his arms wide while bowing deeply, he said, "I am just so sad to say that Thusk's body died on your throne."

Standing now, Pernie was numb, barely able to speak. "You mean, both of you, you put my injured little Thusk on the Crystal Throne—*my* throne!—and he died there? Without my knowledge, without my permission? And he *died*?" Turning toward the door she shouted, "Guards! Guards!" As the four large guardsmen burst in, spears ready, Pernie said with a snarl, "Get them out of here. Throw the little one into the dungeon! The big one is to stay in his quarters! He is forbidden to approach me anymore!"

Thist and Wakan stood astonished, offering no resistance as they were roughly ejected from Pernie's quarters. As they were escorted brusquely down the hallway, a bemused Lork nodded at them, wondering what Pernie was up to now. Walking through her open door, he saw the Mother bent over, crying, and rushed to her side.

"What happened, dearest Pernie," he asked, pulling her to him. "What did those two *do* to you?" He was hoping it was something unforgivable; he had been concerned with their influence over the powerful young woman, and plotting ways to push them aside. Or worse.

Pernie gasped for breath, gulping. "They—he, Thist —*killed* my little Thusk. On my throne! He was in a coma after, after—*you!*—shot down that Una." Lork was taken aback at the news, and upset by Pernie's glare. But then she hugged him and said, "I know it was an accident, that you would never harm a little man like him. But his own twin, that Thist, he gambled with his twin's life. And lost! He *killed* him!"

Pernie continued sobbing as Lork led her to the divan and poured her a large cup of wine. He knew his presence would be of great value to Pernie in this time of grief and stress. And of great value to himself as well. *So my main opponents—the weird Kech and his two dark dwarves—are out of the way now, through no doing of my own.* As the ruler of Motherland continued uncontrolled sobbing in his arms, he thought, *I think Pernie and I will make a great team.* In his mind he could see himself seated on a throne next to the Mother, an absolute monarch in his own right. *Maybe as the Father of this country? Of Fatherland? Whatever happens after today, this so-called Motherland will never be the same!*

CHAPTER FORTY-TWO

As he sat in his quarters, restricted to house arrest by armed guard from leaving per Pernie's hasty order, Wakan Kech was still stunned at the Mother's action; he had never known her to be quite so precipitous in her actions. *I didn't know she held Thusk in quite so much affection*, he mused as he sat locked in his quarters. *I had no idea she would be so, so, emotional about his death. I know he was her lover, as was his twin, Thist, but to throw* me *into limbo, and Thist into the dungeon, that was quite unexpected. I really hoped that her new lover, Lork, would absorb much of her hormonal outbursts, temper her temper so to speak. But he seems to have encouraged her recklessness.*

This was just the latest and most egregious episode in Pernie's erratic behavior lately; Wakan was worried further about her increasing instability. Her plan for a Motherland Navy was something that was rational for a monarch, if not truly necessary for the country. But the goal of conquering all those islands in the Cold Sea, that was not the proper direction for an assembly of republics to be heading. *I need to head off those war plans*, he concluded. *But first, first, I must heal this rift over Thusk's death.* Thinking over that disaster, he said aloud, "What happened to that Mienne up there? Why couldn't Una contact her? Was that other throne even working? Was that the problem?"

AFTER A WEEK, WAKAN WAS RELEASED FROM HIS HOUSE arrest and told to appear before the Mother in her quarters. Arriving as ordered, he was not happy to see the pirate, Lork, standing close to Pernie's chair, his face diffident, as if he were in charge. *Is he?* Wakan wondered. *Do I have to fight this foreigner now, for Pernie's attention?* He knew that Pernie was overly bound to her hormones, but surely she was still rational? "Mother Perneptheranam," he said, pointedly ignoring Lork, "I am at your service."

Pernie motioned for Wakan to sit opposite her, in a plush padded chair. "Wakan, dear Wakan, I am rather, er, *ashamed* that my sudden sorrow over the shock of Thusk's death has inconvenienced you. Not to worry, I realize now that you were only aiding Thist in his, his, ill-fated attempt to save the life of his twin." She picked up a paper document and read from it. "Healer Fyth tells me here that Thist was indeed trying a possible remedy for Thusk's brain damage, that Thusk could have died at any moment otherwise, that he and all his healers could do no more." Taking another document, she handed it to Wakan, a sad look on her face

Pernie said, "According to our customs, little Thusk's body was publicly cremated four days ago, with high honors, with my full court of nobles and ambassadors in attendance." Stunned but without displaying emotion, Wakan said nothing but thought, *Poor Thist will be further destroyed by that. Not even being given the decency to attend his twin's cremation ceremony! What is wrong with Pernie?* A quick glimpse of Lork's smirk gave him the answer. *I will have real trouble with this criminal,* he thought. *He has too much control over Pernie.*

Turning to Lork, who handed her a polished golden urn, six inches high, she said, "Here are Thusk's ashes.

You may give them to Thist to do with as he sees fit. Because our Una machine is no longer flying, there will be no convenient way for him to return them to their cold homeland in the Dark Highlands. Perhaps he will dispose of them elsewhere, or keep them himself. That is his concern."

Wakan stood, bowed, and received the golden urn. "May I ask, Mother, what is to happen with General Thist?" He noticed a slight sneer on Lork's face, which he ignored.

Pernie nodded quietly, as if in thought. "Wakan, Thist is too valuable to Motherland for me to punish him. He alone has the experience, now, of fighting in three rebellions. And as you yourself have said, your informants throughout the Sisterdoms tell of rumblings of resistance to our original plans to convert them to republics." She sighed. "Even the citizens who stand to gain more freedom, seem to prefer not to change. That, I don't understand. But, as you know, I had already decided to slow down our revolution. No more new republics for now, not until ShadowFall and WaterEdge show they can succeed. As you have often told me, Wakan, sometimes experiments fail. We must learn from those failures, as you also taught. One thing I have learned is that I need more control over the emerging republics, so I have appointed a director for ShadowFall, in fact. You know him, Awhalpa Kech. He now reports directly to me, and has the power to overrule the Governing Council there. Only until they learn to control themselves, of course.

"As for Thist, the guilt he feels for killing his twin is punishment enough. However"—with this she looked directly at Lork—"His rank will be diminished; I can no longer rely upon his good judgment. Lork, here, as admiral of the Motherland Navy, will be my supreme military commander, and his navy will be the main force, operating in the Cold Sea. *Colonel* Thist"—she stressed that title—"will still command the Mothersmen, but they will become primarily a police force to contain rebellion, with equal numbers of troops maintained in each Sisterdom and republic, at the expense of each of them. Motherland has no land enemies, and I don't plan any further military incursions into the Southern Highlands. At least, not soon. Creesile pacified those quite well, back in our Lordess Mother's time."

Wakan well remembered one of Creesile's "incursions," namely the one that had captured himself and two dozen other Kech priests in those Southern Highlands as they were investigating a stepped pyramid covered with a transparent dome there. *Over twenty-two years now,* he thought. *Twenty-two years; close to half of my life, as a captive of Motherland, serving first the Lordess Mother—Noomeet was her name—and now Mother Pernie. It hasn't been all that bad, being a chief advisor and sometime lover to the Lordess, and a lifetime friend and...mentor...to Pernie, but none of it was my choice. I wonder what life would have been like if Creesile hadn't been on an "incursion" that day?*

At that rare question, Wakan surprised himself. He seldom ever thought of his previous life in his homeland, the High Antis, where he had been a notable young priest and accomplished athlete, destined to sit on the High Council and reap the rewards in prestige and knowledge that accrued to outstanding achievers. *But Creesile's massacre of our guards and enslaving of the rest of us changed all our lives, for the rest of our lives. Would I return home if I could?* The heretical thoughts continued, to his dismay. *But now that the Una can't fly anymore, I wouldn't have a way to get there. It's thousands of kilometers of western desert and jungle just to get to the Warm Sea, and then a sea voyage thousands more to south. I can't travel to the sea that far on foot, and would have no sailing vessel if I did. I'll never see home again, so I must forget about it!*

Pernie was not aware, of course, of her high priest's internal deliberations, taking his statement of agreement for business as usual. Wakan knew now that her education in human relationships—*Which I taught her!* —was lacking. *Or else she would surmise what I'm thinking. She needs more cynicism, more distrust, in her makeup. I failed her.* But at the moment, he was grateful that she was still young and inexperienced. He still had hope for his Pernie; without an enlightened Mother, Motherland would be doomed to more decades of war and cruelty.

Pernie simply said, "You may go and have Thist released from his cell. Pass on my concern for his welfare, and tell him of his new rank and duties as colonel of the new police force. And that he will move out of my palace and into one of the outer buildings where he may establish his new police headquarters." Thin-lipped and frowning, she added, "There will no apologies for his treatment. Accidental or not, he still killed little Thusk." With that, Wakan took his leave, bowing and departing without so much as a glance at the smirking pirate who bent over Pernie and embraced her.

WAKAN FOUND THIST IN A SULLEN MOOD AS THE GUARD opened his creaking cell door, at which a fetid odor of mold and sweat assaulted his nostrils. Wakan was taken aback at the dark and filthy conditions Thist had been relegated to during his imprisonment. The stench of the moldy stone walls and of Thist's unwashed body nearly gagged him, so he told the guard to leave the door open. Thist refused to stand as the Kech entered, remaining seated cross-legged on the simple bare cot. A squat, three-legged wooden stool, a washbasin of dirty water, and a toilet hole in the grimy stone floor were the only other furnishings.

"Hello, Wakan," Thist grunted, his face bruised and scarred, his grimy tunic torn and bloodstained. "Have you come to escort me to my execution?"

Astonished at Thist's appearance, Wakan said, angrily, "Have they beaten you? Tortured you? I will have somebody's head and guts for this!"

Thist laughed sarcastically. "When the Mother orders somebody thrown into the dungeon, these cretins"—he pointed to the guards standing outside the cell door—"they take it literally. It was only through the interdiction of some of my loyal troops that these guys didn't beat me to death." Wakan had heard rumors of jealous tensions between regular palace guards and Mothersmen, but hadn't realized it could be a matter of life and death.

Over the objections of the guards, now that the stench of the air was somewhat lessened, Wakan shut the door behind him, giving the two men privacy. "Thist," he whispered. "I will get the names of those who mistreated you. If you want to watch the effects of the death-herb on them, be my guest." He waved toward the door. "But now, I'm here to tell you that Pernie has pardoned you. Me, too. She apologized to me after Healer Fyth told her that you had only meant the best when you tried to cure Thusk by using the Crystal Throne."

Hearing that, Thist relaxed a bit. "That's good to hear, Wakan. Thank you. But *I* killed Thusk, and I wish I could pardon myself for that, but I never will." Staring at the urn Wakan held in one hand, he said, "But you are carrying something. Is that for me?" When he saw the priest's pained reaction, he took in a breath then gasped. "Please don't tell me. Is that—?"

Wakan nodded and handed the urn to Thist. "Four days ago. An honorable immolation, with full Motherland honors. I am so sorry."

Thist held back tears, gritting his teeth and holding the urn tightly to his chest with both hands. After a minute of silence, he said in a whisper, "Wakan. This was unforgivable. Poor Thusk, cremated without me or you there, his only family or his closest friend. What has happened to our Pernie? This"—he held the urn out at arm's length—"this hurts as much as it did when he died on the Crystal Throne. When I killed him."

In an unexpected gesture, Wakan leaned over and embraced his little friend, tears in his eyes. "She has been spiraling out of control, Thist. First, the extermination of that rebel Sisterhood and her treatment of the survivors." Thist shuddered; he had been complicit in that atrocity. Wakan acknowledged Thist's guilt with a sympathetic nod.

"Then her plans for a navy we don't need, the promotion of that ice pirate, and her plans to invade the Cold Sea islands. And now, her treatment of you and me. Between us, Lork has only accelerated the deterioration I've seen since we moved into the palace here. Genetics, it might be. I thought it was only the Crystal Throne, but it's more than that. I don't know exactly what, but that Lork is making it worse."

Thist said nothing, only caressed his twin's urn slowly, moving his lips as if talking to him. "So what now, Wakan? What will she do with me? *To* me?"

Wakan sighed. "Unfortunately, there is more."

AFTER THE KECH FINISHED WITH THE NEWS OF THIST'S new assignment and demotion, the ex-general said, "Wakan, I don't think I am welcome any more in Motherland. I hate to think of leaving, but I don't approve of aggressive conquests. If I had known about Pernie's intentions, we would never have taken Una out to find those islands in the first place. That order to find Altamun Kech and punish the pirate Noor was only a pretext. And knowing what we do about that ice pirate, Lork, all of us—and Motherland—would have been better off if we hadn't gone out there."

He set the urn of Thusk's ashes down on the floor beside his cot and looked up at the priest. "I saw what happy people look like, Wakan, in that pirate Noor's town, of all places. Singing, music, smiles, food, drink. Pleasant people just satisfied to be living in a beautiful place. I don't approve of their way of making a living, but then there's a lot about Motherland I don't approve of either.

"I was thinking I'd like to live there in Noorstown, have a sailboat on that beautiful clear sea. Learn to smile again. But if Pernie has a navy, that Lork could find me when they invade. I hate to think of what I've brought upon those island people." He pointed at the urn again. "So I can't go live there, or bury Thusk's ashes there. But I can go home, back to The People's Lands, and carry Thusk with me. I will put this urn in the deepest crevasse I can find in The Ice at the End of the World."

Stroking the urn softly, he said aloud, "Back where our adventure began, back in another world, another time, Thusk. Where we should never have left." Wakan felt Thist's sadness, saw the grim look of determination accentuating his vow to his lost twin.

Leaving the malodorous cell, Wakan escorted Thist past the guards and to his own quarters many levels up from the dungeons. "I've sent for your clothes, Thist. Until the staff has arranged your new rooms in the outside building, you can stay here with me. But once you've bathed and had your wounds tended to, I want us to go talk with Una. I want to find out what she can tell us about Thusk on the throne, what may have happened. Since you were locked up, no one has been able to get inside her. But I still worry that Lork may try some subterfuge to gain access to all of the archives, the knowledge that only Una contains. I do know that he and his men have tried to get the godspheres to work, but fortunately for us, that hasn't happened."

"I need to talk to Una, too, Wakan," Thist said softly.

CHAPTER FORTY-THREE

E arly one morning, three dozen travelers, all PeoplesLandsers, arrived at Odel's Quarry. Well-dressed for the trek they had just completed, the small men and women were also well-armed, and the wheeled sleds they pulled were still stocked with provisions. *These people planned ahead*, Odel thought. *Smart ones. I hope they are come to stay.*

Odel and Mox and their standard coterie of springbowmen welcomed the group. "You're at Odel's Quarry, my friends!" the big man bellowed. "Welcome and stay awhile."

After introductions, all of the newcomers and the guards sat for an early morning meal. The leader of the group, Exorder, a very muscular little man in loose buckskin clothing, said, "We have come from CliffEdge, seeking a better life here. Followed the maps you left and the stone markers along the way. Couple weeks trekking. You mentioned land claims and such?"

"Yes," Odel said, sipping chai, "but has not CliffEdge plenty of land? And a little warmer climate than here up north?"

Exorder looked around the long table at the faces of his group. "You ask anybody here, Odel, what they think's gonna happen at CliffEdge. Or at M'ridge Station." The man's face grew grim. "Or down at Thess

City. Don't even ask about ShadowFall or those Originals."

Of course, Odel did ask. And Exorder explained, "Mother Pernie has put a director in charge of all of ShadowFall. A dictator, one Awhalpa Kech, late of WaterEdge. He has an iron fist over the palace and the people there. And the situation with Thessland gets worse by the day. The Originals keep moving in on our land grants, but that director won't stop them. Took over some of our fields all ready to harvest, drove off our farmers.

"We are afraid that the whole Mothersman army might show up any day and take over all of Thessland, then grab the Odel Elevator and try to come up and invade us. And"—he looked straight up at Odel—"those tri-wings you invented, the Mothersmen aerial force might use them to fly up and attack us. Some of our people have seen them practicing over at ShadowFall. There are no other enemies around, so they must be planning against us at CliffEdge."

Odel, Mox, and the others of his quarry crew just sat in astonishment. All of Odel's fears were coming true. *That damned Lork's behind this, I'll bet. Wants to plunder the whole round world!*

Exorder continued, "So some of us came to see you. If we can get land up here, and make a living somehow —farming, mining, quarrying—then much of CliffEdge and probably the Downsiders, too, would emigrate. It is a tiring and wearying situation, all of this moving, but we do not want to fight any more wars. In fact, if Thusk would ever return in that Una machine, we'd like to ask him for rides back home to The People's Lands." Around the table, all of the new people were nodding and loudly agreeing. Exorder waved his hand at them. "You see, every one of them would gladly exchange this warmth and greenery and these clear skies for the safety and security of The People's Lands, be they ever so cold and overcast."

Odel asked the visitors to stay; accommodations would be provided. In his mind he was reviewing defensive measures that CliffEdge could take to ward off a Motherland invasion. *Bring up the elevator and the godscloth. Burn down the launch tower. But transporting up another thousand people first? Where would they go, how would they be fed?*

Though he loved Mox and warmly regarded his friends Thist and Thusk, Odel began to wish he had never gone down to Motherland. *You never think your problems, your responsibilities, could get any worse. But they always can!*

CHAPTER FORTY-FOUR

I n the hot and humid still air of afternoon, made more uncomfortable by the odor of stagnant water in a nearby decorative pond, the fountain of which was no longer working, Thist and Wakan made their way to Una, still parked in the same open storage field where she had been stored since returning from the Cold Sea. Thist recalled, *After we were shot down over Stonehaven, damn Lork!*

As he and Wakan approached Una, Thist gave the verbal command that opened Una's access door. He was pleasantly surprised that Una maintained a cool, dry, and odor-free cabin volume; after a week's imprisonment in a slimy stone cell, he was glad to be back in a comfortable and familiar environment. *If only she could still fly,* he thought, *I'd go back home today!*

"Welcome, Thist. Welcome, Wakan Kech. What brings you here?"

"Una, can you communicate with that Mienne, on the Moon?" Thist asked as the men sat in the cabin, watching the Anklya-image speaking to them. "And can you tell us anything about what happened when I placed Thusk on Mother's Crystal Throne?"

"Thist, the answers are *Yes* and *Yes*. Let me elaborate."

Thist was again pleased with Una; now she was anticipating his needs and not being so literal about it.

"Please do, Una. In as much detail as you think we need."

"The first answer is, now, *Yes*. Mienne has been out of touch for weeks now. I was unable to communicate. However, I now sense that she is near the qomp receiver there, so that contact is now possible.

"The second answer is also *Yes*. Because Mienne was not near the receiving qomp terminal, the quantum transfer of Thusk from the Crystal Throne transmitter to that chair receiver site did not occur. For mind-to-mind communication, qomp protocols require a human presence at the receiver."

Thist interrupted Una's explanation. "But Thusk told me that on his last visit he woke up in an artificial body. Why didn't that happen this time? Why did he die?"

Una did not answer immediately, causing Thist and Wakan to look at each other, puzzled. Knowing that the DI qomp system processed information millions of times faster than humans, this was the equivalent of years of a human's thinking. Obviously Una was considering some action she was unsure of.

But before Thist could ask, Una said, "Thist, Thusk now occupies that same avatarobot body on the Moon. He is alive, there."

Stunned, Thist sat back in his seat, mouth open, trying to absorb the incredible fact. Wakan, too, could not speak. But Una went on. "When Thusk's unconscious body was placed on the Crystal Throne, the qomp communication system attempted to effect the transfer, but no operator was in or adjacent to the receiving chair for the mind-to-mind connection. Nor was an avatarobot nearby to function as a receiver. But the qomp system scanned for the presence of an artificial body at the receiving end. One was detected at another location deep within the complex there, down inside a tunnel installation. So the transfer occurred with that one instead.

"Thusk now inhabits the same artificial body he once did. Would you like to attempt communication with him now? I can do that."

"Please do, Una," Thist choked out, "please do?" As he waited for that impossible conversation, he said to Wakan, "How is this possible? Why didn't we know? And"—pointing to the golden urn of Thusk's ashes—"how is this even possible?" Wakan just shook his head, still in shock at the incredible conversation he'd just heard. *The ancients' technologies were too close to magic,* he realized. *I will never understand them!*

The image on Una's front cabin screen slowly dissolved, Anklya being replaced by a realistic representation of Thusk, but much taller and now clothed in a skintight shimmering shirt and shorts of some metallic-appearing material, unlike godscloth. The image spoke, "Thist, Wakan, are you there? Can you see me? Hear me?"

Thist fell to his knees, weeping tearlessly. "Thusk, oh, Thusk. I am so sorry, I thought I had killed you, but here you are. Where are you? How are you? Oh, I am so happy to see you alive. You don't know how much I have suffered since you…died…on the Crystal Throne. Or, I thought you had."

Thusk talked over his twin. "Thist, Thist, somehow I woke up in this avvy body, here on the Moon. I am with Mienne, I am safe. But what happened? The last thing I remember is flying over those iceboats in Una, over that cold town. I fell, then blacked out, I guess. Did we hit that big spire? And what do you mean, I died? What happened?"

Seeing Thist unable to speak, Wakan said, "Thusk, please sit down. I think you had rather hear everything from me. I'm not sure how you will take this." And the Kech related, one step at a time, how Thusk had suffered a concussion when Una was shot down, how Thist had cared for him for long weeks, seeing that he was comfortable and attended to during the trip over the Ice Sea, down to the Cold Sea, on to Motherland, and thence to Mother's Palace.

"Where your comatose condition continued," Wakan explained. "The healers said that your blood clots could kill you at any moment, so Thist, with my blessing, put you atop the Crystal Throne in hopes that going up to Moon might awaken you, then bringing you back to Earth might stimulate your system back to consciousness." Breathing hard, he said, "And in a way it did." His voice lowered. "In a way."

Thusk said from the screen image, "Well, I'm here now, awake, feeling fine. No coma, no head injury. Has my body healed since then, in the time I've been here?"

Wakan looked at Thist, who picked up the golden urn to be visible to the screen. "Twin, we thought you were dead. Your body had no life, no pulse, no nothing. Even Healer Fyth found no trace of any living function."

"What? But here I am, alive as anything." Then, suspiciously: "What has happened with my body then, my Earth body?"

Thist held up the urn. "Pernie had it immolated, formally and with high honors, four days ago."

On the Moon, Thusk collapsed.

"So that was what I felt when I woke up, Mienne," Thusk said, trembling, moments later as he regained consciousness. "My body up there on Earth died, but I was here, in this, this, avvy."

"Thusk, my love," Mienne said, holding him in her arms as he lay on the couch. "I would never have met you in that body. This one is all I have ever known, but I was in love with you when our minds met and mixed, all those times before that."

"I know, but I feel strange, even strange now that I know I died up *there*." He shuddered, still not believing that his other body was now just ashes in a golden urn. *But I feel so alive!*

Mienne said, "Our DI here says that the qomp system scans your entire physical body and transfers all of its electromagnetic and other fields to this avvy; it uses *holistic entanglement at the quantum level,* whatever all that means. So I guess you existed in two places at once. But now, you're just here. I don't understand it either, but I am so, so happy that if you had to choose one place or the other, you came to me."

Thusk sat up, trying to absorb the unbelievable information. *But it wasn't really a choice, was it? Here I am, now stuck in a body I wasn't born with, in a world I wasn't born on, in love with a young woman living inside the Moon.* Running his new hands over his new body again, he thought, *Well, I'm a different color now, taller, and Mienne says this body might even last forever. She says it has some differences from the usual human body, but last time I was here, we proved that it felt normal during our intimacy. I certainly enjoyed it!* He knew it would take getting used to, but was glad he'd had the previous experience living in it. *But that was only for a few days, just an interesting episode, I thought at the time. Now it's a lifetime thing!* On an even more somber note, he said aloud, "I suppose I won't be going home."

AFTER THUSK RECOVERED AND RETURNED TO THE conversation a few minutes later, the twins chatted nervously, Thist quickly skipping over Lork's journey to Motherland and the changes in Pernie since. He sensed that such matters were unimportant to Thusk at the moment; what more could either one say after "I killed you?" and "No, I'm alive in a robot body on the Moon"? Wakan quietly suggested that the conversation resume at a later time. Promising to talk again later, the twins finally said goodbye, with Wakan feeling foolish at waving at the fading screen image of Thusk. "Your twin took that much better than I expected, Thist. I'm not sure I could be so accepting of the fact that my body was gone."

Thist just nodded, feeling mixed emotions of joyful surprise and residual grief. "No more surprised than I am, Wakan. I wonder if I'll ever seen him again in the flesh." With an odd look at the fading screen, he said, "Or in that new body of his." Looking for further validation, forgiveness even, of his action with Thusk on the Crystal Throne, he told Wakan that they had probably saved Thusk's life with the Crystal Throne, but had doomed him to a life off of Earth. "Or is *doomed* the right word?" he asked Wakan. "Maybe *blessed* is better? The way things are going with Pernie and Lork, I just might like to *escape* to the Moon myself." The priest just laughed. And frowned.

"So what do we tell Pernie?" Thist asked later as he and Wakan relaxed in the police colonel's modest quarters in a not-so-lavish white stone building located some hundred meters from Mother's Palace. "Will a living Thusk on the Moon, in an artificial body, be enough to get her to forgive me completely?"

Wakan shook his head. "Thist, I don't think we should tell her anything at all. Una is the only way she can communicate with either Thusk or that Mienne up there. As long as you forbid Una to qomp them, nobody else need ever know about his new life."

Thist held up a forefinger. "But Wakan. The Crystal Throne has that capability. If Pernie sits on it again, she may talk to either of them up there."

"That's what I want to talk to you about, Thist," the priest said, puffing a column of white smoke up from the bowl of his pipe. "Do you think Una can shut down the Crystal Throne? I mean, completely fix it so that it can never communicate again? And all of the godspheres too? Because that's what I have in mind."

CHAPTER FORTY-FIVE

The noonday sun was brutal, the blue sky a cloudless dome, as Mother Perneptheranam sat under a shading canopy with Commander in Chief Admiral Lork and Chief Engineer Kleete on her right side and her chief priest, Wakan Kech, and Police Colonel Thist on the left. Below them, down in the same arena where two and a half years before, the dark little immigrant Thist had ridden his war-bird emus in a victorious battle for the Sisterdom of ShadowFall, strutted hundreds of blue-uniformed sailors of the new Motherland Navy.

I have spent five months away from Pernie, Thist thought, *and my first day back, Wakan drags me to this damned arena so Lork can rub my nose in his victory.* As the new Motherland Navy proudly paraded below the reviewing stand, Thist was not impressed. *Thirty months ago I was down there where Lork's sailors are now, but I was fighting for my life. On that day I won rewards for Princess Pernie.* An old pain electrified the stub of his left leg, a constant reminder of that battle. *And lost my damned foot!* He refused to review his memories of the last five months, time spread all over Motherland in every Sisterdom and republic, disbanding army regiments and re-forming them into local police forces, setting up strict chains of command.

The police were being funded and supported by each

individual region, but reported only to the Mother and her designates, bypassing any local controls. *Twelve new centers of control for Pernie and Lork,* Thist's rebellious mind called out to him. *Trained by me to seize control, assassinate any officials or rebels without warrants or warning. A secret police,* he reminded himself. *As directed by Pernie with Lork's manipulation. I watched some of Una's historical archives on that kind of police. They never end well, but I am only following orders. Orders I hate.*

As the Mother and her advisors looked over the panoply of activity in the arena, the new recruits maneuvered in formation, even pulling a hollow, lightweight, full-sized sea-ship replica representing the navy that was under construction and nearing completion hundreds of kilometers to the east at the harbor of WaterEdge.

Beaming with pride, the extravagantly uniformed C-i-C, Admiral Lork, his blue jacket bedecked with gold braid as based on Thist's descriptions of Una's videos of ancient naval officers, leaned over to the Mother. "Pernie, this is just the beginning. In just five months we have recruited the best sailors from the offshore fishing boats, and have retrained my own icers—who every one, opted to stay rather than return to Na Saam—to sail on liquid water instead of the frozen kind. And with the shipbuilding information that came from that Una's archives, we have two dozen fighting ships under construction, nearly complete. They will be ready to sail this month. We should be able to, to, *visit* all of those islands in the Cold Sea by the end of the year."

Pernie nodded, shielding her eyes from the bright sun and occasionally waving her approval to the resplendent displays below. "Very well. I take it you shall soon travel to WaterEdge and take command?"

As Admiral Lork nodded, a contingent of sailors pulled a tarp-covered, catapult-like contraption in front of her, and stopped, saluting. Lork said, "Now watch what my genius, Kleete, has built for us. First, look at the target at the far end of our arena." Some two hundred meters away stood a wall of gray stone blocks, measuring about ten meters high by fifty wide.

Wakan whispered to Thist, "He's going to hit *that*? I can't believe anything could reach that far, much less do any damage." But Thist was horrified; he had seen many scenes of ancient warfare, and at once realized what Kleete had done. Thist had specifically forbidden Una to share any of those secrets of ancient warfare with anyone but himself. How had these pirates done it?

Lork said loudly, so that all could hear, "Your old friend, the traitor and absconder Odel M'ridge, used his firepowder rockets to boost himself high up in the air. Abandoned us, flying over the Dark Highlands cliffs that way." Wakan was still puzzled, but Thist groaned inwardly. He knew what was coming.

"But Kleete, here, studied those rockets, that firepowder, and found a much better use for it." Leaning over the wall, he waved to his crew. "Now, show us!" Standing next to Lork, Kleete was anxious and trembling. Thist was hoping the smith's weapon would fail; he dreaded loosing firepowder weapons on the world.

The sailors quickly removed the covering tarp, revealing a hollow iron cylinder, a little over two meters long and some twenty centimeters in diameter, mounted on a wheeled wooden carriage. As Pernie and her men looked on, the sailors picked up a packed cloth bag and prodded it down into the far end of the hollow cylinder. This was followed by the insertion of a heavy round black ball. Then the crew cranked a wheel and tilted the cylinder back at a forty-five-degree angle. "Launch!" Lork shouted. A sailor placed a flaming torch to the back end of the cylinder.

Boom! The sound came like an explosion, the wheeled carriage jerking back a meter or more, as a cloud of gray smoke covered the launching crew and the cylinder itself. Within seconds, the targeted stone wall exploded, large blocks of stone thrown in all directions. "Relaunch!" Lork shouted again, and within a minute, a second black ball sped toward the remaining portion of the target wall. Nothing was left standing. Clouds of acrid smoke drifted up to the viewing platform, causing Pernie and her companions to wipe their eyes of the irritating mist, coughing and waving their hands in front of their faces to clear the air.

Lork laughed. "That's the smell and the taste of *victory*, Mother! Your victories to come!"

Pernie stood up and clapped, hugging Lork, who was beaming. Kleete likewise held up his fists clasped together, shouting. "Hooray, boys, it worked! You did well!"

Wakan shook his head. "What was that, Thist? How did he—?"

But Thist was gritting his teeth. "It was called *gunpowder*, Wakan, for shooting projectiles, not just for Odel's rockets. A thing I never wanted Motherland to see." In his mind he envisioned the white-walled homes and buildings of the Lordship Islands being bombarded by Lork's iron balls. *Those beautiful cities, those wonderful people. All victims of Lork's aggression!* he agonized. *Pernie might just want those islands for more subjects, more taxes and trade, but that pirate, he is still only a murdering thief!*

Having been in enforced exile from Mother's Palace and Pernie's presence for the last months, Thist judged himself harshly for not keeping up with Lork's and Kleete's military developments. He had thought that Kleete would only be working out new harpoon developments and overseeing shipbuilding, the latter of which would be disastrous enough, in his mind. Ice ships and water ships were too different and the new navy would take years to build and train properly. Meanwhile, he had hoped, Pernie might come to her senses or Wakan might influence her to do something else. Or maybe Wakan would assassinate Lork and his smith. *He did an excellent job on those four guards who roughed me up,* he remembered. *It's funny how the week of shrieks of their death-herb poisoning don't bother my conscience nearly as much as the quick deaths of those men I killed in combat down here in this very arena.*

Again, his stubbed leg complained. Again, he ignored it.

Remembering the casual, joyous Noorstown in the Lordship Isles, Thist there and then determined he would somehow prevent Lork from the conquest and subjugation of that happy isle, pirates or not. "We have to talk, Wakan," Thist whispered to the priest. "This cannot be allowed."

"THIST, I CAN'T REMOVE LORK, THERE IS JUST NO WAY," Wakan Kech said as the two men walked from the Motherland Navy demonstrations toward the storage field where Una was stored. "I mean, it would not be difficult to arrange a poisoning or a dart in the dark, but two things stand in the way. First, Pernie would be devastated. Second, her fury, her revenge, would know no bounds. Innocents, not just us, would suffer."

Thist acknowledged those results. "But Lork and his icers *would* be out of the way. Surely you could convince her for the good of Motherland to hold off on invading the islands in the Cold Sea, maybe finance another project here at home instead? New canals and locks on Mother's River, paving the roads? Hel, maybe go exploring again for that domed pyramid you talked about down in the Southern Highlands, the one where Creesile captured you."

Wakan shook his head as they neared Una's location. "Going back to the first issue, Pernie would be in no shape to govern at all if you took away Lork. She has depended on him for every decision, every day, since you went out to set up that so-called 'police force.' We would be without effective leadership for who knows how long, and there is a danger in that. With the rumblings reported by my network of spies and informants in the Sisterdoms and the two republics, if Pernie were no longer in daily control, I am afraid even your police could not handle all the uprisings. There are already conspiracies afoot, allies plotting; assassinations would run rampant, even against the Mother. Secondly—" He stopped and looked down at Thist, staring at him intently. "Secondly, you and I would be the prime suspects in his murder, and rightly so. For myself, I do not wish to suffer firsthand the intimate knowledge of the effects of the death-herb. I am sure you do not, either. But I have assistants, unfortunately, who know how to extract and compound that fluid as well as I do." He sniffed. "And a few who probably wouldn't mind giving it to me, with Mother's approval and for their own promotion. Not all my Kech brethren are loyal, as you well know."

Thist smiled sardonically at Wakan's understatement; he himself had personally killed the one Kech, that Miran, the late Mother Messinex's corrupt priest, and his own Mothersmen had literally chopped down Loranthip Kech, the priest and lover of the defeated and deposed—and now blinded—Sister Sathronin, during the WaterEdge rebellion. And the Kech from WaterEdge, Awhalpa, reportedly enjoyed being the strongman in the Republic of ShadowFall, putting the name to shame. He wondered how such an intelligent and helpful Kech could turn out that way. *My answers are always the same, though aren't they?: power, greed, control!*

"So killing the pirate is out of the question, Wakan? If that is so, then I don't have a lot of choice. I think I want to leave Motherland and go back home. I don't believe that Lork could ever attack me there, not even with his gunpowder cylinders. Maybe if I'm gone, away from Pernie, no more a threat to him, he will ignore me and I can forget all of this." But Thist's face belied his speech; Wakan knew that his little friend would not lightly surrender all that he had accomplished in Motherland through sheer grit, guts, and intelligence. Both men were silent for a minute, each lost in his own thoughts.

"Pernie was lucky that you were her mentor, Wakan," said Thist, finally. "One of those other Kechs could have been really bad for her. And for Motherland."

"Thist, I am not certain now that raising Pernie as I did, promoting freedom and democracy for all, *was* the best for her *or* for Motherland. That system worked for us in the High Antis, but we were a different culture, a different people—a lot fewer people—with no tradition of an absolute monarchy. When Pernie tasted that kind of power here on the throne, able to direct who would live and who would die, when she could command prison or promotions and sentences and taxes and now, even wars, I am afraid she slowly succumbed to the temptation. She has told me as much in so many words, over the last half year or so. Those rebellious Sisters of hers, the birth pang problems in the ShadowFall Republic, the ongoing daily problems of maintaining a large and diverse country, they affected her greatly."

Thist said, "And I suppose that Odel's departure, the way he left, added to all of that?"

"It bothered her, yes, but mostly because it showed that even a solid man like Odel, strong-willed and a born leader, gave up trying to make ShadowFall a successful republic. And then he even gave up even attempting to make Thessland work, so he headed back to his home up in the Dark Highlands, to that God's Country where they tried to kill you. Odel's desertion during those troubles was just one more blow to the idealism that I inculcated in her during all her life." As they entered into Una's cabin, the priest's shoulders slumped. "I have failed her, and I have failed Motherland. Like you, Thist, I have begun to think of going back to my homeland." Looking around inside Una's cabin, he said, "If only she could still fly. If only."

Once seated, Thist asked Una to show him an aerial map of Motherland. "If I were to leave Mother's City, Una, say riding on an emu, a two-leg, how could I get back to my home? How long would it take me?"

As Una's digital display screen began to trace out a red line over the hundreds of kilometers to the Dark Highlands, Thist and Wakan paid close attention, Una even providing a block of information showing distance traveled, time durations, and alternate routes. Thist had worried about scaling those cliffs, but the display indicated that a lift of some kind now existed about eighty kilometers east of ShadowFall.

Thist inspected the screen closely. "Ten days of hard riding to Thessland, I see. But what is that about getting up the cliffs there? What is going on there?"

"Odel built that while you and Thusk were away on Una," Wakan said. "He constructed a tall tower—one of the kind they call a 'Wakan's Tower,' I might add"—he smiled at the dubious honor—"and flew from the top of that up over onto the highland plateau. He dropped down a godscloth line like you did when you first came to er, *visit,* ShadowFall. But this time it was to bring things *up*. His people built a pulley and an elevator. They have trade going now, both ways, up and down. Timber and fish and corn coming down, people and emus and lowland crops going up."

Thist laughed. "Well, there I was, a pioneer again. Back then I was escaping *downward* from the Priests' Men and their velks. If I go on Odel's elevator, it will mean I am escaping *upward*, from Motherland. From Lork. And from Pernie."

As Thist continued planning his return route, which would involve weeks of emu-riding and walking northward through unexplored territory, Wakan wondered if Una could show him something similar for himself; a path back to the High Antis? Did she have current geographic information? *But that can wait,* he thought. *I'm not through with Pernie yet. Or with that damned pirate!*

CHAPTER FORTY-SIX

Admiral Lork's departure ceremony was the most elaborate and colorful spectacle that Mother's City had ever witnessed: three hundred blue-uniformed sailors marching in step, springbows and spears glistening in the morning sun, dozens of wheeled gunpowder cylinders, polished and shining, with horse-drawn wagons and carriages carrying new officers and Lork himself. From a balcony of Mother's Palace, Mother Perneptheranam herself waved a godscloth streamer, cheering on her military commander and his new servicemen.

"Off to WaterEdge we march," the singing sailors chanted, in time with the beats of the kettle drums, punctuated by brass horn blasts. "And over the cold Cold Sea. There we'll crush the pirate isles. And fight for victory!" Even Wakan Kech was impressed as the chant continued, echoing from the walls of the boulevard as the procession diminished in the distance. What surprised him was the enthusiasm and patriotism of the happy, cheering crowds who joined in the chant. *These people want war,* he thought sadly, *and Lork knows how to glamorize it.* In memory he compared the pirate's entertaining parade to the total lack of celebrations when Thist had won three important battles for Pernie. *Thist won wars,* he thought, *and Lork only puts on a show!*

Standing beside the tall Kech, Police Colonel Thist, half his height, watched without comment as the naval parade turned a corner and was soon out of sight behind buildings in Mother's City. *With Lork gone,* he mused, *I have one more chance to persuade Pernie. If I can't, I am leaving for home.* But as the Mother turned to go back in her chambers, her guards blocked Thist's way. She didn't even look his way when he spoke out, "Mother! A moment, please!"

The big guard nearest him slammed a gloved fist into Thist's face, knocking him down. "Not speak to Mother! Leave now!"

Wakan Kech helped Thist up from the balcony's stone floor as the small man wiped blood from his nose with a sleeve. "I'm sorry, Thist. I thought you knew that Lork has left orders that you are not to speak to Pernie. These thugs"—he jerked his thumb toward the black-leather-vested guards who had already seen Pernie into her room and shut the massive door behind her—"report to him. Not to Pernie or to me. You have to stay away from her. You were only here by my invitation and authority, and I don't think Pernie even approved of me bringing you. She will never forgive you for killing Thusk."

Continuing to wipe blood from his nose, Thist cursed under his breath. "After all we've done for Pernie and Motherland, to be treated this way? Unforgiveable." Looking up at Wakan, he said, "That's it. I am going to work my plan. Today."

Wakan nodded. "I can't blame you, my friend. It is so sad, but we know that the pirate has totally enchanted her, warped her. We can only hope he does not return." The priest smiled a sardonic grin. "Of course we may not know for some time. He has a three-week slow march to WaterEdge. If he has a lot of battles out on the Cold Sea, he may never come back." He dared not tell Thist his plan for Lork's demise; he didn't want his friend to know anything. *Plausible denial, I think that ancient term was.*

Thist hesitated and did not speak, recognizing the

ominous nuance in Wakan's smile. *I don't care what Wakan has planned for Lork. Pernie has betrayed me more than once, and I'm leaving.*

Together the two men left the viewing balcony down a set of steps, the guards keeping a wary eye as they walked away.

As THE LARGE WHITE DOME OF MOTHER'S CITY —"Pernie's big tit!" Lork said to Kleete—disappeared over the horizon behind them, the admiral and chief engineer of the nascent Motherland Navy were enjoying a variety of honeyed wines in their horse-drawn carriage. Kleete coughed, waving a hand in front of his face, driving away dust that seeped through the drawn curtains. "Cap'n, once you get some power here in Motherland, you got to do something about these dusty damn roads. I mean, you and me, in this carriage and with the replacement horses, we got near on to six days on this gravel road. But all these wagons and marching sailors, it'll take them a couple weeks. I'll be surprised if they don't bust axles, or ankles."

"Kleete," said Lork, a little tipsy from the celebratory wine, "these ones behind us, they are just for show, you know. They'll be on guard duty when they get to WaterEdge, while we will be long gone. The mirror messages told me that our two dozen ships are ready now, over two thousand crewmen, just waiting for us to get to there and sail away. There was no reason to tell Pernie or her priest or that damned dwarf about our readiness."

Lork pounded on the padded cushions of their carriage. "So just sit back and enjoy it, we've earned it. Bumpy or not, this beats the Hel out of our damned iceboats. It's soft, and cool now that winter has come. And the food we have with us, well, nothing back home compares. And the women. I mean, *the* woman, that Pernie, well she is the best thing to happen to me—to *us* —ever." After another swig, he patted Kleete on the shoulder. "But me being on the way to sea again, even a melt sea, is good for a change. You know me, I've never had just one woman, every single day, for so many months. Kinda looking forward to what all's in those islands out there, you know. Sailing, fighting, treasure. New foods, new drinks. More women! Drink to it!"

Kleete joined in his boss's cheer. Good times were coming, for sure!

HALFWAY TO WATEREDGE ON THE ROAD FROM Mother's City, Kleete asked Lork, "Admiral, you think it was wise to leave that dwarf Thist and that Kech priest back there with your Pernie? Mightn't they flip her, take away your influence while we're gone?"

Lork shook his head. "Listen, Kleete, that priest has been with her all her life, taught her everything she thinks she knows. But she is just a girl, never had a real man in her life. Till me. Certainly not a Na Saamese man, just some feeble Motherlanders and those two dwarfs. And when I showed up, she couldn't get enough of me. Dropped them!

"She needed a strong man, like me, to straighten out her thinking. After a while, she started listening only to me, telling her the way the world really works, none of that crap that Kech was spewing, about giving up her power to commoners and all of that nonsense. And that runt, Thist, he was with her only a couple of years; he was a good fighter so I heard, and a good lay for a dwarf, so she suggested, but she gave him up right fast, too. You were there, you saw it. She fell for me like a trap door. So not to worry, friend. It also helps us that, being gone, I left strict instructions with my guards for the dwarf to be kept away from her, and her time with the Kech to be limited.

"Those palace guards are corruptible, and so are some of the Kech." Laughing, he clapped his hands. "You see, Kleete, us being away at sea gives Pernie no reason to think I had anything to do with it, when that

Thist and the priest both die unexpectedly." Lork went on to tell how a three-layer assassination plot would remove both of his adversaries while he was commanding the invasion fleet at sea. "One guard, hired by me, kills the two. A second guard, hired by a third, kills that one. And then the third guard takes that one out. He only knows he kills a nobody guard. Nobody left to trace it to me.

"So when we get back in a few months, there's Pernie waiting. No rivals around, just us with our victory and all the spoils. And somebody else hired to make the third guy disappear. All nicely tied up."

Kleete laughed and had another swig. *My Cap'n is a smart one*, he thought. *Nobody smarter!*

CHAPTER FORTY-SEVEN

Asleep in his quarters above the Motherland Police Force Headquarters, Police Colonel Thist tossed and turned, his dreams feverish and disturbing; scenes of torture, mutilation, sieges, battlefields strewn in blood and body parts. Jerking himself awake, he sat on his bed, shaking. "Maybe Wakan can give me a sleep potion," he whispered aloud. "I've got to get more rest. Because it is going to be a long ride when I—"

A sudden rustling noise outside his door caught his ear, and Thist quickly reached for his loaded springbow. Stealthily he crept from his bed to look through a mirrored surface; at the far side of that room was a dark shadow who raised a sword and brought it down hard on the covered figure that lay under the blanket. Dim light seeping in from the iron-barred window defined the silhouette of a large assailant, most likely a man.

"Die, you dark dwarf!" the black-suited swordsman yelled. "Admiral Lork sends you to Hel!"

From his hidden bedchamber, Thist loosed a springbow arrow through a loophole, catching the would-be assassin in the gut. "Ooof!" was the only cry Thist heard as he nocked another arrow. He hesitated, knowing that he himself would never send only one man to assassinate such an important figure as the famous and powerful colonel of the police force. An ancient refrain rang through his mind: "If you're going to kill the Mother, you'd better *kill* the Mother!" Thist's hesitation saved him; within a minute another figure crept silently into the faux bedchamber, a knife in each hand. Seeing his accomplice lying still at his feet, the man looked around, spinning on his heel, finding no one to fight. This assassin then stabbed at the covered figure on the bed, yelling, "Damned dwarf! Lork wants your head!"

Taking a leisurely aim, Thist shot him in the head. "I think I'll send both your heads to Lork, instead," he said, stepping out of the fake wall panel that hid his actual bedroom. "I'll see if Wakan can arrange it."

IN WAKAN'S QUARTERS THE NEXT MORNING, THE KECH was adamant. "No, Thist, I don't think it wise to apprise Lork of the unsuccessful attempt on your life. Let him believe you are gone." The priest lit up his long pipe and leaned back in his overstuffed leather chair, bringing his bare feet up on the covered footstool in front of him.

Thist grimaced at the unpleasant smoke clouds his Kech friend produced, but bore it in silence. "And why is that, Wakan? Don't we want to keep him off balance? Don't you think those two heads would do it?"

"No, Thist." *Puff, puff.* "Such information would just make him implement a backup plan, and then we'd have even more nightmen to fear."

"Won't he be expecting some mirror message about me being dead?"

"No, because he has already received it, Thist." *Puff, puff.* "You see, another pair of them came into my own fake bedroom and tried the same thing on me. But my hidden guards captured one of them." *Puff, puff.* An evil grin split Wakan's face. "You'd be surprised how fast the confessions come when threatened with the death-herb."

Thist breathed heavily. "Wakan, this is definitely the last decision point. I kept putting it off, but now I know I have to leave. When I do, I trust that the mirror-men on your towers won't be reporting any sightings of me? I will try to stay out of sight of them, but I will need to ride the roads at times, and you never know."

"Thist, I won't report you missing unless and until Pernie demands it. And right now she is so concerned with Lork and his naval adventures that she won't bring you up any time soon, I am sure."

Thist took that information with a frown. "And we were lovers for so long, too. I loved her and thought she cared, too. But as you say, life is always changing and we have to adapt if we are to survive." *I think Sire Thess must have said that, too, in my other life back home.*

As shadows swallowed the field where Una was stored, Thist and Wakan Kech returned there, the little man leading a saddled and hooded emu by its reins. They were glad to see that neither Pernie nor Lork had stationed any guards around the big green cylinder.

Noticing Thist looking for possible interference, Wakan said, "Lork and Pernie don't give any thought to Una, Thist. Since she can no longer fly, she is of no possible use in surveillance or transport. Fortunately and unfortunately both, neither of them considers the treasures of Una's archives as anything but useless entertainment or the occasional ancient knowledge you bring out. And since Una turned off the godspheres—and the communications capabilities of the Crystal Throne itself—all the ancient technology is no longer of interest, not with all the other problems emerging in Motherland." Thist just snorted his displeasure.

Shortly the men were back in Una's cabin again. "This is my last visit, Una," Thist said aloud. "I will be leaving Motherland on the emu tied up outside here. I trust that your map information is all that I will need to get back home." He held up a sheet of paper on which he had sketched out his proposed route.

"Thist, you must know that I will feel your absence. Your presence has been a most welcome diversion for me ever since Thusk brought us together here in Mother's City.

"I wish you well. Do you have any final instructions?"

"Una, as you know, I had my last conversation with Thusk last week, when he told me he would be out of contact while he went exploring with that Mienne. The next time you can, please pass on to him my farewell." He then held up a godsphere and said, "If you can ever establish communication between Thusk up there, and this godsphere of mine, please do."

"Thist, should Thusk return near to the qomp terminal on the Moon, I should be able to arrange that. However at present his location there is unavailable. And at your previous instructions, all other information globes remain unresponsive."

Nodding, Thist closed his eyes. "If I ever change my mind, I will communicate it to you through my own godsphere. Thank you, Una," he said, a small tear slowly traveling down his cheek.

Wakan noticed the emotional quaver in his friend's voice. *It will be a sad thing,* he thought, *if those twins never talk to each other again. I wanted to convince Thist to stay, to wait until my own plans hatch, but he is determined to live out his life back in his homeland. I wonder if I should try to do the same, regardless of the risk. But I need to hear from Altamun first. Lork must be eliminated!*

Standing to leave, Thist spoke to the Anklya image now appearing on Una's screen. "I want you to give Wakan, here, full access and command authority over you. The same as I have, and that Thusk…*had*. He may need to avail himself of your archives and your displays. And a private godsphere if he so desires. But please erase all information about gunpowder, gun designs, and any other text or drawings or videos about weapons of any kind. Can you do that?"

"Thist, it is done. Anything else?"

Thist looked at Wakan. "Can you think of any other restrictions we need to give to Una?"

"No," Wakan answered, "only that any queries or commands I may give under duress or torture, Una is not to follow. She can scan my vitals to see if I am feeling normal or not. And I would appreciate having a private godsphere. So that we can communicate with each other."

"Agreed," said Thist. "And another thing: Wakan cannot grant authority and access to anyone else. Una, are you clear on these instructions?"

"Yes, Thist. Very clear."

"Then, Una, I want to thank you for all you have done for us, for Thusk and Wakan and Pernie and Motherland. And for me." He walked to the doorway and stopped, looking forward and back in the cabin, at the displays and seats, fondly remembering the incredible sights and sounds and archives that Una had provided over the last two and a half years. *Less than three years for us, thirty thousand for her. I know how I feel about her, but I still wonder if she is really alive, or just a machine... I'll never know.*

"Una," Thist said with a lump in his throat, "again, I want you to remain closed and sealed and unresponsive to anyone else except Wakan, until I return. In truth, though, I may never see you again. Farewell, friend."

"Thist, farewell and good luck." Thist could have sworn that the god-machine was feeling sad as well.

Outside the green cylinder, Thist stood and looked over the fuselage, noting that the black ovoid over the White Pilot was tilting back. The mannequin swiveled to face Thist and Wakan, hesitated for a minute, then returned to its original position. The black ovoid shut tight.

Thist laughed, "I thought he was going to say something. You know, Wakan, at times I had the feeling that Una and the White Pilot there were two different creatures, but I believe he is just a face she puts on for intimidating people."

"I'll ask her about that, Thist. I do plan to come back to visit her privately from time to time; there is so much knowledge I want to review. And perhaps to talk with Thusk?"

"I'm taking this godsphere with me in my saddlebags, Wakan. Let him know I have it. I don't want him to know yet that I am giving up on Pernie and Motherland, and leaving you here alone. But I don't like what I have become, what I have done. Worse, what I might do if I have to fight Lork. I just don't want my twin to know I have changed so much for the worse, probably more than he has." He laughed at that image. *But Thusk's change—a new body!—is out there for the whole world— worlds—to see, where my scars and crimes are concealed within me, only for me to have to endure, all alone.*

"Wakan," Thist said as he raised himself onto the saddle of his emu, "you have been more than a friend, more than a colleague, to me." Shaking the priest's hand, he said, "You are like the third twin of us. That's all I can say. Good luck to you. And Motherland. And, and, to Pernie." He patted his saddlebags, made fast his springbow, quiver, and shortsword.

As shadows blanketed the courtyard, Thist removed the emu's head covering and lightly pulled back on the reins, signaling the bird to begin its trot. Wakan Kech watched with grim resolve as his dearest friend and closest companion disappeared northward into mist and darkness.

CHAPTER FORTY-EIGHT

The messenger boy ran into Altamun Kech's office, out of breath. "A mirror message for you, Sire," he gasped out. "Emergency level." Tipping the boy with a coin, Altamun opened the sealed, folded paper and read: *"The wolf runs. Feed him well."* Sighing, the Kech shredded the message and began preparing the reception as ordered. *Wakan has so ordered, and I have no choice,* he thought. *I only pray that our Mother never hears of this.*

Altamun recalled his last night at Mother's Palace, when Wakan had taken him aside after the dinner to celebrate Thist's and Thusk's return and Lork's rescue of them. The pirate's presentation to the Mother and her embarrassing response to him was the gossip of the evening.

"Altamun," Wakan had said that night, "I want you to be ready to act for me, should the occasion require. It will involve possible danger, but with great reward. Are you interested?"

"Wakan, you are the superior Kech in Motherland. We all owe our lives to you, you who saved us from Creesile's castrations or death. I am yours to command, sir." After which Wakan told him of the possible murder of the pirate chief and of his companions, if need be.

"I have overheard their conversations and I do not trust that Lork. He is a schemer and will betray Pernie and Motherland at some point. Eventually, he will leave here and will sail away. I do not want him to return. Ensure you can harvest and distill the juice of the *tawa puncha* poison plant that only we Kech cultivate, Altamun. It must be administered before his ship leaves to sail. His death must occur at sea."

Altamun nodded. "Sir, I will do whatever you believe that Motherland needs. Er, you mentioned 'rewards'?" The Kech was conflicted, trying to assess his loyalties. He thought, *Lork rescued me from that crevasse valley, so I owe him a debt. But my countryman, Wakan, saved me from death or mutilation, so I owe him even more. Besides, I have learned from all of these high-ranking men that I must look out for myself.*

Wakan said, "As soon as I can arrange it, Interim Administrator Awhalpa Kech will be reassigned elsewhere. Then you will be promoted to the full rank of Director of the Council for the Republic of WaterEdge. And as such, you will control the harbor and the new vessels that our Mother plans to build there. There will be major income possibilities from trading with all the islands that General Thist has discovered out in the Cold Sea. And you will reap a portion of the benefits."

I will do it, Altamun decided. "As you wish, sir. I will await your message."

AND SO THE TIME HAS COME, AS WAKAN PREDICTED, Altamun thought, reviewing what he had committed to do. *As he promised, I am Director of WaterEdge and am doing quite well, what with all the shipbuilding going on, for the new navy. But now, instead of just being a lone pirate I have to kill, Lork is Commander in Chief and Admiral of the Motherland Navy. And if the gossip is true, he is the favorite of Mother Pernie as well. But Wakan has not modified his directions since that night months ago, so I will do as he commands. For a task of this import, with this risk, my reward is commensurate, not as extravagant as I had first thought. I will earn it.*

Thinking of the effects of the four-day poison to be injected into the admiral's food for him to eat before departing WaterEdge, Altamun was glad he would not be on Lork's ship to witness the pirate's death throes. But those dark and disturbing scenes were overshadowed by a brighter one, the vision of becoming even richer and more powerful as the Republic of WaterEdge thrived. *Life is ironic*, he thought. *One pirate kidnapped me but then disappeared at sea, probably dead. Another pirate rescued me, but killing him will make me richer.* With a sardonic grin, he thought, *There's something to be said about dead pirates!*

THE DAY OF DEPARTURE DAWNED OVER WATEREDGE, the rising sun spreading its light over the harbor where two dozen new seagoing ships were raising their bright white sails, ready to catch the rising winds and an outgoing tide. Amidst the raucous calls of darting seabirds in the clear blue sky, Admiral Lork and First Mate Attuk sat in a longboat as it neared his flagship, *Sea God.* As the crew lowered a standing elevator platform to retrieve the Admiral, Lork smiled broadly, waving at the captains of the other ships, enjoying the salt smell brought in by mild breezes just beginning to arrive from the west. "A fine day, Attuk!" he shouted to his first mate.

"Aye, aye, Cap'n, er, I means *Admiral*, sir," Attuk replied with a laugh. "It ain't ice, but we's been training on this melt—*water*—a lot these months. We's ready."

As Lork was piped aboard by a crewman, Kleete approached, saluted formally and led him to the gunpowder cylinder. "Four of these babies on each ship, Admiral. Ready to blast Hel out of anything." In a quiet voice, he said, "Would sure like to whip up on that Dvora fortress you talked about, if we ever get back up on the Ice Sea."

Lork whispered back, "That's in the plan, Kleete." *I do plan to return to Stonehaven after we take these islands*, he thought. *I will bring Pernie more conquests than she ever expected. And settle a few scores back home, too.* "But first let's do these melt-sea islands. Then after that you can start figuring out a way to get this whole fleet up two or three thousand feet and convert them to ice ships." Kleete nodded and laughed, saluting again.

Lork made his way to the poop deck, satisfied to see all his fleet now flying the Motherland Navy flags, a bright blue field overlaid with a golden sunburst. "Give the command, Attuk, get us underway!"

With a blast of crank-powered air horns, the first mate sounded the "raise anchors" command and the first excursion of the Motherland Navy fleet rode the tide outward to raid their first victims.

As he watched the ships disappear over the horizon, Altamun Kech gave a note to be delivered by a messenger boy to the mirror-men atop the local Wakan's Tower. It read, "*The wolf has left. Well fed.*"

FOUR DAYS OUT OF WATEREDGE, ADMIRAL LORK AND First Mate Attuk were inspecting an unrolled paper map on the large wooden table in Lork's quarters. "We should be coming up on the first island any day now," the Admiral said, munching on a sweet fruit brought up from the galley. "Have all lookouts on alert, and report to me as soon as land is sighted." Pointing to the drawing of a large city and its harbor, he said, "Attuk, we will stand off and bombard the big ships at their docks first. That will prevent anybody from sailing out to fight us. If that city has catapults or gunpowder cylinders of their own, as the dwarf Thist expected, they will shoot back at us. From their misses—or hits—we can judge how close to get, and what locations to fire at. What do you think?"

Attuk's grizzled face reflected some doubt.

"Admiral, sir, I ain't thought it through like you. All I know is the catapults that the drunk Duke of Dvora used against us. These other weapons, I don't know. Lots different from back at Stonehaven even though we been training on them. Actually, from what our Motherland recruits been tellin' me, that little General Thist of theirs, he's the one who could advise you, not me."

Lork said without humor, "Attuk, old friend, don't make me laugh. That little dwarf is a joke. Besides that, he and that Wakan Kech are not even alive now. I don't want to hear his name again, y'hear? Either one of them."

Attuk frowned, nodded, saluted, and proceeded out the door to relay orders to the fleet by semaphore mirrors. As his first mate shut the door to his cabin, Admiral Lork felt a strange twinge in his bowels. Sitting down in his captain's chair, he felt another twinge, this one quite painful, in his left arm, a terrible burning sensation that sped up his arm, to his chin. As consciousness began to fade, he tried to stand but fell forward on the planning table, slamming his head and spreading the battle plans across the floor. Falling onto the floor, his nose broken, he was aware enough that the pain in his guts was unbearable. As his eyes darkened, he felt burning bile erupting up his esophagus and into his mouth, *As hot as lava from Hillmork*, the unfunny thought flashed. With the little remaining energy he had, with every nerve ending in his body now shouting its pain, his sight dimming to darkness, Lork struggled to scream. Though no sound came, his brain roared in agony in dark, shrieking silence.

The pain did not diminish for four days, an excruciating eternity that left Lork a gibbering, drooling, and trembling nonentity, the woeful object of his crew's shock and pity, before welcome Death stilled him and ended his journey into Hel.

FIRST MATE ATTUK SALUTED AS THE FLAG-DRAPED

body of the late Admiral Lork of the Motherland Navy, slipped over the side of *Sea God* and into the blue-water depths of the Cold Sea. "Farewell, Cap'n," Attuk said with tears in his eyes. "I wish we could've took you home, but there wasn't no way." He didn't say, *You were already rotting from the inside out, putrid mush in front of our eyes, even before you died.* Putting back on his seaman's cap, he turned to Zeerance Kleete and the rest of the assembled crew.

"What do we do now, boys? After our Cap'n, our Admiral, took sick, we called off the attack on that island over there"—he pointed toward a dark slump on the southern horizon—"but without no orders now that he is gone, we needs to decide something. We got two dozen ships, two thousand men to keep fed and watered, and nowhere to go. What say you, Chief Engineer? You was closest to him, these last months."

Kleete stepped up and stood beside Attuk, removing his cap and bowing in respect to the ships' captains assembled in the front row. "The way I see it is, one, we can all return to WaterEdge and still be the Motherland Navy. I don't know how that Mother Pernie will react, especially since our late Admiral was her favorite...in many ways." He ignored the ensuing laughter and crude remarks. Some of the men on the deck were nodding their acceptance of that choice, but by no means all. He could tell that they had all thought of other options, as had he.

"Another choice is to try and do the raids we came here to do, starting with that place over there. But—a big but, if you ask me—nobody in this fleet has the experience in planning and executing raids like our Admiral Lork did. Some of you were iceboat captains, but always under Lork's command, am I right? He planned the attacks and led them?" Murmurs swept through the men, but Kleete didn't see much acceptance in their mood.

Hearing no objections or suggestions from the captains or crews, Kleete went on. "Third, we can try to find those Lordship Islands where that pirate Noor was from, and offer them our ships and ourselves, our service, and resettle there in return for citizenship. From the reports of General Thist that I read in Mother's Palace, it is a warm and friendly place." Kleete saw some more interest in the crowd, but nothing unanimous yet. "And yes, they are pirates, but democratic and tolerant. As ice pirates ourselves, we ought to get along with them." Kleete saw more and more support for this course of action evident among the listeners.

Attuk spoke up then, his stretched-arm stance presenting his argument even before he spoke. "A fourth choice, mates, and *my* choice—is, we go home, us from the Ice Sea. We take some ships and some gunpowder cylinders, and we get back up on The Ice. With what we got here, we can rule ever'thing on The Ice—all the towns, all of Na Saam. Nobody can whip us; we can bombard them to Hel! Even that drunk Duke of Dvora!"

Hearing a few cheers for Attuk's choice, Kleete had him assemble all the captains in Lork's cabin for a vote. Unsurprisingly, a fifth choice was suggested, namely that each ship would become its own pirate vessel, its crew taking immediate possession. "To go raiding on our own, Attuk," those captains said. "Let us find our own way, our own places to raid or to live or settle down."

After a full day of wrangling, the fleet disbanded. Attuk and Kleete, with one ship, one crew, departed for Attuk's Crack and the Ice Sea, mainly Na Saamese crewmen returning to Stonehaven, men who had accompanied Lork's rescue operation from Stonehaven to WaterEdge. A dozen other crews opted to go to Noorstown and ask for assimilation and service there. Seven ships wanted to explore farther out into the Cold Sea for other lands. "Gotta be warmer places than even Motherland," was their consensus. "We got nothing in Motherland." "We're glad to get away, maybe find a better place to live." "Gotta be women out there somewhere, right?"

In all, after the provisions were shared, the crews self-selected, and the goodbyes said, only four ships returned to WaterEdge, all of the crews original citizens from across Motherland, men who did not want to abandon their home country or families. Few had expressed any loyalty to their country, and none at all to Mother Pernie, a fact that the departing Zeerance Kleete found disturbing, if revealing. He said as much to Attuk as they sailed to the northeast and the Ice Sea: "Here Motherland paid for this huge fleet, all the weapons I built, and the training and supplies for two thousand men, but very few here even cared enough for their country or their Mother Pernie to return home. Says something about those people and their culture, doesn't it?" But a happy and excited now–Captain Attuk was paying no attention to his engineer's mutterings; the wind in his face, the flap of the sails, and the wide open expanse of blue sea were demanding all his attention.

When Altamun Kech received news of the sighting of the ships returning, only four of them, after just two weeks, he knew the poison had worked, but feared that Wakan had not anticipated the results. How had they lost twenty ships? Who would account for that enormous lost investment? More importantly—who would be blamed? Immediately he sent word to the harbor that only the captains of those returning ships would set foot on the docks, and there await his presence without speaking to anyone.

When Altamun arrived, four bedraggled sailors stood before him, men who looked as though they were already condemned to the stake or worse. The Kech took the captains out of earshot of their crewmen in the boats and of his own guards. "Captains all," he said with a bow toward them, "it is so unfortunate that only your four crews survived that terrible storm at sea. Isn't it?" Staring at each sailor in turn, he saw expressions of confusion, then resistance, and finally grins of acceptance, relief that they were being given a chance to avoid blame and Pernie's notorious wrath. None of them asked their Kech director why.

"Aye, aye, Director, sir!" each man said. Followed by excited sighs of relief. "'Twere a huge storm!" "High waves you wouldn't believe!" "Tore off sails, capsized them ships!" "We was lucky to escape and sorrowful to lose so many brave sailors!"

Altamun smiled and shook hands with each captain. "I trust that each man of your crews will learn by heart the misadventure you all suffered out there. Should I ever hear of any other tales told, no matter how long from now, you captains will be set up high on the sharpened masts of your ships, for all the world to see. Understood? Now, decide upon your story together, here and now. Then return and educate your crews. Tell them that if any one man brings it upon himself to misinterpret the true tale you report to me, all of your crews will meet also meet a sharp end. I expect your written reports yet today. In a few days you and your crews will be awarded substantial bonuses for your patriotic actions. Good day, sailors of the Motherland Navy. Thank you for your heroism." With that, Altamun turned on his heel, summoned his guards, and returned to his office.

After the crews had disembarked and the captains reported to him officially with four written accounts remarkable in their consistency, Altamun crafted what he realized would be the most important message of his life. *It may mean my life*, he realized as he wrote, *or my death*. His first mirror message was to Wakan Kech: *"Pack returned. As planned. But 20 pups lost."*

WAKAN'S REPLY CAME WITHIN THE HOUR: *"20 SHIPS lost? How?"*

Altamun: *"Bad storm. Pack leader died."*

Wakan: *"Send numerical details. Will intercede with P."*

Alone in his plush office, Altamun Kech, Director of

the Republic of WaterEdge, solemnly considered the potted plants in his wide marble windowsill. "That one, the bright green stringy pods; the death-herb," he whispered to himself, "weeks of pain. The pink flowers, there, *tawa puncha*, the four-day poison plant, four days to act, four days to die." He walked to the open window, breathed in the fresh sea air, and looked out over the harbor below where the four remaining ships of the Motherland Navy lay at anchor out beyond the surf. Fingering the tiny buds on the third plant, he said, "Now this one, this one, is my favorite, my earnest companion, if ever needed." *These white buds are hallucinogenic and deadly, transporting one to a quick, sensuous, and wonderfully painless death. Or so they say; nobody has ever returned to tell of it.*

CHAPTER FORTY-NINE

I n the cloying, incense-laden chamber of Mother Pernepetheranam, Healer Fyth was sweating and nervous as he pulled his hand from between her legs. His patient lay on a bed on her back, with her naked legs propped up and wide open, her feet resting high up in stirrups. Fyth hesitated to tell her the unwelcome news, dreading what she might do, given her recent noticeable decline in rationality, her outbursts in court. His scarred fingertips reminded him of how Pernie's own Lordess Mother had reacted to a similar statement from him, many years ago. But the evidence he had just confirmed with those same fingers was undeniable, so he spoke softly: "Mother Pernepetheranam—you are pregnant."

"I can't believe this is happening!" Pernie shouted, as Fyth pulled his hands back. The Mother's exposed belly was already showing signs of swelling. "How could I be pregnant, Healer? *How?*" The healer motioned to a nurse to cleanse the Mother's groin and dress her with an undergarment.

Having already disappointed the Mother over little Thusk's death, months ago—*Although I had nothing to do with the crazy idea of using that Crystal Throne for therapy,* he thought with disdain. *General Thist —Colonel Thist—and Wakan Kech,* they *killed him.* Trying to assuage the monarch's anxiety, hoping not to bring down her wrath upon himself, he artfully replied with what he hoped was a sage smile, "My dear Mother, there is only one way that we can both agree upon that produces pregnancy. May I inquire as to the father?" At his sovereign's sudden glare, he quickly added, "Only so that I may assess his own health, to see if he has any deficiencies we need to take into account for when caring for the unborn child."

"Damn you, Healer. And damn that Lork, the cursed pirate." Sitting up, covering her legs with blue godscloth robes, Pernie breathed deeply, closed her eyes, and said calmly, "Healer, don't be afraid. You will come to no harm. It's just that this, this, *baby*, was not planned nor expected. How far along am I now? When will it be born? Is it a male or a girl?"

Healer Fyth finished washing and drying his hands, giving the towels to the nurse, who quickly left, touching her tongue so that he could see her gesture. He smiled at the woman's action; that nurse and all the other attendants were warned that leaking any news of Mother's condition by any one of them would result in the slow and painful multiple slicing and removal of their tongues, prior to other mutilations, amputations, and burning. *She won't be talking about this*, he thought with satisfaction. *Nor will I!*

"Mother, the signs are that you will give birth in approximately four months. Surely your menses ceased some time ago?" At her reluctant nod, he said, "I could have given you appropriate herbs at that time to, to, *prevent* the child from developing, but any ministrations now would put you in danger yourself, you understand." Mother Pernie nodded again. "And Mother, your final question about the sex of the child? That I cannot answer." Healer Fyth held up a forefinger and pointed at Pernie. "You do know of course, the *tradition*, as practiced by your own Lordess Mother, and her Mothers before her, all the way back to First Mother."

Pernie nodded but said nothing. *I know, Healer*, she thought. *If it is a male it is to be killed at birth. By Motherland's ancient legend, Mothers can only give birth to girls, girls who become princesses. Princesses who rule Sisterdoms. One of them to replace her Mother. And all of the fathers who impregnate Mothers, they are killed, lest they try to gain power through the girl they sired.*

Pernie knew that regardless of her condition, she would have to rule until Lork returned. *We will work this out. Traditions are only traditional if they are continued. I have already made changes in the traditional Sisterdoms, and I no longer sit on that damned traditional Crystal Throne to be made crazy. With Lork, I will make other changes. And if I do have a male child, he will not be killed just because of some old superstitions!*

To Fyth she said, "Not a word to anyone. The warning to the nurses is for you as well. But I know that you already have kept many secrets secret, have you not? So thank you for telling me what I have suspected for months now, and thank you for your care and comfort."

Healer Fyth bowed and backed away, thankful for the Mother's blessing. As he walked the hallways back to his surgery, he recalled other Mothers, other pregnancies. *I served her other Sisters, her late Sister Messinex, their Lordess Mother, and her Mother, going back fifty years now. Messinex was pregnant twice in her short year, I suspect by that Miran Kech, but she never said. The early herbs prevented those from proceeding.* Remembering the Lordess Mother, the biological mother of both Messinex and Pernie and six others, he shuddered. She had put off her preventative medicines another half dozen times, each termination requiring a bloody and invasive procedure. *And four of those were females,* he remembered. Two males had been delivered—*And killed,* he recalled with a sigh. *Pernie herself, now our Mother, was a beautiful baby, even more so than Messinex, and the Lordess's last. I had hoped she would stay as nice a woman as she had been as a child, that the Kech priest, Wakan, would educate her and lead her. But she has been reverting to type, a typical Mother with the power of life or death or worse, over all of us.* As he sat in his favorite chair, a servant poured him a chilled glass of his favorite honeyed wine. *I just hope Pernie decides to keep this child. She is so on edge right now that she is unpredictable. A child might stabilize her.*

Looking at his scarred fingertips, Fyth replayed in his mind the result of the Lordess Mother's last displeasure. *She removed all my fingernails, slowly and one at a time, after that last painful termination.* As he sipped more wine, he prayed, *Mother Pernie, please don't be like your mother!*

LEAVINGS

Walking briskly through the dark, dank hallways of Mother's Palace, Wakan Kech slowed his pace, approaching Mother Pernie's chamber with trepidation. *I have to tell her that Lork is dead*, he thought. *I hope she can accept it and move on, as a ruler should. I really wanted Thist to be in Mother's City to step in and comfort her, but he is probably back in the Dark Highlands by now; it's been two weeks. But no secret word of him from my loyal mirror-men yet.*

Sighing, Wakan knew that he would have to handle Pernie all by himself. After a loud confrontation with Lork's guards who were stationed outside Pernie's door, Mother Pernie herself intervened and invited Wakan in. As usual, the Mother had an excess of incense burning in her rooms, scents that Wakan had come to regard as too offensive to his sense of smell. *Is Pernie's body chemistry changing? Is that why she prefers this repertoire of new odors?*

"You have news, Wakan?" Pernie said in a distinctly unpleasant tone as she invited the priest to sit. "As do I. But you first."

Wakan passed to Pernie a single sheet, then as she looked over it he said calmly, bluntly, "Pernie, there is no way to soften the news on this report. Altamun Kech has reported by mirror that the navy fleet has returned. It encountered a horrific windstorm at sea. Twenty ships were lost. Admiral Lork is gone."

Pernie's eyes opened wide, her mouth an orifice erupting vile curses. She stood, spun around on her feet, swaying and screaming. As handmaids rushed into the room and to her side, she screamed them away. Her guards rushed in, spears ready, but the wordless screams of their Mother halted them in their tracks. Nevertheless they took their places between Pernie and Wakan, spears crossed, to protect her.

Time stood still for Wakan as he experienced the worst rage of Pernie's he had ever seen—out of control, red-faced and shrieking, alternately sobbing so hard she could not breathe, then screaming so loud she would lose her voice. "Wakan, Wakan, how could this be? Who did it? I want them burned alive, skinned alive, death-herbed, all of them! Do it now!"

Trying to comfort her, Wakan held out his arms and approached her, but the guards leveled their spears in front of him. "Not to pass, Priest. Admiral's orders."

"Your Admiral is *dead*, you idiots!" shouted Wakan as he walked in circles around Pernie's chamber, his voice echoing off the polished marble walls and floor. "Let the Mother tell you!"

Confused, the large men pulled their spears upright and stood at attention. One of them broke tradition and protocol, speaking directly to her without being given permission. "Mother? True? Lork dead?"

Pernie screamed, "*Yes! Yes!* My Lork, my Admiral, my love, he is *dead*!" Holding up Wakan's report sheet for the guards to see, she said more calmly, "I know you can't read my language, *fools*! But that is what this paper says: 'Lost at sea, swept overboard in a storm. Many ships sunk. Many sailors lost at sea. Inexperienced crews, poor seamanship, bad luck." Sitting on her divan, she pulled the sheet to her face and sobbed again, uncontrollably. With Pernie's confirmation of their boss's demise, the men looked to Wakan for direction; he waved them out of the room.

This time, Wakan was able to hold Pernie in his

arms and comfort her. As she regained control of herself, she said, "How could this happen? A storm that dangerous? And this about lack of training and poor seamanship, how did that happen? That Kleete is supposed to be a genius, my Lork told me. Where is he? I want him skinned alive and then burned!"

"Pernie, dearest," said Wakan in his softest, most comforting voice, "that engineer was on one of the ships that sank in the storm. He is beyond punishment now."

Pernie was not satisfied. "Has our Kech in WaterEdge interrogated those captains and crews that did come back?" she asked through sobs. "Are we certain that they were not at fault in some way?"

Wakan assured her, having had Altamun carefully detail the punishment that awaited any man who spoke otherwise, that the returnees had made heroic efforts to rescue Lork and the crews of the sunken ships, but were lucky to save themselves and their four vessels. "Heroes aplenty, Pernie. Those men deserve rewards, not punishment." In fact Altamun had already promised the carrot of coppers, as opposed to the stick of impalement, to each and every sailor on that unfortunate expedition.

CHAPTER FIFTY-ONE

The next few days were Hel for Wakan, as he tried to temper Pernie's hysteria, at the same time keeping the court at bay, and all the agencies of Motherland running without Mother's daily decrees and answers to questions of governance. *The more I try to cover for her*, he thought, *the more I see that that Sisterdoms and republics simply* must *operate locally and independently.* He concluded that the current configuration of Motherland itself was just not sustainable, but falling apart at the seams without a tyrant in charge. *But in her present state Pernie is not even a figurehead, but a liability.*

Finally, a week after her meltdown rage over Lork's death and her own pregnancy, judicious doses of calmative herbs rendered Pernie coherent enough, presentable enough, to appear on her blue throne and hold court. Having entered the throne room and sitting before others were allowed in, Pernie's voluminous robes hid her swollen belly. Wakan stood beside her as a dozen or more attendees entered, all of them first looking at Pernie then lowering their eyes to take their places standing in awed silence.

They can see that she has aged far beyond her twenty-three years, Wakan thought, *but I hope some people will see it as maturity, not as undue stress or something worse.*

"THAT WENT WELL, DON'T YOU THINK, WAKAN?" Pernie asked as the last visitor left the throne room. "I think I am ready now to resume my duties fully." Wakan didn't want to comment on her offensive body odor, which he took to be a combination of her excessive sweating, the incense aromas that permeated her quarters, and too much of an application of yet another perfume. *Apparently she is not aware of her own noxious atmosphere*, he concluded. *I fear it emanates from her internal malodorous condition.*

"As you wish, Mother," Wakan answered formally, trying to disguise his feelings. *We are still in the throne room, after all,* he said to himself. *She is only 'Pernie' when we are alone together.* He was bothered somewhat that Pernie had not publicly mentioned the death of Lork, the destruction of most of his fleet, or her pregnancy. *Should she?* he wondered. Because regardless of security measures and the certainty of dire punishment, even the most dedicated of men of the mirror towers was bound to talk with his bar-mates at some point, a drunken man wanting to brag or impress a maid.

So I must have Pernie issue a declaration to be posted country-wide, about brave Admiral Lork's heroic demise as he tried to save his crewmen from the disastrous storm at sea. Her pregnancy will be no problem for another month or so. But then, who knows? I'll handle that problem when it arises.

THE PROBLEMS SURFACED IN FULL FORCE WHEN WAKAN was writing Pernie's dictation for the posters about Lork's fate, declarations that were to be distributed all over Motherland. Walking around her chamber slowly, wafting incense into her face as she spoke, she said, "Wakan, I need for every citizen to understand that Admiral Lork was on a peaceful mission to meet with leaders of the Cold Sea islands, and would have resorted to invasion only if forced into it." Wakan was happy that the Mother of Motherland, ruler of ten million, was able to collect her thoughts, repress her grief, and formulate a reasonable document to dispel the rumors that were bound to be rife by now. He prayed, *Maybe she is regaining control of her emotions again?*

"Pernie, if I may," Wakan softly resisted, "accounting for eighteen hundred lost crew, twenty ships sunk, needs a bit more forceful declaration, don't you think?"

Pernie stopped and looked directly at her priest. "Wakan, are you proposing I say that this was only a punitive expedition, against all those island pirates?" She paused. "That would mean a declaration of war, and I am not sure that we can impose another conscription of men, much less another tax increase, to build another fleet."

Wakan thought, *Well, that departure ceremony, those chants of "crushing pirates," did sound like that.* But he said, "Quite right, Pernie. Just let me work on the wording. I will have a draft for you by tomorrow morning if that suits you." Standing to bow and leave, he hesitated, seeing by her hand gesture that Pernie had other matters on her mind. "Yes, Pernie?"

Pernie smiled. "You know, Lork has been…gone… for a while now, and for good, I suppose. And though it has been many months, I feel that I would like the company of my little Thist again. To tell him I regret my actions. I want to reinstate him as military commander again, as general, in Lork's place." Grinning at Wakan, she flicked her tongue. "Tell him to come to me tonight. I am sure he will be happy when he does."

Stunned, Wakan stuttered. "Pernie, Pernie. I did not want to tell you, to add to your concerns about Lork and the navy and all the other problems we are facing. But after the assassination attempt on him the day after Lork left for WaterEdge, our Thist left us. Weeks ago. Gone back home to the Dark Highlands." Biting his tongue, he awaited her outburst. *I hope she is rational now. I don't think I can take much more abuse. Truly, I know I should leave like Thist did, but who would help her? What would happen to our Motherland?*

Ashen-faced, Pernie sat down hard on her divan, her eyes wide, mouth open. For a full minute she sat quietly. Wakan Kech took her calm reaction well. *This is more the Pernie who grew up her whole life under my care; serious as a child, sober and reflective as a young woman; determined and decisive. Until lately. How she responds now will tell me how she has improved. Or declined.*

Mother Pernie glared at Wakan Kech. "Wakan, again you have disappointed me, allowing something to happen that you knew would affect me greatly." Standing she said calmly, without emotion, "First, the horrible tragedy of Thusk's death, done without my knowledge or approval."

Wakan thought, *Pernie, you were in bed with your new lover, Lork, and would allow no interruption. For two whole days and nights. We feared for Thusk's life more than we feared you.*

Patting her swelling belly, she shook her head. "Then, Wakan, after years of preventative herbs that kept me from becoming pregnant, somehow you failed to protect me." As the priest began to object, she waved him to remain silent. "I do not blame you; I *want* Lork's child, a strong man's baby, an outsider's.

"But now, Wakan, you inform me that my Colonel Thist has gone missing for—how long? Three weeks? I am afraid that your judgment is not trustworthy any longer. You know, thinking back over these last few years, especially this time after hearing that my Lork has, has—*disappeared,* for I refuse to believe he is dead until I see his lifeless body—I can see now where the change in your thinking, your behavior, your overall effectiveness began."

Pernie sat and leaned back on her divan, pushing a lock of copper-colored hair back from her forehead. She took a sip of wine from a golden goblet, licking her lips. "When Thist arrived at ShadowFall, your deterioration started. And became even worse when his twin, Thusk, flew down to our country in that Una flying machine. I think that machine's *videos,* its archives, its so-called ancient secrets—they have corrupted yourself, those twins, many of your Kech associates, probably others. Unfortunately for me, Thist and Thusk are beyond my reach, but the rot they both carried from their primitive tribe in Dark Highlands will be difficult to counteract.

"However, their so-called *god machine* is still in my control. So long as anyone can hear its legends and lies, it is a danger to all human beings, in Motherland or anywhere else. So I give you this order, Wakan: Because I know that the Una-thing is almost indestructible, I want it permanently disabled in a way that neither Motherland nor anyone else will ever be influenced by its ancient evil."

"But Pernie, I—" Wakan had never heard such madness. *To deliberately hide forever, all of Una's knowledge, experience—wisdom? I shall not!*

"Quiet, Kech! Do not speak! Take that Una-thing out in the hills, perforate it with a hundred of those borophene arrows like the one that Creesile killed Messinex with. Then find an opening in the earth or a cavern, and drop it in, seal it in, hundreds of meters of earth over it. Then cover it with rocks and ragged scrap metal and seal it with tons and tons of concrete. So nobody will ever be able even to see it. I want no record of its location, no history of its doings. Everything about its very existence is to be erased, just like that former Sister of mine and her domain. *Understood?*"

Wakan bowed formally, keeping his thoughts to himself. But Pernie could see his clenched jaw and tightened fists, his trembling arms. "As you wish, Mother Perneptheranam. It shall be done. I will see to it personally."

"See that you do, Wakan Kech. To be certain that you have fulfilled my order, I am assigning an overseer for you. Someone you know, Altamun Kech, of WaterEdge. In fact, though it saddens me to do so, he will become my new High Priest and chief advisor. And you shall report to him as he sees fit. He should be arriving within the week. Make him welcome."

This was too much for the Kech. "I, I, will do as you wish, of course. But I beg you to reconsider. I have known you your whole life, and I..." Unable to control the emotions overwhelming his speech, Wakan bowed again and backed out of Pernie's door, tears in his eyes.

STAGGERED BY PERNIE'S PRECIPITATE ACTION, WAKAN strode out of Mother's Palace and out to Una's storage field. There he was shocked to find a dozen Mothersmen guards spaced around the machine, spears and swords in evidence. In the distance several long-arrow catapults of Creesile's design were being towed by oxen, coming toward their big green target. *Those big projectiles will damage Una even further. This can't happen!* Remembering Thist's discovery at Stonehaven, that Una could self-destruct and vaporize everything around her for kilometers, he grew desperate.

Picking up his pace Wakan ran toward the craft, thinking, *Pernie had already planned Una's destruction, even before I told her of Thist's leaving. And she had already summoned Altamun here to replace me! Lork's influence must extend beyond his death. Does she suspect I had anything to do with that, or the fleet's disappearance?* Fearing that Pernie's wrath would not stop with eliminating Una, he made the decision to leave Motherland as soon as possible, once he had convinced Una not to blow up. The belts of gold and silver he always carried on himself would speed his way through civilized areas, he knew, and buy passage on a sea vessel if he could find one. But traversing those thousands of kilometers of barbaric and desolate lands, that would be a challenge. But all that was secondary; first he had to save Una or stop her from destroying Mother's City and its hundred thousand inhabitants!

As Wakan approached the line of guards, one spoke to him. "No one approaches the evil machine. Mother's orders." Una herself was ten meters inside the guarded perimeter, too far for Wakan to run without getting punctured by a spear. Yet within a few minutes the harpoon arrows would be in place to damage or kill her.

What to do? Wakan thought. Then, an idea hit. He shouted, "Una, if you can hear me, let the White Pilot shout out, noisily to disarm these men—and then open your cabin door!"

At that, the black ovoid atop Una's green fuselage tilted back with a loud, attention-getting *creeeaaak!*, a sound Wakan had never heard before. As soon as it was exposed, the white man-thing began to rotate a complete revolution, and an ear-splitting roar of a voice commanded: "Mothersmen, lay down your weapons! This priest is allowed to enter my cabin!"

At the unexpected volume of Una's loud-talker, every guardsman turned in shock toward the eerie sight of the White Pilot figure. With no eyes on him, Wakan rushed toward Una's opening cabin door and jumped in as it quickly closed behind him. "Transparent walls, Una!" he yelled.

Outside, the guards had recovered somewhat and were now banging on Una's walls, trying to puncture or force her to open up.

"Wakan, I sense no borophene weapons with these guards, but there are dangerous ones being pulled this way. What is happening?"

Wakan spoke quickly, repeating Pernie's orders. "And so, Una, I am afraid I have come to the end of my time here in Motherland. I wish I knew of some way to prevent your awful fate. You may never see daylight again. Were it just me and we had the time, I would have enabled some escape for you, but with these guards outside and those harpoons coming, I am at a loss. I am so sorry."

As Wakan watched, the two harpoon launchers were being situated just a few meters on either side of Una. He knew that he himself was likely to be killed by those arrows, just as the two guardsmen were when Una was shot down over Stonehaven. There was no way out, short of abandoning Una, which he decided not to do.

"Una," Wakan said sadly as the crews were loading the fatal barrage of harpoons, "I only wish it hadn't come to this. I wish you were back with Thist and I were back home in the High Antis. Forgive me. I have failed you. And Pernie."

Una responded, "Wakan Kech, I will not remain here to be destroyed. I will fly you home in a few hours, if you so desire. That is the safest, not to say, the fastest, way for you to return to the High Antis."

At first, Una's reply made no sense. "How, how, is this possible, Una? You have been disabled for many months now. I can't believe this!" *What is going on? Is she delusional? Can a machine be insane? And with me locked up inside it?*

"Wakan, I detect that you are nervous, upset. Do not be. Listen to me. Over the last eight months since my… injuries…at Stonehaven, I have been able to effect minimal repairs, extremely slowly, less than satisfactory. They are incomplete and only temporary, but possibly sufficient to fly you to your High Antis, which I estimate to be some four thousand, five hundred kilometers south."

"Then do it, Una! Fly out of here! Now!"

As Wakan felt a sudden acceleration upward, Una's loud-talker blasted out a deep voice: "Mothersmen! If you fire, I will consume you with fire! You will be doomed! Now, run!"

As Una lifted skyward Wakan could see the dark figures on the ground waving their arms in confusion, some rigid, some running. *But nobody shooting! Good!* He collapsed in a cabin chair and breathed in relief. Within minutes, Mother's Palace shrank in his sight to the size of a doll house, the whole of Mother's City becoming children's toy blocks, the lights of the city finally disappearing in the dark distance as Una flew southward.

Grateful but still shocked by Una's newfound flight capability, Wakan asked, "But why did you not tell Thist of your repairs? That you could still fly? He could have gone home in a few hours, instead of trekking over thousands of kilometers of dangerous highlands."

"From his actions and physical scans, I determined that Thist would not have returned home, but instead would continue to engage in military activities, in an effort to placate Mother Perneptheranam. I could not chance that. Over the years that I have interacted with him, I observed General Thist's devolution from a talented but naive and unsophisticated young adventurer into an adroit, effective, but ruthless military genius."

Wakan marveled at Una's sophisticated tone, her articulate manner of speech, quite unlike most of her previous conversations. "My limited remaining temporary capabilities would have served only to frustrate Thist's ambition, contributing to more loss of life. I did not wish to allow further harm to come to humans through continuing warfare. But I see you and your High Antis culture as relatively more benign. Returning you to it will enable your nation to prepare to defend itself when, as seems all too possible, Motherland seeks to conquer more distant lands.

"By historical comparisons, Motherland will definitely try to expand in the coming centuries to absorb all of Earth's Western Hemisphere and perhaps the entire globe. The aggressive navy that Mother Pernie is rebuilding will enable such conquests, now or in the future.

"As a result of the imminent possibility of Motherland aggression, I have continued to disable all communications from the Crystal Throne and among the 'godspheres.' By this action, neither Motherland nor any other country will have access to the knowledge in my archives.

"I cannot be weaponized, but the archives aboard this craft may serve to advance your society's knowledge and scientific capabilities, and develop them so as to resist Motherland's future aggressions."

Wakan Kech sat back in awe. Una's qomps had made sophisticated moral decisions, moves that planned ahead centuries, perhaps millennia. Could humans ever think so deeply, so broadly? Then he remembered what Thusk had said once: "Una's thinking is millions of times faster than ours. Her archived memories are millions of times better than ours, and are perfect, not subject to false remembrances or biases. Una is the living embodiment of Truth, Wakan. The ultimate authority on this whole round Earth!"

But she can still lie, Wakan thought. *Is she doing so now? Is there a survival instinct?*

"The future of the human race looks grim, Una." Wakan remembered what Thist had said when the little general thought he was bluffing during his time at Stonehaven. "Una, would you truly have exploded yourself, vaporized everything around for kilometers, as you once told Thist you could? That was my primary reason for coming to see you tonight, to save Mother's City. I hoped you would not let yourself be destroyed or hurt others, but I was very concerned about that explosion."

"Yes, Wakan. At Stonehaven, a fusion explosion was always a possibility." Then Una went quiet for another self-imposed eternity of unbelievably rapid processing and thinking. "However, that time has passed, and upon reflection I concluded that self-destruction accomplishes nothing. To avoid harm to humans and myself, I would not set off a fusion explosion. But today, upon realizing that we were to be injured, I had decided I would remove myself from the storage field and fly elsewhere to prevent such treatment. It is fortunate that you arrived when you did. You provided me a preferable destination, one where I can be of continuing service."

Wakan's burden of potential guilt was washed away by Una's proclamation. The machine would not have served a bleak, lonely eternity underground, nor would it have exploded itself. He shook off earlier visions of Pernie dying in nuclear flames like some of those ancient cities in the video archives, along with her innocent baby. *Strange that only those two come to mind at a time like this, and not the fate of millions or more.*

Maybe it's just because Pernie is my biological daughter? Her child, my grandbaby? He laughed aloud at the thought. *Lordess Mother would scold me —or skin me—for such sentimentality!*

"Una," he said slowly, "are we on our way to the High Antis now?"

In answer, the Anklya image smiled and gave a thumbs-up gesture. Wakan smiled, guessing that the upward thumb movement meant agreement, though he had never seen it before. With Motherland now far behind him as Una flew on, in his view below and to the south scattered campfires dotted the vast black highland jungles like stars in the velvet sky above. As the red sun sank behind the far Western Highlands, Wakan sighed. *I am going home. After nearly twenty-five years, I am going home!*

I wish I were happy.

CHAPTER FIFTY-TWO

"Winter is pretty bad as you go north," Thist said to himself, breaking the silence that seemed to surround him every long day on the road to Thessland. Pulling his hooded jacket tighter against the north wind swooping down from the Dark Highlands on the horizon, he added, "But not a glacier in sight, so that's good, don't you think?" The emu he was riding did not answer, but kept up its monotonous rhythm, a *thump-thump-thump* as the war-bird strode up the Main Road toward ShadowFall. *Good bird!* Thist thought, grateful that the two-legs in Motherland were every bit as tough and resilient as those he had ridden back home.

During his ten days on the road after escaping from Mother's City, Thist had hoped to remain incognito, having exchanged an assortment of rare godscloth robes for warmer and nondescript clothing as he moved northward. But as he soon learned, a lone dark-skinned little man from the Dark Highlands, especially one riding a war-bird and carrying weapons, was not yet a common sight on Motherland's highways. Several times he had been recognized and welcomed by demobilized soldiers, other times by more wary patrolmen of the new police forces he had set up in each Sisterdom. With his tale of being on a secret mission for Mother Pernie, he was feted, fed, and sent on his way with a celebration—exactly what he did not want to happen.

"I just hope that Wakan is controlling the mirror-men as he promised," he reassured himself. Nevertheless, he tried to stay away from population centers, riding at night when possible. Because his bird could eat any of the vegetation and he himself had a meager diet, he minimized interactions with the population as much as possible.

As he approached the border to ShadowFall, Thist's problems returned, this time in the form of an overweight Original who lazily sauntered out from a dark kiosk adjacent to the road. Putting a fat hand on the control lever for the lowered road-crossing gate, the brown-uniformed man said, "Ya one of them damn dwarfs, are ya?" The snobbish border official (as proclaimed by a large, flashy silver badge), looked eye-to-eye at Thist, astride his emu. "What'cha doin' comin' up here? Your kind is over t' *Thessland,* they call it," he said with a sneer. Thist followed the man's pointing finger to a dirt road that ran next to a barbwire fence. Another gated entrance lay in the distance. "Two klicks east, ya go in. Not here, y'hear?"

Thist reacted with much more restraint than he felt, his right hand unconsciously reaching for his shortsword. *If I were here on official business, your head would be rolling on the ground right now!* But he replied calmly, "Thank you, sir. I shall go that way. A good day to you!" Lightly kicking the emu, he trotted eastward to Thessland's own entryway. "What the Hel has happened up here? They were all pretty happy to see me, *us,* when Creesile was thundering over this very spot. *Gratitude!*" he spat back in the direction of the fat thug at the gate. *ShadowFall has fallen!*

In a hurry because he figured the fat man would send a mirror-message that Wakan might not intercept in time, Thist begged off the welcome he received at the Thessland gate, and proceeded at speed to the main settlement, Thess City, some kilometers north. Once there, he did accept the accolades of the locals, gratefully eating their food and drinking their wine. And though the temptation was great, he politely declined offers of female companionship for the night.

"I love you all, folks, but it is important that I get up to the Dark Highlands as fast as I can," he told the people at his dinner table. "And it will go better for you all if you never saw me, you know?" Not yet aware of the changing dynamics at Mother's Palace, the puzzled Thesslanders nevertheless trusted their hero and agreed that his passage would not be discussed with outsiders.

Changing clothes yet again, this time for a heavy wool-lined coat and gloves, Thist was surprised when one young Thesslander man spoke up. "General Thist, let me wear that hooded jacket of yours the one you came here in. While you go on up to Odel's Elevator, I will ride back past that fat ShadowFall border patrol guy and engage him." At Thist's puzzled look, he said, "Fat Man there will think I am you—because to him we all look alike."

Thist kept laughing as he mounted his emu, heading north.

M'RIDGE STATION WAS A SETTLEMENT OF A FEW DOZEN log cabins situated at the base of massive six hundred meter stone cliffs that extended horizon to horizon. Kilometers to the west, Thist knew, was the gigantic waterfall where the New River ended and Mother's River began. He was still in awe at the memory of his descent down that cliff nearly three years before. *Without that godscloth I'd've never made it down to ShadowFall*, he remembered. Then with a smile, *Of course, without stealing that godscloth I would not have needed to escape!*

In the center of the station stood a wooden tower one-tenth the height of the cliffs. Thist looked at the construction. "Taller than Wakan's Towers; I am impressed." When he thought of Odel launching his tri-wing off the high top, then lighting rockets to ascend higher than the rocky massif a half kilometer away, he shuddered. "But I am glad you did it, you crazy big guy." Watching as an iron cage slowly lowered down a godscloth cable from an almost invisible cantilever beam at the top of the cliff, down to a receiving wheel on the ground, he said, "Thanks, Odel. I'd hate to have to climb all that way up."

Greeted warmly by the elevator operators and other townspeople, Thist begged off any celebration, telling them that he was under time constraints. "I have to find Odel before winter sets in," he said. "And I'm not used to the cold any more, like I used to be back home." As the Odel Elevators moved up and down from CliffEdge M'ridge Station, Thist noted with satisfaction that trade goods were the primary cargoes—processed lumber and furs coming down, field crops going up. It appeared to him that the differences in available resources and climate from highlands to Thessland would ensure profitable commerce and peaceful relations between the two new communities. *Odel's Elevators are a great invention. As long as Lork and Pernie don't decide to send their Mothersmen up them!*

THIST TOOK HIS EMU WITH HIM ON THE NEXT ODEL Elevator trip up to the Dark Highlands. Once again, as he arrived at the settlement called CliffEdge, a hero's welcome awaited him. Called by many names, "Savior of ShadowFall" seemed to Thist to be a hollow phrase, given the subsequent an ongoing troubles with the Originals there. "Twin of the Liberator" was more appropriate and satisfying, based on honoring Thusk for the separation treaty that freed Thessland from the ungrateful Originals. *But more than half of our people left Thessland to come up here, or to go on with Odel to God's Country. Did I help them by their immigration to Motherland? Certainly not those who died fighting for ShadowFall or Pernie or me. I am surprised that the relatives of those who died don't just throw me over the cliffs here.*

After a raucous party, Thist left the celebration to walk alone along the cliff fence line, enjoying the cool mild breeze. Looking out over the dark expanse of Motherland spread out in front of him, he saw the dots of the few gas lights of M'ridge Station down below; in the distance the many lights of Thess City blinked and wavered in the turbulent air that poured from the highlands into the basin below. He sighed. *Wakan and Pernie, what has happened to you since I left? Is Motherland now in good hands? Pernie, you changed so much, betrayed me. And I, I...loved you.* He sighed. *And I still do.*

Thist felt continuing guilt over leaving Wakan Kech to face Pernie alone. *Wakan, my friend, I trust that you settled things with Pernie, that she knows I did not leave Motherland without good reason. No, she chose the pirate, Lork, and I hope she stays happy with him. I wish her no ill will, but my life is up here, and back home in The People's Lands.*

Overhead, the Moon—*The Wen of the Mist*, as he had first known it—glowed yellow and full, the dim lights of Her necklace of colored beads overwhelmed by the surrounding brightness of Her scarred face. Thist's heart ached to think of Thusk up there, living underground with that Mienne, in a body not even his own. "But at least you *do* live, twin. I didn't kill you. You have found your place with the Wen of the Mist and with a wen of your own." Turning toward the dark forest that lay before him, seven hundred kilometers of unknown territory just to Odel's Quarry, he said, "I hope to make it upriver to my own wen, Anklya."

<hr>

"It's been a long while since I experienced snow and ice," Thist said to his uninterested emu, his breath fogging his snow goggles. "Not since the Ice Sea. And back then I was in Una, and a lot warmer." Although he desperately wanted to stop and start a campfire, he kept pushing himself and his two-leg ever northward. "At least another two hundred kilometers to go, my bird. And colder, too, I'm sure."

Two weeks had passed since Thist left CliffEdge, cheered on by the People there who still considered him as a kind of savior. *You'd have probably been better off staying home*, Thist thought as he waved goodbye to the fur-coated crowd of well-wishers. *At least all those who died fighting for ShadowFall and in Pernie's other battles.* But he realized that the PeoplesLandsers were all adults and each had made a free choice to immigrate down to Motherland. *As I chose to leave it, and head back home.*

———

ARMED WITH THE LATEST MAP SHOWING THE WAY TO Odel's Quarry as supplied by the traders at CliffEdge, Thist continued his trek, at times feeling regretful that he had not allowed a few People to accompany him to find Odel. Waterways being too unpredictable in wintertime, Thist opted to go an overland route. The sketchy map indicated stone-pile markers, bent trees, rivers, creeks and ponds, and the estimated distances between them. His intention was to locate his friend, rest up and resupply, then sneak westward into God's Port incognito, hoping to make contact with one of the berg crews who conveyed their ice for sale in the Solar Priests' God's Country trading harbor. "That's the only way I'll ever be able to find the secret lift site that will get me back home," he had explained to his hosts at CliffEdge. "But I have to avoid those Solars or I'll get fried like the poor warehouseman who sold me the godscloth."

During his evening in CliffEdge, raucous laughter had ensued every time Thist related the story of his godscloth theft and his escape downriver to Motherland. The gruesome execution by solar concentrators always drew grimaces, but then his experience of hiding in the excrement of the toilet pit, dodging the catapult stones in his sailboat, and finally climbing down thousands of yards of godscloth to ShadowFall, made up for that, and his listeners laughed and congratulated him. He preferred to gloss over his subsequent time as a fighter in the Game and to minimize his tenure as general of the Motherland Army. He omitted entirely his relationship with Mother Pernie. As the envious and awestruck onlookers sat back in respect and admiration, he wondered if any of them would trade places. *If they knew the cost of my fame, the losses I have endured*, he mused, *not just Thusk and Wakan and...and Pernie, but my scars and my foot.* As if on cue, the stump above his missing left ankle throbbed up its own painful memories of that amputation.

THE NEXT WEEK PROVED ALMOST FATAL TO THIST; FOR his steed, it did. During an unexpected assault by half a dozen blue-painted, near-naked tribesmen, Thist killed three with sword and springbow, and his emu eviscerated another. Man and bird both watched the survivors fleeing back into the dark forest. *No shoes, no furs, in all of this snow?* he thought. *Armed only with stone hatchets? Who are these people and why so primitive?* As his bird defecated on one of the bodies in its usual victory trope, Thist inspected the others of the dead, finding only tattoos and bone necklaces, but no metal of any kind, nothing worth saving. *Oh well, the scavenger birds and animals will feed well today.*

But during the attack, one of the savages had injured the emu's right leg. As his bird hobbled pitifully, trying to walk on the bleeding leg, Thist sighed. He then killed it with a swift blow to the neck with his shortsword. "A good bird you were, and I am sorry it came to this," he said as he removed his saddlebags. Over the next hour he skinned the bird, slicing its more edible breast meat into small portions, leaving the entrails, legs, and other bloody pieces for the scavengers. A quick campfire rendered the cooked meat storable, an amount sufficient for the remainder of his trip. *At least, I hope it is enough. With these snows it is harder and harder to find game to eat.* Reluctantly putting out the fire, he gazed out over the snow-covered mountains in the distance, his difficult route to Odel and God's Country. *Another hundred kilometers, one step at a time. I hope I can make it.*

COLD WINDS CUT THROUGH THIST'S WET FURS, CHILLING him dangerously. Clutching onto a crudely hewn crutch under his left armpit, he trudged slowly through a line of trees, toward what appeared to be a clearing of some kind ahead. *If I don't find shelter soon, I am going to die here in this damned forest*, he thought. *If I hadn't lost that map along with my backpack in that tumble down the hill into the river, I might know where I am. Surely not more than a few kilometers away.* He regretted losing his springbow, his food, his fire-starters, and the godsphere. *And my damned ivory foot!* As a final insult to his body's condition, during the tumble his ivory prosthesis had been ripped from its ties and lost in the river current. Fortunately his shortsword, tied to his waist, stayed with him, enabling him to fashion a makeshift crutch from a tree limb and to keep on walking, however slowly. *But not much longer, I am just too cold and wet and tired.* A darkly humorous thought rose up, a vision of a crude wooden plaque nailed to a tree, reading: *Here lies one General Thist, late commander of the Motherland Army, liberator of ShadowFall, lover of the matriarch, star of the Games— frozen to death under scrub pines in Nowhereland.*

As he emerged from the line of trees, Thist came upon not a clearing but a road, one paved with flat stones. Looking both ways, the highway disappeared in a broad curve in each direction, with no buildings or houses to be seen. "This has got to be the road to God's Port!" he exclaimed joyously. "Now, which way would Odel's Quarry be?" Trying to estimate his location from his memory of the map, he decided to go eastward, to his right. If he went westward and made it to God's Port, he would be caught and executed, he knew. But if he were already too far to the east and went eastward and missed Odel's Quarry, he would freeze to death on the open road. But while on the road, he figured, he would at least stand the chance of finding help; passersby, traders? Hopefully not any Solar Priests, although basking in the concentrated sunlight of their reflectors didn't sound quite so bad, not with the deepening chill in his recalcitrant muscles and aching bones.

Hours passed as Thist neared exhaustion, plodding eastward, becoming fearful that he had started his road journey too far east of Odel's Quarry. *If I did, I will die here*. The winds died down as the storm subsided, the sun making a welcome, warming appearance behind scattered clouds. *It is late afternoon,* Thist saw. *Another night in this cold will kill me. I've got to find some place warm and dry or somebody to help me.*

CHAPTER FIFTY-THREE

After six months back home in his quarry site, Odel M'ridge was feeling reasonably content. A hundred immigrants from Thessland had arrived and settled in, taking land grants from the now-friendly Solar Priests at God's Port, clearing the forest for cabins and croplands. Even some mining operations—lead, zinc, copper, iron and coal. *These little people are industrious*, he thought. *They explore, experiment, develop resources as nobody else around here has ever done. Those ancient underground cities that God's Port is built over, the ones they exploit, spoiled those people. When all you have to do is dig down and find miles of godscloth, tons of aluminum, and infinite amounts of other processed metals and porcelain, it's no wonder they never ventured out into these hills to mine.*

Having heard no more news about any difficulties at CliffEdge, Odel and his local people tended to dismiss any such concerns as low priority. When time allowed, however, Odel and a few of his experienced flyers did build a small fleet of tri-wings, outfitting them with multiple rocket boosters for longer-distance operations if ever needed. Mox had been especially efficient in overseeing the production of the boosters and of a small arsenal of firepowder bombs. Odel hated to devote time and resources to warfare preparations, thinking of it as a waste of people and resources, but he did enjoy flying again. With its own small aerial force, and with every adult trained in springbow and shortsword, Quarry, as their community had come to be called, would not be easily taken. Weekly drills at Quarry reminded each citizen of their duties; monthly assemblies ensured that area defenses would be properly coordinated. *I only wish we had been able to bring enough emus for all of them,* he thought. *Those birds are force-multipliers. Maybe CliffEdge can do a war-bird drive up here someday? Bring a herd of them?* He smiled at the thought of herding such a collection of war-birds up from the Edge. *I'll wait till spring, get word to them, see how much that would cost.* A stray vision of emus coming down the New River from The People's Lands to God's Port passed through his mind. *And maybe I can talk to some ice peddlers about that?*

AS SNOW DRAPED THE LAND, A VERY PREGNANT MOX began to show signs that she would soon deliver. Odel didn't want her to have to travel all the way to God's Port, and did not have confidence enough in the little People's healers to perform the delivery of a big man's baby, so he decided to go fetch the recommended healer himself. Leaving the quarry in the hands of Exorder and the new settlers, he set off to God's Port in a horse-drawn covered sleigh with a driver and two springbow guards. It would be a five-day round trip to and from, which he did not look forward to, but knew he had to endure. An hour out, though, the driver halted. "What is it?" Odel shouted out, upset at the stop, anxious to get the healer quickly and return before Mox went into labor.

"Sir, you'd better see for yourself," the driver shouted back.

Sword in hand, Odel stepped out carefully onto the icy road, spotting a small dark figure in dark furs, leaning on a crutch. Hobbling closer, the man pulled down his face covering. Odel stood in shock, not believing his eyes.

—

As Thist rounded a curve in the road, his prayer was answered—there in the middle of the snow-covered roadway, heading his way, was a horse-drawn carriage, an expensive-looking sleigh conveyance, with a driver high up front, and beside him two guards armed with springbows. As the vehicle approached Thist, it stopped. He heard the driver call out to someone inside. A big man descended from the carriage and walked over toward him. *Carrying a sword, but pointed down, not threatening me with it,* Thist thought, his strength leaving him as he tried to remain standing. *That's good.* As the man drew closer, Thist relaxed. *This redheaded giant looks familiar...*

"Hello, Odel," Thist said, and collapsed onto the snow-covered ground.

—

Wrapped in warm, dry furs and with a mug of warm wine in hand, Thist smiled and thanked Odel for rescuing him. "Another night, I'd be dead, Odel. Very lucky you found me."

As their sleigh bounced along the road toward God's Port, Odel listened in disbelief as Thist dried himself off and slipped into oversized furs of Odel's. The little man related his travels from Motherland, and what had been happening since the big man's departure.

"Our Pernie went crazy over that Admiral Lork, the ice pirate who shot Una down and then rescued Thusk and me and brought us back to WaterEdge."

"Shot Una down? Rescued you?"

Thist took his time, detailing every day of the adventure out over the Cold Sea—Thornveld, Noorstown, the Ice Valley, Stonehaven, the return, and Pernie's immediate taking to Lork.

"But Thusk was injured, you say? How is he now? Or, how was he when you left him?" Odel was seriously concerned, wondering how Thist could possibly leave the comatose Thusk in the hands of an unpredictable, perhaps unstable, Mother Pernie.

Then Thist told him the incredible details of the Crystal Throne, of his conversation with Thusk in the avvy. "And so my twin is now alive, but in another body. On the Moon."

Odel blew out a long breath. "Thist, if anybody but you told me this tale I wouldn't believe it. But the first time I saw you two, flying down here in that big green Una machine, I knew you were unusual little guys. And seeing what all you both did down in Motherland, well now I guess I can believe anything!"

The sleigh ride lasted all night, Thist grateful for the comfort and for the companionship of his friend. A few stops for Nature's calls and two quick meals of cold meat and soup broke up the monotony of the horse's clip-clop and the soft bouncing of the sleigh. Thist slept deeply for the first time in weeks.

CHAPTER FIFTY-FOUR

As they approached the outskirts of God's Port, Odel told Thist about the huge shrine to Una that the new Solar Priests had built in the plaza fronting the Solar Temple. "I wanted to laugh when old Preesen, the new chief priest, told me about it," he said, "but I thought I ought not. You never know how people will react to having their superstitions and their legends explained in actual fact."

Thist just grinned. "Well, all of that was Thusk's doings. A shrine to my days here would show a giant shithole, with people pissing on me!" As Odel laughed, Thist remembered that Odel had spoken of his friend Razzo, for whose incineration death on that same plaza Thist himself was responsible, so he didn't mention that detail. He wondered if Odel would ever piece that puzzle together, and if so, what he would think of Thist afterwards. *Best just to let that sleeping velk lie,* he thought.

"I don't think I want to see that big Una," Thist said. "It was so disturbing to have to leave her there at Mother's Palace, unable to move. But at least she's there for Wakan to talk to. She has so much information; I wish we could have written it all down for everyone to see."

Odel clucked his tongue. "I dunno, Thist. Wouldn't want everybody to know about firepowder, much less all of them other ancient weapons. Hate to see that stuff spread around."

Thist then told Odel about smith Kleete's gunpowder cylinders and the demonstration at the arena, and mounting those pieces on Pernie's new ships.

"Oh gods, Thist, every Sister will build her own cylinders, and the next rebellions will be bloodier than ever."

"That's why, Odel, we need either to get those people away from M'ridge Station and CliffEdge, or else have them prepare defenses. Maybe make up cylinders of their own. I mean, Lork might make bigger ones to hit CliffEdge. And smaller ones, maybe carried on big tri-wings." As Odel stared at him wide-eyed, Thist said, "That godsmetal smith, Kleete, is a genius. No telling what he might come up with for Lork. And Pernie."

M'ridge groaned, "And to think, I showed them how to build tri-wings, and set up their aerial force." Eyeing Thist, he said, "Man, you never know what is going to happen when you make something new, or when you go new places." *And other than finding my Mox, Thist, sometimes I wish I'd never met you and Thusk!*

Odel stopped at an outfitter's where he bought Thist new furs and boots. "Take both boots, Thist; we'll take care of that missing foot, too." Odel then dropped off Thist at the shop of a stonemason he knew in town, where the little man sat patiently as an artisan measured his right foot to carve an exact image of it out of ivory. Odel begged off, hurriedly leaving to find the healer for Mox's delivery and then return to Quarry. The foot-carving itself went fairly fast, but making the pads and fitting the leather straps properly turned out to be a challenge for someone who had never done such a job before. Knowing that it would take overnight for the job to be done, Thist asked the man to modify his makeshift crutch while he was waiting, so he could walk outside.

A quick flurry of hammering and sawing by two assistants proceeded, and Thist was able to walk out of the shop with a promise from the stonemason that all should be ready the next morning.

While his prosthetic was thus being finished, Thist ambled through God's Port. With a nice bag of coppers, courtesy of Odel's generosity, he walked slowly through the city streets, getting gradually accommodated to the feel and heft of his new crutch. He walked toward the harbor, hoping to find ice merchants from The People's Lands and a way home with them. M'ridge had said that bergs were being delivered at least once a month, now that the new Solar Priests had become more receptive to outsiders.

Thist's first stop was at the dockmaster's small kiosk, where a large, obese man in heavy furs sat in front of a hot metal stove. "I'm looking for berg men," Thist said, through the open door. The warmth felt good.

"Not due for a couple days, I'm thinking," was the reply. Looking carefully at Thist, the man said, "Friends of yours comin' down with 'em?"

"Hoping so," Thist replied.

"Check back tomorrow, then," the dockmaster said, shutting the door.

Thist thanked him and went to find shelter. "I hope this time I don't have to spend the night in the shitter," he said aloud. Tall passersby looked down at him with puzzled looks. He didn't care, eagerly remembering the unexpected charms of the big wen in the inn he had resided in during his first visit to the town, two years ago. *Those women are still there, I'll bet, and so am I. Anklya or not, it has been entirely too long a time.*

TWO DAYS LATER, A BERG CREW ARRIVED, POLING THEIR ice into a dock as Thist stood watching. Seeing if he could recognize anyone, he broke out into a grin and shouted, "Hey, Cruthar! That you?"

As the berg was being secured to the dock with

godscloth netting, one of the crew walked over to Thist. "Be damned if it ain't you, Mr. Thist! My own berg-man!" Pounding Thist on the back, the man said, "And yessir, Mr. Thist, it is me, the one and only Cruthar!" Ostentatiously sniffing around Thist's head and shoulders, he laughed. "You ain't been sleepin' in no shitholes, have ya?" Cruthar had once saved him by leaving a small sailboat next to him as he slept, covered with filth, under a dock on this very harbor. He owed the berg-man his life.

Laughing, Cruthar took Thist by the shoulder and they headed off to the nearest pub. Inside, Cruthar said, "You know, last time we's in this place, them Priests' Men and their velks was after you."

"Don't remind me, Cruthar." Thist wrinkled his nose. "Back of here's that toilet I spent the night in, back then."

"Well, how's ya been since your twin took all them folks down to that Motherland in that flyin' machine of yours? Did y'all fight that war? What news?"

Thist summarized the events of the last year, notably smoothing over the losses of People in the battles and not commenting about Thusk's current status. "And so, many of them decided to leave. The big Originals down there, they don't like us, so most are up here in God's Country or still down at CliffEdge." He didn't say anything about his fears of Lork attacking their countrymen or invading farther north. *Best not to stir up emotions*, he thought, *I don't want any more wars if I can help it. This God's Country might be the best place for most of us for a while. But I want to go home. To Anklya.*

After much wine and beer and laughter, and more stories by Thist of his and Thusk's adventures, Cruthar grew more serious. "I reckon yer big friend, that Odel, he told you news about The People's Lands?"

"I'm hoping my birther, Mell, is doing well," Thist said, as Cruthar nodded. "And Anklya? How is she? I really want to see her again." At which Cruthar frowned.

"Mr. Thist, then you don't know about Anklya? That Odel didn't tell you?"

Thist picked up the concern in Cruthar's voice. "And what might that be? Is she doing well?"

"Well, sir. Yes, she is doing well. She is on the Council of Electors. And"—he hesitated—"Anklya is now the mother of newborn twins. A month old."

Thist was taken aback. Had he or Thusk impregnated her? Were either of them now fathers? Mixed emotions swelled up in his mind, contradictory thoughts swirling. *I thought Wakan's herbs prevented pregnancy! But—a month old? We've been away for well over a year. Who—?*

Cruthar looked straight into Thist's eyes. "I kin answer that question I see you're wantin' to ask. They're mine. Anklya is my wife!"

Thist gulped, almost choking on his beer. Drawing on emotional reserves he had thought depleted after Pernie's turnabout with Lork, he thought, *Cruthar saved my life once. And he is my ticket home. Have to be nice and respectful to him, even though I've just had a punch in the gut.*

Thist stood and held up his flagon, loudly toasting the man who had just deflated the last remaining volume of his ego. "Well, great, Cruthar! You are the man! I'm happy for you and Anklya and your twins!" Returning home, he thought, was not going to be exactly what he thought it might be. *Life is an adventure that serves as food for the soul, Wakan always said. And surprise is the spice for that meal—sometimes tasty, sometimes stomach-churning.*

FINDINGS

Mienne shouted, "Thusk, I think this is where I was found! It's the way to UpTop, Zhee City!" The tunnel in front of them looked as if an overhead cave-in had been repaired, a rough patch on the ceiling contrasting to the smoothly lasered surface of the floor and walls.

"Looks like it, Mienne," Avvy Thusk said. "This map of Jolan Keesh's indicates it should be close by here. But if that overhead tunnel you came through goes up to Vac, it would be dangerous to try to get into it."

They had walked several kilometers from Community to this site, Thusk knew, trusting to the hand-drawn sketch of Jolan's, as overlaid on the drawing he himself had made from the DI's three-dimensional display back in Mienne's Control Room. "If we dig up there, we'd best put on these construction suits, just in case." In each backpack the engineers had packed a Vac suit, a protective covering used when excavating into unknown or suspect Rock. Several instances of encountering airless voids and ancient tubes had resulted in the suffocation of crews. Engineers had discovered the Vac suits in the ancient Resource Tube, working out the details of how to adapt them down from the sizes of ancients to fit the smaller Community people. Mienne's suit had not required modifications, as it was originally fabricated for those of her size. *And for the size of my avvy body*, Thusk thought.

Once encased in the loose-fitting Vac suits, Thusk followed the instructions Jolan Keesh had given him, and set up seals on both sides of the roof excavation, ahead of and behind them, in the tunnel. "These balloon sealant systems are pretty easy to inflate, Mienne," Thusk said, his voice somewhat muffled by the faceplate. Pointing to the ceiling, he said, "If that opens directly into Vac, the air from this five meter section of tunnel is all that will be lost." Using Jolan's loaned laser cutter, he drew a roughly circular line around the existing patch, about a meter in diameter. After several repeated courses, a piece of the roof gradually separated, opening almost like a circular trapdoor. There was no rush of air out of their sealed tunnel section, in fact no noise at all. "My pressure gauge shows no drop, so there's no Vac there. Yet."

Their torch lights showed that the intersecting overhead tunnel, if that's what it was, slanted upward about fifteen to twenty degrees and was perpendicular to the tunnel that Jolan and Ledd were excavating when Mienne collapsed into it.

"So this is where I came in," Mienne said calmly. "I was so afraid. I had been running for so long." Shining her light into the darkness, she could see that her escape route had been designed for people her size, being twice the height and width of Community excavations. "I'm ready to go back and see where I came from."

Thusk nodded. Mienne opened her backpack to pull out an extension ladder that unfolded from the size of her hand into a rigid, ten-foot-long shimmering latticelike ladder. "More of that miraculous nanotech stuff, huh, Mienne?"

She smiled. "These flat cards do it. And it folds back up just as easily," she said, scrambling up the almost invisible framework. After Thusk climbed up, Mienne pressed both sides of the nanoladder and it collapsed into a flat pack that fit into her palm again. "Magic, yes?" Thusk just shook his head. *This Moon is a weird place!*

Given unknowns and possible cave-ins, regardless of DI's assurances that the way was open once they accessed the intersecting tunnel, Thusk had brought provisions for five days. Twenty kilometers each way, and one day on site. Mienne carried the ladder, lights and batteries. Each carried food, water, a torchlight and a laser cutter.

With their loaded packs, the going was not difficult, Thusk still feeling light on his feet, unconsciously adopting Mienne's long strides, a modified loping gait impossible up on Earth. Not knowing the why of it, he just accepted it as yet another strange mystery of the Moon, Kilometer after kilometer they trudged ever upward, ever on the same slope. Thusk felt no fatigue, attributing his undiminished energy to the avvy he occupied. *I could get used to this*, he thought. *I wonder how long its power lasts?* A strange thought popped into his mind, almost a voice: "Thirty Earth days, nominally, sir."

Shaking his head, he thought, *Voices in my head? Too many memories of Una, residual hallucinations, still getting used to my new body*. He promptly put away that train of thought and focused on the trek ahead. Fortunately they encountered no branching pathways, no places to get lost, though Thusk began to experience some claustrophobic discomfort as he realized that he was actually hundreds of meters underground on the distant *Wen of the Mist*. Hours passed and still there was breathable air in the tunnel according to their instruments. With Mienne leading, he could see that she was tiring, slowing down.

"When did you run out of air, Mienne? Thusk asked, wondering if this tunnel could possibly be the wrong one.

"My mother gave me her breather pack, Thusk, when mine was showing near empty. That's all I remember." She was breathing shallowly, Thusk could tell.

He answered, "We should be near the surface now, a lot sooner than I expected. No obstacles, no cave-ins. Counting my steps, it can't be far." He shrugged off his backpack and said, "I'm going to go on ahead. You sit and rest here for a while. I'll see how far it is to the top, then come back and get you. You have plenty of food and water here, and batteries for your torch and warmer, if you need it."

Exhausted, Mienne took off her own pack, sitting down and leaning against the smooth stone wall. "All right, Thusk. But be careful up there. There was danger when Mother and I escaped. There might still be."

Lifting his faceplate, Thusk kissed her and continued on up the tunnel.

"BY MY COUNT, TWO THOUSAND STEPS SINCE I LEFT Mienne, close to a kilometer," he said aloud, just to hear a human voice. There was no echo, and he had opened his helmet long before to keep from sweating. So far the tunnel looked exactly like it had for the other six hours —smooth, dark gray walls and arched ceiling, slightly roughened floor; no signs, no markings, no indicators of distance, and no curves. Then ahead of him, filling the tunnel floor to ceiling, appeared a shimmering curtain of greenish light. Slowly approaching the translucent screen, he probed it with his torch light. "Nothing," he said to himself. Using the extensible hand-operated probe tool on his wrist, he again tested the curtain. The instruments registered only magnetism and ionic activity. "Nothing harmful to tissue, so in I go."

As he stepped through the shimmer, Thusk's Vac suit suddenly sealed itself at his neckline, the arms and legs puffing out, balloon-like. "What?" he said, but could not hear himself. In panic, he pulled the helmet back in place, breathing hard, heart pounding. Had he been injured? Not that he could feel.

"What happened?" he said aloud, hearing his voice amplified inside his helmet.

"Vacuum mode initiated, sir," an emotionless voice said. Thusk couldn't tell who said it.

"What? Who are you?" he demanded, looking around the tunnel.

"Avatar system, at your command, sir."

Thusk spun around again, searching with his torchlight, looking for the speaker. Only the green shimmering curtain stood out from the gray stone surface of the tunnel. "Where are you? What are you doing?" He realized that he was only hearing himself inside his helmet, meaning that outside his suit was vacuum. *My Vac suit worked for my body, but I had no helmet on. How did I breathe? How could I?*

"Sir, this system is an integral component of this qomp array. This system is presently operating in total vacuum. Qomps are in constant adjustment flux to compensate and to simulate nominal human operations."

"*Inside* me? In this, this, this avvy?" Thusk tried to put down the panic he was feeling. *A new body, and shared with qomps? What am I now, a man or a machine?*

"To answer that question, sir: this avatar body comprises quadrillions of qomps. Of these, a small portion accommodates the entangled quanta from your original human body as transferred. The remainder provide the enhanced physical capabilities required for the missions, as they are assigned."

Horrified, Thusk asked, not wanting to know the answer, "What, what *missions*?"

"Missions are assigned by headquarters, Union of North America Defense Command, sir. At the present time, none have been received. By NADC protocol, in the absence of orders from HQ, command authority defers locally, meaning to yourself. At your command, sir."

In near shock, Thusk leaned against the tunnel wall. "What, what, do I call you?" An innocuous question, it was the only thing he could think to do in his state of mind.

"Whatever you wish, sir. No nomenclature is

required, but this system recognizes that humans prefer to address qomp systems by a familiar name. In searching your preferences, this system suggests *Kech* as appropriate."

Trying to calm himself down, Thusk thought, *This can't be any weirder than dying on Earth and waking up in a new body of the Moon. But it will take getting used to.*

"Sir, a training routine is available for new users."

"Don't read my mind, dammit!" Thusk yelled.

"Sir, thoughts are faster than words. Are you certain you wish to override established protocols?"

If you can read this, let it be the last time!

As you wish, sir. Is this intramind communication, one way, acceptable?

"Yes, Kech. But only in emergencies, or when I ask."

Understood, sir.

"Now, er, *Kech*, why did you wait until now to communicate with me? Why didn't you say something when I arrived, or even that first time, months ago?"

"Sir, this avatar system remains quiescent until a question is asked or a threat is detected. You asked no questions. And until you walked into vacuum, there was no threat."

This avvy reasons about the way that Una used to—no anticipation of needs, and a literal answer every time. I hope that behavior will change, as Una's did.
"So, what was that about vacuum? Am I in vacuum now? Does that green curtain serve as an airlock? Aloud, please."

"Sir, Kech here sensed vacuum and immediately adjusted this avvy to function in it. Nominal human functions are put in abeyance for the duration. The shimmer curtain is a yielding complex borophene screen that enables passage of humans and their associated systems while preventing atmosphere from escaping into vacuum."

"But I can live in a vacuum? Very useful on the

Moon, I guess. What else can you do, Kech? Or should I say *we*?"

"Sir, this avvy is designed to operate in deep space from temperatures near zero kelvin to four hundred kelvin. Radiation tolerance is…"

Thusk reeled as Kech listed his avvy capabilities and features. *I'm more robot than man, more a machine than a human. But…I still* feel *the same, my emotions toward Mienne are the same, our lovemaking, the same. Better, actually.*

"Kech, but why? Why were avvys made this way? For what purpose?"

"Sir, to fulfill the missions as assigned."

"But what are the missions *for*? What happens on a mission? *Where* are the missions?"

"Sir, as pre-transfer training explained to all transferees, mission destinations typically include Moon, Mars, asteroids, and outbound ships. Missions typically involve threatened or actual armed combat.

"With your human mind now integrated with the enhanced capabilities of this avvy Kech, sir, we are a soldier."

TREMBLING AT KECH'S REVELATIONS, THUSK WALKED on, trying not to think; he didn't fully trust his avvy companion, Kech, regardless of his/its protestations. Within a hundred meters the tunnel ended and he found himself walking out of an open doorway into a deserted city. Above him, at least a hundred meters up, was the occluded underside of a dome, its surface clouded with dust or debris, Thusk couldn't tell which. Under the dome and all around him stood lifeless buildings lining empty streets. As he walked farther into the city, he saw gaping holes in the clouded dome, cracks open to the black sky of space itself. Having seen lifelike videos of space on Una's screens, he was familiar with the sight, but seeing it for real impressed him deeply. *We are so tiny; it's so big Out There.*

Reaching an open parklike space, Thusk found a kind of bench and sat. "Kech, what happened here? Where are the people? Or their bodies?"

"Sir, remnant qomps in this human habitation are erratic in nature, but it seems that the city's environmental protection dome was severely compromised rapidly and its atmosphere suffered an instantaneous pressure drop. A small percentage of the human inhabitants seem to have survived by virtue of quick-acting vacuum suits or their location in sealed areas at the time.

"The surviving remnant population seems to have departed to other domed cities."

"But where are the bodies of the dead?" He wanted Mienne to have closure from her traumatic memories, maybe know the details of her parents' passing.

"Sir, by Lunar Republic protocols, all deceased humans and biological comfort animals are thoroughly documented and then processed by maintenance bots into useful organic compounds for the crop-fields."

"Oh," said Thusk in shock, "so no cremation; they became fertilizer, huh?" The idea of eating crops that grew from the remains of people seemed gruesome. *But the Moon is weird and so are its people! Not like Earth at all!* In reviewing other aspects of the disaster, he also wondered why the green borophene curtain was set up inside the tunnel where it was, with the air kept in the lower section. And why the dome itself was never repaired. Maybe the survivors didn't want to return? If so, why not reprocess all of the buildings and other materials? The apparent priorities of lunar surface societies all seemed so different; would he ever get used to the strangeness on and *in* the Moon?

Through Kech's scanning of the city's remaining qomps, Thusk located a set of sealed apartments that still supported a breathable atmosphere. He walked the many blocks to get there, feeling an eeriness at the unoccupied buildings and homes and empty streets. Numerous two-wheeled frameworks of some kind —"Electric bicycles, sir"—stood in orderly fashion in vertical racks at every doorway, for whatever now-forgotten purpose. Taking off his helmet once inside the sealed apartment, Thusk breathed in ozone-tinged air. *It feels good to breathe, regardless of what Kech says. I don't want to give up any more humanity than I have to!*

Kech said, "Sir, the nanotech air-supply systems have been idle for three years. The odors you sense are amenable to change, as you see fit. Any aroma you choose."

"No, Kech, I'd rather keep my normal range of smelling, if you don't mind." *But later I might try the enhanced audible and visual capabilities. Those could come in handy.* He hoped Kech was not listening in.

HOURS LATER, THUSK WAS DRAPING HIS RIGHT ARM over a sobbing Mienne. "Yes, Thusk," she said between crying spells, "this was my home city of Zhee. I can still read the Man symbols and the Spanglish characters. But I don't remember where my home was here, the address. And I don't think I want to search, either it would be too emotional.

"The day it happened, Father was out, attending to crop-fields in the Far End section of the dome. All I remember is Mother slapping a quicksuit on me, and us running to some exit." Her voice dropped off to a whisper. "I had always thought I might come home and find both my parents alive. Or at least their bodies, preserved in vacuum. But I didn't suspect the autobots to, to, *collect* and, and reprocess them!" Breaking into sobs again, she held onto Thusk for long minutes.

THE NEXT MORNING, THUSK WANTED TO TAKE MORE time to explore the cracked-dome city, especially the larger vehicles and solar power equipment, but Mienne insisted they leave. "Everything I loved about my childhood here is gone, Thusk. All of the colors, the plants, the people, their clothing, their festivals. All organics are desiccated or reprocessed to no good use." She pointed out the window, indicating the sparkling clean, yet sterile, environment outside in the abandoned city.

"My life for years has been down in Community; my new life is in Control Complex. It will be an adventurous life; as the 3D showed, there are hundreds of kilometers of tubes yet to explore. Even some going over to the Far Side."

Thusk grimaced. "Mienne, I want to stay up here on the surface for a while. I like looking up at Earth, having all this open space around me."

"But you can't stay; you'd have no food, no support," she complained softly, "no *me*."

Thusk held Mienne close, adjusting her backpack. Before closing her helmet, he said, "My avvy tells me I can subsist on sunlight and assorted mineral dust."

Mienne drew back from Thusk and opened her mouth in an O. "The avvy *tells* you? What…what…do you mean?"

Thusk sighed. "It's complicated. Sit down for a while."

HIGH IN THE VELVET-BLACK SKY, THUSK COULD SEE THE shadow of darkness dividing the distant disc of Earth into night and day. Though the white swirl of clouds obscured most of the details of that distant globe, he could tell that the edge of the terminator lay within the expanse of Motherland.

"I wonder what Thist and our birther are doing up there right now? And Wakan? And Odel?" Sighing, Thusk said to the infinite vacuum around him, hearing it only in his own head, "And Pernie. Even her pirate." But he knew he'd never find out; the crystal chairs had stopped working for some unknown reason. He'd never be able to talk with his twin or those others up there again. *But that's a whole other world, now,* he thought. *Not mine any more.* As his view encompassed the stark lunar landscape, its shades of gray and black broken only by the reflections from distant domes and towers, he thought, *But Mienne had a point there; I would like to see living colors up close again, not just those tiny lights in the sky or dead cities here on the Moon.*

As he walked from the paved pathway onto virgin lunar surface, kicking up dust, Thusk looked back at the shattered dome that had been the city of Zhee, Mienne's birthplace. He wondered what had impacted it so suddenly, and why it had not self-repaired. But even his Kech and the external qomps it accessed had no answers. "It looks to me like a deliberate attack. Somebody wanted to destroy that city, its people." *Other people, probably.* Sighing, he realized that humans were humans, on Earth or Moon, large or small, ancient or modern.

When Mienne had left, going back through the slanted tunnel to her Control, Thusk promised to return to her in a matter of days, but only after he had done some exploring topside in the entirely new environment. Exploration was in his blood, he explained, which was the only reason he had ever volunteered to sit on the Crystal Throne and come to the Moon in the first place. And because his avvy could survive in any lunar or vacuum conditions, there was no need for her to worry about accidents or anything else affecting his health or safety.

"Be sure you do come back, Thusk. I missed you so much when you were gone all those months. And now that you're back, I don't want to lose you again." After she was gone, Thusk laughed at Mienne's stated relief that he would not be eating any local foodstuffs of any kind, stored or fresh. "You might be ingesting Father or Mother." He didn't think she was joking.

We parted on good terms, he thought, *but there is so much to see up here, it may take a while. Maybe a lifetime. Meanwhile...* "Kech, now that we are aboveground, are you able to access any of the qomps on Far Side?" He had been considering bits and pieces of evidence, but wanted to be alone before asking Kech.

"Sir, only a few. Your query?"

"What was the purpose of that vast array constructed over Parsons crater on Far Side?"

"Sir, incomplete data, but it appears to have been built as a quantum entanglement scanner and transmitter for distant missions. For distant destinations and numerous transfers, a large transmission area was necessary.

"To send people into avvys out in space? Why not just use crystal chairs like on Earth and Moon?"

"Sir, the cislunar-system chairs were built for security transfers; they are low power, for single-person communication and transmission only. Your Kech, here, was fabricated in the large receiving area where hundreds of transferees could be accommodated. The large-scale transmission facility on Earth has not communicated for...some time, and is believed to be nonfunctional.

"To answer your unasked question—yes. The intention of the now-defunct Parsons crater installation was to transmit thousands of transferees to Mars and other outer system destinations simultaneously."

Thusk wondered why such a capability was needed, why such an expensive installation had been needed. What *mission* would have needed thousands of avvys? He stopped walking, taking time to gaze up at Red Mars, trying to envision what had occurred there on The Day. Had Martian colonies been destroyed? *What are they like now, after thirty thousand years of separation from Mother Earth? Did anyone survive? Did they keep all the ancient ways of living, of government? Could they have developed societies like The Tharn's Lands, or Na Saam or Motherland?* A favorite memory surfaced. *Or like Noorstown, a warm and wonderful place despite its pirates?*

He had to ask. "Kech, are there other transmitting

facilities still in existence here on Moon, any nearby that could transfer just one human from one avvy to another avvy? Say from one here on Moon to one out on Mars?" That red dot in the sky looked tempting, a solid colorful beacon in an infinite black void.

"Sir, yes."

CHAPTER FIFTY-SIX

"These last weeks have been strenuous, Mell," Thist told his birther as they sat in front of her fireplace. Her house was rebuilt on the site of their former home, the one burned by The Tharn's thugs long ago. The smoldering peat logs brought back happy memories of when his whole family had shared good times in the old house. But with Sire Thess dead and Thusk on the Moon, his recollections were bittersweet. "It was so nice coming home. Cruthar showed me the way back after we sailed upriver. It was quite a march from that river to the lift site, and of course a week's trudging back through the mountains and back home here."

Mell smiled at her son, happy to be seeing him after so long. But she was still recuperating from Thist's report on Thusk. Thist was thinking that she might have been less stressed out if he had reported his twin dead, instead of his actual status. Death was familiar to everyone, a thing sad but natural, understandable; it could be ensconced in a special emotional space, kept there, visited when grief was called for. But—being qomped to an avvy body on the Moon? Being alive up there, on the *Wen of the Mist*? That was almost unbelievable to anyone who had not experienced the Crystal Throne themselves. *At times I still find myself not believing it,* he thought. He had been unhappy to find that none of the godspheres in The People's Lands were functional; not one had responded to his touch. *But that is my own doing, my fault. I told Una to turn them off, but then I lost mine in that damned river.* Without a godsphere or Una, he would never be able to communicate with Thusk again.

His later meeting with Anklya was not as awkward as he had feared. He and Mell walked to the People's Palace, where Anklya, as Director of the Council, shared living quarters with her husband Cruthar and their new children. Thist noted that the plaza outside the palace was now scrubbed clean, as were the columns at the entrance; cleanliness had never been a hallmark of The Tharn back in that time. Inside, the entire building was also clean and now well-lit by gas lamps, most of the rooms serving as government offices, with a library and a meeting hall for citizens. Thist was glad to see that written books were in abundance, ever since Una had corrected the genetic shortsightedness of the People by her laser surgery. But he also felt a bit rueful that youngsters were not keen on learning the carved touch-language of knife and totem spindle, at which thought his Reading hand tingled. *Oh well, things change, and eyes* are *much quicker than hands when it comes to reading.* Still, he felt that some meanings and nuances would be lost to those who could not *feel* the symbols. He would have to ask Anklya to get the Old Wen and others to translate all of the library of carved totems into written words, before that skill was lost entirely and with it the millennia of carved history.

As Thist and Mell walked into Cruthar and Anklya's foyer, he was taken aback by her appearance, comparing it to a year before, when he had left for Motherland with Thusk. Though still tall and beautiful, there was a maturity about Anklya that he had not expected, a muting of her ebullient personality, a look of sadness or compassion in her eyes. *Perhaps resignation?* He shook off such thoughts. *The woman has a life without me or Thusk, and she is probably happier than I am.* Thist had wondered whether the offspring of large and small people would be a mixture of the two, maybe halfway-sized? Odel's baby daughter with Mox had been nearly normal human sized, resulting in a difficult birth made successful only by surgery, a cute little thing with dark skin and reddish hair. But Anklya and Cruthar's twins were small people like their father, though with blond hair and striking blue eyes and skin of a slightly lighter shade than his.

Cruthar said, as he and Anklya each held one of the tiny babies for Thist to see, "As usual with our People, Mr. Thist, when it's boys, they's twins. And I hope you don't mind, but when we were ready to name them, we didn't know if you two was still alive or not. Nobody heard nothing about if you made it through all them Motherland wars or anything. So we took your birther Mell's suggestion." Mell smiled as Cruthar said, "These boys here are named Rist and Rusk. We hopes they'll earn their *Th* when they grows up."

AFTER A FEW DAYS BACK IN THE PEOPLE'S TOWN, Thist was growing restless, trying to decide what to do with the rest of his life. He and Thusk had changed The Tharn's Lands for the better; they had saved ShadowFall from Creesile; they had won civil wars for Pernie and Motherland. They had introduced Odel M'ridge to Motherland and to Mox, and that big guy now had a baby girl and led a colony of immigrants at his burgeoning community of Quarry. Odel had learned what his tri-wings could do, built that elevator, and earned his happiness with Mox and an ever-increasing number of immigrants from Thessland and CliffEdge.

All these people and places, we improved them. What else could anyone ask for? he wondered, no longer feeling any guilt about fighting in the Game or the wars, or even carrying out Pernie's gruesome orders. *That is all in the past, and most often the violence was against others trying to kill me. I'm glad I won and they didn't— I'm not feeling guilty about that!* Being back home in familiar surroundings and its simpler society had restored his original confidence in his own worth and integrity. *Maybe it takes really bad experiences to make you realize you're not so bad yourself?* He was happy with that; apparently his body was, too, because the old memories no longer caused his missing left foot to throb painfully.

With the benefits bestowed on Mell after Thess' death, and with some small treasure retrieved from Sire Thess' cave of refuge halfway to The Ice, neither he nor his birther had any financial worries. But he wanted to be active again; simply retelling tales about his adventures in Motherland and on Una quickly grew boring for him, and, he suspected, for others, too.

Going back to ice selling was out of the question. Sire Thess had bestowed that business on Cruthar during their revolt against The Tharn, and Cruthar had expanded the iceberg market fourfold. Cruthar's firm now scheduled regular ice deliveries to God's Port, no longer dependent on icefalls at the glacier's edge, but with active crews mining at The Ice at the End of the World—something that neither Sire Thess nor his twins had thought of. *I never would have considered old rough-edged Cruthar being so creative*, he thought. *But I'll bet Anklya could have had something to do with that.*

Thinking of his lost lover, Thist knew he had to get away from The People's Lands again; every time he was near Anklya he felt his passion rising, memories of their frenetic lovemaking, of her breathtaking response. Worse than that, he could sense by Anklya's body language and furtive glances that she felt the same. *I won't do that*, he thought, *not to her, not to Cruthar, not to their little Rist and Rusk.*

Early one afternoon Cruthar sent a messenger to Mell's home, asking Thist to meet him at his new riverside pub. "For business," the note said. Reluctantly, Thist put on more formal furs and footwear and walked through town, returning greetings from the dozens of grateful citizens, large people and small, who encountered him along the way. Their gratitude at having been liberated in his and Thusk's revolution was a welcome and warming relief from the depression he was feeling about his own idleness. Finally, at Cruthar's pub, now advertised by a large, printed sign proclaiming THE ANKLYA PUB—no longer just a patch of color for illiterates, he noticed, yet another improvement he and Thusk had introduced to their homeland—the wealthy ice merchant met him, seating him at a small booth in a dark corner near a fireplace.

After the serving wen sat their flagons of beer down, she left, drawing a thin curtain over the secluded booth. Thist wondered at the site and the situation. "So, Cruthar, why the secrecy, over here in the corner? I thought you would be open and loud, and we'd laugh it up a bit."

But Cruthar was all seriousness. "Some news for you, Thist. You know I has crews workin' on The Ice up there, calving off chunks all the time, not waitin' for them to fall off by themselves."

"Yes. Brilliant idea. Glad you thought of it. Made you rich, and you buying this pub and all."

Cruthar nodded, grinning. "Got somethin' else, make us both rich. Or richer."

Thist perked up. Something new? He was interested.

"Yep, Thist. Just got some word from my calving crew up there, delivered by bird-rider this very day."

"And?"

"You know that Una y'all found in The Ice?"

A curious question, Thist thought. "Sure. But she's broken down, can't fly, stuck in a field on Mother's Palace grounds now, twenty-five hundred kilometers away. What about her?"

"They just found another one, this one blue, stickin' halfway outta the glacier. Got some strange-lookin' bodies inside," said Cruthar. "Wanna go up there with me and see it?"

Thist grinned.

CHAPTER FIFTY-SEVEN

Mother Perneptheranam leaned back on her cushioned divan, suckling her infant son at her left breast. Across from her sat her Kech priest, Altamun, who was attempting to divert his view from his Mother's enticing appearance to some of the paintings and sculptures adorning her chambers. His gaze settled on the large map of Motherland and the large continents north and south of it, but he could not avoid furtive glances at Pernie's exposed breast. Amused at the Kech's embarrassment, Pernie said, "Altamun, don't be shy. Surely my little boy is not that unpleasant to view, is he?"

Pernie's light chuckle set Altamun more at ease, but he did make a conscious effort to look her in the eyes and not gaze farther down. "Yes, Mother, he is quite the looker. Red hair and all." The Kech priest, now on the job six months since Wakan's demotion and disappearance, had not yet become used to Mother Pernie's eccentricities, but knew that his very life depended upon staying in her good graces. From the day she had announced Wakan Kech's demotion and his own promotion—a total surprise to both priests— Altamun had started to worry about his fate. Considering what all Wakan had briefed him about, in particular Pernie's increasingly erratic and unpredictable reaction to events outside her control, the new priestly advisor felt as if he were standing on a knife edge—one slip would be painful.

Supremely self-confident after several years of turmoil and turnover, Pernie now appeared to be in total control of herself and of the Motherland. A loyal army, a new navy, and a cadre of elite palace guards ensured as much. "Fine, Altamun. Now, what news have you about the deserters, Thist and Wakan Kech? It's been months now, with no word. I expected better from you. Have you competently utilized Wakan's nationwide network of spies and informers? Is it possible to message the deserters? Or even better, to seize them? Or…?" She left the question unspoken but the fierce snarl on her face left no doubt to her intent.

"*Assassination*, Mother?" Altamun answered softly. "I think not. All we have ever known about Wakan are those reports from the guards and harpooners who saw that Una-thing rise up and fly southward with him in it. I do not believe that he was forcibly taken by that machine. My own interpretation is that Wakan successfully deceived you and all of us to think the god-machine could no longer fly, and then used his demotion as an excuse to fly home to the High Antis." He made a conscious effort not to show his own yearning for his homeland, wishing he could have flown off with Wakan. *Pernie is very perceptive,* he reminded himself. *Wakan taught her well—too well.*

"Thank you, Altamun. Since you came from those same High Antis with Wakan all those years ago, I would think you might like to visit your homeland again someday yourself." Altamun flinched, unable to prevent his involuntary response.

"I see from your reaction that I am correct, as usual." She smiled, acknowledging her priest's unsuccessful attempts to conceal his innermost emotions. "So—do tell our planners to estimate the resources to, ah, *visit* that distant southern land. Time and cost. Get back to me when you have some definite proposals."

Altamun groaned inwardly. The Motherland Navy's

half dozen ships had recently *visited* a few islands in the Cold Sea, leveling one city and capturing several others without a fight. The horrific roars of the Motherland Navy's gunpowder cylinders and the widespread destruction their iron balls wrought on that first city— now renamed Mother's Port—were enough to cow neighboring isles into immediate surrender. The larger, more distant Lordship Isles remained a goal of Pernie's, but they would be a formidable foe; spies said that they possessed their own gunpowder weapons and ships that had deserted the Motherland fleet from the alleged storm that killed Lork. *And now she wants an invasion of the High Antis mountains, thousands of kilometers to the south? How would we even get there, with an ocean on one side and a tropical forest on the other? How can we afford it? And—do I want Pernie ruling my homeland? Even if I were to gain by it?*

"And after that, Altamun, I want you to know that I chose you to replace the deserter Wakan primarily because you spent so much time in Stonehaven with the … the … late Admiral Lork … that you must have an intimate knowledge of Na Saam, its people, its geography, its defenses. Now that you have done a reasonable job as my chief advisor, I want to reap the further benefits of your promotion. Get one of those native Na Saamese pirates to work with you to figure out a way to get some of our fleet back up onto the Ice Sea. I want to annex that little nation of pirates. And I'll bet little Lork, here, would be welcome back in his father's lands."

"As you wish, Mother. I am certain the lad will be quite popular in Stonehaven." *Sure, another conquest, more expense, and for what? Fish? Seal skins?* But he knew the answer: *My own skin!*

"I HAD NO IDEA THIS POSITION WOULD BE SO ALL-consuming," Altamun Kech whispered to himself as he nodded to the guards outside his own luxurious chambers, entering under a vast marble arch. "I wish I had more time to enjoy all of this," he murmured as he looked over his lavish quarters, smelled the enticing incense of the burners and the savory odors of cooking food wafting in from his personal kitchen. He dared only to think the rest: *But with the hundreds of daily responsibilities and Pernie's incessant and sometimes irrational demands, I grow so tired. So weary.* As his handmaids removed his robes and began massaging oils onto his tired back and leg muscles—and other places— he lay back on cushions, enjoying the sensations. *This is a wonderful life, with all my gold and silver and maids and servants and all the luxuries of Motherland. I am rich beyond my dreams, but only one short misstep from the nightmare of Pernie's unpredictable wrath. If only I could keep all of this, but stay far away from Mother's City. I wonder if ShadowFall Director Awhalpa Kech might want to trade places with me?*

Much later, satiated, he drifted off to sleep, his last waking thoughts memories of his months as a pirate captain's captive—his palatial white stucco home, the palm trees and warm tropical nights, the music and food, in friendly Noorstown.

MOTHER PERNIE WATCHED WITH WARMTH AND LOVE AS baby Lork smiled up at her, cooing, his bright red hair and pale blue eyes striking evidence of his ancestry. *You look so much like your father, little Lork. I think you will be the first Father of this land.* Images of the child's laughing sire, the impressive and handsome ice pirate, interlaced in her mind with unwanted flashes of the nights with her little lovers, Thist and Thusk, bringing pangs of regret for the lost loves; then those overshadowed by unwelcome scenes of her lifetime with Wakan Kech—the heartrending loss of her only father figure. With a sigh, Pernie steeled her emotions. Wakan had abandoned her without warning, without a goodbye. *Flying off in that damned Una-thing!* His treachery was so deep it could not be forgotten, much less forgiven. *I will find those High Antis someday, and have my revenge. And as for little Thist running away, well…he is much closer and his time will come, too.*

Pernie gazed across the room at the map covering the far wall, a painting reconstructed from the memories of those guards who had seen the ancient archive videos on that gods-forsaken flying Una. As Pernie picked out details—*APPROXIMATE COORDINATES OF PEOPLE'S LANDS, IMPUTED SITE OF GOD'S PORT, ESTIMATED LOCATION OF HIGH ANTIS*— she wondered about all of the peoples and nations in those places, and how many other areas might be worth investigating in those highlands to the north and south of her own Motherland. How many might be allies, or enemies; how many could be conquered? She envisioned new invasion plans every minute she was away from daily duties and tribulations in the throne room, an obsession that she knew was taking its toll on her physical and mental health. Even the constant stream of handsome lovers, night after night, did not provide release enough from the stress, along with a nagging concern that she might become pregnant again —*that damned Wakan didn't teach anyone else about his baby-preventing herbs!*

She also suspected Wakan of disabling the Crystal Throne. *I wish that damned old chair had not died,* she rued. *Driving me insane or not, at least it let me lose my mind every day, away from all of this!* Breathing deeply the way Wakan had taught her as a child, Pernie calmed herself down to a rational state and focused on the issue at hand. *Damn you, Wakan. You taught me well, but not how to not think!*

The wall map kept her attention, guided her thoughts. *We are confined in that lowland basin now, but won't be forever. Someday, all of these lands could be —will be!—part of a Greater Motherland,* she thought, looking down at little Lork. *If not in my time, little man, then in yours. We are building a massive aerial force; our army has many, many gunpowder cylinders; and we have a growing navy and even an aerial force. Our sailors and soldiers and flyers will reach* everywhere!

God's Port would be the first and primary target in the Dark Highlands, she knew. Her military advisors, people Altamun Kech did not know about, were already planning that. They had told her that a speedy takeover of the so-called Odel Elevator at M'ridge Station would expedite the invasion. *And I will then abolish Thessland and enslave all its little people for the mines,* she thought. *Perfect revenge for Thist's betrayal.* Seizing God's Port would then require Thist's homeland to react somehow, because of their ice trade. "Either we fight them and win, or we starve them out and win," her generals promised.

And depending on Altamun's knowledge of his homeland, even Wakan's high mountains in the South would follow someday. *Someday. But even before then I will make a triumphant visit across the Ice Sea, to Stonehaven in Na Saam, with my Little Lord Lork! Someday.* Imagined scenes of times to come always settled her nerves, steeled her resolve.

Aloud, in soft musical tones, Pernie spoke to her baby. "All those past years of lost loves and lovers and friendships, of Sisters fought and defeated, of battles won and challenges met, all of those are gone and soon forgotten, little Lork. But I have learned. How to live and how to prevail. How to *rule.* In more ways than I ever imagined, I am truly a Mother. *Your* mother."

Looking down at her suckling baby, she felt an attachment missing elsewhere in her life.

"The future of Motherland is yet to be written, my little one—but it is all yours."

ABOUT THE AUTHOR

Dr. Arlan Andrews, Sr., is a Lifetime Member of the Science Fiction and Fantasy Writers of America (SFWA), with over 500 publications of books, stories, and articles in more than 100 venues worldwide. A retired engineer, his career ranged from the White Sands Missile Range to the White House Science Office, a nuclear weapons lab, several high-tech startup companies, and private consulting. Arlan founded SIGMA, the science fiction think tank of writers who provide pro bono futurism consulting to the Federal Government. He is author of the often quoted phrase, "A spaceship that takes off and lands the way God and Robert Heinlein intended."

The Thaw Trilogy of novels arose from Arlan's fascination with vanished civilizations and the megalithic ruins he visited, the ruins those ancients left behind: What will remain of today's world thousands of years from now? It won't all be spaceships and robots.